A LONG SHADOW

Sempronius Scipio and Elagabalus.
CE 221 to 222.

By Gordon Anthony

ISBN-13: 979-8685415059

Chapter 1
The Beggar

By African standards, it was a cool day, but I'd still spent the hottest part of the early afternoon relaxing in the bath house. It was, I told myself, a just reward for having sealed an excellent deal with the legionary quartermaster who had come seeking cavalry mounts. Since my estate – or more properly my wife's estate – breeds some of the finest horses to be found anywhere in the Empire, I'd been able to secure a good price for the seven geldings and twelve fillies Collinus and I had brought up to the city. In fact, I'd managed to wring such a good price out of the seasoned and cynical horse trader that even Collinus had been impressed.

"The Lady Aurelia will be pleased," he told me, which was as fine a compliment as the tall, hard-eyed Berber had ever given me.

We'd capped that by selling six dozen amphorae of olive oil to a trader who supplied the local homes and businesses as well as handling exports to Rome itself, and we'd been well rewarded for that too. Leptis Magna produces a lot of olive oil, but ours was as fine as any, and the trader had been suitably impressed with the quality.

So I'd treated myself to an afternoon of relaxation before the long journey back home. Meanwhile Collinus had gone to the market to purchase some of the more exotic supplies our own fields could not provide. I left him to that chore. He'd been doing it for years, so he knew what sort of stuff Circe liked, and I had no wish to be out and about during the hottest part of the day.

After I'd towelled myself dry and dressed in my cream-coloured tunic of finely woven wool, I buckled my old leather belt around my waist, slipped my sandals on, then stepped back out into the bustle of Leptis Magna and went looking for Collinus.

It wasn't likely to be a difficult search since we'd agreed to meet outside the south gate of the city, so I was feeling quite relaxed as I strolled through the crowded forum towards the main road leading into the interior of the province. The forum always busy, so navigating across it was a slow process, but I didn't mind. Life, after all, was good.

I had passed my thirty-first birthday only a couple of months earlier, and I felt as physically fit as I had ever done, even in my youth. Long days working on the estate had helped me control my waistline despite having access to more and better quality food than I could ever recall. I had a gorgeous wife who was, incidentally, ludicrously wealthy, and I had two young children who, despite their tender years, still managed to get the better of me more often than not. Circe said I was too soft with them, but I didn't care.

There was quite a crowd of people milling around in front of me so, to avoid them, I moved slightly to my left, into the shade provided by the tall buildings which line the southern side of the forum. This brought me close to the steps of the temple of Serapis where a beggar was sitting, a small rectangle of tatty cloth laid on the ground at his feet in the hope that passers-by would place some coins on it.

I was feeling benevolent thanks to the warm glow from my hours in the bath house and the general air of wellbeing, so I dipped my fingers into my purse and pulled out a few bronze *asses*. I stooped to drop the coins on the cloth as I passed the beggar, holding my breath as I did so because his filthy rags and grimy body were giving off quite a potent aroma.

He was a big man, with long, untidy hair and an unkempt beard, the hair all matted and tangled so it was difficult to tell whether its grey appearance was due to natural processes or the layer of dust it had collected. I noticed he had a scar on his cheek, and I guessed he might be an old soldier. He was certainly large enough, although he looked as if he hadn't eaten a decent meal in weeks.

"Thank you, Sir," he mumbled as I placed the coins on his rag. He spoke in Latin rather than the local Punic, but that wasn't unusual for Leptis Magna. The city may retain a lot of its ancient Phoenician roots, but it's also a very Roman city.

Feeling even more of a warm glow after my act of charity, I moved on, but I had barely taken two steps when the beggar called after me, his voice now urgent and surprised.

"Scipio? Is that you?"

Perhaps I had been feeling too warm and fuzzy, but I admit my steps faltered slightly when I heard that. However, I recovered quickly and continued on my way, managing not to look back at him.

It didn't work. I heard him – and smelled him – coming up behind me. His large, gnarled hand gripped my shoulder and he pulled me around to face him. Up close, he was even bigger than I had first thought. He was much broader in the shoulder than me, and he was a head taller as well.

He was also very angry.

"It is you! Sempronius Scipio!"

I slapped his hand away, conscious that we were attracting attention from the nearest pedestrians.

"You are mistaken," I told him haughtily, putting on my plummiest aristocratic accent. "My name is Valerius Cantiacus."

I almost reeled back at the stink of his breath when he leaned close to growl, "No it's not! I know you! We thought you were dead! But you ran out on us!"

I blinked, studying his face for any signs that I knew this man, but he was so covered in grime, and his face surrounded by so much hair, I could make no connection. However, it was obvious he knew me from my former life, so I needed to shut him up. He might have lowered his voice to hiss his accusations, but we were still attracting some very acute looks from the bystanders around us.

Steeling myself to ignore the pungency of his stench, I smiled and said softly, "I don't think we should speak here."

"I don't want to speak to you at all!" he rasped.

He was fast for a big man. I barely had time to register that his right hand had bunched into a fist and was aiming for my belly. Fortunately, I had not forgotten all the *pankration* lessons I had learned in my friend's gymnasium in Ephesus. I may have been out of practice, but I managed to block the punch with my left forearm. After that, instinct took over. I swivelled to my left and rammed my right elbow into his stomach, hearing the satisfying whoosh of air as his lungs emptied. Then I backhanded a punch to his face, sending him sprawling backwards onto the cobbles.

I heard shouts of astonishment and alarm from the watching crowd, but I ignored them as I hurriedly tried to decide what to do next.

3

My friend, Hannibal, who had taught me the art of *pankration* fighting, would have advised me to kick the guy in the head and finish the fight for certain.

"Always kick a man when he's down," he used to tell me. "That way, he won't get back up again."

A wiser alternative would have been to tug my tunic back into shape, smile at the crowd, tell them the man was drunk, and walk away.

Instead, I bent down, grabbed the front of his stained and ragged tunic, and pulled him up into a sitting position.

He groaned, his eyes screwed tightly shut as he fought off the pain. I'd caught him a hefty blow on the nose, and the back of his head had hit the cobbles with considerable force, so I couldn't blame him for being out of it for a moment.

Bending down, I hissed in his ear, "Who are you? Tell me quickly or I'll have you sent to the arena for the lions to chew on."

I could see him tensing his thigh muscles as he prepared to kick at me, so I clenched my fingers around his throat and whispered, "I know how to kill a man with my bare hands, so don't bother trying anything. Just tell me who you are. Then we can talk. It's that or the lions."

I don't know what I expected, but the one thing I hadn't anticipated was that he would start crying. I mean, Roman men are not given to tears even at the worst of times, and a big lump like this didn't strike me as having a soft personality. But the tears were unmistakable, and his chest began to heave as he tried to stifle a sob.

I was so surprised I let go of his throat and straightened up. Looking down at him, I could not recall when I had last seen such a pitiable sight.

He sat there, his hands now clamped over his face as if to conceal his shame, while his shoulders continued to heave as he fought to regain his composure.

Behind me, someone said, "We should summon the *vigiles*."

"There's no need for that," I said, twisting round to address the gawpers. "It's just a little misunderstanding."

The frowns on the faces of the onlookers remained in place, but at least nobody was running off to summon the *vigiles*. That was the last thing I wanted.

I turned back to the beggar.

"You," I told him, "need a wash and a change of clothes. Come with me. We'll get you cleaned up and then you can tell me who you are. Now, you'd better get up. You are attracting a lot of attention which neither of us wants. Here, take my hand."

It took a moment or two before he removed his hands from his face. Then, disdaining my offer of assistance, he pushed himself to his feet with the air of a man who had been utterly defeated by life.

He wiped away the dampness from his cheeks, sniffing as he did so. Then he gazed at me with lost, accusing eyes.

"Have I fallen so far?" he asked me miserably. "Do you really not recognise me?"

I shook my head.

"I'm sorry. But you are going to have to remind me."

He gave a weary sigh. All the fight and anger seemed to have drained from him, and all that was left was sorrow and bitterness.

Half laughing, half crying, he sighed, "I was one of the best in the army, and a scrawny, pampered little shit like you put me down. I'm glad none of my old unit were here to see that."

"Don't take it too badly," I told him. "I had some special training, and you're not exactly in the best shape at the moment. But for Neptune's sake tell me who you are."

Blinking his eyes dry, he let out a long, slow breath of resignation.

"I'm Aelius Caecus," he told me. "Centurion Aelius Caecus. Or I was."

I gaped at him, the memories flooding back as I tried to picture this ragged, filthy human being in the guise of one of the Emperor's elite soldiers. When I'd last seen Aelius Caecus, he'd been dressed in the armour of a Praetorian, and he'd been one of the toughest men I'd ever come across.

I mentally stripped away the beard from his face and tried to see him with short, close-cropped hair.

5

Yes, I recalled the flat features and the scar on his cheek, a memento from a campaign in Armenia.

"Caecus?" I gasped.

A spark flashed in his eyes as he nodded.

"And you, you bastard, ran out on us."

"It wasn't like that," I told him.

"No? Then how was it? How did you end up here when you were sent to find the proof the Emperor wanted?"

"It's a long story," I told him. "Just like yours, I expect. But we can't talk here. Come with me and we'll get you cleaned and fed."

I suppose the onlookers must have been very confused, but I ignored them. I didn't visit the city very often, so I don't suppose many of them knew who I was, even under my locally assumed name. Still, the pair of us must have made an odd sight; me with my expensive tunic, him wearing rags. Fortunately, the bath house was not far away, so we left the gawkers and went inside.

I handed Caecus more coins. In all the excitement, we'd forgotten the few *asses* I'd left on his begging cloth, but I was a rich man, so I had plenty more, including silver denarii.

"Have a thorough wash," I told him. "Then get your hair cut and your beard shaved off. Or, if you want to keep it, at least have it trimmed. And make sure you get rid of any lice and fleas."

He glared at me, but accepted the money and nodded.

"I'll go and buy you a fresh tunic," I continued. Then, looking down at his tattered footwear, I added, "And another pair of sandals."

For a moment, the old, hard stare of Centurion Caecus fixed on me.

"If you are going to run out on me, Scipio," he said menacingly, "I'll come after you. You know that, don't you?"

"I'll come back," I promised. "As long as you call me Valerius Cantiacus. That's my name now."

I left him arguing with the bath attendants who weren't keen on letting him soil their pools with his grime, and went out to purchase some new clothes for him. I had to guess at the size, but I also purchased a leather belt he could fasten around his waist to take up any slack if the tunic was too big for him. Finding a fresh loincloth wasn't so much of a problem, but the sandals were more difficult to judge.

Returning to the bath house, I went to the changing room and took a seat. Caecus turned up after about a quarter of an hour, looking clean but with his hair and beard still long. I saw the scars on his body, reminders of his career, and I also noticed how much weight he had lost.

"Here you go," I said as I tossed him the new clothing.

He dressed quickly, and I was pleased to see my guess had not been too far out. The tunic fitted well, although the sandals were rather too big for him, even with the straps pulled tight.

"You might grow into them," I told him.

He scowled at that, the reminder of the sort of quip the Legions' quartermasters use perhaps being unwelcome.

Once he was dressed, we moved to one of the outer courtyards where I waited while Caecus sat on a stool and allowed a barber to trim his beard and cut his hair short.

"I'd like to keep the beard," he explained. "But a short one will do."

Beards have been fashionable among Romans for a long time, ever since Emperor Hadrian grew one to conceal his acne, but most soldiers still preferred to be clean-shaven. The legend tells us having a beard in combat gave your enemy a chance to grab it and pull at your face, so Roman soldiers normally fought with their cheeks and chin shaved. Caecus, though, was no longer a soldier, so perhaps he had decided to adopt a more fashionable look.

Even with his beard, the transformation was incredible once the tangled mass of hair had been cut short and tidied. I now saw the man I had known four years earlier, although it was still strange to see him in a civilian tunic rather than Praetorian armour and a Centurion's plumed helmet.

He'd lost a lot of weight, but he was hardly frail. There were still plenty of muscle beneath his tanned skin, and I reckoned all he needed was a few decent meals to return him to his former vigour. His age was difficult to estimate, but he had been a veteran officer in the Praetorian Guard, so I guessed he must be well into his forties. His ragged appearance had made him seem older, but the freshly shorn Caecus seemed almost rejuvenated.

"Now we will get you some food," I told him. "But you'll need to eat on the move. I need to get back home, and it's a couple of hours' ride."

He didn't argue. I purchased some spiced bread, a couple of pears, some olives and a handful of almonds. It was an eclectic mix, but at least Caecus could eat while we walked.

"You don't live in town?" he asked between hungry mouthfuls.

"No. We have an estate about fifteen miles inland."

"We?"

"My wife, Aurelia, owns it."

"I should have guessed there would be a woman involved," he muttered. "Turn your head, did she?"

"Something like that," I admitted.

We found Collinus waiting patiently just outside the south gate. He was sitting against the city wall, his head covered by the folds of the Arab headgear he always wore. Even in the full glare of the sun, he seemed annoyingly cool. A little way beyond him, two horses were tethered, each saddled and waiting for its rider. There were also around three dozen mules, all with their backs loaded by amphorae, sacks or wooden boxes. Eight brawny slaves stood watching over them, their resigned forms perking up when they saw me walking towards them. I suppose I had kept them waiting rather a long time.

Collinus rose smoothly to his feet as we approached. The ivory hilt of his dagger protruded from the red sash around his waist, and I saw his right hand flicker towards it as he studied my companion.

"Hello, Collinus," I said airily. "Sorry I'm late. This is Aelius Caecus. He's an old friend."

That didn't really describe my relationship with Caecus very accurately. We'd actually only encountered one another twice before, and our relationship hadn't exactly been companionable because Caecus had been a soldier, while I'd been an imperial spy. Soldiers generally disapprove of spies, even the ones who are on their own side, and Caecus had been no exception, although our shared experiences had led us to respect each other even if we hadn't been bosom pals.

"Caecus," I said to him. "This is Collinus."

8

The two men nodded greetings but did not clasp forearms in the traditional style. Collinus had the excuse of being, on the face of it at least, a barbarian, while Caecus obviously didn't trust anyone.

Collinus gave no indication of being concerned by Caecus' unexpected presence. His face remained impassive as he said, "We should leave now. It will be dark in a few hours."

"Can you have another mule freed up so Caecus can ride?" I suggested.

Collinus inclined his head in a slight bow, then strolled off to pass the instruction to the slaves. One of the loaded mules was soon divested of its baggage which was distributed among the other beasts. The rasping sounds of the mules' protests accompanied the task, but Caecus was soon presented with a mule he could sit on. Naturally, there was no saddle, but he sat astride the blanket which had been left on the animal's back, his feet dangling close to the ground on either side.

"I could walk," he said sourly.

"It's a long way," I informed him.

"Not as far as I've walked already," he grunted. Still, he did not dismount and, when Collinus and I hauled ourselves into the saddles of our horses, he followed close behind.

The slaves also sat on mules, and they prodded the rest of our long caravan into motion. We had sold our herd of horses and our amphorae of olive oil, and now we would return to the villa with supplies of wine, cloth, spices, trinkets and tools. Our estate produced most of our food and some other essentials, but we specialised in horses and olive oil, so there was always a need to trade for other goods we could not provide for ourselves.

We headed south, following what began as a paved road but which would eventually deteriorate into a trackway. Collinus rode in silence, knowing I would tell him more about Caecus when I was ready.

We'd travelled a couple of miles before I ventured, "Caecus was a Praetorian. He knows my real name."

Collinus gave the briefest of nods, but he remained silent, clearly waiting for more information.

I told him, "I met him in Alexandria. And he was a witness to Caracalla's assassination."

The Roman propensity for adding or changing names can be confusing. Caecus and I had both served an Emperor who had been known as Antoninus for most of his life, but the nickname of Caracalla had been given to him by his troops, and it had stuck. On the two occasions when I had encountered Caecus, we'd been trying to foil plots to assassinate Caracalla. In Alexandria, we had succeeded, but our second attempt had failed. Collinus knew why, but even these revelations did not appear to perturb the grim-eyed Berber. All he did was purse his lips while he considered my news.

After a moment, he turned his head to look at me, his expression solemn.

In a low voice, he asked me, "Do you want me to kill him?"

It was the sort of question I'd come to expect from Collinus. He was in his fifties now, but he was still agile and very, very deadly with that dagger he always carried.

"No. I want to hear what he has to say."

Collinus gave a slight nod. Technically, he was one of my freedmen, but we both understood that he was Circe's man first and foremost. He acquiesced to my orders because I was married to her, but all three of us knew that he would always put her safety above anything else. If he thought I was putting her in danger by bringing a former Praetorian to our home, he'd ignore whatever I told him to do.

He was the same now. With a grave nod of his head, he said, "Very well. We shall hear his story. Then I will kill him."

Chapter 2
The Rising Sun

Our estate lies near the edge of the fertile zone which lies between the coast and the desert. We are very fortunate that there is a fresh water spring which provides plenty of irrigation, so the fields and meadows are lush in comparison to the barren, stony areas surrounding our lands, particularly to the south where rocky, scrub-covered hills form a demarcation line between the civilised area and the desert where nomadic Berber people still live in the manner of their ancestors.

One of the customs these nomads follow is attacking travelling caravans which might promise a chance of plunder. That was why Collinus and I were keen to get home before nightfall. We knew the road, and we could have followed it even by starlight, but the risks of encountering bandits rose considerably once the sun went down. Even full daylight was not always a deterrent, which was why we had brought eight of our burliest slaves to guard the convoy of mules. They each had a very stout club close at hand, as did I. I'm not one for carrying a sword, but facing an armed bandit with my bare hands isn't something I'd ever want to do. Collinus, of course, had his long-bladed dagger, and he knew precisely how to use it.

Fortunately, the journey passed without incident, and I breathed a little easier as we turned off the main road. We passed between groves of olive trees, then crested a low rise to gaze down on the wide expanse of fields and meadows which belonged to the lady known to most people as Aurelia, but to me as Circe in honour of the name she'd used when I'd first met her in Ephesus.

In fact, she used lots of names, depending on what she was trying to accomplish at any given time. The one name she never used was the one she had inherited from her parents. Only a handful of people knew her true identity, and we weren't going to tell anyone else, especially not a former Praetorian like Caecus.

Circe came to meet us herself, my four year old son, Sextus Valerius, standing beside her with wide eyes, and our toddler daughter, Valeria, held at her shoulder. Julianus, our *major domo*, was also there, and he immediately took charge of overseeing the storage of the cargo we had brought back with us. A veritable army of slaves were employed to carry out this task with brisk, smooth efficiency.

Circe, dark-haired, tall, slender and elegant, focused her attention on Caecus, as I'd known she would. I made the introductions once we had dismounted.

Circe smiled, "You are welcome in our home, Aelius Caecus," but I knew as well as she did that the extent of our welcome would very much depend on what story the former soldier had to tell.

"You've done all right for yourself," was his only comment to me as I led him into the villa.

It was impossible to deny that. Circe, as I've mentioned, was very wealthy indeed, and our two-storey villa was extremely comfortable without being too ostentatious. It was built in a square, with a garden of flowers and shrubs at the centre. The garden also contained a well which provided our drinking water. Tasteful statues of gods and goddesses provided the ornamentation, while the interior decoration consisted of wildlife frescoes painted on plain, white walls.

I gave little Valeria a hug and a kiss, but she seemed more interested in the unpacking of the goods we had brought back, while little Sextus looked at Caecus with suspicious eyes. We rarely had visitors out here, not only because we lived some way distant from the city and any neighbouring farmsteads, but because we liked to keep ourselves to ourselves. Given Circe's history – and mine, come to that – we felt it was safer that way.

We had returned just in time. The sun sank rapidly below the horizon, day giving way to night with a rapidity I had become accustomed to. Oil lamps and candles were being lit throughout the villa, so we headed indoors, making for the dining room which was situated on the ground floor. We actually had a couple of dining areas, a small, private one and a much larger room for entertaining guests. Since we rarely had guests, we normally used the smaller room, and this is where Circe led us. When I say it is small, that is relatively speaking, for there was plenty of room for three large couches set out around low tables in the traditional Roman triclinium style. Each couch could easily accommodate three people, although there were rarely more than Circe and I, with Collinus occasionally joining us.

Today there were four of us. While Collinus, Caecus and I washed away the dust of the journey using warm water and towels, Circe handed the children over to her female slaves who would put them to bed. Then I settled down on a couch beside her while Collinus and Caecus each had a couch to themselves.

"You are late," Circe remarked without accusation. "I was beginning to wonder if you'd decided to stay overnight in the city."

"It's my fault," I admitted. "I bumped into Caecus in the forum."

Caecus regarded me with those baleful eyes I remembered so well. He was obviously wondering whether I was about to reveal that he'd broken down in tears, but I had already decided to keep that little snippet for when I was alone with Circe.

Slaves were bringing through large platters of food. It wasn't an extravagant meal, and the cooks had needed to flesh it out a bit when they discovered we had a guest, but there was always plenty to eat in our home. This time it was roasted quails in a date sauce as the main course, with plenty additional sweetmeats and some of the new wine Collinus had bought in the city.

As always, we talked only of trivial things until the slaves had departed. Circe and I agreed that people who spoke in front of slaves as if they were inanimate objects needed a lesson in humanity. Slaves might be low in status, but they are still people. And if you want to keep something secret, talking in front of them is one sure way of letting word spread.

Julianus was on hand, though. He stood patiently near the door to the kitchens. He was a freedman, a Nubian who had once been a slave but who had displayed such alertness and intelligence that Circe had freed him years ago. We trusted him implicitly, and he ran the household with supreme efficiency. He also insisted on pouring refills of wine for us even though Circe had often told him we were perfectly capable of doing this for ourselves. Julianus, though, would take offence if we demeaned ourselves by performing such a menial task, so he was on hand whenever we needed a refill.

Caecus, I noticed, was still hungry. I wondered when he had last eaten a decent meal, and I worried he might make himself ill if he gorged too much on an empty stomach, but he tucked in with gusto.

Circe had already given orders for a guest room to be prepared for him. These rooms were on the ground floor, as were the slaves' quarters and the working rooms containing things like looms for making cloth, while the upper floor was reserved for our private chambers and, for the past four years, children's play rooms.

Circe said, "So, husband, how do you and Aelius Caecus come to know one another?"

I chose my words carefully as I replied, "We first met in Alexandria."

Circe gave a slow, thoughtful nod. She knew all about the massacre in Alexandria when Emperor Caracalla had set his Legions loose on the citizens. She knew about it because she'd been there. It was a touchy subject between us because, at the time, she and I had found ourselves on opposite sides of the ultimately doomed rebellion, so I hurriedly glossed over this episode.

"Then we met again when Macrinus was proclaimed Emperor."

Again, I didn't need to say too much. Marcus Opellius Macrinus had been the Praetorian Prefect under Caracalla. When Caracalla was assassinated, Macrinus stepped up and took the imperial throne, largely because there was nobody else remotely qualified for the position.

To be honest, although I had been an imperial spy, I held no great loyalty towards Caracalla. He was a bloodthirsty, untrustworthy tyrant, and his passing was mourned mostly by the soldiers because he'd always paid them well. Few other people regretted his demise, and I had thought Macrinus had the makings of a fine Emperor despite not being from a Senatorial background.

Our conversation with Caecus, though, was treading on dangerous territory, and even though Circe was able to conceal her feelings, I could tell she was concerned about me having brought the former Praetorian into our home.

I told her, "Caecus recognised me. I thought it would be better if we could talk in absolute privacy, so I brought him back here. Also, he was obviously down on his luck."

Caecus muttered, "And it's partly your fault, Scipio."

"Call me Valerius Cantiacus," I reminded him.

"Why? Who are you hiding from? Macrinus is dead."

It was a good point, and I had no real answer except that secrecy had become a way of life for me.

I shrugged, "I adopted the name when I first came here. It's how the locals know me."

Caecus was not deterred by this statement.

He said, "You took the name because you didn't want Macrinus to find you. He sent you on a mission, and you vanished."

I could not deny that, so I didn't bother trying.

I told him, "The mission he sent me on was a fool's errand. I could not find the evidence he wanted. Even if I had, it would have been too late in any case. I heard the stories of Julia Maesa's coup before I could return."

That was a highly selective interpretation of events, but it was all I was prepared to tell Caecus.

I'd known the conversation would go this way, but I needed to guide him away from the true facts. My problem was that there are two versions of how Macrinus came to power. There's the version everyone believes, and then there's the truth.

The story most folk know is that a prophet from Africa pronounced that Macrinus would overthrow Caracalla and seize power for himself. Word of this prophecy was heard by the imperial spy network, and a message was sent to the Emperor reporting it. But Caracalla had been busy planning a war with Parthia, so he had left instructions that all messages were to be read by Macrinus who was acting as his deputy. The story goes that, when Macrinus read the report, he knew Caracalla would have him executed as soon as he learned of the prophecy, so Macrinus bribed a soldier named Martialis to murder Caracalla. As soon as the deed was done, he'd had Martialis killed to cover up the plot.

That's the version most people believe, but Caecus and I knew it was only partly correct. Macrinus had indeed read the warning message. I'd been there when he had opened the scroll because I was the one who had delivered it. But, instead of hatching a plot, Macrinus, accompanied by me, Caecus and a dozen or so Praetorians, had galloped off to find the Emperor and explain why the alleged prophecy was nonsense. We'd actually succeeded in that mission, but then things had taken a very unexpected turn. With dozens of soldiers nearby, Martialis had marched up to Caracalla and stabbed him to death before being cut down by the Emperor's bodyguards. His motives for the deed were unclear, with several theories being put forward. At the time, I'd been as confused as anyone as to why Martialis had murdered the Emperor, but I'd learned the full story later. The trouble was, I could not tell Caecus because it was a secret Circe and I wished to keep to ourselves.

So I told Caecus, "You know Martialis acted alone."

"So it seems," he admitted reluctantly. "But Macrinus suspected Julia Maesa was behind the scheme. She probably wanted to get rid of both Macrinus and Caracalla, but Martialis bungled the assassinations."

He was more correct than he knew, but I assured him, "There was no evidence to support Maesa's involvement."

"You were sent to find the proof," he reminded me.

"There was no proof," I insisted. "I was sent to find the prophet to learn who had put him up to it, but the man had disappeared long before we even heard of his prophecy. By the time I had finished looking for him, it was already too late."

Again, that was only partly true, and I felt bad for deceiving Caecus, but I could not afford to tell him the whole truth.

With a resigned sigh, he admitted, "Aye, it probably was a foolish task to set you. Maesa would have covered her tracks well."

He relaxed slightly, which was a good sign as far as I was concerned. During my time as an imperial spy, I had learned how to deceive people when I was on a mission, but lying to Caecus left a bad taste in my mouth, and I wanted to shift the conversation away from my own actions.

Looking around at our surroundings, he asked, "So how did you end up here?"

"My searching brought me this way, and I fell in love," I told him by way of explanation, reaching down to squeeze Circe's shoulder as I did so.

Circe placed her own hand on top of mine to return the sentiment then, smiling her gentle smile, she asked Caecus, "So can you tell us what really happened after Caracalla's death? We hear rumours, of course, but we are a long way from the centre of things, and I've always treated official announcements with some scepticism."

Caecus took a long drink of wine, then held up his cup for Julianus to refill. He took a deep breath before recounting his story.

"You know Caracalla was at war with Parthia?" he began.

"Yes," I nodded. "He'd gathered quite an army."

Caecus went on, "The trouble was, Macrinus was no general. I liked the man, and I respected him, but he wasn't a soldier. The Parthians damn near beat us, and we were only saved when our reserves charged out of our camp and broke up their attack before they could encircle us."

"I heard Macrinus made peace with Artabanus of Parthia," I commented, relieved that the discussion had moved on at last.

"Yes," Caecus nodded. "He paid a big indemnity, blamed the hostilities on Caracalla, and settled a peace deal. The troops weren't too happy but, after the mauling they'd had, they were at first on his side."

He took another drink of wine before continuing, "But then he paid money to barbarians up on the Danube front, and that was the beginning of the trouble. He'd bought peace, but he'd run out of money, so he had to find some savings. What he did was cut the legionary pay for new recruits back to the old level."

"I take it the soldiers weren't happy about that?" I guessed.

Circe frowned, "Why not? Those already in service didn't lose any pay."

Caecus explained, "But it created a two-tier system. New recruits were being asked to do the same work as veterans but for half the pay. And the older troops began to wonder how long it would be before their own pay was cut. So none of them were happy. Losing battles always makes men miserable, and everything Macrinus did just turned them more against him."

"The Senate didn't like him either, so we heard," Circe put in. "He was from an equestrian family, so the snobs in Rome probably thought he wasn't noble enough."

"Aye," Caecus agreed glumly. "But it was the army that did for him."

His disapproving stare fixed on me again as he went on, "Julia Maesa was stirring up trouble. I wouldn't be surprised if she was behind a lot of the rumours criticising Macrinus."

"He should have kept her and her whole brood under lock and key," I remarked.

"He should have had the whole lot of them executed," Caecus said with feeling.

Circe asked, "Why didn't he?"

"Partly because he was an honourable man," Caecus replied. "But mostly because that would have upset the soldiers even more. Maesa and her family were the last remnants of the Severan dynasty, even if it was only by marriage. If he'd had them killed, he wouldn't have lasted as long as he did."

I nodded my understanding. Julia Maesa, the woman who kept cropping up in our conversation, came from a very wealthy and influential family from Syria. Her younger sister, Julia Domna, had married Emperor Septimius Severus and had been Caracalla's step-mother. Domna had died of a cancer shortly after Caracalla's murder, leaving Julia Maesa as the family matriarch. She was as ambitious and cunning as any person I'd ever met, and I knew she had long been plotting to have one of her grandsons appointed as Caracalla's heir. Things had not gone as she had hoped because Macrinus had seized power after Caracalla's death, but that had not deterred her, and we all knew she had achieved her aim eventually. What I didn't know was precisely how she had accomplished that feat.

Caecus continued, "Eventually, when everyone was grumbling, she paraded her grandson in front of the Third Legion and told them he was actually Caracalla's son."

"She really said that?" I gaped. "I thought that was just gossip."

"No, that's exactly what she told them."

"And they believed it?"

"Men will believe anything if it suits their cause," Caecus grunted. "Let's face it, everyone knew Caracalla had been …" he paused as he sought for a more polite word than the one he had been about to use, "… sleeping with his stepmother. To believe he had also had an affair with his cousin, Julia Soaemias, wasn't so hard to accept."

I nodded. As I mentioned, the imperial family had a rather complex background. It was widely believed that Caracalla had been carrying on a long-term affair with his step-mother, Julia Domna. Circe insisted it was true, and she had some inside knowledge.

But Domna's was not the only scandalous relationship in the Julia family. Her niece, Maesa's elder daughter, Soaemias, had a reputation for taking and discarding lovers on a whim. Bearing that in mind, it was perhaps no surprise that the disgruntled soldiers had been happy to accept that her son, Verius, could be the child of their beloved former Emperor, Caracalla. Incest between cousins, it seemed, bothered the troops far less than rumours about how their pay might be slashed if Macrinus remained in charge of the empire.

"Maesa proclaimed her grandson as Emperor," Caecus informed us. "And the Third Legion backed him. They thought he was a link to the Severan dynasty, you see, and the Severans had always looked after the army."

He shook his head in disgust as he went on, "The boy was still a child, barely fourteen years old, and he always dressed and acted like a girl, but still the idiots of the Third thought he would make a better Emperor than Macrinus."

I thought he might be about to make another remark about my failure to find any evidence that Julia Maesa had been plotting against Macrinus from the start, but he merely gave another grunt of disgust.

"What Maesa did only serves to prove she is a scheming bitch," he growled. "She backed up her lies with donations of gold, and the Third Legion lapped it all up. Of course, Macrinus sent troops to put down the revolt, but some of them joined Maesa's cause, and the rest were killed or put to flight. The same happened in the second battle, and Macrinus was captured."

19

"I heard he escaped," I ventured, prompting him to continue.

He gave a sad grin as he agreed, "Aye, a few of us remained loyal. We broke him out and tried to get him to Rome. There was a chance the Senate might back him rather than a child as Emperor, especially if he turned up in person and demanded their support. But it was a risky journey, so he sent some men with his wife and son to try to get to Parthia where Artabanus would keep them safe."

I thought he might break into tears again as he sighed, "But it was no good. We were caught. Macrinus was killed, and I heard his wife and son were also executed."

That filled me with sorrow. I'd briefly known Macrinus' wife and young son, and I'd liked them. Contemplating their last moments was horrible. They had paid the price for Macrinus' inability to outwit Julia Maesa.

Regarding Caecus with genuine sympathy, I guessed, "You were with him when it happened?"

"I took a blow to my head during the last fight," he confided as he touched a finger to his left temple. "They left me for dead. When I came to my senses, all that was left of Macrinus was a headless corpse."

"I'm sorry," I told him. "I liked Macrinus. I wish I could have done more to help, but I failed him."

"So did I," Caecus sighed, his voice thick with emotion. "It's not a feeling I am used to."

Gently, Circe put in, "Macrinus made his own choices. We cannot absolve him of all responsibility for how things turned out."

Caecus gave another gloomy nod, then downed another gulp of wine.

Circe asked him, "So what did you do after that?"

After taking yet another swig of wine, Caecus told us, "I took off my armour, and I began walking. I had nowhere to go, and no real reason to stay alive."

"Do you have no home town to go to?" Circe enquired.

He shook his head.

"The army was my home. But I wanted to get as far away from recent events as I could, so I had this daft notion I should go to Mauretania. It's almost as out of the way as Britannia, and it's a damn sight warmer."

He gave an embarrassed shrug.

"Like I said, I wasn't really thinking straight, but I knew I should get away from Syria. It wasn't a safe place for someone who had remained loyal to a defeated Emperor, so I just started walking. It's taken me three years to get as far as Leptis Magna."

He held our gaze as he explained, "I turned into a beggar. Sometimes I stayed in a town for weeks, doing menial labour, other times I slept rough on the road or scavenged in fields and forests. To be honest, I can't explain everywhere I've been. I did spend a few months in Alexandria. They were looking for men to help them rebuild the homes destroyed in the sack."

"It's a long walk from Antioch to Mauretania," I murmured.

That was no understatement.

Mauretania is the province which lies at the western end of the African coast, near the Pillars of Hercules and the Atlantic Ocean. To get there from Syria on foot meant walking the entire length of the Mediterranean coastline of Africa.

"You have suffered a great deal," Circe told him. "But you are welcome to stay here as long as you like."

It was probably the kindest thing anyone had said to the veteran soldier for years. He was trying to retain his outward posture of a hard man, but I could see his attitude soften under the influence of the wine and Circe's genuine display of sympathy.

"The worst thing," he sighed, "is that the Third Legion soon realised how stupid they'd been and they decided to revolt. It was too late by then, of course, and Maesa sent more legions to destroy them. The Third was disbanded and the ringleaders put to death."

He shook his head in disgust, then turned his gaze back to me.

"I have nothing much to live for," he told me. "Everything went wrong, and it can't be fixed now. Julia Maesa got her way, but it will be the ruin of the empire. The boy who now wears the Purple is not worthy of being Emperor. He's a puppet of his grandmother, and he acts like a girl, prancing around half naked all the time. Did you know he is High Priest of the sun god,

Elagabalus? They dragged the black stone all the way to Rome so he could put it in a temple and have everyone worship it. They are even calling him Elagabalus himself."

I'd heard all this. Julia Maesa, her mission accomplished, had taken her scheming brood to Rome, transporting the worship of Elagabalus at the same time. Legend says that a black pillar of stone fell from the sky at some time in the distant past, and this monument is worshipped as the physical embodiment of the sun god, Elagabalus. Now, our boy Emperor had taken the same name in honour of his patron deity, and worship of Elagabalus was overtaking the old gods of Rome.

Caecus admitted, "Sometimes I think it would have been better if I'd walked to Rome and killed the young brat myself. At least it would have avenged Macrinus."

"It wouldn't have solved anything," I told him.

"I know. All it would have done is trigger another civil war. The empire has had enough of that. But it sickens me that a child who acts like a painted harlot should now wear the Purple because of my failure."

"You couldn't have fought the Third Legion on your own," Circe pointed out. "The blame does not lie with you. And even if Scipio had discovered some evidence of Maesa's treachery, there is no guarantee things would be any different. As soon as she thought she was in danger, Maesa would have raised a revolt anyway. You said yourself that the soldiers were already unhappy with Macrinus. I suspect things would have turned out much the same whatever any of us did or did not do."

"I suppose you are right," Caecus sighed. "But I don't like losing."

There was a long silence before Circe said, "Aelius Caecus, we all understand your bitterness and sorrow. But you have suffered enough. You should rest here and regain your strength. If you wish, you could work for us, and we will pay you."

Caecus blinked drunkenly as he stared at her.

"Work for you? Doing what?"

"I am sure you have many skills," Circe replied. "But the first thing is to recover your proper fitness. You look half starved. So you will be our guest for as long as you wish."

Caecus nodded gravely, "Thank you, Lady. You are very kind. I will admit I am tired, sore and weak. But I will work to earn my pay. I have had enough of begging for charity."

Circe smiled her broadest smile, her tanned face lighting up.

"Then Julianus will show you to your room, and we will speak again in the morning. I am sure we can find plenty for you to help with around the estate."

Caecus rose to his feet, his movements a little unsteady. I guessed he had not drunk strong wine for some time, and it had clearly gone to his head.

He stood still for a moment, looking down at me.

Speaking very solemnly, he said, "I am sorry for the way I reacted when I saw you in the forum. It's just that it brought back a lot of bad memories. I felt angry, and I needed someone to blame."

I didn't know how much it had cost him to say that, but I knew it couldn't have been easy for him.

"I understand," I told him.

He gave a bow, then followed Julianus out of the dining room.

Once he was gone, Collinus spoke for the first time.

"He could be dangerous," the Berber said softly. "If he learns the full truth behind Caracalla's death, he will be angry. It would be better to kill him now."

I shook my head vigorously.

"No. I have seen too much killing. Caecus was a good soldier and a decent enough man in his own way. We owe him another chance."

"We owe him nothing," Collinus said flatly.

"Our deeds had consequences, "I pointed out. "Caecus is a victim of those consequences."

Circe put in, "What happened in the past does not really matter. What matters is that he needs help, and we are in a position to provide it."

I said, "I want no more deaths on my hands. Rome is far away, and we have a good life here. Let Caecus share it if that is what he wants."

"Very well," Collinus shrugged. "As long as he never learns the truth. I will keep my dagger close at hand in case he does."

Chapter 3
The Letter

The next morning, I showed Caecus all around our estate, pointing out the wine press, the tannery, the stables and cattle byres, the pens for the goats and sheep, the bee hives and the fields where we grew wheat, oats, barley and enough variety of vegetables to keep our cooks happy.

Moving on, I pointed, "And over there we have some fig trees and, of course, our olive groves."

"It's quite a place," Caecus murmured. "But what do you want me to do?"

"What are you good at?" I asked him.

"Killing barbarians," he replied, his expression stony.

"There aren't too many of them around here," I smiled, pretending I had taken his comment as a joke. "We do get the occasional bit of trouble from the Berbers, but they mostly leave us in peace. Besides, they are technically citizens of the empire, not barbarians."

Caecus grunted, "I joined the army when I was a lad. I rose through the ranks to be a Centurion, then I joined the Praetorians. Soldiering is all I know."

"But you'll have learned a lot of other skills in the Legions," I countered. "I bet you know how to build roads, walls and houses."

He gave a slow, ponderous nod.

"Yes, I did a lot of that. I wasn't an engineer, but I picked up a lot of the basics."

"Then you can help me keep the estate in good condition, and you can help with the irrigation ditches. We have a fresh water spring which feeds all the channels, but they need to be maintained. And I have no experience of engineering or construction."

Caecus' eyes lit up at that, and he showed a keener interest as we continued our tour, noting the position of the spring which fed our fields and the layout of the myriad irrigation channels.

As we completed our circuit, we approached the villa from the rear. About a hundred paces from the back wall was another large building, a single-storey complex built in a square around a central, cobbled courtyard which had its own well.

"What's that?" Caecus asked me.

"The slaves' quarters," I told him.

He stopped walking, taking time to study the building with expert eyes. The walls were plain, but there were rows of painted wooden shutters for each window, and the roof was tiled. There was little in the way of ornamentation, but it was still a very fine building.

"It's better than most barracks I've stayed in," he frowned. "How many slaves do you have?"

"One hundred and eighty three adults who work the fields and tend the livestock," I replied. "Plus nine children under the age of fourteen. There are another twenty-seven in the villa, but I see you've spotted our next problem. This place is becoming crowded, so we need to design and build another set of quarters."

"It looks big enough to me," he grunted.

"Only because they are crowded together in small rooms."

Caecus looked at me as if I were some sort of simpleton.

"So what?" he frowned. "They are slaves. You treat them too lightly. I noticed your overseers don't even carry whips."

"That's right. Aurelia believes slaves should be well treated."

Before he could make any comment on Circe's liberal attitude, I added, "And so do I. We encourage them all to share in the benefits of what the estate produces. You've seen for yourself how much we grow here. Happy slaves who know they are going to benefit from that will work more willingly."

Caecus blew air down his nose in one of his customary snorts.

"They're more likely to run away if you are too soft on them," he opined with the certainty of a lifetime's experience.

I smiled as I informed him, "Actually, we have very few runaways. Of course, the fact that we are out near the desert helps, but most of our slaves know they are well off."

"So what do you do if one does run away?"

"We try to find him. Or her, although the women rarely try anything like that. And if we do find the runaway, we sell him at the first opportunity."

I didn't say to him that it had taken me a little while to adjust to Circe's attitude towards her slaves. Every Roman has slaves, you see, and many of the wealthiest possess thousands rather than the modest two hundred or so we had on our estate, and some owners treat their slaves very poorly indeed.

As an imperial spy, I'd not often had a personal slave, but I had been around plenty during my time working in the imperial palace in Antioch. I hadn't really thought much about them as individuals or about slavery as an institution until I had married Circe. But she had made me wonder how I would have felt if I had been enslaved. Once she'd made me think about that, it wasn't long before I was committed to following her example.

"We don't keep trouble-makers," I informed Caecus. "If any slave starts causing problems, we take them to Leptis Magna and sell them. I very much doubt any of them will find a better life under some other master."

"Why don't you just set them all free, then?" he demanded.

"That would ruin us," I told him. "The whole economy of the empire relies on slavery, and we're no exception. But that doesn't mean we should treat our slaves harshly."

Caecus nodded. He clearly still thought we treated our slaves far too leniently, but I warned him that he would need to fit in to our way of life, so he kept his opinions to himself.

Over the next few weeks, he gradually settled in. The decent food and having tasks to accomplish transformed him from a surly house guest into a slightly less surly but extremely focused and driven man with a mission.

"If you want a new slave barracks, let's do it properly," he decided.

I don't think any of the other freedmen liked him overly much. He was, at heart, still a centurion, and his attitude reflected that, but he impressed everyone with his hard work. He measured out a site where a new barracks block could be built, then discussed the design with me and Circe, jotting down what materials and manpower we would need to complete the project.

"He's certainly very efficient," Collinus observed once Caecus had gone to mark out the plot.

Circe, who was looking particularly radiant in a shimmering gown of green silk, said, "I'm glad he came here. It will do him good, as well as benefitting us."

"Yes," I agreed. "He has a purpose in life again."

I admired Caecus, but he was a difficult man to like. He was, in many ways, still Centurion Caecus, and I supposed he would remain so. He always seemed slightly apart from the rest of the household, generally keeping himself to himself. He'd certainly never revealed what his *praenomen* was. That personal name, whether it be Marcus or Quintus or Gaius, was normally reserved for use by close friends and family. Caecus had not told us his *praenomen,* which revealed he did not regard us as close enough to him.

Not yet, at any rate.

With the plans made, Caecus was keen to get on with the building work. He and I took a trip to the city to purchase some of the materials we would need.

We needed to order roof tiles, bricks, window shutters, cobbles and paving slabs, plus all the ingredients for cement and a lot of timber to build the frames. We needed doors, beds, tables and chairs, so we spent a couple of days in Leptis Magna, touring the various tradesmen's businesses and bargaining for what we wanted. Caecus was very helpful in that because his intimidating bulk and gorgon stare persuaded one or two of the tradesfolk to give us very good prices.

It was nearing the winter season by this time. There had been a few showers of rain, and the summer's baking heat had lessened considerably, but that meant it was a good time to get on with the new building. The harvest was in, so we had quite a few slaves who would be free to help with the labouring.

I sometimes made clumsy attempts to help with the work, but other aspects of the estate also needed my attention. We had hundreds of horses to care for, as well as cattle, sheep and goats. We also had a few geese and chickens, and there was always a need to hunt for wild game.

I was a novice when it came to hunting. Some upper class Romans enjoy Africa for the hunting which they regard as a sport.

We did it to provide some variety to our diet, and it was here that Collinus was in his element. He seemed to have an uncanny knack of knowing when and where wild goats or flocks of birds would be located. I accompanied him when I could, but I always left him to lead the expedition.

So the weeks became months, and Caecus' project began to take shape while the daily life of the estate continued around the construction. I felt very content, and I particularly enjoyed the Saturnalia festival which marked the turning point of the year as December gave way to January. Saturnalia always involved a great deal of feasting and merriment. One of the features was the day when the roles of slaves and masters were reversed, so Circe and I served dinner for our house slaves, while the field slaves were given enough food and wine to fill their bellies several times over.

Collinus tended to make himself scarce during such revelries. He might have lived most of his life as a Roman citizen, but he still disdained some of our more raucous behaviour. Caecus, though, surprised everyone by joining in the fun, and even sang a few of the Legions' marching songs once the wine had loosened his tongue. Even Circe laughed, although she pretended to be shocked by the bawdy lyrics.

So another year began, and I was happy.

Until the letter arrived.

It reached me a week after Saturnalia. It was delivered by a driver who had brought several dozen clay tiles on the back of his ox-drawn wagon as part of the building materials we had ordered.

"Valerius Cantiacus?" he asked when Caecus and I went to meet him.

"That's me."

He handed over a rather battered pouch made of otter fur which had been stitched shut to keep its contents safe from prying eyes and the elements. There was a small label attached which bore my name in faded ink above the simple address of, "Leptis Magna". Normally, such letters are delivered to a local temple until they are collected, but someone had used their initiative and sent it on via one of the frequent wagons which were now bringing all sorts of building supplies out to our estate.

There is no public message service in the empire. Imperial messengers dash around all over the place carrying official documents, and it is sometimes possible to bribe one of them to carry a personal letter, but unless you want to send a slave hundreds of miles to deliver a message, most written documents are simply passed to a trader who happens to be going to, or near, the destination. Such letters can pass through several hands before they reach the intended recipient, and often take months to arrive.

I paid the man for his trouble, then left Caecus to take care of the delivery of goods, taking my package into the villa where I carried it up to my private study.

I cut open the stitching and pulled out a thick, folded wad of parchment. This had been wrapped in a linen cloth and had also been sealed with a large blob of red wax. I recognised the seal which confirmed my suspicion that this was a letter from my mother.

I'm afraid it's time for further explanations. If you thought my life was already complicated, there is even more to it. You see, I had been content to change my name and let the world believe Sextus Sempronius Secundus Scipio had died while on some mission on behalf of Emperor Macrinus, but I could not have let my mother believe that. She was one of only two people in Rome who knew the full truth about me and Circe, and I had always known I must let her know I was still alive.

Of course, I could not write it out in a letter in case it fell into the wrong hands, so I'd sent a coded message to the only other person I'd entrusted with the full story of my relationship with Circe. That was my friend Fronto, who happened to work for the imperial spy network. He was based on the Palatine Hill in Rome where he and a small army of scribes had sent and received messages on behalf of the Emperor's network of informers. In fact, it had been Fronto who had first recruited me into the service, telling me all about Sempronius Rufus, the spy master who was usually referred to by his codename of "The Juggler". Most importantly for my story, Fronto had devised a special code which he and I used to exchange information. I had used that code to tell him I was still alive and where I was. I'd also told him to warn my mother that she would receive a letter from someone named Valerius Cantiacus who was a friend of her dead son. Since then, my mother and I had carried on a long-distance, if rather infrequent, exchange of letters.

This latest parchment, though, contained an additional message which fell out when I broke the seal and unfolded the thick document. This smaller letter was instantly recognisable as a coded message from Fronto.

My heart skipped a beat when I saw it. Fronto rarely wrote to me, so this suggested something out of the ordinary had happened.

I was in two minds as to whether to read my mother's letter first or to decode the message from Fronto. After some dithering, I decided to read the main letter because decoding Fronto's scribbles was likely to take a long time.

So I settled in a comfortable armchair beside the open window and began to read.

"To Sextus Valerius Cantiacus, from your friend Zoe."

My mother, as you can tell from her name, is from the east. She'd been born in Syria, and had been taken back to Rome by my father when he retired from the Legions. It had been a way for her to escape the grinding poverty she had been born into, and she had become a model Roman wife, although she had ensured that I learned all about the history of the east. She had also taught me how to speak her native Aramaic, which was one of the reasons I had been so useful as an imperial spy. When my knowledge of a local language was allied to the dark looks I'd inherited from her, it had allowed me to pass as a native during some long expeditions into Parthian territory.

Pushing those memories to the back of my mind, I read on. There were the usual wishes of health for me and my family before she got to the main reason for her letter.

"I am writing to ask for your help," she informed me. "I know you have some experience of investigating crimes, and I do not know who else to turn to."

With a growing sense of foreboding, I continued to take in the neat writing. It had probably been penned by one of her slaves, for my mother had never learned to read or write properly.

"My son, Sextus Sempronius Primus, has received death threats. He had assured me they were the work of pranksters and were not to be taken seriously, but yesterday he was attacked in the streets and barely survived with his life. He was badly injured and, although the doctor we summoned says he will live, it will take him some time to recover. What nobody can assure me of is that his attackers will not try again, and their next attempt may succeed."

I was feeling distinctly uncomfortable by this time, but I kept reading.

The letter went on, "My dearest friend Cantiacus, I need your help. Please, I beg you, come to Rome and help discover who was behind this attack. I implore you, for the sake of our friendship, come to my aid. I fear not just for the life of my son, but for my grandchildren."

She signed off with the usual formalities, but it was an odd letter. Normally, my mother filled pages with inconsequential tales of my brother's family. This time, it was a short appeal for help.

Just then, the door curtain was pulled aside and Circe walked into my study. She has her own private office where she insists on keeping a very close eye on the estate's financial affairs, but news of a letter from Rome was bound to attract her attention.

"Is something wrong?" she asked as soon as she saw the expression on my face.

"I'm not sure," I replied, handing her the letter.

She read it quickly, her face growing increasingly concerned.

"We must go and help!" she told me.

"Why? Primus is an ass. If someone beat him up, he probably deserved it."

"Scipio! You can't talk that way about your own brother."

"Yes I can. The greedy bastard inherited everything when our father died, and he made it very clear indeed that I was not welcome in his house. If I was in Rome, I'd have happily helped give him a good kicking."

Circe frowned at me.

"That was all a long time ago," she declared. "You were still only a teenager."

"Yes, and I haven't spoken to Primus since the day I left home all those years ago. I don't really want to see him again now."

"Then we must go for your mother's sake. She is obviously very frightened."

"That puzzles me, too. It's not as if Primus is short of ready cash. If someone is out to get him, I'm sure he is perfectly capable of finding out who is responsible."

Circe gave me another of her stern looks.

"Not if he is badly hurt," she told me. "Or perhaps he doesn't know anyone who could carry out such an investigation."

"He should report it to the *vigiles*," I returned. "That's their job."

Circe's expression told me what she thought of the men who were supposed to investigate crimes in Rome.

"We both know they don't spend much time on things like that," she countered. "We really ought to go, and you know it."

I scowled. The thought of returning to Rome was bad enough, but doing it to help my brother made it even worse.

Circe went on, "You cannot leave your mother in danger. We must try to help her."

"It's not easy as that," I argued. "There are a lot of very powerful people in Rome who think I'm dead. If they find out I'm still alive, who knows what might happen?"

"You are worrying over nothing," Circe declared. "You are in no danger from Julia Maesa. As Caecus said, it was Macrinus you were hiding from, and he has been dead these past four years."

"But what about you?" I shot back. "You've spent your whole life hiding from imperial vengeance, and I dare say Julia Maesa wouldn't regard you as a friend. You were supposed to persuade Martialis to kill Macrinus as well as Caracalla."

"It's not my fault it didn't turn out that way," she protested, her eyes glaring at me.

We were in danger of falling out over our respective roles in Caracalla's assassination, but Circe sighed, waving a hand as if to dismiss the matter.

"Let's not fight over all that," she decided. "It doesn't really matter now. As for travelling to Rome, Julia Maesa has never met me, and she doesn't know my name."

"Which name?" I smirked. "You have so many."

"None of them," she grinned back. "She only ever met Collinus, and he was in disguise. So it's perfectly safe for us to go to Rome."

33

"Being near the imperial family is never safe," I warned.

"They won't even know we are there," she insisted. "This is a private matter."

I knew when I was beaten, so I simply held up the smaller parchment.

"I haven't read Fronto's message yet."

"Then let's read it now," she told me.

So I sat down and began decoding the letter from my friend. Apart from the date written neatly at the foot of the message, it looked like a meaningless list of random letters which made no sense at all. It had been a while since I'd needed to decipher one of these, but I quickly got into the swing of it. Picking up a wax tablet and a stylus, I explained to Circe, "The letter is dated three days before the Ides of November. That means we need to adjust each letter by fourteen, counting forwards through the Latin alphabet."

"Fourteen?" she frowned.

"Three for the days and eleven for the number of the month."

She nodded, "I see. That's quite a calculation."

"It's even more complicated than that," I told her. "The letter is written in columns, not across the page from left to right."

It was indeed a complex code, but I soon began scratching out the translated message while Circe peered over my shoulder.

"Dear Sextus," Fronto began, using my personal *praenomen*. "You will see from your mother's message that your brother, Primus, is in some trouble. I know this is unlikely to persuade you to return to Rome, but you should know that the danger is also to his family, including your mother. There have been many threats made, including one to burn the house down. I know you care little for Primus, but I genuinely believe you should come here. I believe your mother has at last recognised what you and I have known for a long time about Primus. He has become wealthy, and I fear he may use that wealth to take drastic action once he recovers from his injuries. This can only result in an escalation of whatever feud lies behind the attack.

"Your mother is a proud woman, but I do believe that she would be prepared to leave Rome if you asked her to travel to Africa with you. Primus' behaviour has shocked her, but she is reluctant to take any drastic steps on her own initiative. I think it would be good for her, and for you, if you came to Rome and used the excuse of tracking down Primus' attackers to give you time to persuade her to return home with you."

Well, that put rather a different complexion on things. I sighed and read on.

"I know you will have reservations about coming back," Fronto wrote, "but I do not think you need fear. Things have changed since our new Emperor took the throne. The Juggler no longer controls the spy network. He, like many others, was replaced. Those who now run the empire have too many things on their minds to concern themselves over you, especially if you confine yourself to helping with a private matter."

That, I thought, was easy for Fronto to say. It wasn't his neck on the line.

Circe said, "Well, that settles it. We must go."

I reached out to hold her hand, putting it to my lips to gently kiss the backs of her fingers.

"It could still be very dangerous," I warned. "It sounds like we could be walking into the middle of a gang war."

"Stop making excuses!" she told me. "We must go. Your mother needs you."

"Fronto may be wrong," I cautioned. "She might prefer to stay in Rome. She has lived there most of her life."

"We won't know until we ask her," Circe pointed out.

"And you wouldn't mind her coming to live with us?"

"Of course not!" she insisted.

"I suppose I should go, then."

With a triumphant smile, Circe beamed, "Good. And don't tell me you wouldn't love a chance to lord it over your brother. He's done well for himself, but you are even richer than he is. I know you'd like to let him see that."

"Scoring points over my brother is not important," I lied.

Then another thought struck me.

I said, "We can't go just now, though. It's far too late in the season. We'd probably end up drowning when the ship sinks in a storm."

Circe treated me to her smile again.

"Trade and commerce do not cease entirely in the winter months," she reminded me. "Lots of ships continue to sail."

"And lots of them sink," I retorted.

It was no good. I could see the gleam in her eyes, and I knew we would be travelling to Rome whatever I said. Circe had spent a lot of her life involved in travelling as well as in intrigue. Since I'd found her, I thought she had been content to settle down, but I could now tell that it was the prospect of excitement which appealed to her.

"The children stay here," I said as forcefully as I could.

"No. They should meet their grandmother."

"They'll meet her when she comes back here," I argued.

"If she comes," Circe countered. "Seeing her grandchildren might help persuade her."

"It might put her off," I muttered, earning me an angry glare.

"Don't be silly," she scolded. "The children should come with us. Family is important, Scipio, and they are all I have."

I knew that wasn't strictly true, but Circe had been estranged from her few surviving relatives for more than two decades, and the reasons for their falling out were even more valid than my own disagreement with Primus.

"We will leave as soon as I can arrange passage," she informed me in a tone which denied any possibility of argument.

And so ended the peaceful days of my quiet retirement. Rome beckoned once again, and I had no option but to answer the call.

Chapter 4
Journey

It did not take long to find a ship to take us to Rome. This was because one of Circe's many business investments was in a small fleet of merchant ships. All she needed to do was have one of the slaves carry a letter to the shipping contractor in Leptis Magna, and a boat was quickly found to take us on our journey.

Circe's wide range of business interests never ceases to amaze me. Under Roman law, I could have insisted she pass control of all her financial affairs over to me as soon as we married, but I had left everything with her. The truth was that she was far more capable of controlling the purse strings than I was, so I was happy to let her carry on, even if this did result in occasional surprises like the production of maritime transport at such short notice.

"Some ships' captains don't like transporting passengers," I reminded her.

"This one won't mind," she replied archly. "Not if he knows what's good for him. I own the ship, you see."

So that matter was settled, although it didn't stop me fretting about the risk of travelling in winter. The Mediterranean can be a dangerous place for sailing vessels. In fact, during the first war against Carthage more than four hundred years ago, Rome had lost more warships to storms than to enemy action. Entire fleets had been sunk by Neptune. That was why I really would have preferred to wait a few months before setting off, but Circe refused to be swayed.

"If your mother is in danger," she told me, "the least we can do is risk a little bad weather."

I feared we might experience rather more than a few squalls, but Circe was determined we should go, so that left me only one other problem.

Caecus had done a wonderful job of building our new slave quarters. The wooden frame had been erected, brick and plaster walls raised, and the tiled roof put in place. There was still a lot of internal work to be done, but the basic structure of the new building, including drains, had been completed. Caecus, I knew, was content, but now I had to tell him we were planning to travel to Rome.

"Do you want to come with us?" I asked him when I went out to take a look at how the construction work was progressing. "It is entirely up to you. You are welcome to stay here and look after the estate while we are away."

He answered my question with one of his own.

"Do you want me to come with you?"

I said, "The issue is whether you want to come. It's your decision."

"But you believe there may be some danger?"

"The greatest danger is drowning on the way," I shrugged. "I'm not sure about the rest of it. My brother does seem to have got himself mixed up with something risky, though."

"And you will investigate this on your own?"

"I'll need to go through the motions for my mother's sake," I told him. "As for doing it on my own, Collinus will be coming."

As I'd hoped, that was the clinching argument. Caecus and Collinus had developed quite a rivalry over the past weeks, and I suspected Caecus would not want to be left out if Collinus was accompanying us.

There was a gleam in the former Centurion's eyes when he said, "Then I'll go with you too. Julianus can take care of the estate without any interference from me. And I can leave Longus to take care of finishing the work here."

I smiled. Longus was one of our freedmen overseers. He was a short, squat Gaul whose only major fault was a tendency to become drunk. He'd been assigned to assist Caecus with supervising the building work, and he'd managed to stay sober ever since the first occasion when Caecus had found him sleeping off a hangover instead of being on the site. Caecus had dragged him from his bed and thrown him into one of the irrigation channels, holding his head under water until Longus had spluttered his submission. There had been no further trouble with any of the building crew, and it was a good sign that Caecus now trusted the little Gaul enough to leave him in charge.

Not that this prevented Caecus laying down the law when he gave Longus his final instructions.

"I expect the place to be ready by the time I get back," he growled at the little Gaul. "If it's not done right, I'll use your head as a battering ram to demolish it so we can start again."

I must admit I was glad Caecus was coming with us. He was very tough and extremely competent, and having him watch my back if I did need to go places where I'd need some muscle was a great comfort.

Other aspects of the journey still troubled me, though. I had argued long and hard with Circe about bringing the children, but she refused to leave them behind. We also had a sizeable train of slaves to help us. Our son's tutor, a Greek named Hermion, accompanied us very reluctantly, while two of the younger female slaves were available to help Circe with the children. Her old servant Helena was deemed too elderly to travel, which seemed to upset the old woman since she regarded our children as something akin to her own grandchildren. I wondered what sort of clashes that might result in if my mother did return with us. Helena's influence meant that young Sextus' speech was already a mix of Latin and Punic, while Hermion had begun teaching him Greek. Being young, the boy took it all in his stride, but his conversation was often peppered with words from all three languages in one statement.

Not that I minded Helena. She'd been rather distant with me at first, but she now treated me with a modicum of respect, and she had certainly helped me learn how to speak Punic.

Even without Helena, though, I felt our group was unnecessarily large. Circe insisted we should take a dozen male slaves to carry our luggage. Caecus, Collinus and I travelled light, each of us cramming our essential belongings into small packs, but Circe had brought six large and heavy wooden trunks.

"What's all that?" I asked her.

"The bare minimum," she told me. "You wanted to be inconspicuous, so I cut down on everything except the absolute necessities."

In fairness to Circe, I'd seen wealthy Romans insist on having a baggage train of a hundred mules and as many slaves to accompany them on a journey, so by those standards, Circe really had restrained herself.

There were other surprises in store for me before we set off. Collinus had abandoned his usual Berber robes and was dressed in a Roman-style tunic and cloak. I blinked when I saw him, but he acted as if his new appearance was perfectly normal. Which, when I thought about it, it was. Nobody would give him a second glance in Rome. As long as he kept his dagger concealed, that was.

"Blades aren't allowed in Rome," I informed him.

"Most people carry knives for eating," he countered in his calm, authoritative way.

"Yes, but you could eat an elephant with that thing," I said. "Best keep it out of sight."

He gave a cool nod, but he tucked the dagger behind his back where a cloak would conceal it. That, I knew, was the best I could hope for. Collinus never went anywhere without that blade.

As for the ship which would take us to Rome, it was a medium sized, two-masted merchant vessel with four passenger cabins. Circe and I shared one with our children, Collinus and Caecus had one each on the grounds we felt it best to keep them apart, and the fourth was given over to the female slaves. The male slaves were given makeshift beds in the hold which contained only a small cargo of olive oil.

The captain, a bald, broad-shouldered man with a squint in one eye, was called Lepidus. He was ingratiatingly polite, and made no quibble about undertaking such a long voyage in the worst season of the year, nor did he complain about having most of the cargo space given over to our slaves and baggage.

"The Lady Aurelia has made sure we won't lose any money on the trip," he told me.

"But will we reach Rome safely?" I asked anxiously.

He shrugged, "We shall make all the necessary sacrifices to Neptune, but I expect we may still need to take shelter if the sea gets rough. But I can assure you we'll be careful. The most dangerous part is crossing from Carthage to Sicily. That's open sea for three days at least, depending on the wind. If we survive that, we'll probably be fine."

40

I didn't much care for his use of 'if' and 'probably', but I wasn't in much position to protest since I spent the first few days hanging over the rail being very seasick. I'm normally fine on a sea voyage, but I had never really sailed in rough weather before, so this trip was unusually miserable for me.

I wasn't the only sufferer. Most of the slaves felt the effects of the rolling, pitching ship too. Caecus was also looking rather green, although he did manage to retain the contents of his stomach. But he stayed on deck most of the time, only taking shelter during the not infrequent squalls of wind and rain which battered us as we made our slow way along the African coast.
Naturally, Circe and Collinus, as well as our children, seemed entirely unaffected by the rough seas. For the rest of us, the voyage was very unpleasant.

It was also very long. In summertime, the captain would have been confident of completing the journey in less than three weeks, but it took nearly twice as long for us to reach Ostia, Rome's nearest sea port. We'd battled against the prevailing wind as we travelled west along the northern coast of Africa, and had sometimes been forced to seek refuge for a couple of days until a storm blew itself out. Once we'd reached Carthage, though, things improved. With a fair wind driving us on, we shot northwards, reaching Sicily without mishap, and after that it was a case of following the western coast of Italia northwards until we reached Ostia.

"I told you we would get here safely," Circe smiled at me as I stumbled ashore, my legs wobbling as I adjusted to the feel of solid earth beneath my feet.

It was late in the afternoon, so we decided to spend the night in Ostia before travelling on towards Rome. It's a journey of around twenty miles, and I reckoned it would take an entire day, so we found a decent inn where we paid an extortionate amount for rooms for the night. With her usual foresight, Circe had ensured that we had plenty of silver with us. Each of the locked trunks of baggage contained a bag of coins in addition to the spare clothing and accessories she had packed.

Ostia is a big place. It's the busiest port in the Roman world apart from Alexandria. In fact, since Caracalla set his Legions loose on Alexandria in a fit of imperial pique, Ostia may well have taken over as number one. There are a couple of harbours, and even in winter ships come and go all the time. It's also the base for a large part of the imperial fleet whose main purpose nowadays is to transport soldiers from one part of the empire to another. There are no enemy fleets to battle, and piracy was more or less stamped out a couple of centuries ago.

The town itself is a thriving place, almost a miniature of Rome with its temples, forum and large merchant complexes where the various trades gather to exchange goods and news. There are also massive warehouses where the grain shipped from Egypt and Africa is stored before being transported to Rome to be doled out to the poorer citizens. In short, Ostia plays a critical part in the daily running of the empire.

Naturally, the town has plenty of hostelries catering for travellers. Even so, it can sometimes be difficult to find rooms because of the sheer level of the demand, but we had arrived at their quietest time of the year, so we had our pick. In keeping with our stated intention of retaining a low profile, we selected a mid-range establishment where we could eat a decent meal and sleep on relatively comfortable and clean beds.

The next day, after a breakfast of porridge and fruit juice, we made for Rome. Caecus had hired three wagons. Pulled by lumbering oxen, they were very slow, but they were able to haul all our luggage and slaves. Circe and I rode in a proper carriage with Caecus, Collinus and our children. Collinus gave the appearance of disinterest and spent much of the journey with his eyes closed, apparently dozing, while Caecus seemed lost in thought. Young Sextus spent most of the journey sitting on my knee and staring out of the window. He wasn't normally a voluble or expressive lad, but he chattered away to me, asking all about the things we passed on the road.

"I was born in Rome," I informed him. "And my mother still lives there."

He considered this for a moment, then asked, "Does she have a big house?"

Young children, I was learning, have very different views of the world than adults. It seemed Sextus wasn't at all interested in my family history, only in their material wealth.

"Yes, she does," I told him. "My brother lives there too, along with his family. You will soon meet your cousins."

Luckily for me, he didn't appear all that interested in his cousins either. It was just as well since I had never even met Primus' wife, let alone his son and daughter. I knew from my mother's letters that they were older than my children by a couple of years, but they remained strangers as far as I was concerned.

I can't say it was the most interesting trip I'd ever made. The carriage was hot and stuffy, especially when Valeria soiled herself, and we moved at a slow pace to allow the oxen to keep up, so the day did rather drag. We made a couple of stops, taking lunch at a roadside inn, then travelled on throughout the afternoon.

Large, wheeled vehicles aren't allowed within Rome's city limits during daytime, so we paid the drivers, dismounted and unloaded our belongings. The slaves hefted the trunks, two of them to each crate, while the rest of us slung our packs on our backs, and we entered the heart of the empire.

We'd followed the *Via Ostiensis* which runs near the River Tiber all the way from Ostia to Rome, so we now passed through the Field of Mars which, in days long past, used to be an open space where the army of the Republic had trained and exercised for war. These days, while there is still some open space, much of it is as built up as any other part of the city. I made a point of leading us past some of the most significant buildings, notably the Altar of Peace, the mausoleum of Augustus, the Theatre of Pompey where good old Julius Caesar had met his bloody end, and the magnificent Pantheon built by Hadrian, with its huge, marble columns and enormous dome. All of these lie outside the old city walls because Rome is so powerful it no longer needs to rely on defensive walls for protection. The old defences, said to have been built hundreds of years ago by King Servius Tullius, are still there, so we passed beneath the arch of the Raedusculam Gate, then turned north, by-passing the centre of the city to head up to the Quirinal Hill.

We could have hired litters to carry us, but we decided to walk because it wasn't very far from the Field of Mars to the Quirinal in the north of the city. The walk also allowed us to drive off the last stiffness from weeks at sea.

I ended up carrying Sextus on my shoulders, while Valeria was passed between Circe and her two slaves, clinging onto their necks as she gazed at the noisy, smelly bustle all around us. She even contributed to the cacophony with some loud wails of her own when she decided she was hungry.

It was a slow walk, and I was beginning to regret not having hired a litter by the time we eventually trudged up the long street on the Quirinal Hill towards my brother's house.

I had spent much of the day wondering what sort of reception we would receive and wondering, too, how I should act when I met Primus. I wasn't looking forward to that particular encounter, and Circe knew it.

"Don't let him bully you," she advised softly as we tramped up the cobbled lane between high houses.

The Quirinal has never been the most affluent part of the city, but I'd noticed an improvement the last time I'd been here a few years ago. There were still plenty of the tall, four or five-storey tenements which are ubiquitous throughout the empire, but there were grander homes as well, all of them intermingled.

"That's Fronto's house," I said as we passed one of the larger homes, a two-storey structure which I knew was built around a central peristyle garden. I was tempted to knock on the door, but we had been on the road all day, and evening was advancing, so we carried on further up the narrow street.

A surprise awaited me. My father, who had retired from the army as a Centurion, had bought a moderately sized house up here when he had returned to Rome from Syria. He had told me he had grown up on the Quirinal and wanted to return to show his old neighbours how well he had done for himself. He had achieved this by buying a house rather than renting rooms in one of the tenements where he had grown up. When I asked him which neighbours he meant, he had grumbled something about most of them having already moved away or died, but he'd still stayed up here in the northern part of the city, probably because, having made his decision, he was too stubborn to change his mind.

The house was still there, its front wall bearing a solid door and shutters on high windows. Security is important in Rome, so having large windows on the street-facing side was never a good idea. What struck me, though, was the building next door.

Where there had once been a four-storey tenement, there was now a very large house, its red roof tiles just visible over the ten-foot high stone wall which surrounded it. This place had large double doors which presumably led into an entrance courtyard, but little else could be seen of it. The wall was aligned with the corner of my brother's house, effectively joining the two properties together.

I stopped, momentarily confused. The old door was still where I remembered, but it was obvious that my old home was now relegated to the status of a small part of a much larger dwelling.

"Mother mentioned Primus was having an extension built," I told Circe. "But that's a lot bigger than I imagined."

"Yes," she nodded. "It's almost as big as the slave quarters Caecus designed for us."

I couldn't help laughing at that.

"I'll need to remember that one," I grinned. "Come on, let's see who is at home."

Chapter 5
Dinner

I ignored the double doors of what was obviously the main entrance and strode towards the door I remembered from my childhood. I can't explain exactly why I did this, but something inside me was telling me not to conform to whatever it was Primus wanted his visitors to do.

I noticed the door was a new one, or at least not the same one I recalled. I thumped on the thick oak several times before I heard a scuffling of footsteps from the other side. These were followed by the unmistakable sounds of bolts being withdrawn. Then the door swung open to reveal a muscle-bound, shaven-headed man who held a heavy cudgel in his right hand.

"Use the main door," he growled, his eyes scanning us for any signs of threatening behaviour.

"Why?" I asked him as politely as I could in the circumstances.

"All Sempronius Primus' visitors must use the main door," he informed me.

"But we're not here to visit Sempronius Primus," I told him. "We are here at the invitation of the Lady Zoe. This is her house, isn't it?"

He seemed unsure how to respond, but he was saved from answering by the arrival of an elderly man with stooped shoulders, grey hair and blinking eyes who came up behind him and leaned around to peer out at me.

It had been more than fifteen years since I'd seen him, but I knew him instantly.

"Hello, Lucius," I said in greeting. "I'm here to see my mother."

This made the old man and his younger companion gape at me in surprise. Then Lucius gasped, "By Jupiter! It's young Master Sextus! The Lady said you would come, but I didn't really believe it."

He paused, his watery gaze taking in Circe and the long queue of attendants standing behind me.

"You'd better come in," he decided, pushing the club-wielding guard aside and opening the door fully to let us in.

As I stepped into the house, I gave the man with the club a triumphant smile. He glowered back at me, but made no move to prevent us entering the house.

I led the way into the atrium. Nothing much had changed. The decoration had been freshened up, but white walls don't need a great deal of maintenance. I remembered my father had always wanted to have a mosaic floor laid in the atrium, but he'd never quite raised the finances to have that work undertaken. Primus didn't seem to have bothered either. Even the busts of our ancestors had been removed, leaving the atrium feeling rather bare. The room was cool because it was on the northern side of the house, and the presence of the pool which gathered rain water helped keep the temperature bearable even on the hottest days. Now, with winter upon us, it was decidedly chilly.

Lucius fluttered his hands while the rest of our group filed slowly in, the slaves grateful to dump the heavy trunks on the paved floor.

The guy with the club locked and bolted the door, then scurried off, presumably to report our arrival.

"I will inform the Mistress that you are here," Lucius declared, which suggested Club Man was going to speak to Primus. That was interesting.

It was then that my mother appeared. Against all formal protocol, she came in through the door which led to the main part of the old house. She'd obviously heard us arriving and had come to see what was causing all the noise.

"Sextus!" she beamed as she hurried over to greet me, her arms wide. We embraced for a long time, and I thought she was trying hard to fight back tears. When she did pull away, though, her face was alight with pleasure.

My mother had always been slightly built, and the years had not altered this. Small of stature, she had an inner glow and an elegance about her which I suddenly realised reminded me of Circe even though the two women were unalike in any other way. My mother's dark hair revealed a few hints of grey, but she still seemed much the same as she always had, with the exception of a few additional wrinkles on her tanned face.

She smiled broadly as she turned to Circe.

"And you must be Aurelia," she said. "Or should I call you Circe?"

"Either will do," Circe replied as she, too, gave my mother a hug.

Yes, I thought as I looked on. Circe was tall and slim, and her complexion was fairer than my mother's darker features, but there was definitely a similarity there. What, I wondered, did that say about me?

Then, naturally, my mother spent an age gushing over our children. Young Sextus regarded her with solemn eyes and bore her hugs and kisses with almost stoic indifference, then he moved to stand behind Circe, holding onto her long dress as he peered cautiously around her to keep a wary eye on the grandmother he had never met and who was behaving in a most un-Roman manner.

Valeria, on the other hand, giggled when she was passed over to my mother's embrace, then tried to pull her ear rings out, resulting in much hilarity.

I introduced Collinus, Caecus and Hermion who were all freedmen and, because I knew what my mother was like, I then named all the slaves.

"I hope you have room for all of us," I said.

She waved a hand to tell me not to worry.

"I have the whole of this place to myself these days," she informed us. "Primus and his family moved into the new house next door. There is a connecting passage, and his kitchen staff provide my meals, but I'm left here with only Lucius and Justina, so there is plenty of room."

"You have a door guard as well," I pointed out.

She shrugged, "Oh, Primus always has one of his men on duty there. Not that I get many visitors these days. But let's get you settled in and then we can talk."

The duty man in question returned, a sour expression on his craggy face. He looked us over with a jaundiced eye, then purposefully walked past and made his way to the small room nearest the front door.

My mother completely ignored him. She began giving orders to Lucius while her other slave, a middle-aged, plump little woman named Justina, was summoned and then sent off to the kitchens with orders to have a meal prepared.

"And have fresh bed linen brought!" my mother shouted after her. "We will need beds made up in all the rooms."

I'd almost forgotten the verbal whirlwind my mother could emit. Pointing and waving her hands, she showed the slaves where to take our trunks – which turned out to be the room on the upper floor where I had slept as a boy. Other rooms were set aside for Collinus, Caecus and Hermion, while a couple of rooms leading off the atrium, which had once been the rather pompously named reception rooms, were given over to the slaves. By the standards of most homes in the city, this was luxury for our attendants. Most households had cellars where tiny cubicles, each with a stone shelf, were allocated as slave sleeping chambers. The shelf was the bed, and an old blanket was the best most slaves could hope for. Here, in my mother's home, our retinue was being treated almost royally.

Circe was delighted with the room we had been given. There was a large, comfortable bed, plenty of room for our baggage, and a door leading out onto a balcony which overlooked the small garden at the rear of the house. The late evening sun was bathing this in a warm, orange glow. I joined her on the balcony, slipping one arm around her waist while I used my other hand to keep a tight hold on Valeria to prevent her attempting to climb the wooden railing. Out here the noise of the city still reached us as we looked beyond the garden wall to the vista of rooftops crowding the upper slope of the Quirinal. If we had been closer to the top of the hill, we might have caught a glimpse of the Tiber off to our left, but here, about half way up the southern slope, all we could see were hundreds of buildings perched on the hill which legend said had once been the home of the Sabines, a tribe who had been Rome's first enemies in the days when Romulus had established his new city on what was now known as the Palatine. I had sometimes tried to imagine the lives of all the people who had ever lived on this spot, wondering what stories they might tell. All of those individual lives made up the story of Rome, greatest of all cities, and I confess that standing here again after so many years filled me with a confusing array of emotions. This had been my home, but it was almost like a foreign place to me now.

The garden was a square patch of gravel with large wooden tubs which contained shrubs and bushes. Near the back wall grew two olive trees which, in summer, provided a little shade for the stone benches at their feet. Closer to us were a couple of raised beds of earth which I recalled were used for growing herbs for the kitchen. It was hauntingly familiar, yet seemed a lot smaller and more confined than I remembered.

"So this is where you grew up," Circe said as she gazed all around, taking in the view.

"Yes, although quite a few things have changed. The shrubs in the garden are taller now. You used to be able to see the gate in the back wall from here. And, of course, that used to be a tall tenement."

I nodded to my right where the substantial bulk of Primus' new home now stood, a wall with several windows facing us. Primus certainly hadn't stinted on the construction. The place looked solidly expensive, and the roof tiles still retained their red hue, not yet having been faded by the Italian sun.

"Did you notice the graffiti on the front wall of the house?" Circe asked me.

"Not really. Most walls in Rome have graffiti of some sort or other. It's a tradition."

"Yes, I'd noticed that. But some of the comments on your brother's house were rather different to the other scribbles I saw on the way here."

"Different? How?"

"Oh, you know. 'Sempronius Primus is a crook', 'Primus deserves a knife in the back'. That sort of thing. They'd been whitewashed over, but the words were coming through again. And there was a newer one which hadn't been covered. It was a very crude image of a headless corpse."

My response to this was interrupted when my mother bustled in, followed by a couple of young slave girls. They carried bundles of fresh bed linen and began making up the bed for us.

"The children can sleep next door," my mother announced. "Come and take a look. There is room for your personal slaves there as well if you want."

So we had a quick tour of the place, with Circe smiling and nodding as my mother regaled her with tales of what each room had formerly been used for. Most of them were almost empty now and smelled rather musty, so she had the shutters opened to admit some fresh air.

"I'll have curtains put up to stop mosquitos getting in," she promised. "Now, come down for dinner while the beds are made up for you."

Circe insisted on staying with the children who were tired and needed to get to bed, so I followed my mother downstairs. As we made our way to the dining room, a burly man with short, dark hair and a stubbled beard appeared, stepping in front of us and blocking our path.

He gave a tiny bow, his body bending slightly at the waist, but there was more condescension than respect in the gesture.

Unfazed by his surly attitude, my mother said brightly, "Mardonius, this is my son, Sextus Sempronius Scipio."

Turning to me, she explained, "Mardonius is Primus' *major domo*."

I gave the man a nod. It wasn't clear whether he was a freedman or a slave, but he was certainly a large fellow, so I treated him with some wary respect.

He said, "My master has a guest this evening. He hopes to speak to you later. Or perhaps tomorrow. I am sure you will want to rest after your long journey."

"Yes," I replied, leaving my intentions vague.

He studied me for a moment, then nodded and turned away, striding towards a door which hadn't existed when I had lived in this house as a boy.

"That's the way to Primus' house?" I guessed.

"Yes," my mother confirmed, her mouth set in a tight line. "And that was Mardonius. He's not a pleasant man."

"I can't say I took to him," I agreed.

"And he is a lot nicer than some of the other brutes Primus has working for him now."

"Because of what has happened?"

"Yes," she sighed. "He has always had a fondness for having hefty servants, but he's recruited quite a few extra bodyguards since the attack."

She glanced around, noticed a couple of kitchen slaves delivering plates to the dining room, and said softly, "We can talk over dinner. Once Primus' slaves have left us."

That, I thought, struck a very jarring note indeed, and I recalled Fronto's letter in which he'd suggested my mother had, at long last, given up on my brother. I was tempted to say something, but Circe and I had agreed that it would be best to take our time to feel our way. If we charged in and told my mother she must come back to Africa with us, she was stubborn enough to dig her heels in.

"We should take our time to work on her," Circe had advised. "And you need to find out what it is Primus is up to. Knowing that may help us convince your mother to return home with us."

So all I did was squeeze my mother's arm in a gesture of support, then follow her into the dining room where we waited until the others joined us.

Like our own dining room back home, this spacious chamber was set out in the traditional *triclinium* style, with three long couches placed around a series of low tables so that slaves could bring and remove dishes from the open end of the square layout. My mother reclined on the couch at the head of the table, Circe and I shared the one to her right, while Caecus and Collinus shared the other. Hermion, Circe informed me, had decided to eat in his room. From the quick glance she gave me, I suspected she had made this decision for him.

I had to admit that Primus' cooks had done a good job at such short notice. There were traditional Roman dishes like stuffed dormice, and also baked trout, lamb strips, a roasted pheasant, oysters, mushrooms, cabbage and bowls of lentils. There was also a pot of pungent *garum*, the fish sauce which was so popular all across the empire. Bread, honey and fruit preserves completed the repast, while the wine was as good as any our own estate could offer.

At first, the chat was all very informal, with my mother insisting Circe should call her Zoe, and asking all about our journey. I let Circe do the talking because I was enjoying seeing the two of them sparring in the way mothers and daughters-in-law always do. It soon became clear, though, that they were in danger of forming some sort of alliance against me. Fortunately, the conversation moved on as my mother began asking Collinus and Caecus about themselves.

"Scipio never mentioned you in his letters," she said, shooting me a disapproving frown.

Collinus merely said, "I am a humble servant."

He rarely said much at any time, and Caecus seemed uncomfortable in these surroundings, but Circe came to their rescue, saying, "Collinus has been with me since I was a girl. He joined my father's service when he was a boy himself, and was appointed to take care of me. He has done so ever since."

Moving on quickly, she explained, "Aelius Caecus joined us only recently. He and Scipio met a few years ago when Caecus was in the army. He's retired now."

"He's even bigger than some of Primus' guards," my mother observed, a comment which I was astonished to note brought a tinge of a flush to Caecus' rough-hewn face.

Circe cast a meaningful glance towards the slaves, Lucius and Justina, who were standing behind my mother's couch, ready to refill wine cups when needed. My mother noticed her look, but carried on as if the two slaves were invisible.

She asked, "Did I do wrong to tell Mardonius your real name?"

I shrugged, "I suppose Primus would have told him in any event. But as far as the rest of the city is concerned, I'm Sextus Valerius Cantiacus."

"Yes," my mother smiled. "And you didn't need to send that secret message to Fronto to warn me. I would have known it was you if you'd written directly to me using that name."

Circe's delicate eyebrows arched when she heard this.

"I didn't know the name had any significance," she said, treating me to an accusatory frown.

I gave a helpless shrug, while my mother laughed, "Oh, yes, although I don't suppose anyone except young Tiberius Fronto or I would understand it."

In response to Circe's inquisitive stare, she explained, "When Sextus was a young boy, there was another young lad who lived in the tenement next door. He was a sorry little thing, as skinny as a stylus, and always dressed in ragged clothes. His name was Gnaeus Valerius."

A shadow of regret passed over her face as she went on, "Then, one day, he just disappeared. Nobody ever found out what happened to him. But his father was a drunk, and a violent one. Valerius' mother often had bruises on her arms and even her face once or twice. The boy was often beaten, and I had words with the father on more than one occasion, but he wasn't the sort to listen."

She sighed as she said, "I have often wished I'd done more to help the lad, but it was no use."

"You think the father killed the boy?" Circe gasped.

My mother shrugged, "Who knows? There were always gangs roaming the streets at night. There still are, come to that. Maybe he fell foul of some hooligans. Or perhaps he ran away, although I doubt it. He wouldn't have left his mother."

"So what happened?"

"Valerius' mother left a short time after the boy's disappearance. She walked out, though, and everyone saw her go. I don't know what happened to her, but I hope she found a better life than the one she'd led up to then."

"And the father?"

My mother's voice held a hint of satisfaction as she reported, "He fell down the tenement steps one night when he was drunk. He broke his neck. An accident, so people said."

I said nothing. I remembered little Valerius, and I also remembered the satisfied looks on the faces of the neighbours when his father 'accidentally' fell down the stairs. It was justice of a sort, I suppose, although the old drunk had always maintained he knew nothing about his son's disappearance.

Looking at me, Circe said, "So Valerius disappeared without a trace? That's why you chose that name when you wanted to drop out of sight?"

"It seemed appropriate," I nodded.

"And Cantiacus?"

"That's even easier to explain," my mother smiled. "You see, Sextus' father was descended from a Briton who had belonged to a tribe known as the Cantiaci. He was brought to Rome as a slave, but he was freed when his master died. That was Sextus' great-grandfather, but the story was passed down through the generations."

"It's nice to know what lies behind a name," Circe smiled.

I almost laughed aloud. In the years I had known her, she'd adopted more names than I could keep up with. Upper class Romans add names or even change them to suit their political allegiances, so there was nothing particularly unusual about our habit of using pseudonyms, although our reasons for doing so were more out of a desire to keep our true identities secret. I wasn't sure that would work now we were in Rome, but I still didn't particularly want anyone in authority finding out my real name.

I decided it was time to change the subject. Taking a sip of wine to wash down a spicy piece of meat, I asked, "So why don't you tell us why you asked us here? You said Primus was being threatened and had been beaten up. He's obviously still alive, and he has plenty of heavies to keep him safe, so what's going on?"

My mother's expression grew serious as she informed me, "You know Primus has always wanted to be wealthy and powerful. He's built up a lot of business ventures, and he's made a lot of money, but he's also made plenty of enemies. It seems one of those is determined to do away with him."

"Which one?"

"I don't know. And if Primus does, he hasn't told me. He refuses to discuss the subject with me."

"So how did he manage to get himself beaten up if he has all these bodyguards?"

"He didn't have as many until then," she explained. "Even so, he always had a retinue of guards when he went out. But it was purely down to bad luck. He'd been at some private function, visiting a Senator he'd been trying to impress. Hortensia had been with him, but she had left early, so Primus sent most of the guards back with her."

Hortensia, I knew, was my brother's wife. I knew very little about her as he'd married her long after I'd left Rome in search of adventure.

My mother continued, "He only had two men with him, and it was a very dark night. They were almost home when they were attacked by a dozen men armed with clubs."

"Where, exactly, did it happen?" I asked.

She told me, "At the junction with the *Via Salaria*, just a couple of hundred paces up the road."

"They were waiting for him?"

My mother nodded, "Apparently they called out his name before they attacked."

"So it wasn't a random mugging, then?"

"Definitely not," she said.

"So what happened next?"

She explained, "The guards said later that the thugs weren't very tough, but there were so many of them it soon turned into a running battle. Primus became separated from his guards, and three men set on him. They broke his arm, several ribs, and his left leg. That still hasn't healed properly, so he can hardly walk even after all this time. And he took an awful blow to the head."

She pursed her lips, then continued, "Luckily for him, a squad of *vigiles* turned up, so the gang ran off before they could kill him."

"Were none of them caught?"

She shook her head.

"I don't think the *vigiles* were keen on running through dark alleyways at night."

I gave a shrug. The *vigiles'* main task is making sure fires do not break out in the city. They are also supposed to investigate crimes, but most of them view that as a much lower priority, and their lack of interest in chasing Primus' attackers was hardly surprising.

I asked, "Did Primus recognise any of the men who attacked him?"

"He says not."

"Has anything else happened?"

"Not really. But there's been a lot of abusive graffiti, and we've had stones thrown in through open windows."

"That was probably just kids," I replied. "We all used to do that when we were young."

"Did you?" my mother frowned.

"It was a long time ago," I shrugged. "But is that all that's happened?"

"It's enough!" my mother declared. "Some of the graffiti threatened to burn the house down."

That, I knew, was more serious. Fire is an ever-present threat in the city, which is why the *vigiles* have patrols out every night watching for any burning buildings. When so much cooking is done indoors on open fires, the *vigiles* are kept busy.

I asked, "But, aside from the threats, has there been any other attack?"

"Not that I know of," my mother admitted. "But Primus is keeping very much to himself these days. There are lots of comings and goings, but he never tells me anything. Perhaps he will tell you more when you see him."

I still wasn't looking forward to that inevitable confrontation, but I put it to one side for the moment.

"What has Primus done about the situation? Fronto suggested he was gearing up for a street war."

My mother explained, "As I mentioned, he's recruited more bodyguards, including several ex-gladiators. Primus won't tell me what they've been up to, but one of the guards had a black eye and kept his arm in a sling for a couple of weeks, and others have been nursing bruises."

"It all sounds very stupid," Circe put in.

My mother said, "But also very dangerous. I'm not allowed to go out unless I have half a dozen of Primus' men to escort me."

"So you want me to find out who he is waging this war against?" I asked. "But what do you expect me to do about it?"

"Stop it," she said simply.

"I doubt I can stop a gang war on my own," I told her.

"You could try," my mother insisted with the certainty of so many mothers addressing their sons.

Circe ventured, "I'm sure Scipio will do his best to find out what is going on. Whether he can stop it will depend on what he learns."

My mother gave a sad nod, then looked bleakly down into her wine cup. I think she understood, and I also think she was torn. She had lived most of her life in Rome, becoming a Roman matron who had raised her two children as best she could. Primus had always been our father's favourite, while she had tended to favour me while still trying to treat us as equally as possible. When I had left Rome, though, she had been left alone with Primus, and I felt a

57

pang of guilt that I had not really considered what that might have cost her.

Hoping to distract her, I put in, "What about Fronto? How is he doing?"

My mother shook off her pensiveness to say, "Oh, poor Fronto. He lost his position in the palace. When the new Emperor arrived, everyone who had worked for Sempronius Rufus was replaced."

She smiled as she added, "It seems the new Emperor wants his own spies."

"So what is Fronto doing now?" I asked, worried for my friend. He'd inherited a decent house from his father, but I knew he wasn't rich. It was his employment in the imperial spy network which had kept him solvent.

"Nothing very much," my mother told me. "I've seen him a few times, and he always smiles and tells me he's looking into various things, but I don't think he's had any luck finding a new career."

"I'll go and see him tomorrow," I decided.

Caecus, who had remained silent throughout the meal, suddenly asked, "What about the rest of us? What do we do?"

"You can come with me," I told him. "If there is some sort of gang war going on, I'd like a bit of protection in case someone is watching the house."

Nodding his approval, Caecus bared his teeth in a feral grin.

"Collinus will do the same for Circe," I said, probably unnecessarily. Collinus always watched over Circe's safety.

"And what will I do?" Circe asked. "I'm not going to sit around spinning wool all day."

"No," I agreed. "I'm sure we will meet Primus and his family tomorrow. You should make friends with Hortensia."

Circe gave me a grin as she asked, "Because husbands tell their wives things they don't tell other people?"

"Exactly. See what you can find out about this war he's got himself involved in."

My mother smiled and said, "There! You have a plan already. If anyone can find out who was behind the attack, I know you can."

I smiled back at her, keeping my thoughts to myself. Finding out who was battling Primus probably wouldn't be very difficult. It was stopping the escalating war that would be the problem.

Circe stretched lazily and put her hand to her mouth to stifle a yawn.

"It is getting late," she said. "I think, if you don't mind, Zoe, we should retire for the evening."

"Of course," my mother replied. "I'll get Justina to light your way upstairs."

We all rose. I kissed my mother goodnight, then we left the dining room and walked across the hall to the stairs. As we did so, a figure stepped out of a shadowy recess. I sensed both Collinus and Caecus moving quickly up beside me, but I held up my hand to stop them when I recognised the rugged face of Mardonius, the *major domo*.

"Sextus Secundus?" he said as he approached me. "My Master would like to speak to you. In private."

I bridled a little at his use of my personal *Praenomen* which should only be used by close friends and family, and also at his use of my old *cognomen* of Secundus, which I detested, but I guessed Primus had told him to address me in that fashion in order to annoy me, so I simply nodded my agreement.

Still, I felt my stomach give a lurch at the thought of meeting Primus, but I knew I had to face my nemesis at some point, so I said, "All right. Lead on."

To Circe and the others, I said, "I'll see you soon."

For some reason, I wasn't entirely convinced by that statement. Perhaps it was the thought of seeing my brother again after all these years, or perhaps it was the looming antagonism behind Mardonius' smirking gaze, but I felt as if I was about to walk into a trap.

"Welcome home," I muttered as I followed the hulking servant through the door which led to Primus' lair.

59

Chapter 6
Primus

Mardonius led me through what I now knew was the connecting door, and I stepped into another world.

The house beyond the doorway was, I had to admit, magnificent. Another man was waiting for us, holding an oil lamp which provided sufficient light for me to see the neatly plastered walls painted with martial frescoes, and to confirm what my ears were telling me as our footsteps echoed around the tiled passage. This house had been built on an entirely different scale to the place where I had grown up and where my mother now lived in near-isolation. Our old house had been one of the better ones on the Quirinal, but Primus had obviously decided to go even further up-market.

We passed through an echoing atrium, where I caught a glimpse of the busts and face masks of our ancestors or, at least, the few ancestors Primus was prepared to admit to. The paucity of mementoes showed that he probably shared my father's distaste for any reminder of our barbarian heritage.

There were other statues, too. Bronze, ivory and marble figurines were very much in evidence, ranging in height from a hand's length to almost half my own height. They all portrayed heroes, gods and goddesses. This wasn't unusual, and our own villa had similar statuettes, although I couldn't help thinking Circe's taste was rather better, since she used such decorations minimally, while Primus' home was full of the damned things. His collection included a small statuette of Priapus, a fertility god whose representations always showed him with an enormous erection. Circe was of the opinion that men who displayed Priapus statues were attempting to over-compensate for their own insecurities, while women who enjoyed owning these figurines were silently laughing at the men who expressed admiration for the god's phallic proportions. I smiled to myself as I mentally slotted Primus into the category of insecure men. That, I mused, might help me get through the impending ordeal without losing my temper.

I followed Mardonius and his large companion in silence. One thing I was beginning to appreciate was that my brother certainly chose his attendants for their bulk. The two men dwarfed me, although the guy with the lamp wasn't all that tall. His fleshy build suggested he might be one of the former gladiators my mother had mentioned. Many gladiators are famous for being, if not fat, then certainly bulked up with padding. The logic behind this is that their vital organs are protected by layers of muscles and fat, thus giving them a greater chance of surviving a stab wound. I have no idea whether it works in practice, but most gladiators seem to believe it. I suppose there might be something to the theory, since some gladiators do survive their time in the arena. It's a very dangerous career, but those few who do manage to live through it are always sure of finding employment as a bodyguard. Primus certainly seemed to have tapped into that market.

We passed through another door and stepped out into what was obviously a central courtyard. In many houses, this would have been given over to a garden surrounded by colonnaded porticos, but this was a small gravel-lined space with, at its centre, another *impluvium* pool for gathering rain water. At a guess, I reckoned Primus had discovered he did not have a large enough plot of land to build his house around a spacious garden, so had settled for a smaller space to give a nod to custom.

That apart, though, he hadn't stinted on much else. I could tell that the doors and shutters were of high quality, and some of the decorative columns which lined the tiny garden certainly looked like genuine marble. Once we moved back inside, the other thing that struck me was that the interior doorways all had actual wooden doors instead of the much cheaper, and therefore more common, hanging curtains.

The rear of the house obviously contained Primus' private rooms, and we soon stopped at one of the heavy doors.

Mardonius knocked, pushed the door open and announced, "Sempronius Secundus to see you, Sir."

He stood aside, ushering me in. With mounting trepidation, I went through the doorway and into a surprisingly comfortable room. Several oil lamps provided a warm, cosy glow, giving enough light to see the place well. I noticed a couple of shuttered windows high up on the walls, one to the rear and one to my left, so I guessed this room was at the rear corner of the house. It was a decent size without being overly large. The floor had a mosaic of geometric designs in several colours, and the walls bore pictures of mythical scenes from old legends, mostly depictions of powerful gods and heroes. Knowing my brother, that wasn't a surprise. Representations of power would be just the sort of thing he'd like around him.

There was a large dresser to one side of the room, a low table in the centre and a couple of well padded armchairs beside it.

And there, on the far side of the table, the illumination from several lamps revealed a long couch on which sat a huge man.

I hadn't seen Primus since I was a teenager. He was several years older than me, and he'd always had a bigger build, but now he was even larger. Unlike the attendants I'd seen so far, though, his bulk showed little evidence of being formed by muscles. His stomach bulged under his tunic, his arms and legs were like flabby tree trunks, and his eyes peered out at me from a face which had more than the usual number of chins. His hair, not as dark as mine, was neatly trimmed in the Roman style, and I saw he wore several gold rings on his fleshy fingers. My first impression was that he resembled a great, fat toad sitting beside a pool, waiting for flies to come within reach of his tongue.

"Hello, Secundus," he said, his voice so familiar despite the years since I had last heard it. It was full of confident authority and patronising scorn, just as I remembered.

"Hello, Primus," I replied, refusing to give him the satisfaction of knowing how much his use of my old *cognomen* annoyed me. He knew perfectly well how much I detested it, but that was because it was a symptom of our sibling rivalry.

It all stemmed from my father's obsession with being a good Roman. I think the taint of barbarian ancestry had really bothered the old man, even though very few people in Rome ever cared where a person came from as long as they adopted Roman ways. My father certainly became a Roman with wholehearted determination. That extended to the names he gave my brother and me.

Because our ex-slave ancestor had been freed by a man with the *nomen* of Sempronius, we all had that as our family name.

62

I didn't have any sisters but, if I had, they'd all have been called Sempronia.

When my brother was born in the month of August, my father gave him the *praenomen* of Sextus because August used to be the sixth month of the year in the old Roman calendar. That calendar had been altered by Julius Caesar a couple of hundred years earlier, but that didn't prevent my father following the old tradition.

Boys are sometimes given a *cognomen* at an early age, perhaps to copy their father's well known name, or if they have some distinguishing trait of their own. For example, a boy with very dark hair might be called Niger, or a boy who says very little might be known as Tacitus. Often, though, the *cognomen* is earned later in life, and is sometimes even chosen by the boy himself.

I had no such luck. When I was born a few years after my brother, my birthday also happened to fall in August. My father, being a man of limited imagination, promptly named me Sextus as well. To differentiate between us, he simply applied the *cognomen* of Primus to his elder son and Secundus to the younger. To me, being officially referred to as the "Second" was a sign that I was regarded as of lesser importance and, when added to the way my father treated us, it only served to foster my resentment. That was why, years later, I had happily adopted the *cognomen* of Scipio. A friend of mine named Hannibal had given it to me as a joke when I managed to throw him to the floor during a *pankration* exercise bout. Ever since then, I'd much preferred to be known as Sempronius Scipio.

Until I became Valerius Cantiacus, that is.

Of course, Valerius Cantiacus was a wealthy and successful man, and not someone who would be overawed by these surroundings, nor the fat character sitting there waiting for him, so I strode across the room, my right hand extended in greeting.

Primus made no effort to rise to his feet, and I saw why when I drew closer to him. His left leg was heavily bandaged, with long, wooden splints bracing it on either side. He did, though, reach out to clasp my forearm in greeting. Needless to say, he squeezed hard, hoping to make me wince. I squeezed back, pressing my thumb into his flesh until he released his grip. I held his gaze the whole time, letting him know I was not intimidated.

Or, at least, that I was not going to appear intimidated which isn't quite the same thing.

Without being asked, I settled myself in one of the armchairs and faced him across the low table. There was a wine pitcher on the table, along with two silver cups. I made a point of looking at them, but Primus made no move or offer.

"You've been entertaining?" I guessed, supposing that these were the remnants from his last visitor.

"A business acquaintance," he said dismissively, letting me know he didn't consider me worthy of being provided with further information, nor of being offered wine.

He stared at me for a long moment, and I just smiled back at him.

"Everyone thought you were dead," he said eventually.

"Everyone was wrong," I replied, stating the obvious.

"Mother knew the truth," he muttered. "She didn't deign to tell me until recently."

"I asked her to keep it quiet," I told him. "Besides, I thought it might make you happy to think I was dead."

His lips twitched in a cruel smile, so I added, "I'm sorry to disappoint you."

He didn't bother trying to hide his displeasure as he demanded, "So why are you here?"

"Mother asked me to visit," I replied casually.

His lips sputtered a rasp of scorn.

"She said she had written to you. She has some notion that I am unable to take care of myself. But I don't need anyone's help, least of all yours."

"That suits me," I said amiably. "I don't much fancy getting stuck in the middle of a street war. I'll treat this as a holiday."

His eyes narrowed as he studied me for signs that I was being disingenuous. Leaning back in my chair, I waved my hand airily at our surroundings.

"You've done a nice job here," I told him. "Mother did tell me you were having some extension work done, but she didn't say it was on this sort of scale."

"It's nothing special," he replied with the air of a man who knew he was being deliberately modest. "I have a villa down near the Alban Mount which is much more impressive."

Show off, I thought.

I kept smiling as I said, "That sounds nice. But it was a stroke of luck that you managed to buy the old tenement which used to be here."

"Luck had little to do with it," he told me, his face unreadable.

I guessed that meant bribes or coercion had been involved. Or possibly both.

I remarked, "Owning property is the big thing, isn't it?"

"Yes."

"I hear it's very profitable," I continued. "Although you obviously don't earn any rent on this place."

"I have other properties," he said when I left a long silence for him to fill.

"Yes, Mother told me in one of her letters that you own quite a few properties now. Is that right?"

Primus scowled as he nodded. I suspect he didn't like the thought that our mother had been sharing news of his financial affairs. Not that he was the only wealthy person investing in land and buildings. Owning a tenement block or two could bring in a very healthy income for rich landlords because demand always outstripped supply in Rome.

"And you've certainly got a very nice house here," I smiled, my tone full of innocent admiration. "But what about the block which used to be here?"

"What about it?" he scowled.

"What happened to all the people who used to live in it?"

He blinked for a moment, then shook his head.

"How in Hades' name should I know? I bought the place and told them to move out. They went."

"So any one of them could be behind these attacks on you?" I suggested.

"I thought you were here for a holiday?" he rasped.

"I am. But I need go through the motions to keep Mother happy. Also, I'd like to be reassured about the safety of my family."

"Yes, I hear your wife and children came with you," he grunted.

"It's a family holiday," I assured him. "But if you are waging a war against one of your many enemies, I'd quite like to know who to avoid. Or, even better, who I should speak to so I can let them know I'm only here to visit Mother."

He spat, "I see your years in the imperial service didn't improve your intelligence. The people I'm up against won't care about that."

"So you know who it is?"

"Of course I do," he asserted.

"So tell me. Then I can get Mother off my back. She wants me to stop the trouble. I'd like to be able to tell her I tried and failed. Then I can go home and forget all about this."

I waited. He said nothing, just stared at me with those beady eyes.

After a few moments, I said, "Look at it this way, Primus. If you tell me who was behind the attack, I can go and talk to them. If you're lucky, they'll stick a knife in my ribs and you'll be rid of me for good."

He retorted, "You won't sound so cheerful when they actually do that, Secundus."

"The name is Cantiacus," I told him. "Valerius Cantiacus. Perhaps you could tell your thugs that."

"Why should I?"

"Because, while it may be unlikely, if certain people on the Palatine learned that Sempronius Scipio is in Rome, you might find yourself visited by a cohort of Praetorians."

I'd said it mostly in jest, but my words had a very unexpected effect. Primus went very still and the blood seemed to drain from his face. It could have been a trick of the flickering light, but he looked suddenly very ill indeed.

Almost feverishly, he leaned forwards, reached out to grab the cup nearest to him and gulped down its remaining contents.

After licking his lips and sitting back, he recovered enough to say, "You're not funny, Secundus. You shouldn't make jokes like that. Things in Rome are … delicate."

"Oh? In what way?"

"In the way they always are when there is a madman wearing the purple," he said in a low, hissing voice. "There are spies everywhere, and anyone suspected of saying anything disloyal can be denounced."

"Then you'd best let it be known that your visitor is Valerius Cantiacus, an old acquaintance from Africa. He's here on holiday and you kindly offered to put him up for a few weeks."

"A few weeks!?" he blurted, his eyes narrowing suspiciously.

"You don't expect me to travel back in the middle of winter?" I grinned happily. "It's far too dangerous."

"You sailed here," he pointed out sulkily.

"And I was as sick as a dog for the entire voyage," I informed him.

He muttered, "I must make an offering of thanks to Neptune for that small mercy."

I let him have that one. It wasn't a bad riposte by Primus' standards, although it must be said he'd had more than fifteen years to improve his repartee.

I asked, "So who was behind the attack on you? Are you going to give me a name?"

He considered this for a moment, then sighed, "Gaius Marius Vindex."

"And where would I find him?"

Smiling smugly, Primus informed me, "He runs a gang on the Viminal. There are several smaller gangs, but his is the largest and most powerful. You know the sort of stuff. Extortion and protection rackets. He's also bought up a lot of the lower class properties."

I nodded encouragingly, prompting him to continue.

"Vindex got upset when I moved into what he sees as his patch."

"Moved in? How?"

"I bought a tenement block he was interested in."

"Legally?"

"Of course!"

I raised my eyebrows, then Primus shrugged as he admitted, "The previous landlord died. I made sure his Executors sold the property to me."

"I see."

I put a lot into those two words, mostly to needle him. It worked.

"It's how business is done in Rome!" he spluttered angrily. "The only thing I am guilty of is paying the Executors a larger bribe than the one Vindex offered."

"So Vindex is pissed, and now he wants you out?"

"Obviously."

"So why didn't you tell Mother? She's been worried sick."

"It's my business," he growled. "Not hers."

I didn't bother arguing. Women have a very reduced role in traditional Roman families. Primus was a classic example of the Roman patriarch, and he probably saw nothing wrong with this attitude.

Glossing over his misogyny, I asked, "I take it you've had a few tussles with Vindex already?"

"There have been a few minor skirmishes, that's all. Nothing serious. Yet."

"Apart from when you were almost beaten to death? What exactly happened that night?"

"That's what really started it," Primus growled. "But it won't be the end of things, I can promise you that."

"You're sure it was Vindex?"

"Who else would it be?"

"That's what Mother wants me to find out."

Primus snorted in disparagement.

"I know it was Vindex," He stated. "And you'd best stay out of it if you know what's good for you. Like you said, you could accidentally find yourself in the middle of a street war."

"You could always report the matter to the City Prefect," I suggested. "The Urban Cohorts are under his control and could stop any trouble."

"They wouldn't take any action against Vindex, though," he argued. "All they'd do is flood the streets with soldiers for a few days. In the long run, that would solve nothing."

I nodded. He was probably right about that. Justice in Rome is often left to individual citizens, and the authorities don't get involved unless things go too far. The *vigiles* wouldn't be interested in any case. Their role is to investigate individual

68

crimes, which they generally do in a rather perfunctory way, but they aren't responsible for keeping public order. That's the job of the Urban Cohorts. These troops are separate from the Praetorians, whose role is to guard the imperial family, and they are under the command of the City Prefect. But they generally don't bother with breaking up fights unless the trouble turns into a riot.

"Go and see Vindex if you like," Primus told me. "But I won't pay for your funeral."

From his tone and the smirk on his face, I knew he was daring me to get involved. What was worse, I knew I'd accept the challenge.

Looking meaningfully at his injured leg, I said, "From here, it looks as if it's you who got caught. Still, I'm glad to see you are recovering. I hope the leg mends soon."

He made no response, so I went on, "Now tell me how I can find this fellow Vindex."

Grinning maliciously, Primus suggested, "You could try wandering around the Viminal like a tourist and asking for him. He'll soon send someone to deal with you."

"That's an idea," I nodded. "Not a very good one, but it is an idea. I tell you what, why don't you have one of your thugs show me this tenement building the dispute is over? I'm sure I can take it from there."

I could see all sorts of calculations going on behind his eyes, but his lips curled into a smile as he nodded, "I'll do that. First thing tomorrow."

"Excellent!" I beamed. "Now, if you will excuse me, I'd better get to bed. Aurelia probably won't let me get much sleep, but I might snatch a couple of hours. No, you needn't bother to get up."

Grinning at my own puerile jibe, I rose to my feet, walked casually to the door and left the fat slob in his power-obsessed lair. I hoped I'd given him the impression that Circe and I would be participating in bouts of energetic sex all night, but I hadn't actually lied when I'd told him she would not let me get much sleep. That's because I knew without a doubt that she'd question me about what we had discussed, and then she'd start making plans.

With any luck, those plans would focus on how to keep me alive when I met one of Rome's gang lords.

Chapter 7
Meeting the Gang

Circe was not happy. She was lying in bed, still wide awake and eager to hear what I had learned from Primus, but her mood turned sour once I'd told her what he'd said.

"What were you thinking?" she demanded. "You can't go searching for a gang boss just because your brother dared you to!"

"But if Vindex really is behind the trouble, I can confirm it quickly enough without getting involved in any gang war. Then we can go home."

"It's too dangerous!" she insisted. "You don't know what you will be walking into."

"I've walked into tough spots before," I reminded her.

That was a mistake.

In a scarily icy tone which I knew all too well, she asked, "Would you walk out into the garden at night if Primus dared you to?"

"The garden?"

"Yes, that place just beneath our balcony."

I had an uneasy feeling about where she was going with this.

I said, "That would depend on what you are about to tell me."

"Exactly!" she declared triumphantly. "You'd be making a mistake. He keeps a dog which is let out at nights to deter thieves."

"A big dog, I presume?"

"That's what your mother says. She told me it is called Dentes."

"Teeth?" I frowned. "The dog is called Teeth?"

She told me, "Perhaps Fangs would be a better way to think of it."

"Then I'll stay out of the garden at night. I'd rather be in bed with you in any case."

That didn't earn me any sort of reprieve.

"Which is precisely my point," she told me as she poked me in the ribs. "Once you know what you face, you can take steps to avoid danger. You know nothing about Vindex."

"I know his type. Besides, I can't very well back out. I need to show Mother that I am trying to help her."

"You could always tell her Primus has revealed the name of the culprit. That's what she wanted to know."

"She also wants me to try to stop it."

Circe rolled her eyes as she said, "You know you won't be able to do that if Primus is determined to continue the feud."

"I won't know until I've at least made some sort of effort," I argued.

"You are being ridiculous!" she sighed. "The real reason you are being so stubborn is that you feel the need to prove something to your brother."

"That too," I confessed grudgingly.

Circe let out a long sigh.

"Surely you can see how stupid you are being?" she demanded.

I wanted to argue, but I knew she was right. Primus had managed to get to me even though I'd been determined to remain cool and detached.

"All right," I said. "I'll go to the Viminal, but all I'll do is scout around a bit and see if I can get any information on Vindex."

"You won't go seeking him out?" Circe asked, rolling onto her side to look at me.

"No. It will be a scouting mission. Nothing more. I'll find out as much as I can, then I can report back to Mother and let her know what we are up against."

"That had better be a promise," Circe warned.

"It is," I assured her.

Reluctantly – very reluctantly – she said, "I suppose that would give us some extra ammunition when trying to persuade her to come back to Leptis Magna with us."

"Yes," I grinned. "It certainly would."

We sealed the deal with a kiss. Then we sealed it further with some more intimate action which, as I'd told Primus, kept me awake half the night.

72

We met the rest of Primus' family the following morning, probably because my mother arranged it. Once we were up and about, she ushered us all through the connecting door and into what she described as the family room of Primus' dwelling. This was a large, spacious chamber with doors leading out into the central courtyard, and elegantly furnished with stools, chairs and small tables.

Primus was there, sitting propped against a wall, a pair of crutches close at hand. He was polite, but only just, when I introduced our group to him. His main interest seemed to be Caecus, whom he kept eyeing as if considering whether the ex-Centurion was big enough to warrant being invited to join his gang of heavies. He did, though, cast an appraising eye over Circe, which she ignored but which only served to rile me.

Then we met Hortensia, who turned out to be a small, rather nervous woman who spoke so softly it was often difficult to make out what she was saying. She was quite pretty although she appeared older than I would have imagined. Perhaps living with Primus had aged her.

Their children were a daughter named Sempronia who was seven years old and rather precocious, and a boy named Quintus Sempronius who was only a few months older than our own son, Sextus. Not that this gave the boys much in common, because young Quintus looked as if he was already in competition with his father to see who could be the fattest male in the house. It soon became obvious that the two boys did not get on. Perhaps they had inherited the mutual dislike shared by their fathers.

Naturally, Circe and my mother managed, between them, to keep the occasion lively while we all tucked into bowls of porridge and slices of freshly baked bread smeared with honey and sprinkled with cinnamon.

Circe, going under her formal name of Aurelia, said to Hortensia, "You have a lovely house here."

I smiled inwardly when she failed to mention it was smaller than the new slave quarters Caecus had designed for us, but the two women, accompanied by my mother, decided to take a tour of the property.

"I'm going out for a while," I told Circe. "Caecus and Collinus can come with me."

She gave me a cool look which I knew was intended to remind me of the promise I'd made.

"All right," she said, her tone distant. "We may go shopping later."

Shopping was, she had informed me earlier, a way women liked to bond. She had insisted it would give her an opportunity to extract some gossip from Hortensia, but I was fairly sure that was only an excuse to allow her to spend a lot of silver in the markets.

Once the women had set off on their tour and the slaves had hustled the children away, I turned to Primus.

"Can you give us a guide to show us where your tenement is?"

Affecting disinterest, he sent a slave to summon one of his bodyguards.

"Gallicus will show you the way," he told me.

Gallicus looked like another ex-gladiator. He wasn't particularly tall, about the same height as me, in fact, but he was solidly built and looked as tough as old boots. His bare arms bore the silvery traces of several old wounds which could only have been inflicted by sharp blades. He didn't say much at all as he led us through the house, into the entrance courtyard and out through the double doors which, I noticed, were guarded by another two burly guards.

Out in the street it was a dull day, with overcast skies and a chill breeze. We all tugged our cloaks a bit tighter. There had been some overnight rain, so the cobbles were damp and slick, but I noticed Primus already had a slave armed with a brush and a bucket of whitewash painting a section of his front wall.

Intrigued, I ignored Gallicus' impatient wave of his hand and went over to speak to the slave.

"Has there been another slogan painted?" I asked him, noticing he'd already painted a fresh patch of whitewash over most of whatever graffiti had been added during the night.

"Just kids being rude," the slave mumbled unconvincingly.

"What did it say?"

He shrugged, continuing to daub the wall to obscure the last couple of letters.

"I can't read," he informed me. "I just paint over whatever is written here."

"Does it happen every night?"

He gave another shrug.

"Not always."

I had the distinct impression he'd been told not to talk to me, so I thanked him and turned back to my companions. Was it merely a case of Primus being house-proud and wanting no graffiti marring the pristine whiteness of his outer walls? If so, the slave would have a job for life because graffiti is as much a part of Roman life as circuses and the grain dole. Every man who stands for political office hires people to daub slogans supporting him, and those graffiti usually attract unflattering comments from supporters of rival candidates. But if Circe was right, the comments scrawled on Primus' house had little to do with politics.

Gallicus was scowling impatiently, so I waved my arm theatrically and told him, "Lead on."

He barely said a word as he led us down the hill, heading in a roughly easterly direction. The streets were busy because, even in winter, most Romans spend the majority of their time out of doors. When you share a room with ten other adults, the indoor life doesn't hold many attractions.

The Viminal Hill is the one next to the Quirinal. It lies a little to the south-east, so we walked down into the dip between the two hills, then gradually climbed into the maze of streets and lanes on the Viminal. Of course, unless you know Rome, it can be difficult to tell where one of the ancient hills ends and the next one begins. Much of the city is built up, so it's usually hard to see any further than the end of whichever street you are on. We passed tavernas serving hot food, shops selling all sorts of goods, workshops where potters, carpenters and leather-workers plied their trade, and the ubiquitous tenements, many of which looked to be in danger of imminent collapse.

It was to one of these that Gallicus led us. It was quite unremarkable, a five-storey block reached via a narrow, dingy and smelly alley. The lower floor had walls of brick, but I was fairly sure the upper storeys would be made of wood and plaster, and probably very old wood at that, considering the way the whole building seemed to lean over the alley as if seeking support from the tenement across the way.

"This is it?" I asked Gallicus.

75

He nodded.

"It hardly looks worth fighting over," I sighed as I surveyed the peeling plaster and warped shutters on the windows.

Gallicus made no comment, so I asked him, "Has there been much trouble? I hear a few of your pals received some bruises?"

His hard eyes betrayed little emotion as he told me, "We had a bit of a scrap with some of Vindex's lads. It was nothing serious. They ran off when they realised they were up against experienced fighters."

"So things have settled down?"

"For the moment."

"Is it all right if I take a look inside?"

"Go ahead," he shrugged, his disinterest plain.

I told Collinus to keep watch outside while Caecus and I ventured into the building. It was typical of the type, with doors leading off small landings on every floor. The wooden steps creaked as we climbed, and we could hear voices, sometimes raised voices, from behind some of the doors which looked as if they were made of thin strips of cheap plywood.

A couple of young children, barefoot and almost naked, scampered down past us as we ascended, their shrill voices indicating that one had stolen something which the other was going to kick his effing head in for.

"Nice place," I murmured as I stepped to one side to let the charging infants pass.

"It's likely to collapse before long," Caecus opined.

He scratched a fingernail against the nearest wall. Plaster flaked away, as did some of the wood beneath.

"It's rotten," he told me.

"I wonder what rent Primus charges?" I mused.

"Too much," Caecus grunted. "Some of these look like decent sized apartments, but I'll bet most are overcrowded."

I nodded, "And if a landlord knows there are several people contributing to the rent, he puts up the weekly rate."

"Is that how it's done?" Caecus frowned.

"I suspect so."

Caecus scratched his chin as he remarked, "But he'll surely lose money if the place falls down."

"Not necessarily. It will give him a chance to put up another cheap place, maybe with an extra storey on top, and charge higher rents because it's a newer building."

Caecus, who had seen a lot in his life, nevertheless seemed surprised by this. He shook his head.

"I never had to worry about that sort of thing in the Army," he confessed. "But I suppose the rich didn't get rich by being nice to poor folk."

"That, I nodded, "is as true a word as has ever been spoken. Come on, I've seen enough."

We tramped down the creaking stairs and went back outside to find Collinus waiting patiently while Gallicus was fidgeting nervously.

"Is there a problem?" I asked him.

"I don't like being here on my own," he hissed in reply.

"You're not on your own," I pointed out.

Perhaps I spoke rather more forcefully than I should have done, but the visit to the tenement had left me feeling depressed and angry. Primus was getting rich from other people's poverty, and that annoyed me.

I suppose I'd expected Gallicus to be cowed by my irritable mood, but all he did was cast a scornful eye over me and my companions.

"Two old men and a weedy thing like you won't be much use if Vindex's lads find us here," he informed me coldly.

"Are they likely to find us here?" I enquired.

"Eventually. I'm sure someone will pass the word to him. It's not as if you look like locals."

I looked down at my expensive cloak and tunic. He was right. We didn't exactly blend in. In my career as a spy, I'd normally travelled on my own and had made a habit of wearing old, tattered outfits. But now I was Valerius Cantiacus, so I wore much more expensive clothing.

I said, "I suppose we could hang around until they find us, but I'd rather be a bit more circumspect."

Eyeing me with a frown, Gallicus asked, "What do you intend to do? The boss told me to bring you here, but he didn't say anything about walking around Vindex's patch."

"We're not looking for trouble," I assured him. "All we're going to do is snoop around a bit. But you don't need to come. Just point us in the right direction."

Pointing down the narrow alley, he said, "Go back out to the main street, then keep heading east. There's a fountain in a square. Hang around there for a few minutes and you'll get all the answers you want."

"Great. Thanks. See you later."

He followed us back along the alley to the main street, then he stopped while Collinus, Caecus and I headed eastwards.

"Is he following?" I asked Collinus.

"No. He's just standing there."

He's probably waiting to hear the screams before he runs back and tells Primus we've been attacked."

"Let's hope he has a long wait," Caecus murmured.

"We'll be fine," I assured him. "All we are going to do is nose around a little bit."

"What do you hope to learn?" he asked.

"I'd like to know what the local gossip is regarding Vindex and Primus."

"I doubt anyone will speak to us," Caecus grunted. "People tend to keep their mouths shut about stuff like that."

"Maybe so, but we won't learn anything if we don't poke around a bit."

I'm pretty sure Caecus wasn't convinced by my confident mood, but he had been a soldier, so marching into danger was nothing new for him.

As for Collinus, he might be getting on in years, but he displayed no signs of being concerned, and I found his imperturbability reassuring.

We walked on through the bustle. It's a funny thing about Rome that, of all the cities in the empire, its layout doesn't much follow the grid pattern we've imposed elsewhere. It's probably because the city is so ancient that, like Athens, its streets can become a bewildering maze. This time, though, we were on a main road, one of the wider avenues which led pretty much all the way across the low summit of the Viminal. I honestly felt perfectly safe. In my career as a spy, I'd spent several weeks in Parthia nosing around in disguise and I'd rarely had much trouble. I reckoned Rome should be a lot easier than that.

We reached the fountain Gallicus had mentioned, an ornate statue of a group of nymphs, each holding a vase from which flowed fresh water provided by one of the city's many aqueducts. This water-bearing bridge soared high overhead, its many arches supporting the vital channel which brought the essential water into the heart of the city.

Below the aqueduct was a stone-lined pool where people were splashing, washing and gathering buckets of water. It wasn't the most hygienic scene I'd ever witnessed, but everyone seemed happy enough.

The square was crowded. There were several business establishments and a couple of tavernas and wine shops, along with a handful of street vendors selling odds and ends like yarn and needles, children's toys and fresh fruit. In short, it was a typical Roman scene on a typical Roman day.

We paused at the entrance to the square, taking a few moments to look around.

"Let's split up," I decided. "We can cover more ground, and it won't be as intimidating for the locals if we don't go mob-handed."

"Are you sure that is wise?" Collinus asked. "The Lady ordered me to keep you safe."

"Then you can take a seat outside one of the wine shops where you can keep an eye on things. Caecus, why don't you browse the local shops and see if you can pick up any gossip."

Caecus gave a less than enthusiastic nod, but Collinus asked, "What are you going to do?"

"I'm going to visit that wine shop over there. It looks like the biggest one, so it's probably quite popular."

The place I'd indicated was on the right of the square from where we stood. It had a brightly coloured sign daubed on the wall above the open door, the red painted letters proclaiming it to be "Xeno's", and it had several tables set outside where a handful of local worthies were sipping at cups while they engaged in conversation or watched the world go by.

I glanced up to gauge the position of the sun.

79

"It's about the fourth hour," I guessed. "Let's meet back here in an hour."

"I doubt it will take that long," Caecus muttered.

"It depends on how many drinks I need to buy to loosen tongues," I told him.

We separated. Collinus moved towards a smaller wine shop opposite the one I had selected, Caecus sauntered off towards the fountain, while I strolled over to Xeno's. It looked like a pleasant place, although the building itself was old, and there were several gloomy tenements running the length of a narrow alleyway which led down the side of the wine shop. Still, it looked like an unusually large establishment. It probably wouldn't be all that busy at this early hour, but perhaps that might allow me to engage the owner in conversation without being interrupted.

I passed the outside tables, attracting no attention from the elderly men who were sitting around a table playing dice. If I had no luck inside, I reckoned they'd be a good bet for obtaining information.

I stepped through the open door into a surprisingly quiet room. There were around a dozen tables, only two of which were occupied. To my right sat two middle-aged men who were engaged in a quiet conversation, while a large table to my left was occupied by four young men, all of whom studied me with what I can only describe as malevolent interest. I ignored them and walked on to the counter.

A slim teenage girl was clearing away platters and cups from an empty table. She scurried round the counter and vanished through one of two doors. The only other member of staff I saw was a big, swarthy individual who wore a long apron over his tunic. The garment did little to conceal his bulging paunch. Behind him stood shelves of wine jars and cups, while I could smell something cooking from beyond the door where the girl had passed through.

The chap gave me an appraising look and asked, "Can I help you?"

"A cup of your finest," I said, dipping my fingers into my purse.

"I've got a lovely one from Etruria," he informed me. "It's expensive, though. One cup will cost you a whole *denarius*."

"That sounds good," I smiled, passing over the silver coin. "If it's not up to the price, I'll want a refund."

That earned me a blank stare, but he took the coin, then poured a cup for me.

I tasted it.

"Not bad at all," I said approvingly.

"Good," he replied. "Because we don't give refunds."

I laughed to let him know I hadn't been serious.

Then I asked, "Are you Xeno?"

He shook his head.

"There's no Xeno. It's just a name."

"I see. So what should I call you?"

He frowned as if suspecting I was up to something nefarious, but grudgingly said, "I'm Balbo."

"Pleased to meet you," I smiled. "Why don't you join me in a drink? This stuff is very good."

For a moment, his eyes flicked beyond my shoulder, then he gave a slow nod.

"I don't mind if I do," he said.

I fished out another *denarius* from my dwindling purse and laid it on the counter while he poured another cup.

"I'm Valerius Cantiacus," I informed him. "I've not been in Rome for many years. I don't remember this place."

He gave a shrug, obviously playing hard to get. Hard to get information out of, that is. I began to suspect I'd need to try the old boys outside, but I decided to persevere for a little longer. In any wine shop, the man behind the counter hears all sorts of things.

"A lot has changed in the city," I continued, adopting the manner of a tourist. "I have heard rather a lot about our new Emperor."

"He's not that new," Balbo sniffed. "He's been here a couple of years now."

"So what is he like?"

"I wouldn't know," he said. "He never comes in here."

I laughed, and so did some of the young men at the table behind me. I did not look round. From the glimpse I had caught of them as I passed their table, I reckoned they were not likely to be particularly helpful. Still, it was disappointing that they were taking such an obvious interest in me.

Keeping my attention on Balbo, I asked, "So who does come in here? A nice place like this must attract the custom of some of the local worthies."

Balbo frowned. Once again, his eyes flicked past me, and I began to get an uneasy feeling about this place.

"Just locals," he mumbled, paying more attention to his cup than to me.

"Well, it's a nice place, so I expect you are busy at meal times."

He said nothing.

Behind me, I heard a chair scrape back, and I became aware of someone moving up behind me. It could have been one of the young men coming to order more drinks, but something warned me it was more than that. I turned slowly, coming face to face with a pair of the coldest eyes I'd ever seen.

Those eyes belonged to a man in his early twenties. He was medium-sized but well muscled, his strong chin covered by a couple of days' worth of stubble. His green tunic was worn but clean, and I noticed he wore a couple of silver rings on his fingers.

But his eyes demanded my attention, distracting me from the fact that his three companions had also risen to their feet and had spread out in a line behind him. Two were obviously still teenagers, while the third was an absolute giant, possibly the biggest man I'd ever seen. His face looked ludicrously young, and I doubted whether he'd ever needed to shave, which suggested he still had some growing left in him. That was a terrifying thought, because he towered over his companions.

I was dimly aware of the other two occupants of the shop hastily standing up and leaving. That was not a good sign.

Still smiling, I asked the cold-eyed man, "Can I help you? Would you like to join me in a cup of wine?"

His voice was as chilly as the icy blue of his eyes as he hissed, "Who are you?"

"I'm Valerius Cantiacus," I told him.

"And why are you asking all these questions?"

"I was just making conversation," I said, making sure to hold his gaze to show him I wasn't as scared as I felt. One man I could handle if it came to a fight. Four would be impossible, especially with the ox-like brute being one of the four.

"You're new in town?" the leader wanted to know.

"That's right. I've been away for nearly twenty years."

"And you're staying locally?"

"Does that matter?"

His teeth appeared as he made a grimace of a smile.

"That depends," he said.

"On what?"

"On what answer you give. You see, we don't like nosy toffs coming around our place and asking questions."

I should have made something up, tossed my purse on the counter and invited them to drink themselves senseless on me, but I decided to take a risk. I'd promised Circe I would be careful, but this situation had not been of my making. And if my response caused any trouble, I was fairly confident I could grapple the leader and throw him into his pals. That would give me enough time to reach the door. Collinus would be watching, so that would help even the odds.

I said, "As a matter of fact, I'm staying on the Quirinal at the home of an old acquaintance. His name is Sempronius Primus."

The leader's eyes widened, and one of his companions, a fair-haired youth with a pimply complexion, rasped, "Let's teach him a lesson, Hestius."

The leader, presumably Hestius, held up his right hand.

"Not yet, Albius."

I put on a puzzled expression and asked, "What's wrong? Do you know Sempronius Primus?"

"Oh, we know him all right."

I decided to try to bluff it out. It didn't take a genius to figure out I'd stumbled into a place frequented by some of Vindex's men, but I thought there might still be a way I could extricate myself without causing any trouble.

I said, "You have my sympathy, then. Primus is still as much of an arsehole as he was when I knew him twenty years ago."

That made them hesitate, so I pressed on.

"He told me he was having some trouble with one of the local gangs up here," I told Hestius. "I expect he was exaggerating as usual, but he claimed some lads from the Viminal beat him up a couple of months ago. That wouldn't have been you, by any chance?"

All of them frowned, even the big lump whose thought processes seemed to run several seconds behind the others.

I forced a grin as I told them, "Because if it was you, I'd really like to buy you all a drink."

The three youngsters looked confused, but Hestius was obviously capable of reaching his own decisions.

He told me, "I think you'd better speak to the Boss."

I had no time to think of a response. As soon as he'd spoken, Balbo's hand clamped down on my shoulder, and I felt the sharp blade of a knife at my throat.

Chapter 8
Vindex

"Search him," Hestius ordered the youth named Albius.

As the young man stepped towards me, a malicious grin on his beardless face, Hestius turned to his other companions.

"Venantius, watch the door. Polus, make sure our guest doesn't try to leave."

Polus, I reckoned, was a joke name because it means "little" or "small", and it was the complete opposite of the hulking young brute who obediently blocked my route to the exit while his regular-sized pal walked across the room and pushed the door shut.

Not that I was in a position to try anything. Balbo's knife was still pricking the flesh of my throat, so I didn't dare move. Albius gleefully patted me down, checking my cloak for inside pockets. He found nothing except my purse tied to my belt. He ripped it off, snapping the ties, and tipped the contents into his palm.

"Is this all you've got?" he asked me.

"You're the one who just searched me," I replied coldly.

That saved me telling a lie. You see, my old belt was just about the only thing I'd kept from my days as a spy. It was a wide band of thick leather, with a plain buckle and no ornamentation. It didn't look anything special at all, yet it contained several secret slots cut into the leather on its inner side. Here I could keep folded scraps of parchment and a few extra coins. What Albius didn't know was that I had half a dozen golden *aurei* stashed there. They weren't the diluted tat of Caracalla either, but older coins with a higher gold content.

Frowning at the few silvers and coppers he had found, Albius poured them into his own purse.

Hestius, meanwhile, had walked around the counter behind me. I heard a door open and close. After that, we all stood perfectly still for what seemed an eternity. At least, most of us did. Albius hopped from foot to foot as if trying to decide whether he could get away with punching me a few times.

"You think you're smart, don't you?" he rasped as he pushed his face close to mine.

I did not answer. He was, I knew, merely a hired thug. Hestius had gone to talk to a person he had called "the Boss", so I was not about to waste my breath talking to a callow upstart like Albius. Besides, I was wondering whether Collinus might find it suspicious that someone had closed the door to the wine shop. What would I do if he came to investigate?

"Balbo," I said soothingly, "if I promise not to make a run for it, will you take that knife away?"

"Not a chance," he replied gruffly. "Not until Hestius says so."

So I stood there, trying not to move, until I heard the door open behind me once again.

"Bring him," I heard Hestius say.

The blade was removed from my neck, and I breathed more easily, but Albius and the giant Polus each took one of my arms and marched me around the counter.

"Open the front door, Venantius," Hestius called. "Business as usual."

Then he turned and led the way along a short corridor which led to the rear of the building. I was shoved roughly after him, Albius obviously unsure whether he could mistreat me, but unwilling to let me have too easy a time.

There were two more doors leading off to the right. Hestius led us to the second, pushing it open, then stepping inside. I was again shoved hard in the back, almost knocking me into the frame of the door, but I ignored Albius' obvious attempts to antagonise me. I knew I would need to save all my wits for whoever waited in this room.

It was a spacious office, with a large desk and several wooden chairs spaced around the walls. Racks of pigeonholes contained rolled scrolls, each tagged and labelled, and there was a dresser on the wall opposite the desk. Thick rugs of Persian design covered the floor, and there were panels on the walls with paintings of idyllic woodland scenes.

It was all very tasteful, and all very much in contrast to the appearance of the man who sat behind the desk.

He was in his sixties, I guessed, with a hard face, his skin lined and weather-beaten like old leather. His nose had obviously been broken at some distant time in the past, and I noticed a couple of long scars on his bare arms. His brown eyes glared at me as Hestius stood aside to take up position behind me, along with Albius and the giant Polus.

There was another man in the room. He was leaning casually against the wall to my right, his arms folded across his chest as he looked on with what might have been amusement. He was in his thirties, with brown hair and neatly trimmed beard. Lean and tough-looking, he nevertheless gave off an air of more refinement than any of the others. That struck me as odd. His stance suggested he was a bodyguard, but his appearance did not quite match.

I had no time to consider the jarring note he struck because the grey-haired man behind the desk said, "I hear you have been asking about Sempronius Primus. Tell me why."

I took a calming breath before replying.

"Actually, I know quite a bit about Sempronius Primus," I told him. "What I was asking about was whether there is any truth to the story he told me."

"Don't get smart with me!" he barked, his right hand jabbing a finger at me. "I can have the lads break some of your bones if I feel like it. Now, what's your game? Why are you asking questions?"

"Because I'm staying with that pompous ass Sempronius Primus, and it seems he's gearing up for a war. I've only just arrived in the city after twenty years away, and I'd like to know what I'm stuck in the middle of."

"Do you expect me to believe that?" he snorted.

"It's the truth," I lied as convincingly as I could. "All I said to your boys is that, if they were the ones who had beaten Primus up, I'd like to buy them a drink."

"You're staying with him, and you want him hurt?" the old man scowled disbelievingly.

"I'm staying with him because I knew him when I was a boy. I also knew his mother. She was the one who offered to put me up while I'm in Rome. But she's worried by the attack and all the threats."

"What threats?" he asked, frowning.

"The ones someone is scrawling on the walls of his house at night."

The man's face remained hard and virtually unreadable, but there was a flicker in his eyes which suggested he had no idea what I was talking about. He glanced towards the bearded man who was regarding me with an expression of curious interest. He gave a shrug and a casual shake of his head, confirming my suspicion that my words had meant nothing to them.

"So you haven't been scribbling threats on Primus' house?" I asked.

"What would be the point of that?" the older man scowled.

"To frighten him."

"Is he frightened?"

"No, I can't say he is."

He nodded as if to validate his argument. Then, his expression hard and menacing, he rasped, "Never mind that. How do I know you're not a spy he's sent here?"

"You don't," I had to admit. "Except that a genuine spy wouldn't come in and start talking about Sempronius Primus, would he?"

"He might if he wanted to curry favour with us by pretending to dislike Primus."

"Then I can't win, can I? Whatever I say, you're not going to believe me."

He shot me an evil smile as he grinned, "No, I'm not."

I suggested, "Well, I suppose you could always go and ask Primus what he thinks of me."

This time, I caught a glimpse of the bearded man chuckling softly to himself.

The man at the desk snapped, "You are wasting my time! I think I'll get Polus to snap a few of your fingers. Then you might start telling me the truth."

The way he spoke, I believed him. The sheer menace he emitted was palpable, so I decided I might as well take a chance.

I said, "No, it's you who is wasting my time. I came to talk to Gaius Marius Vindex, not to you."

He stiffened, his eyes blazing.

"I am Marius Vindex!" he shouted.

Speaking firmly, I said, "No, I don't think you are."

Turning my head, I nodded towards the bearded man.

"I think he's Marius Vindex."

There was a moment's silence, then the man with the beard grinned.

"What gave it away?" he asked me. "I've always thought Petronax makes a very convincing gang boss."

"He does. But you are the one wearing gold rings on your fingers. And you don't glower the way most bodyguards do. You weren't trying to intimidate me."

He nodded gravely.

"I must remember that," he said conversationally. "But don't Hestius and his boys intimidate you?"

"Them?" I scoffed. "Hardly."

I heard Albius hiss an angry insult, but Vindex held up a warning hand.

"No!" he barked, preventing the young hooligan from delivering any blows.

Petronax, the grey-haired villain, rose from his chair, offering it to Vindex who smoothly exchanged places with him.

"So," the gang boss said once he had settled into his chair, "you just want to know what you've walked into. Is that right?"

"That's right. Was it you who had Primus beaten up a couple of months ago?"

"No," he said. "And I don't know anything about any threats being painted on his house either."

I said, "Well, to return your friend's question, why should I believe you?"

Vindex was not at all offended. He was a smooth character all right; not at all what you would imagine if you pictured the leader of one of Rome's street gangs. These guys were tough, vicious and ruthless. So far, Vindex seemed more like a businessman, but I knew it would be dangerous to underestimate him. Nobody reached the top of the criminal world by being a nice guy.

Smiling, he told me, "You can believe me because, if I wanted Primus dealt with, I'd do it properly. From what I heard, that beating he got was done by a bunch of amateurs. I wouldn't make the mistake of letting him live."

Now I detected the steel in this man. It was perhaps more chilling than the more obvious malevolence of Petronax.

"All right," I nodded. "In that case, I don't suppose you have any idea who was responsible? It couldn't have been some of your lads who decided to act on their own initiative?"

His eyes grew hard as he informed me, "None of them would dare. Not if they know what's good for them. No, I have no idea who carried out the attack, and I don't really care."

He might have been a villain, yet I believed him. He had no reason to lie about something like that. Most thugs would be happy to boast of what they had done to their opponents.

I said, "Fair enough. Thank you for telling me. But you ought to know Primus thinks it was you. He's gearing up for a war, and he's recruiting ex-soldiers and former gladiators."

"Are you trying to scare me?" Vindex asked.

"No, I'm simply warning you. Like I said, Primus is an ass. I'd happily see him beaten up, but I don't want anyone to die as a result of a squabble over some run-down tenements."

There was a definite edge to Vindex's voice as he said, "Then tell him to stay out of my patch. He has the Quirinal. I'm happy to let him have that, but if he comes to the Viminal, he'll regret it."

"I'll tell him, but I doubt he'll listen to me."

"That's his problem," Vindex shrugged.

I was desperate to get out of this place. I could feel a trickle of sweat running down my back, and my palms were damp. I'd blundered right into Vindex's lair, and I was not confident of my chances of getting out alive no matter how much I bad-mouthed Primus.

Acting cool and confident, I said, "Then I don't think we have much more to say to one another, so I'd best be going."

"Do you think you can just walk out of here?" Vindex asked.

"I've already paid my ransom," I told him.

He frowned, so I explained, "Young Albius there took my purse. I'm sure he intends to share it with the rest of you. He's cleaned me out."

I could sense every eye turning towards Albius, but Vindex remained unflappable.

90

"I like you, Valerius Cantiacus. You've got some balls, and I admire that. But I'm thinking I need to send Sempronius Primus some sort of message."

Now the sweat on my back turned to ice. I had visions of the *vigiles* finding my mutilated body in a gutter somewhere. And that was one of the least unpleasant images I conjured in my mind.

Somehow, I managed to remain calm as I told him, "That would be playing into Primus' hands, you know. I told you, he and I do not like one another at all. He'd love it if something happened to me. Not only would he be rid of me, he'd be able to use that as an excuse to launch an all out attack on you for harming one of his guests. I know you feel confident you can deal with him, but it wouldn't be good for business, would it?"

Albius could not contain himself.

He blurted, "Let me gut him, Boss!"

Irritably, Vindex snapped, "Shut up, Albius!"

Albius relapsed into a sullen silence. Petronax, meanwhile, was giving me the evil eye as if he agreed with the youngster, but Vindex continued to study me coolly.

He said, "If I let you walk out of here in one piece, some people might regard that as a sign of weakness. I can't have anyone thinking I'm weak. You must understand that."

"Or they might view it as a sign of strength," I countered. "It shows you are confident in your own position."

He gave the slightest of nods, then remarked, "What puzzles me, Valerius Cantiacus, is why you aren't on your knees begging me for mercy."

"Would it do any good?" I asked.

"No, probably not."

"Then I won't waste my breath."

"I think you are a dangerous man," he told me.

"I'm no danger to you," I assured him. "I have no interest in your fight with Primus. All I was asked to do was find out who attacked him. If it wasn't you, then I'll need to look elsewhere. For now, I'll deliver your message, then I'll keep out of your way."

From where he stood at the side of the room, Petronax growled, "I think we should teach this smug little prick a lesson."

I thought Vindex was about to agree, but then we heard raised voices from the main room of the shop. I recognised Caecus' Centurion's bark, and I could not help but grin.

"That will be my friends come looking for me," I informed Vindex. "I think it would be best for everyone if I left with them."

There was more shouting, a loud crash as if something heavy had fallen, and a girl screamed in fright.

"Polus!" Vindex snapped. "Go and sort it out."

The giant lumbered round, heading for the door. He barely had time to pull it open before Collinus appeared, his long-bladed dagger flashing up until the needle point was just below Polus' chin. The big man hesitated, then Collinus prodded him back into the room, allowing the looming bulk of Caecus to appear in the doorway. The former Praetorian held a broken chair leg in each hand, and had a look of cold fury on his face as his eyes scanned the room.

Nobody moved. Albius was probably just stupid enough to try something, but Hestius had the good sense to put a hand on his arm and hiss at him to remain calm.

I said to Vindex, "There's no need for any trouble. We'll leave now."

He eyed me coldly, but gave a nod.

"Go, then. But be warned. If any of you come back to the Viminal, it won't go easy on you. Do you understand?"

I nodded, then edged to the door. Caecus led the way, with Collinus and his dagger bringing up the rear. As soon as we were in the corridor, he pulled the door shut, then we made for the exit as quickly as we could.

Chapter 9
Respite

"I got fed up waiting," Caecus explained as we hurried away from the square as fast as we could without actually breaking into a jog. "None of the locals were prepared to talk, but a couple of folk shot meaningful glances at Xeno's when I mentioned Vindex. So Collinus and I decided we would take a closer look at the place."

"I'm glad you did," I gasped, my pulse racing wildly now that I had time to reflect on just how much danger I had been in.

Caecus continued, "We decided we'd just buy a couple of drinks and sit quietly, not letting on we knew you, but we knew something was wrong as soon as we went in and saw the place was empty."

"How did you know where I was?" I asked between gulps of air.

"I had to knock a couple of heads together," he grinned.

I had been in such a hurry to get out of Xeno's that I hadn't noticed what had become of Balbo and Venantius. Presumably Caecus had knocked their heads together so firmly they were still out cold.

"The kitchen girl told us where to find you as soon as she saw Collinus' dagger," Caecus explained.

"I owe both of you my thanks," I said sincerely. "I don't think I could have got out of there in one piece. They were about to begin doing nasty things to me."

As concisely as I could, I recounted what had happened during my encounter with Vindex. By the time I'd finished the tale, we had reached the foot of the Quirinal, where I insisted we stopped at the first wine shop we came across.

"I really do need a drink now," I told them. "Does anyone have any money?"

"I'll pay," Caecus grunted.

I ordered a jug, and we sat at a table just inside the door where I hoped we would not be overheard by the proprietor.

It took a while for my hands to stop trembling as reaction set in, but a couple of cups of wine restored my equilibrium.

"What now?" Caecus wanted to know.

"I'm going to see my friend Fronto."

"Do you need us?" Caecus asked. "I wouldn't mind taking a look around the city."

I shrugged, "Get me safely to Fronto, then you can do what you like for the day. Just don't draw anyone's attention to yourself. Play the part of a tourist, but don't take any risks."

"Look who's talking," Caecus muttered.

I had no answer to that, so all I did was give him a weak smile.

"It was just bad luck," I told him. "But at least we now know Vindex probably wasn't behind the attack after all."

Collinus asked, "Do you think your brother misled you deliberately?"

I gave a shrug. I wouldn't have put it past Primus to set me up like that.

"It doesn't matter," I replied.

"It would matter to me," Collinus observed, his eyes hard.

"I can't prove it anyway," I told him. "So let's move on."

Caecus wondered, "If it wasn't Vindex, then who did beat your brother up? It wasn't just some casual muggers, was it?"

"I have no idea who it was," I admitted. "But that's a problem for later. I've had too much excitement already today, so I'm going to see what I can learn from my old friend, Fronto."

Before I could make a move, Collinus leaned forward to whisper, "There is something else you should know. There was someone following us this morning."

"What? Who?"

He shrugged, "I do not know who. I thought I'd noticed someone trailing us when we went to the Viminal to visit that tenement, then I saw him again while I was sitting in the square waiting for you."

Caecus scowled, "You never mentioned it."

Collinus said, "There was no time. I noticed him watching you as you spoke to the local traders, and I saw him keeping a close watch on the wine shop where Scipio had gone. I decided to see if I could find out who he was."

Collinus gave us an apologetic smile as he admitted, "Unfortunately, he was a clever one. He saw me as I tried to approach him through the crowd, and he hurried off. I returned to the fountain, which was when we noticed something odd was going on in Xeno's."

Caecus scowled, but I asked Collinus, "What about this man you saw? What did he look like?"

"A small man, but with an ample stomach. Yet he moved quickly and lightly. His age is difficult to estimate because he wore a hat with a broad brim which kept his face in shadow. From the way he moved, I'd guess he was not young, but I cannot be certain. He was dressed in ordinary clothing. Nothing fancy, so he blended in."

Caecus ventured, "He was probably one of Vindex's men."

"Possibly," Collinus agreed, although his tone suggested he doubted it.

His dark eyes bored into me as he warned, "You need to be careful, I think."

I nodded. This was a very unwelcome development.

After a moment, I let out a long, slow breath.

"Let's all keep an eye out," I decided. "But there is no point in speculating about who he might be."

Caecus shot me a very sceptical look when I said that, but neither he nor Collinus argued.

"Come on," I said. "I need to talk to Fronto."

I drained my cup and we set off back up the sloping streets of the Quirinal. We reached Fronto's house without incident, and I knocked on the door.

The slave who answered was a slightly-built, middle-aged man with rounded shoulders and a rather hangdog expression complemented by a pair of weary eyes. He didn't recognise me, but he confirmed his master was in and invited me to wait in one of the reception rooms. I told Caecus and Collinus I'd see them later. The two of them went their separate ways, and I went inside to wait for Fronto.

I was soon ushered into his study where he came to greet me, a broad smile on his face.

"Sextus! You came! I wasn't sure you would risk it."

We clasped forearms and he showed me to a comfortable chair while he sent his slaves off to bring refreshments. I'd already had more than my usual daily amount of wine, but I couldn't refuse the offer when I was in Fronto's company.

I'd known Tiberius Sestius Fronto all my life. We were the same age and had grown up together. As boys, we had treated each other's homes as our own, and we'd shared many foolish escapades. Even after I'd left home in righteous indignation when Primus inherited the bulk of my father's estate, I'd still kept in touch with Fronto, and he was the one person I knew I could always rely on.

Looking at him now, I thought he seemed to have aged since I'd last seen him a few years earlier. His hair was thinning, and his normally youthful face now appeared to have gained several worry lines despite his obvious delight at seeing me.

"When did you get here?" he asked.

"Yesterday. I think it gave Primus a bit of a shock."

He laughed, and the boy I had known reappeared in that happy face.

"You'll have your work cut out if you're going to stop him getting into more trouble," Fronto said. "He has a knack of falling out with people."

"Tell me about it. I've just come from a very scary chat with a thug called Marius Vindex."

"Vindex?" Fronto gaped, his stance suddenly frozen. "You've met him?"

"You know him?" I countered.

Fronto nodded, "I recall his name. We used to keep tabs on all the local thugs, you know. It wasn't really my area of responsibility, but I heard him mentioned during some of our meetings with the City Prefect and the Tribunes of the Urban Cohorts."

"He's a rising star, then?"

Fronto shrugged, "I don't know enough about him, but I seem to recall he's got the Viminal area pretty much under his control. I can't believe you've been to see him. Not so soon, at any rate."

"It wasn't exactly intentional," I assured him.

Briefly, I recounted my story for him.

"You're just as mad as ever, Sextus," Fronto sighed. "And just as lucky. Most people don't come away from that sort of thing without having a few fingers cut off at the very least."

"He was threatening to cut off rather more than that," I smiled.

Fronto chuckled, although I could tell my tale had worried him. Then he asked the same question Caecus had posed earlier.

"So if it wasn't Vindex, who did attack Primus?"

I told him, "I was rather hoping you might be able to shed some light on that for me."

He shook his head.

"I'm sorry, Sextus. I only heard about it after the event. It was the topic of a lot of gossip, but nobody knew any real facts. The gang who attacked him all got away, and they left no clues as to their identities."

"Then I may have my work cut out if I am to find them," I sighed.

"Why bother?" Fronto challenged. "Nobody around here cares all that much for Primus, you know. You should let him sort out his own problems."

"I'd like to, but he seems to think it was Vindex, and he's planning revenge."

"He's just as much of an idiot as he always was," Fronto sighed.

"I know. But if it wasn't Vindex, I think I need to try to find out who was responsible. I've got to let my mother believe I'm trying to help."

"She's miserable, you know," he informed me. "As I said in my letter, I think she would go back to Africa with you if you ask her."

"Yes, we'll do that. But we wanted to settle in first. Circe didn't think it would go down too well if that was the first thing we said when we got here."

Fronto shrugged, "Perhaps that is sensible."

"Besides which, it's the wrong time of year to be making another long voyage. We'll be in Rome for a few weeks at least."

"It will be good to have you around," Fronto smiled.

I asked him, "So what has been happening? How are things with you?"

He sat back, giving a slight shrug.

After a moment, he admitted, "I lost my position in the imperial household. Our new Emperor decided he wanted a complete change of staff, so the whole section was cleared out. He put his own people in to replace us."

"So what are you doing now?"

"Nothing very much so far," he confessed. "But there's plenty of time for me to find something to occupy me. I've got some savings, but I haven't quite decided what to try."

I could understand Fronto's dilemma. Many Romans curried the favour of a rich patron who would dispense money, gifts and invite them to dinner. In return, they support their patron in his business and political endeavours. Fronto, whose father had been relatively prosperous without ever attaining sufficient wealth to be classed among the equestrian ranks, had been fortunate enough to find a position in the imperial household where he'd helped Sempronius Rufus build up the Emperor's spy network. He had no need of a patron when he was working for the palace, but without that employment, he had no other skills and no rich benefactor to fall back on.

"You'll need to do something," I pointed out rather lamely.

"I know," he sighed. "But nobody wants a former palace official who is out of favour, especially one who used to work for the Juggler."

"Then you should go into business for yourself," I told him.

"It's a question of identifying the right opportunity," he replied evasively. "I've got my eye on one or two businesses I could maybe invest in, but I don't know an awful lot about trade, so I've not yet been able to make up my mind where to start."

Something in his manner told me he was making light of a serious situation, but I knew his pride must be hurting, so I didn't want to press him too hard.

I smiled, "Well, if you ever need help, let me know. Circe is very rich, you know."

Perhaps I shouldn't have said that. He gave me a very serious look as he said, "Thank you, but I need to sort this out for myself."

I knew his mannerisms well enough to recognise that he did not feel ready to discuss his personal affairs in any detail, so I changed the subject.

"What about down on the Palatine? The change of personnel must be causing them problems. The Juggler had built up a huge network of contacts."

"The new men have their own contacts," Fronto informed me. "And their own spies. You should be very careful about what you say and who you say it to."

"It's as bad as that?" I frowned.

Fronto shook his head sadly as he told me, "Actually, it's worse. When I say it was the Emperor who wanted his own men in place, what I meant was it was his grandmother, Julia Maesa, who decided to sweep out all the old staff. Slaves, freedmen and officials like me were all replaced. But since then, the Emperor has been building his own little network of informers, and so has his mother."

"Julia Soaemias? The Emperor's mother? She's plotting against Maesa?"

Fronto shrugged, "I don't know about any actual plots, but none of them seem to trust each other at all. Well, that's not entirely true. Soaemias is still very close to the Emperor, although he doesn't pay much heed to her advice. His lackeys are the sort you would expect, so she's been trying to set up her own web of spies to help him. Maesa still controls the official household, but the Emperor is growing up, and he's been exerting his own authority for the past few months, which means there's a great deal of shifting of allegiances and double dealing."

"It sounds like you are better off out of it," I remarked.

"I certainly am. I can't recall a time when things were so bad on the Palatine."

"How bad is that?"

Fronto lowered his voice slightly as he explained, "Very bad. Haven't you heard about the assassination attempts?"

I shook my head.

"No. That news hadn't reached Leptis Magna by the time we left. What happened?"

"It was complicated," Fronto informed me, "so I'll summarise it for you. It began a couple of weeks ago with rumours that the Emperor had decided to do away with his cousin."

"What?"

"You remember the Emperor has a younger cousin? Alexander, he's called. He's the son of Soaemias' sister, Julia Mamaea."

"I remember him," I nodded, "although he was a child when I last saw him in Antioch."

"He's still a child, really," Fronto told me. "But he's a clever young lad, and he's very popular with the Praetorians."

I could detect the undercurrent in Fronto's words.

I guessed, "But the Emperor isn't quite as popular?"

"That's the problem," Fronto confirmed. "Last year, Julia Maesa, who is grandmother to both boys, of course, persuaded the Emperor to have his cousin named as his heir, so Alexander became Alexander Caesar. Later, though, if you believe the rumours, the Emperor became jealous and stripped Alexander of his position. Then he sent assassins to do away with the boy."

"In the palace?"

"That's right. The Emperor went off to his summer house on the Caelian where he waited for word that his acolytes had done away with Alexander."

"What happened?"

Fronto explained, "It seems the Praetorians didn't obey the Emperor's order to return to their barracks and leave the palace unprotected. They became suspicious of the men he had sent, and they prevented the murder."

"That was lucky for Alexander, but I doubt the Emperor would have been pleased."

"I wouldn't know," Fronto shrugged. "But the Praetorians were furious. A band of them marched off to the summer house determined to execute the Emperor and place Alexander on the imperial throne."

I gaped in amazement. What my friend was telling me appalled me. Caecus had long been of the view that Elagabalus was not fit to be Emperor, but I'd always treated his views with some caution because he had been a loyal follower of Macrinus, so he was naturally biased against the young Emperor. What Fronto was telling me, though, was far worse than I could have imagined.

I observed, "The Emperor is still alive, so I presume he escaped?"

"Yes. Most of his so-called friends abandoned him when they saw the Praetorians coming for him, but a couple of them managed to calm the soldiers and remind them of their oaths of loyalty."

"That worked?" I asked sceptically. Soldiers' oaths were notoriously fragile things.

Fronto nodded, "Yes. Elagabalus is, after all, linked to the Severan dynasty, so that carried a lot of weight with the troops. But the Emperor had to go to the Praetorian Camp and swear to reinstate Alexander and to make no more attempts on his life. He also had to pay the Praetorians a rather large bribe."

"And, in exchange, they let him live?" I ventured.

"That's right. But things have been very tense ever since then."

"I can imagine," I agreed. "Perhaps things would settle a bit if the Emperor produced an heir of his own."

Fronto let out a soft sigh.

"That doesn't seem very likely in the near future," he told me. "He's already been married three or four times. I lost count of the women he's married and divorced without producing any children."

"Three or four marriages?" I frowned.

"At least. And he's still only eighteen years old."

"It all sounds very chaotic," I said in bemusement.

"It certainly is," Fronto nodded wearily. "It's not at all like the old days."

"Speaking of which," I said, "what about the Juggler? What happened to him?"

"He's dead," Fronto replied with a grimace. "He was told he was no longer needed, but I heard he suffered an accident only a few days after he was kicked out."

"An accident? Sempronius Rufus?"

Fronto nodded, "I don't know the details, but I heard his house burned down. By the time the fire was noticed, his bedroom was already well ablaze, and nobody could get near it. I expect he suffocated before the flames reached him, otherwise he would have tried to get out. As it was, they say his body was still lying in the ashes of his bed."

"I'm sorry to hear that," I said. "He was a tough man to please, but he was always fair."

After a moment, I asked, "I don't suppose there's any doubt about it being an accident?"

Fronto shrugged, "Who knows? But, to be honest, if Maesa wanted him dead, she'd have sent a bunch of Praetorians to remove his head. That's happened to plenty of others she wanted rid of. Burning his house isn't really her style."

That made sense. A person who wields absolute authority has no need to conceal deeds like killing political opponents. In the weeks following Julia Maesa's coup, plenty of her enemies had been done away with in rather public ways.

There was a short, introspective silence, then Fronto said, "But enough about imperial politics. It's a depressing subject at the best of times, and these are far from being the best. So tell me about your family. How is Circe anyway?"

"She is very well. In fact, why don't you come and meet her?"

"She's here?"

"I couldn't stop her," I admitted. "The kids are with us, too."

Fronto's smile held a hint of regret, and I mentally kicked myself for that last comment. He and his wife, Faustia, still had no children, and that was obviously something that bothered him.

Pushing that issue aside, I suggested, "Why don't you and Faustia come for dinner tonight? My mother would love to see you, I know. And Circe as well."

Fronto gave a wry laugh. He had met Circe only once, long before either of us knew anything about her. At the time, she'd been laying the groundwork for her self-appointed task of avenging the deaths of her father and step-sister. It had been a long-term project, years in the planning, and part of it had involved her infiltrating the Juggler's spy network. Circe had dazzled the young and very impressionable Fronto who had told her rather more than he should have in his attempts to impress her. He'd failed in his efforts to get her into bed, but meeting her again might prove awkward, especially if his wife happened to be with him.

Warily, I asked him, "Is there a problem? Does Faustia know about you and Circe?"

He held up a hand in denial.

"No! I learned my lesson from that episode. I've never told Faustia anything about Circe or my work."

I knew that last bit was true. When I'd last stayed with Fronto, we had never discussed what we knew about imperial affairs in Faustia's presence.

"So you'll come to dinner?" I prompted.

Fronto thought about it for a moment, then grinned, "That would be nice."

"Excellent! I'm sure my mother can get Primus' kitchen staff to arrange something. Just make sure you come to her door, not the main one."

"You're going to have a dinner at Primus' expense?" Fronto chuckled.

"Why not? I'm trying to save his rotten life. The least he can do is feed me and my family. And friends. And anyone else I feel inclined to invite."

We both laughed.

That was the great thing about Fronto. We could go for years without seeing one another, but could pick up as if only moments had passed since our previous meeting. And one thing we'd always had in common was a dislike of Primus.

Fronto said, "You haven't changed, my friend. You may be insufferably rich now, but you still refuse to follow conventions. And you still take too many risks. You should be careful of Primus. I may not be at the centre of things these days, but I know enough to recognise that he's moving in ever higher circles of society, and he hasn't got there by being nice."

"He's just like Marius Vindex, you mean?"

"It's often hard to tell the difference between underworld bosses and the top echelons of Roman society," Fronto agreed. "They behave in very similar ways. So be careful."

"I can handle Primus," I assured him.

He regarded me seriously as he said softly, "I wasn't only talking about him. You might have escaped from Vindex, but there

103

are a lot of powerful people in Rome, and Primus knows quite a few of them."

"He's not one of Maesa's informers?" I guessed, feeling a chill at the thought.

"Not as far as I know," Fronto assured me. "I'd have warned you not to come if I believed that. But things have changed since I wrote that letter to you. Primus has been cosying up to some important Senators, and who knows where their allegiances lie? With Maesa and Soaemias vying for control of the Emperor, you need to be very careful about what you say and do."

That gave me pause for thought. Everyone seemed to be warning me to tread carefully. I'd always known Rome was a city full of intrigue, but there was a definite feeling of fear surrounding every conversation. The sooner I solved the mystery of who had attacked Primus, the sooner we could head home to Leptis Magna.

But if Vindex wasn't behind the attack on Primus, that left me facing a big problem. The task my mother had set me looked as if it might be more complicated than I'd first thought. If Fronto was right, Primus might have made some very powerful enemies. Enemies I wanted nothing to do with.

Chapter 10
Massages

It was starting to rain when I left Fronto's house. Nevertheless, I took a few moments to take a good look around in case anyone might be watching for me. Apart from a couple of old women heading down the hill and a stray dog sniffing around the gutters, the street was clear, so I walked briskly to my mother's door. Another of Primus' heavies let me in, and I walked through to the back of the house where I found my mother sitting with Valeria on her knee and Sextus at her feet while she told them a children's story in her native Aramaic. Sextus' Greek tutor, Hermion, was sitting close by, his own expression revealing fascination at my mother's use of the language and at the children's response.

Valeria, of course, was far too young to have any clue about what my mother was saying, but she was smiling and burbling at the tone of happiness my mother was employing. Sextus, though, seemed fascinated by what he was hearing. Aramaic was new to him, but it was related to Punic, so I think he was able to pick up a few words. Children's capacity to learn is incredible, and I had no doubt my two would become fluent in Aramaic if they were around my mother for any length of time.

Their play lesson was momentarily interrupted by my arrival. Sextus informed me that his grandmother was teaching him a new language, while Valeria dribbled all over me when I picked her up and gave her a kiss.

"She taught me that language when I was a boy," I told my son as I wiped away Valeria's soggy dribble.

Still holding Valeria, I made my way to the windows at the rear of the house.

This room had a set of double doors which led out to the garden, but the rain had driven everyone inside, and the doors were shut. The windows, thanks to Primus' wealth, had panes of glass, so it was possible to see out while still being protected from the elements. I peered through the thick, murky glass to see a distorted and very wet image of the garden where I had played as a child. The sight recalled several memories, both good and bad.

"We were playing outside," my mother informed me. "But that rain looks as if it could be on for a while."

I turned to give her a questioning look.

"Circe mentioned something about a dog."

"Oh, Dentes. He's kept chained up during the day. Petrus only lets him roam during the night."

"Petrus?"

"He's one of your brother's slaves. He came here as a boy, and he practically raised Dentes from a pup."

"I hope he keeps him under control when the kids are out in the garden."

"I told you. He is chained up all day. Besides, he's very well trained."

"Trained to rip people's throats out, I expect."

My mother smiled, "You never used to worry so much when you were younger."

"I wasn't a father then. Of course I worry."

"So now you know what it is like," she said, smiling to soften the words.

"I'm sorry," I told her. "I suppose I wasn't a very good son to you. Running off like that, I mean."

She did not contradict me, but merely said, "It is often a woman's lot to remain at home and worry while her father, husband, or son goes off to war. At least I knew you had not joined the Army."

"I'm no fighter," I assured her, keeping to myself the riskier adventures I had managed to get myself into during my imperial career.

I was wondering whether this might be an appropriate time to broach the subject of her returning to Africa with us, but she pre-empted my train of thought by standing up and moving to the window on the far side of the door.

"Circe is going to get wet," she observed.

"I take it she's not back yet?"

"Not yet."

"I expect she's bought half the goods on sale in the forum," I sighed. "But I hope she isn't too late getting back. I've invited Fronto and his wife for dinner."

My mother beamed, "That is good. I love Fronto. He's such a sensible boy."

"You didn't used to say that when we got into trouble."

"That's because it was always your fault," she reminded me.

"You could be right," I grinned. "But could I trouble you to organise the dinner? I'm sure the kitchen staff will take orders from you better than from me."

"Leave it to me," she said as she reached out to take Valeria back from me.

"Thanks. Now I need to go and talk to Primus."

"Is there anything I should know?" she asked, her delicate eyebrows arching.

"Nothing too important. We can talk later, once everyone is back."

She wasn't impressed with this, but accepted my reticence, so I left her to summon slaves to get the dinner arranged, and I went in search of my brother.

I ran into the *major domo*, Mardonius, almost as soon as I had passed through the connecting door. He was formal and almost polite as he showed me to Primus' study, a small room adjoining the reception chamber where I'd spoken to my brother the previous evening.

Primus was sitting at a desk scribbling on a wax tablet. He scowled when I entered the room, but reluctantly set the tablet aside and gestured for me to take a seat. He did not tell Mardonius to bring wine, so I guessed this would be a short discussion.

"I've spoken to Vindex," I announced.

Primus regarded me with a sarcastic sneer.

"I doubt that. You're still alive."

"Yes, although it was, I'm sure you'll be pleased to learn, touch and go for a while. You might have warned me he uses that place Xeno's as his base."

"You didn't ask."

"Actually, I think I did," I reminded him.

He merely shrugged, feigning indifference, but I knew him well enough to understand that was just an act.

"Would you like to know what he said?"

"I don't expect it was anything profound," Primus sneered.

"No, but it was interesting. He claimed to know nothing about the attack on you, nor of the slogans being painted on your walls."

"You're an idiot," Primus told me. "Of course he would say that."

"I think he was telling the truth," I stated.

"Yes," Primus nodded sarcastically, "gangsters like Vindex are well known for their truthfulness."

I sighed, "He also said I was to warn you off encroaching on his territory. He said he would deal with you if you tried to muscle in on the Viminal."

Primus snorted a laugh.

"I'm terrified!" he exclaimed. "Vindex doesn't scare me."

"Maybe not, but a street war is going to cause trouble and attract a lot of attention. Sooner or later, the City Prefect will be forced to take notice."

Primus sneered, "I'm not stupid, Secundus. As it happens, I have no interest in acquiring any more properties on the Viminal at the moment. That one came on the market, and I decided to buy it, but I've got other ventures to concentrate on just now."

He leaned forwards, his elbows on the desk, his hands clasped together as he added forcefully, "But I'll deal with Vindex when I'm ready. I'll let him think he's scared me off. Then, when the time comes, he'll regret ever tangling with me."

He glared at me as he added, "As for you, you're an idiot if you believe anything he told you."

Primus wasn't exactly trying to massage my ego, but I remained as patient as I could. It wasn't easy, as he had always been able to rouse my temper.

"Look," I said earnestly, "I think we ought to seriously consider the possibility that he was not responsible for the assault. And if he's not behind the threats against you, it means you have another enemy. Mother wants me to find out who that is."

Primus leaned back in his chair, resting his hands on his fat belly while he continued to stare at me, waiting for me to complete my argument.

I asked him, "I don't suppose you have any suggestions as to who else might have a grudge against you?"

He shook his head.

"Vindex is the only one who would dare."

I frowned, "I honestly don't see Vindex as the sort of man who would be content merely to daub insults on your walls, do you?"

That brought nothing more than a shrug of his shoulders.

I said, "I suppose you've considered posting some men outside at night? You might catch whoever is scribbling on your walls."

"Painted slogans don't bother me," he replied. "I employ men to keep the house safe, not to wander the streets outside."

I persisted, "It really would help if you could give me some more names of possible enemies you might have made. You know, business rivals or the like."

He frowned, "Every businessman makes enemies. How should I know whether any hapless fool holds a grudge because I got the better of him in a deal?"

"Do you always get the better of people in deals?" I asked.

His look suggested his opinion of me hadn't been improved by that question.

He snapped, "Of course I do."

That was Primus. For him, there were only winners and losers. The concept of a mutually beneficial arrangement would simply never occur to him.

"But are any of them likely to hold such a serious grudge? You must have some idea."

"How many times must I tell you?" he rasped, leaning towards me again. "If it wasn't Vindex, I don't know who it could have been. But if it was some poor sap who harbours a grudge, then I really don't care."

That, I knew, was true. He'd always been like that, although the sentiment did not extend to anyone who was more powerful or wealthy than him. Primus was a typical bully, making life a misery for those who were weaker than him, but fawning over anyone he perceived as stronger. He had been like that all through my boyhood, and I expected he'd be the same until his dying day.

I sighed, "All right, have it your way. But could I maybe talk to Mardonius or your other staff? One of them might have some suggestions."

The look he gave me this time suggested he'd be happy to flog any of his staff who dared to have ideas of their own without his permission, but he gave a surly nod.

"Do what you like," he said. "But be quick about it. The sooner you give up on this stupid quest, the better."

"Don't worry," I assured him. "I won't stay here a moment longer than I need to."

There didn't seem much else to say after that, so I stood up and left the room.

Mardonius was waiting outside, possibly to ensure that I returned to my mother's part of the house without pinching any of the valuables.

I told him, "My brother says I can ask you some questions."

Mardonius' saturnine features grew even darker, and I could see he wasn't keen on saying anything.

I sighed, "Why don't you check with him? If he says you can answer questions, you and I can have a chat later."

"All right," he muttered.

"Good man!" I beamed.

Then I opened the connecting door, walked through and slammed it shut behind me, cutting him off.

I doubted I'd get anything from the *major domo*. If he spoke to Primus first, he'd be instructed in what to say, but on the other hand, if he didn't get Primus' permission, he wouldn't say anything at all.

Still, there were more ways than one of obtaining information. It was just a question of knowing who to ask.

As I'd expected, Circe returned home with the slaves who had accompanied her laden down by heavy bags. Still, the look of relief on her face when she saw me made my heart skip a beat.

"How did it go?" she asked in a whisper as she gave me a hug.

"Let's go upstairs and talk," I suggested.

After checking that my mother was still happy to watch the children, Circe led the way up to our room, tugged off her damp clothes, leaving only her under-tunic, then flopped down on the bed with a sigh of relief.

110

"So what happened?" she asked me as she stretched her limbs. "Did you learn anything?"

"Tell me about your day first," I replied. "It looks as if it was a busy one."

"A difficult one, anyway," she sighed. "Hortensia is *so* boring!"

I looked down at her, taking in the sight of her long legs and lithe body.

"No!" she said.

"No what?"

"I know that look," she told me. "And I'm too tired. I've been walking all day, and my feet are aching."

Smiling, I moved to the foot of the bed and began massaging her bare feet. They felt cold and damp after her trek in the rain, so I rubbed them vigorously for a while to warm them up.

"That's nice," she purred.

"So you didn't enjoy your day?" I enquired.

"Oh, I liked seeing the various markets. I bought a few things."

"I noticed. We'll need a second ship to get it all back home."

She ignored that remark.

She said, "What I didn't like was having half a dozen of Primus' thugs following us everywhere."

"You took some of our own slaves with you," I pointed out.

"Yes, but at least they were able to carry stuff for me. Those brutes just plodded around behind us, scaring off anyone who dared come too close."

"Primus was just taking precautions," I suggested.

"I know. But it meant Hortensia was not inclined to say too much."

"About what?"

"About the threats. And you can get back to rubbing my feet. There's nothing wrong with my thighs."

"I know that. They're perfect."

Receiving a scathing look, I obediently spent some more time rubbing her feet before slowly edging up to massage her calves.

She said, "I did learn that Primus got rid of one of his guards a little while ago. A man named Vespillo."

"What caused that?"

Circe explained, "According to Hortensia, Vespillo beat up some of the female slaves."

"Nasty," I observed. "I presume he wanted sex and didn't take refusals well."

"Oh, no," Circe replied. "The slaves had no choice about having sex with him. He was a freedman, after all. But he liked to be rough, and he went too far with a couple of them. Primus warned him, but he did it again, so Primus got rid of him."

I pursed my lips. The lot of young female slaves is rarely a happy one. Many masters don't mind their other slaves or guests having sex with the girls because it can result in the birth of a child who can either be raised as another slave who has been acquired at no cost or, more likely, can be sold in the slave market, bringing in some extra cash. But damaging the goods is generally frowned upon, so it was no wonder Primus had got rid of the fellow.

"Does Hortensia think this Vespillo could have been behind the attack, then?"

"She didn't say as much, but she obviously didn't like him, and she did admit he would be quite capable of using violence."

"He sounds like a nice chap."

"He's a former legionary," Circe said. "I expect that means he's accustomed to looting and raping."

"Don't let Caecus hear you say that," I warned with a smile. "But perhaps we should have a word with Vespillo. Does Hortensia know where he went?"

"Apparently not. But I'm sure you could track him down. You're good at that sort of thing."

"I know," I grinned with lack of modesty. "Did you learn anything else from Hortensia?"

"Nothing much. Only that your brother had a visitor yesterday evening."

"I know he did. I saw the wine cups."

"But did you know the visitor was a Senator?"

"No. Which one?"

"Hortensia didn't know. Primus met the man in private."

"There's nothing unusual about that. And I suppose if Primus has trouble walking, there's no reason why a Senator shouldn't come to visit him. It could have been his patron."

"I suppose so," Circe sighed. "It just annoys me that some women accept such an inferior role in their own house."

"Most Roman women do," I grinned. "It's you who is unusual."

"And don't you forget it!" she laughed. "Now tell me about your day. How did you get on?"

I continued to massage her legs while I told her what had happened. Despite my ministrations, I could feel her tensing up.

"You walked right into his headquarters?" she gasped.

"It was an accident!" I protested. "Primus omitted to tell me where Vindex and his gang hang out. It was pure luck I wandered into the place. But it all turned out well enough in the end."

"Thanks to Collinus and Caecus," she retorted.

"Yes. But at least I discovered Vindex probably isn't the person we are looking for."

"I suppose so," she conceded rather ungraciously.

I knew I needed to earn some credit with her, so I spent a few more minutes rubbing her legs while I explained what Primus had told me.

"Oh, and I invited Fronto and Faustia to come to dinner tonight."

"That will be nice," she sighed dreamily, her eyes closed as she relaxed.

There was a short silence before she murmured, "Your hands seem to have wandered rather a long way up beneath my tunic."

"So they have."

Stretching, I leaned down to kiss her. She obviously wasn't as tired as she'd claimed, because she returned the kiss with considerable enthusiasm, and her arms were soon pulling me down onto the bed. I won't divulge the details of what happened next, but suffice to say it was the most enjoyable time I'd had since we'd left Africa six weeks earlier.

Chapter 11
Multiple Choice

Caecus returned late in the afternoon, his hair and clothes soaked by the rain. He seemed in a sombre mood, but we had no opportunity to exchange news because there were too many slaves around.

"We'll talk after dinner," I told him. "Best not say anything while our guests are here. Fronto knows all about us, but his wife doesn't, so mind what you say in front of her."

Caecus gave a distracted nod, then went to dry off. If I'd been drenched like that, I'd have made sure I went to a bath house for a dip in the hot pool, but I supposed the ex-soldier was accustomed to being out in all weathers. Perhaps he was immune to catching colds.

Collinus, I learned, had been home all afternoon. As his room was across the hall from the one Circe and I shared, I suspect he'd heard our lovemaking, but his inscrutable expression revealed nothing at all. I had never been very sure whether Collinus liked me personally, but he was devoted to Circe, and I suppose he had decided he could put up with me as long as I made her happy. I gave him the same warning I'd given Caecus, to which he responded with a silent nod.

Circe and I spent some time playing with the children before we handed control over to the slave girls who would take care of them at night. One of the girls also helped Circe pin up her hair and find a suitable dress for the evening. I put on a fresh tunic, then went down to wait for Fronto and Faustia.

It was dark and still raining when they arrived, but Fronto was in a good mood. He handed his dripping cloak to old Lucius, then came through to the dining chamber. I made the introductions and we all took our places on the long, wide couches. I had to stifle my amusement at the way Circe and Fronto addressed one another as if they'd never met, but it was easier for them to do that than to explain to Faustia the circumstances of their first encounter.

I must admit Primus' kitchen staff had worked wonders again. We were served more courses of food in such variety I wondered how big his larder was. I also wondered whether he knew we were dining at his expense. I suspected Mardonius would have told him, and I couldn't help smiling at the thought of how my brother must feel at not being invited to a dinner party which was being held in his own house, and for which he was paying. Still, the devious bastard hadn't warned me about Vindex's lair, so I really didn't care what he thought.

Naturally, with ebullient characters like Fronto, Circe and my mother at the table, the conversation did not lag at all. Fronto and I reminisced, with my mother putting in asides which we would have preferred to have kept quiet about but which greatly amused Circe and Faustia.

I quite liked Faustia. She was small and delicate, if not conventionally pretty, but she came from a good family and she seemed a good match for Fronto. He might not have told her any details about his former work, but I gained the impression she may have guessed at more than my friend suspected. If she had, though, she kept it to herself.

Collinus and Caecus were not left out of the conversation, although both men generally preferred to listen rather than to speak. In response to Fronto's curiosity, Collinus gave a brief account of how he had come to serve Circe's father, and how he had been given the role of acting as a personal bodyguard to her when she was still a young girl.

"And he's been taking care of me ever since," Circe explained with a smile.

Then Caecus gave an edited version of his military career and how he had come to join our service. He omitted any mention of being on the losing side in the brief civil war which had overthrown Macrinus, merely saying he had retired from the service after the death of Caracalla.

"And now you are all here in Rome," Faustia remarked. "Tiberius Fronto tells me you are trying to find out who is behind the trouble Sempronius Primus is having."

"That's right," I said cautiously. "Although we haven't really begun our investigation yet."

"It may take you a long time," Faustia smiled, her eyes sparkling with amusement. "Your brother has made rather a lot of enemies."

"So I gather. I suppose all we can do is draw up a list of names, then check them out one at a time."

"Well, it won't be Rusticus," she declared. "So you needn't add his name to your list."

I frowned, "Who is Rusticus?"

Fronto shot a look in my mother's direction, then put in, "You saw him earlier today. He's our door slave."

He paused for effect, then added, "But he used to be the *major domo* here until Primus sold him."

I glanced at my mother who gave me a nod of confirmation.

She sighed, "Primus said he was growing too old, but I think it was because Rusticus is not a big man, and Primus has taken a liking to having strong men around him."

Fronto said, "I'd known Rusticus for years, of course. So when I heard Primus was about to sell him, I bought him."

He gave a shrug as if to dismiss any notion he had acted out of charity, but I knew Fronto and Faustia had more than enough slaves in their large house.

I tried to picture the man in my mind, and I certainly couldn't see him as a potential killer. But even an elderly man could scrawl graffiti on a wall.

"Would you mind if I spoke to him anyway?" I asked.

Faustia exclaimed, "You can't think dear old Rusticus could do anything like that? He's far too gentle."

"I appreciate that," I told her. "But he might be able to give me some information as we build up our list of names. As a former *major domo* here, he must know a fair bit about Primus' business associates."

Faustia relaxed slightly, giving me a resigned nod.

"I understand. Of course you can talk to him."

"Thank you."

I looked at Fronto, but he merely gave me a non-committal shrug.

The evening wound up shortly afterwards, and we said our farewells, sending a couple of slaves to light the way and make sure Fronto and Faustia returned home safely. The rain had stopped, so at least it would be a drier walk than the one they had experienced on their way here.

116

Primus' slaves cleared away the post-dinner debris, leaving only a couple of jugs of wine and our cups. It was growing late, the oil lamps creating dancing shadows on the walls, but we needed to discuss the events of the day and our plans for the morning, so I asked Collinus and Caecus to stay.

My mother also resumed her place, giving me a defiant look as she stretched out on her couch.

"I know more about this house than any of you," she informed me. "And I also know all about you and your true circumstances, so don't think you can keep me out of these discussions. You might think all I'm good for is watching over the children, but I'm sure I'll be able to help."

I gave in without protest, and we lay on the couches, sipping at our wine.

To begin, I gave an account of my encounter with Vindex. Everyone except my mother had heard the story already, so I provided her with a slightly edited version to conceal the danger I had been in. Then I told everyone about my later discussion with Primus.

"So it looks as if we need to compile our own list of names," I told them.

Next, Circe recounted her discussion with Hortensia. This provided Vespillo as the first name for us to consider.

"I remember him," my mother said. "A brute of a man. I rarely saw him, but I was glad when Primus got rid of him. Poor Cassia could barely walk after the beating he gave her."

"Where did he go?" I asked her.

"I'm not sure. But Mardonius would know."

"All right. I will speak to Mardonius tomorrow. And I'll go and talk to Rusticus to see if he can help us with any other names."

I paused, looking across at Collinus and Caecus.

"Before we continue, do either of you have any information you think we should know?"

Caecus, his voice low, said, "Nothing much. I spent most of the day down in the forum. I was just checking the lie of the land. I acted like a newcomer, and asked a lot of questions."

"About what?" I asked him.

"About recent events. It seems the Emperor is not well liked, but nobody was prepared to say anything very specific. There does seem to be tension in the imperial family, though."

That tallied with what Fronto had told me but, other than serving as a reminder to be wary of informers, it didn't really help our investigation.

When I looked at Collinus, he merely said, "We should not forget the man who was following us this morning."

Naturally, Circe's ears pricked up at this. She was lying on the couch beside me, her head near my knees, but I did not need to look down to see her alertness.

"What man?" she demanded, shooting me a frown of disapproval.

"It's probably nothing," I told her.

In response to her continuing stare, Collinus repeated the story he had relayed to me and Caecus earlier in the day.

I could tell from Circe's frown that she was reaching some disturbing conclusions about this episode. Whoever the stranger had been, he almost certainly was not one of Vindex's men. If he had been, he'd have followed me into Xeno's instead of running away when Collinus tried to challenge him. That meant it was more likely to have been an informer working for someone in the palace, and that was something we could have done without.

To allay the mounting tension, I said, "He could have been nothing more than an opportunist pickpocket looking for some newcomers to fleece. Whoever he was, let's use that as a reminder to remain wary when we are out. Keep checking behind you."

I knew I had not reassured my friends at all, so I decided it was time to move the conversation on.

Turning to my mother, I said, "Now, can you tell us who else might have a grudge against Primus? Do you know any of the people he has fallen out with?"

She sighed, "You know your brother. He makes enemies easily. But I have been thinking about it ever since the night he was attacked."

"And?"

"And there are a few names which spring to mind. To begin with, there is Aconius Dardanus.

He's a property factor. He used to collect rents for Primus, but they had a serious falling out a few months ago."

"Over what?" Circe asked.

"I'm not sure, but it was probably money."

"Where can we find him?" I asked.

"He has rooms up near the Colline Gate," my mother told us. "Just off the *Via Salaria*."

That wasn't far away. The Via Salaria was the main route to the eastern coast of the Italian peninsula and the Adriatic Sea, but it began very close to where we were now.

"That's one," I said. "Who else?"

"I suppose I should mention the builder who worked on the new house extension," my mother informed us, "although I really don't think he would have done anything like that. He was such a kind, gentle man."

"But he fell out with Primus?"

"It was more that Primus fell out with him. He was always shouting at poor Tanicus."

"Tanicus? That's the builder's name?"

"Yes. Mallius Tanicus. He and his men did most of the work on the new house."

"Most of it?"

"Primus was not happy with the way things were going. He constantly complained about shoddy workmanship."

"The house looks perfectly good to me," Circe said. "I couldn't fault it."

My mother explained, "Primus brought in someone else to finish the work, and he refused to pay Tanicus what the man asked for. I didn't see the argument myself, but I did hear whispers from the slaves that poor old Tanicus was begging Primus to pay him what he thought he was due, and Primus simply laughed at him and threw him out."

"That sounds like he has a motive," I remarked.

"But Tanicus was not the sort of man who would resort to violence," my mother insisted.

"It depends how desperate he was," Circe ventured.

My mother shook her head.

"I still can't see it. Tanicus simply wasn't like that."

"We'd better talk to him anyway," I sighed. I was beginning to feel the weight of our task pressing on my shoulders. Primus certainly had a knack of falling out with people.

"Where do we find this Mallius Tanicus?" I asked.

My mother replied uncertainly, "I'm not entirely sure. I think he had a builder's yard somewhere out near the Tiber, beyond the Field of Mars."

"It should be easy enough to find," I nodded. "Is there anyone else we should add to the list?"

My mother frowned, "I suppose there's old Helvius Oceanus. He lives in the house across the street. He and Primus have never got on since the man moved in. All the noise of the building work annoyed Oceanus."

"He's an old man, you say?"

"I think he must be nearly seventy now," my mother nodded. "But he has a very young wife."

She hesitated, then sighed, "Primus paid rather a lot of attention to her when she moved in."

"How much attention?" I asked.

"Enough for Oceanus to insist she never saw Primus again."

Circe asked, "Did they have an affair?"

"I don't know for certain, but I think they may have done."

"Does Hortensia know?" Circe enquired.

"She'd have been blind if she hadn't noticed," my mother replied. "But she pretends nothing happened. Perhaps she is right, but I have my doubts."

Caecus murmured, "Living on the other side of the street, he could easily nip across and write on the wall."

Looking at my mother, I asked her, "Is he the sort of man who would do something like that?"

She shrugged, "I don't know him well enough to say. But he's certainly got a short temper."

"Well, at least he's another one who is close at hand. I can talk to him tomorrow."

Circe put in, "Why don't you let me go over? Perhaps I can talk to his wife when he is out. I might learn more than you'd get out of an angry old man."

"That's a good idea," I agreed.

120

"But I'd also like to take the children out to see something of the city," Circe said. "This is supposed to be a holiday, after all."

I guessed she had an ulterior motive for suggesting this, and it was probably along the same lines as Caecus' snooping around the forum, but I knew better than to argue with her.

"As long as Collinus goes with you," I smiled.

Collinus nodded gravely.

"Are there any other names we should know about?" I asked my mother.

"I don't think so. But that's enough to begin with, isn't it?"

"It certainly is. A neighbour, a former *major domo*, a property factor, a builder and an ex-bodyguard."

Circe laughed, "Don't look so miserable, Scipio. You love this sort of thing. But we should go to bed now. It looks as if you are going to have a busy day tomorrow."

That, I thought, was an understatement if ever I'd heard one.

Chapter 12
Rusticus

Collinus was detailed to keep an eye on Circe, so I nominated Caecus to accompany me. If someone was trailing us, I would feel more comfortable with an extra pair of eyes helping me out, not to mention Caecus' imposing frame and menacing air which I hoped would deter anyone from hassling me.

We began by seeking out Mardonius on the grounds that he was close at hand. He wasn't hard to find since he must have been keeping one eye on the connecting door between the two parts of the house. He materialised almost as soon as we emerged from the short corridor beyond the door and stepped into the atrium. When he saw me, his face took on its usual expression of grim disapproval, but that morphed into wariness when he noticed Caecus close behind me. Mardonius may have been a big guy, but Caecus was bigger and a whole lot tougher.

"Good morning!" I beamed. "Did you ask my brother whether you can answer my questions?"

He returned a less than amicable nod.

"Yes."

"Good. I'd like to know about a man who used to be employed here. His name is Vespillo. I understand he left under something of a cloud."

To my surprise, Mardonius seemed to relax slightly when he heard the question. He didn't exactly exude friendliness, but he almost smiled as he confirmed, "Yes, he was one of the Master's guards. He used to be a soldier, or so he said."

"You don't believe he was in the army?" I queried.

"Oh, I'm sure he was. But let's just say I think he exaggerated some of the stories he told."

"That's not unusual," I shrugged. "Do you happen to know where he served, and in which unit?"

"He claimed to have been on the Germania frontier," Mardonius replied. "I don't recall him ever saying which unit he was with."

"It's not important," I told him casually. "What I'd really like to know is what happened to him after he left here. Do you know where he went?"

Mardonius' eyes narrowed slightly as if he was wondering why I wanted to know this. When he couldn't think of a reason not to tell me, he said, "I believe he's working for a Senator. I'm not sure which one."

"It must be somebody who doesn't object to his freedmen roughing up young girls," I murmured.

"I wouldn't know about that, Sir," Mardonius replied stiffly. His manner remained distinctly cool, but at least he'd given me a "Sir".

"Do you have any idea how I might find Vespillo or his new employer?" I asked.

This time, the *major domo's* response was heavy with sarcasm as he told me, "I expect a good place to look for them would be at the Senate House in the forum."

"Of course it would," I agreed, trying to convey the impression he'd correctly identified me as a witless fool. "But how will I recognise him?"

"Vespillo? Well, he's a tough-looking so-and-so. He keeps his hair cropped short. His nose was broken at one time, so it looks rather squashed, and he's lost a finger of his left hand. He claimed a German bit it off."

"Which finger?" I asked, knowing this would be a good way to identify our quarry.

"The smallest one," Mardonius told me, holding up his own left hand and waggling the little finger.

"That's very helpful," I smiled. "Thank you very much."

"Is that all you needed to know, Sir?"

"Why? Is there something else you want to tell me?"

He took half a pace backwards, holding up his hands in denial.

"No. Nothing at all."

"Fine. Then we'll be off. Come on, Caecus, we have a lot to do."

Once outside, I asked Caecus, "What did you make of that?"

123

"I don't trust him at all," Caecus stated with the finality of a man who was accustomed to judging character. "If he'd been in my Century, I'd have kept a close watch on him."

"Yes," I agreed, "I had the distinct impression he was worried I might ask him about something he wanted to keep hidden. I wonder what that could have been?"

Caecus opined, "He'd have lied if you had asked him about whatever it was. Like I say, he's not to be trusted."

I said, "You are forgetting that he works for my brother, who is one of the least trustworthy men you're ever likely to meet."

"Like attracts like," Caecus muttered.

"Very true. Of course, every household has secrets. It could be nothing more than some petty pilfering he's trying to conceal. But I think I'll keep needling him to see if he gives anything away. That will need to wait, though. We have more important things to do."

The first of those things was to visit a bath house. Circe had informed me that Primus had a bathing suite in his house, but I didn't fancy using those facilities.

"It's tiny," Circe had told me. "There's barely room for two people. Only one if it's your brother who is taking a bath."

That had been an unusually personal remark for Circe to make. She's normally very careful not to make derogatory comments about a person's appearance, so it told me she shared my dislike of Primus.

Still, I was feeling very much in need of scrubbing and a shave, so we walked down the hill to a small establishment I remembered from my youth. It wasn't much by Rome's standards, but it was serviceable enough. Caecus and I had a good soak in the hot pool, plunged into the cold pool, lay on tables while slaves used oil and strigils to scrape the dirt and sweat from our bodies, then I paid a barber to trim our hair, shave off my stubble, and trim Caecus' beard.

Refreshed and reinvigorated, we headed back up the Quirinal to Fronto's house. My knock on the door was answered quickly by the very man I'd come to see.

Rusticus peered at me with a look of dismay, his rounded shoulders seeming to slump even further when he recognised me.

"The Master said you would be coming," he sighed wearily as he let us in. "He says to use the main reception room. I'll go and tell him you are here."

In other circumstances, I'd not have trusted my suspect to return. Other men might have shown us into the large, comfortable room leading off the atrium, then made a run for it. Rusticus, though, didn't strike me as that type at all. He seemed resigned to whatever fate befell him.

Sure enough, he and Fronto came into the room a few moments later. Rusticus remained standing while we sat in the padded chairs which bordered a floor mosaic depicting an image of a voluptuous Venus rising from the sea in a giant clam shell, her arms strategically positioned to preserve her modesty.

"Sit down, Rusticus," I said, waving the man to a chair.

He glanced at Fronto for approval, then gingerly perched on the edge of a chair when my friend nodded his assent.

Rusticus was wringing his hands even before I'd started, which made me wonder whether he might be feeling guilty about having taken some revenge against my brother. More likely, he was just very nervous, as the beads of sweat on his upper lip strongly suggested.

Trying to relax him, I smiled, "Do you know who I am?"

He swallowed anxiously before stuttering, "Yes, Sir. You are Valerius Cantiacus, a guest of Sempronius Primus."

"Actually, I'm a guest of his mother," I informed him. "She has asked me to look into some threats which have been made against her son."

"So I understand, Sir," he bobbed, apparently eager to please.

"What I'd like to know is whether you could provide any information on who might be behind those threats."

Rusticus shook his head, lowering his eyes as if unable to meet my gaze.

"I'm sorry, Sir. The trouble started up after I'd left. And, to be perfectly blunt, Sir, there are rather a lot of people who dislike Sempronius Primus."

"I can understand that," I said sympathetically. "He can't have been an easy master to work for."

125

Rusticus made no reply, keeping his eyes firmly fixed on Venus' luscious outline.

I asked him, "How long were you *major domo* there?"

"Five years, Sir."

That, I thought to myself, was long enough to have had all the confidence knocked out of him. A *major domo* holds a very important position in any household, and nervous individuals can't usually cope with the pressure. I wondered whether that was the reason Primus had got rid of him.

"Five years," I nodded. "But you still can't think of anyone who would hate him enough to have him attacked?"

"Not really, Sir. I mean, a lot of people hate him, but whether they would be capable of that sort of thing, I can't say."

"Have you been writing threatening graffiti on his walls?"

He sat upright, his eyes wide with alarm and his hands flapping in agitation.

"No, Sir! I would never do anything like that."

I decided to make my questioning more aggressive. Firing a surprise question at him had rattled him even though it hadn't evoked an admission, but I could tell he wasn't the sort of person who would be able to resist a strong interrogation.

"You have the opportunity," I told him. "You could easily unbolt the door at night, nip up the street, daub a slogan and be back here before anyone missed you."

"No, Sir!" he almost wailed. "I didn't enjoy working for the man, but I have no reason to wish him harm. He no longer owns me, so why should I care?"

I could see his eyes filling with tears, so I sat back, waving at him to calm down.

"All right, Rusticus. I'm sorry. I had to be sure."

Fronto put in, "I trust Rusticus. If he says he is innocent, I believe him."

I knew my friend had said that more for Rusticus' benefit than mine, and the slave gave him a mournful look of gratitude in response.

Changing tack, I asked him, "What about his row with Mallius Tanicus, the builder?"

"What about it, Sir?"

"Did you witness it?"

"Yes, Sir."

"As I understand it, Primus was not happy with the quality of the work. Is that right?"

"Yes, Sir. Sempronius Primus told Mallius Tanicus he would not pay because of shoddy workmanship. The poor builder was in a terrible state, saying he would go out of business if he was not paid."

"He was angry?"

"Yes, but not in the way you mean. He was distressed, but he was no match for Sempronius Primus."

"Do you think he would be capable of resorting to violence to take revenge?"

"I very much doubt it, Sir. He was not that sort of man."

"But his work wasn't up to scratch?"

Rusticus hesitated, chewing his lip and wringing his hands as he plucked up courage. I waited, and he eventually revealed, "There was nothing wrong with Tanicus' work. He and his men did a good job. But Sempronius Primus had some of his slaves go around at night cracking bricks and scoring paintwork. They would bend lead pipes and make dents or cuts in the woodwork, then Primus would blame the builders."

"And he used that as an excuse not to pay them?"

"That's right, Sir. He eventually dismissed Tanicus and brought in another builder, although there was really only finishing work to be done. Tanicus had done most of the important stuff."

"Did he ever pay Tanicus?" I enquired.

Rusticus gave a shrug, "I don't know for sure, Sir, but I don't think so. I heard Tanicus had to sell his business."

I glanced at Fronto and Caecus, but they were both content to let me continue.

I asked the slave, "Do you know where I can find Mallius Tanicus?"

"I'm sorry, Sir. His business used to be just off the *Via Ostiensis*, down near Pottery Mountain, but I have no idea where he will be now that he's sold it."

"What about a property factor named Dardanus? I'm told Primus fell out with him as well."

Rusticus shook his head.

"I know the man, but I know nothing about any disagreement."

"And there was a guard named Vespillo who had a tendency to beat up some of the women slaves."

My prompting only drew another shake of the head.

"I'm sorry, Sir. I've been away from the house for several months now, so I don't know what has happened since then."

"In that case, perhaps you can tell me something else. I believe Primus had a visit from a Senator the other night. Would you happen to know who that might be?"

"No, Sir."

I pursed my lips. This wasn't really helping my investigation at all. I'd never really thought Rusticus could be a suspect, but I'd hoped he could have told me more.

In a final attempt to glean some information, I asked him, "Do you know who Primus' patron is?"

"Oh, yes, Sir. That would be Decimus Herennius Muncius. He's a Senator."

"I see. And where does he live? Do you know?"

"He has a house on the Pincian, Sir."

"That's an expensive part of town."

"Herennius Muncius is very wealthy, Sir."

That made sense. Primus wouldn't attach himself to anyone who was less than obscenely rich. But was this Herennius Muncius the man who had come to visit my brother the other evening? If he had, it was unusual. Wealthy patrons like to process around the city with a train of clients in attendance in order to show off how important they are. Another central part of the whole patronage system is that clients are generally expected to visit their patron's home every day. Was Herennius Muncius the sort of man who would instead visit the home of a client who had suffered an injury? It was possible, I supposed.

I sat back in my chair. I'd run out of ideas, so I looked at Fronto and Caecus, but neither of them had any questions.

I said to Rusticus, "All right. Thank you very much. You've been very helpful."

"Can I go now, Sir?" he asked Fronto.

"Yes. Thank you for your honesty, Rusticus."

The slave stood up, then regarded us with doubt in his eyes.

He hesitated, then asked, "Would you like to lock me in a room tonight, Sir? That way, if anyone scribbles on Sempronius Primus' house, you'll know it wasn't me."

"I don't think there's any need for that," I put in.

Fronto, though, said, "Actually, although I trust Rusticus implicitly, I think he might prefer that he be permitted to prove his innocence."

Rusticus nodded eagerly, "Yes, Sir."

"It's up to you," I shrugged.

Fronto dismissed Rusticus with a wave of his hand, leaving the three of us sitting wondering what we'd learned.

Not very much, in truth.

We spent a couple of minutes going over what Rusticus had told us, and bringing Fronto up to date on what we'd learned from my mother the previous evening. We were just about to leave, when Rusticus reappeared.

"There's a man at the door, Sir. He says he's here to see someone called Scipio. He insists I tell you this."

I felt a shiver of fear run through me as I exchanged a look with Fronto. My friend raised an eyebrow in question, to which I responded with a shake of my head to tell him I had no idea who this visitor might be.

Fronto asked the slave, "Did he give a name?"

"No, Sir. He wouldn't tell me."

"Is he alone?"

"Yes, Sir. He looks a shifty sort, Sir. Shall I send him away?"

Again, Fronto looked at me.

I sighed, "Perhaps we should hear what he has to say."

Fronto nodded, "Show him in, Rusticus."

The slave, clearly confused, gave a bow and departed.

Caecus, moving quickly but smoothly, rose from his chair and took up position a little way from the door. This would put him behind whoever came in. I gave him a smile of thanks, then Fronto and I both stood up, ready to greet whoever this mysterious visitor might be. Who in Rome knew my real name, I wondered?

When the door reopened, it was to admit a short, stout, middle–aged man with broad, flat features and knowing eyes. He moved lightly on his feet despite his bulging waistline, and he was smiling broadly as his perceptive gaze swept over me and Fronto. He must have sensed Caecus' presence, because he shot him a quick look, then turned his attention back to me.

"Well, well," he said pleasantly. "Sextus Sempronius Scipio. You are supposed to be dead."

Fronto and I both gaped at him, but I managed to respond, "So are you."

Because the man facing us was none other than Sempronius Rufus, also known as the Juggler, who had run the imperial spy network for the Emperor Caracalla. Fronto and I had both worked for him, so we knew him well. We could not have mistaken him, and he looked very much alive even though he was supposed to have burned to death in his bed shortly after being dismissed from the palace.

Chapter 13
Back From The Dead

"Sit down," Rufus ordered, assuming control as he had always done.

In his youth, he was reputed to have been a street performer, juggling balls and sticks, and performing acrobatic stunts for the amusement of the crowd. Somehow, he had talked his way into the service of the old Emperor, Septimius Severus. Severus had never been one to follow conventions and had a habit of promoting men on merit rather than on the basis of their family background. As a result, Sempronius Rufus had risen to command the imperial spies, and Caracalla had kept him in that role when he assumed the Purple after the death of his father. Rufus had grown fat during the years of sitting at a desk, but he had always possessed a sharp and cunning mind. He'd run his department with a rod of iron, and I still found myself automatically obeying his command to resume my seat.

Caecus hesitated for a moment, then moved to a chair which placed him close to Rufus.

The old spymaster regarded the former soldier with an amused expression.

"You have the look of Eagles about you," he remarked. "Which unit did you serve with?"

"Tenth Gemina," Caecus replied.

"The Danube front? Rank?"

"Centurion."

Rufus nodded thoughtfully.

"And now you are Scipio's bodyguard?"

"He's my friend," I interjected, pleased that Caecus had not revealed he had been a member of the Praetorian Guard. I had never asked, but I supposed the Tenth Gemina was the Legion he had originally joined before transferring to the elite unit who protected the Emperor.

Rufus and Caecus continued to regard one another with distrust, although Rufus was, as usual, very composed and self-assured.

Having recovered slightly from my initial shock, I studied him more closely. When he had worked at the palace, he had always been clean-shaven, but now he sported the stubble of a couple of days' worth of beard. His hair, dark but with streaks of ginger which had given him his *cognomen*, was in need of trimming, too, falling over his ears in a tangled, untidy mess which added to the air of disreputability he was obviously trying to cultivate. He was dressed in a plain, nondescript tunic and old sandals, and he held a freedman's cap in his hand. That, I thought, was a clever trick. Slaves who have recently been freed often wear a peaked cap to denote their new status. It serves to let those who knew them as slaves to recognise they have been freed. As far as the Juggler was concerned, however, the cap would act as a distraction, since anyone giving him a casual glance would be more likely to notice the headgear than his features. That was one of the tricks he had taught me years ago.

"Wear something people will notice," he had explained. "That way, they won't notice the important things about you."

Which meant he did not want to be noticed, but that did not explain why or how he was here.

"How did you find us?" I demanded.

Still smiling, Rufus said, "I think you should tell me your story first. The last I heard, you had been sent on a mission to discover the identity of a mad prophet who had predicted Caracalla's death."

"I never found him," I lied, holding Rufus' gaze to show my sincerity.

I went on, "It doesn't matter anyway. All that is in the past, and I no longer work for you. Or for the current Emperor. Come to that, neither do you."

Rufus continued to smile as he nodded, "Very well said, young Scipio. I always thought you were a man who could make his own decisions. It's what made you such a good spy, but it also meant you were difficult to control."

"You don't control me now," I shot back. "So why don't you tell us how you come to still be alive, and what you are doing here?"

His eyes roved over each of us in turn, assessing and calculating as always.

Then he said, "I know I am a guest here, but I think my story should wait until I have heard yours. I would guess the tall, good-looking woman is your wife, and the two children are yours?"

I felt my whole body tense. I should have known the Juggler would not come here unless he knew a lot about us already.

"What of it?" I responded guardedly.

Instead of answering, he said, "Your other man, the Arab. He's a sharp one. He almost caught me yesterday."

"So it was you who was following us?" Caecus growled, shifting in his seat.

"I was curious," Rufus shrugged. "You went to see Marius Vindex, I presume? And you came out alive. That was well done, although I should have expected nothing less from Sigma."

"Sigma?" Caecus frowned.

I said, "It was my code name. Sextus Sempronius Scipio. In Greek, they all begin with the letter Sigma."

I could have added that Rufus often called me his namesake because we shared the family name Sempronius, although that did not mean we were related. Back in the dim and distant past, I suppose all the Sempronii were related, but each time one of them freed a slave, the new freedman would assume the family name, so now there were thousands of people with the Sempronius name.

Rufus said, "What I'd like to know is why you are here after having vanished from sight a few years ago. If you tell me that, I'll tell you my tale."

I sighed, slumping back in my chair. After a few moments, I gave him a brief account of my mother's appeal for help.

"I see," Rufus nodded. "That explains why you went to see Vindex. Did you have any luck?"

"I didn't go to see him," I informed him. "All I was doing was scouting around. I went into his place by accident."

Even the normally phlegmatic Rufus looked surprised by this news.

"Truly?" he asked.

"I'm afraid so. As for having any luck, I got out in one piece, which I think was very lucky in the circumstances."

"I see," he said, rubbing his chin pensively. "And did you learn anything of value?"

"I learned not to go to Xeno's," I replied. "But also that Vindex claims to know nothing about the night my brother was beaten up."

"Interesting," he mused, "although I doubt it will have any bearing on their feud."

"What do you know about that?" I probed.

"Only that your brother was trying to move in on Vindex's patch, and their followers have been involved in a couple of altercations. It seems to have settled down recently, though."

I informed him, "Primus says he has other things on his mind at the moment."

"I'm sure he does," Rufus nodded knowingly.

"What is that supposed to mean?"

"I'll tell you in a moment."

"Well, you've heard my story, so why don't you tell us yours?"

"It's a long one," Rufus said pointedly.

Taking the hint, Fronto reached for a small hand bell which stood on a table nearby. He rang, summoning Rusticus who soon had a jug of wine and a plate of dried fruits and pastries delivered.

Rufus took a sip of his wine, bit into a pastry, chewed slowly, then eventually began his explanation.

"You know, of course, that our Emperor, who now goes by the name of Elagabalus, removed me from my post. Or perhaps it would be more truthful to say that his grandmother, Julia Maesa, gave the orders."

Fronto let out a small mumble of discontent at this. He, too, had been a victim of the change of regime.

Rufus went on, "The Emperor was little more than a boy when he came to Rome, dragging along his black stone which he insisted represents his god. He was, and is, more interested in the rituals of worshipping that lump of rock than in governing."

He gave a wry grimace as he added, "Now, he demands that he be worshipped as the earthly embodiment of that same god."

134

Caecus gave a grim nod, while Fronto and I exchanged worried glances. The last Emperor who had insisted on being worshipped as a god was mad Caligula. That hadn't ended well.

Rufus continued, "He has also had every important religious relic moved into his new temple to the Sun God. That means nobody can worship any of the other gods without offering prayers to Elagabalus the god."

I shifted uneasily in my chair. I knew enough about Roman history to understand how unpopular such an action would be.

Yet Rufus had not finished his list of complaints.

He said, "Of course, it is Julia Maesa and her daughter, Soaemias, who really rule the empire. They even sit in the Senate to hear all the discussions, and it is they who tell the Emperor what to do and say."

"Women in the Senate?" I gaped. "What do the Senators think about that?"

"What they think is not what they say," Rufus grinned. "Most of them are too afraid to voice their real opinions. The Praetorians may dislike the Emperor, but they remain loyal to the house of Severus."

Fronto interjected, "Is it true they hung a picture of the Emperor in the Senate House?"

Rufus nodded, "It's true. It was done by Maesa's order. The portrait hangs just behind the statue of Victory, so when the Senators make an offering to the goddess, they are also making an offering to the Emperor."

He explained this in his usual manner, calm and apparently making no judgement, but we all understood the symbolism behind the incident.

"The problem," he told us, "is that the Emperor is growing up. He's nearly eighteen years old now, and he is trying to exert his own authority."

Again, Rufus passed his gaze over all three of us to make sure we were paying attention.

"He has, as I think most people will tell you, also become unstable. His mother, Soaemias, remains devoted to him, but she is trying to control him, while his grandmother, Maesa, is now running an almost entirely separate household. All three are vying to take absolute control, although their priorities are not the same. The result is that plots abound, as do spies and informers."

"And where do you stand in this?" I asked him.

Rufus grinned, "On my own. As I said, I was dismissed. However, a number of former officials who were dismissed suffered fatal accidents after being removed from office. I thought it best to pre-empt that by arranging an accident of my own."

"You burned your own house down?" I guessed.

He nodded, "It seemed the best way to ensure the body they found could not be properly identified."

"Who was it?" I scowled.

Rufus shrugged, "It doesn't matter."

To a man like Rufus, I suppose it probably didn't, but his callousness left a sour taste in my mouth. For him, the ends always justified the means, but perhaps that was why he had risen to a position of high authority while I'd remained a humble drone.

"Since then," he informed us, "I have been watching and waiting, compiling information and attempting to see who is planning what."

"To what end?" I challenged.

"It's what I do," he replied easily. "It makes a pleasant change to be back on the streets again, I must say. As yet, though, I have not decided what to do with what I have learned."

Uncharacteristically, he pulled a face as he admitted, "I am working on the assumption that whoever ultimately seizes power will need the sort of information I can provide, but to be honest, none of the three parties appeal to me. Macrinus should have executed the lot of them when he had the chance."

I glanced at Caecus who said, "Scipio and I have discussed that at length. We agree such a move would have been highly dangerous. As you said, the soldiers are loyal to the house of Severus. Attempting to execute the last remnants of that family would have caused a mutiny in any event."

Rufus considered that for a moment, then nodded, "Perhaps you are right, but I still think he should have tried. Letting them live did not exactly work out well for him, did it? He allowed Maesa time to dish out bribes, and to concoct that ludicrous story about Elagabalus being the son of Caracalla. That was what persuaded the Legions to rebel against Macrinus."

136

I said, "People will believe what they want to believe."

"True, but things have deteriorated since Elagabalus came to power. It is fortunate for the empire that Macrinus made peace with Parthia and the northern barbarians. It has left Maesa free to govern without the need to fight anyone. The problem is that Macrinus drained the Treasury buying peace, so the coinage has been devalued, which has upset a lot of people."

He took another sip of wine, then let out a long sigh before continuing.

"But it is the Emperor's personal habits which will ruin the empire. I've already told you how he prances about in his new temple to the Sun God, but there is more to it than that. He is wilful, which you would expect from a teenage boy with absolute power, but he behaves more like a woman than a man. The empire cannot have a leader like that."

I said, "I know plenty of women who could do a good job of running the empire. I don't like Maesa, but she's very capable."

Rufus nodded, "Yes, you worked with her in Antioch for a while, didn't you?"

"I worked for her sister, Domna, but I met Maesa many times."

"She's capable, all right," Rufus agreed. "But she won't live forever, and the Emperor is bucking against her control. In any case, the people won't stand for a woman actually becoming Emperor."

Fronto put in, "I've heard some rumours, of course, but I don't know whether to believe most of them. You say the Emperor behaves like a woman, yet it is common knowledge he has already married several women."

Rufus gave a grim laugh as he replied, "Yes, he's married and divorced five women in the past two years. One of them, as you may recall, was a Vestal Virgin. He forcibly removed her from the temple and married her without her consent. That did not sit well with the populace, let alone the Senators."

Setting aside the undoubted sacrilege, I gasped, "Five women in two years?"

Rufus waved a hand as he told me, "Oh, I don't think he actually consummated any of the marriages. If he did, nothing came of it. I think he went through with the ceremonies for show. Now he's a bit older, his true nature is being revealed."

"And what is that?"

"He wants to be a woman," Rufus told me. "It's not just a case of wanting to dress like a woman, he actually wants to become one. Last year, he took up with a chariot driver and insisted this was his new husband."

"His husband?" I gaped.

"That's right," Rufus sighed grimly. "There was a formal wedding ceremony, with the Emperor playing the part of the bride. It's also common knowledge in the palace that he was considering having himself castrated but settled for being circumcised. And he's apparently offered a reward to any doctor who can turn him into a woman."

"Physically, you mean?" I gasped.

"That's right. Nobody's been foolish enough to take up that challenge. So far, at any rate."

There was a stunned silence as my friends and I tried to absorb these revelations. Rumours are one thing, but the Juggler was not known for spreading malicious gossip. If he said these tales were true, I was inclined to believe him, no matter how outlandish they might sound.

After a moment, I said, "People have all sorts of tastes. Does this really bar him from being Emperor?"

"Of course it does!" snapped Rufus. "He's dissolute, wasteful and has no interest in governing except that he wants the power to give his friends and hangers-on appointments to high office. He surrounds himself with eunuchs and sycophants, and he offers himself to any man who takes his fancy, even though he's allegedly married to his charioteer."

I was reeling a little by now, but Rufus wasn't finished.

He went on, "He holds extravagant dinners, then sets wild beasts loose in the palace to terrify his guests. Above all, though, you know the Senate won't put up with a man who wants to be a woman. Sooner or later, something serious will happen."

I found all this very disturbing. Personally, it didn't bother me what anyone got up to in their private lives as long as it didn't harm others, but that, I supposed, was the nub of the problem. The Emperor's behaviour might have been eccentric if he was a private individual, but it could be disastrous if it created mayhem in the running of the empire.

Rufus continued, "I presume you have heard that the Emperor recently tried to have his young cousin murdered?"

"Fronto told me about that," I confirmed.

"The boy is unstable," Rufus insisted. "The Senate will not put up with it forever. Neither will the Praetorians. Everything I've told you is true, and it means there is a lot of trouble ahead."

I exhaled slowly while I tried to gather my thoughts.

"I can't see Julia Maesa sitting back and accepting his behaviour," I remarked.

"No, but her position is precarious," the Juggler replied. "Like her daughter, Julia Soaemias, she derives her power from her relationship with the Emperor. Without him, she is nothing. Yet neither she nor Soaemias seem capable of controlling him."

There was another short silence while each of us waited for someone else to say the unthinkable.

Eventually, it was Caecus who growled softly, "Are you saying she is planning to have him killed?"

"I would not discount it," Rufus said in a matter of fact tone. "The Emperor seems to have recognised that his cousin would provide a ready-made heir. That is why Maesa persuaded him to appoint young Alexander as Caesar. He's already made one attempt to get rid of the lad, and I expect he will try again, although he will need to be more subtle next time."

I ventured, "You mean his position is more secure if Alexander is dead?"

"More secure from Maesa's plotting, at any rate," the Juggler agreed.

With a coarse chuckle, he added, "And, if he is married to a man and playing the part of a wife, then the chances of any natural heir being produced are slim to say the least."

There was another moment of silence while we all contemplated the tortuous imperial situation, then I said to Rufus, "This is all very interesting, but what has it got to do with us? Fronto no longer works in the palace, and my home is in Africa. I'm only here to help my mother by finding out who is carrying on this grudge against my brother."

139

Rufus regarded me with an expression of disappointment as he asked, "Haven't you worked that out yet?"

"Clearly not. Why don't you tell me?"

He leaned forward in his chair to say, "It would be unwise to focus all our attention on the imperial household. Others have a vested interest in who runs the empire."

"You mean some Senators are planning to overthrow the whole family?"

"It's a distinct possibility," the Juggler agreed.

. I frowned, "I still don't see what that has to do with me."

Rufus shook his head as if he were a teacher expressing disappointment in a favourite pupil.

Speaking slowly, he said, "I think your brother, Sempronius Primus, is involved in one such plot. I don't know many details, but I've been watching his house for a couple of weeks now. I saw you arrive the other day, and I must admit I was rather startled to see you so alive and well."

"You've been watching the house?"

"That's right. Not all the time, but enough to keep an eye on who has been coming and going."

"And what makes you think Primus is plotting anything other than his own enrichment?"

"Because I'm fairly certain his patron, Herennius Muncius, is part of a group who are planning some sort of coup. And Muncius has been paying frequent visits to Primus' house."

I had a sudden recollection of Primus' reaction to my mentioning attracting interest from the palace. Was that why he had been scared? Was that what Mardonius was hiding?

"You think they intend to place someone else on the throne?" I asked.

In response, Rufus gave a slow nod.

"Who?"

"That's what I am trying to find out. There are no obvious candidates to be Emperor apart from young Alexander, but I doubt he has much support in the Senate. If they stage a coup, I expect they will want to wipe out the entire Severan family."

The thought of so much death and upheaval left me feeling queasy, and I now knew what the Juggler expected from me.

140

"Let me guess," I sighed. "You want me to find out what's going on?"

Rufus grinned, "It took you a while, but you've got there at last. Well done, Scipio."

Ignoring his sarcasm, I demanded, "Why should I? I'll be going home as soon as I track down Primus' attackers."

"You'll do it for two reasons," Rufus told me. "First, you will want to satisfy your own curiosity now that you know your brother is involved. Secondly, you wouldn't want anyone important finding out you are here in Rome."

"And you would tell them?"

Rufus merely shrugged, so I decided to call his bluff.

"Why don't you go ahead and tell Maesa I'm here? She has no reason to have me harmed. In fact, some people might argue that I helped her gain power, even if it wasn't what I intended."

"I wasn't talking about anyone on the Palatine," Rufus informed me, his voice holding that hard, ruthless edge I remembered so well. "I was thinking more of the Praetorians."

I blinked in surprise, and I noticed Caecus tense his body at the mention of his former comrades.

"What have the Praetorians got to do with it?" I asked, feeling a growing sense of helplessness creep over me.

Rufus was entirely relaxed as he explained, "The Praetorians loved Caracalla. The man may have been a ruthless, egotistic maniac, but he was a strong ruler and a good General. The troops adored him, and his memory casts a long shadow. I wonder how they would react if they discovered the part you and your wife played in his murder?"

I was stunned. How did he know about Circe? I had only ever told Fronto and my mother the full story.

Rufus chuckled, "Don't look so dumbfounded, Scipio. I was a spymaster. You don't think I didn't have other reports from Ephesus? You were seen with a young woman who accompanied you to Alexandria, yet you never mentioned her in any of your reports. I must admit it took me a while to work it all out, but seeing you the other day made me think about your disappearance in more detail. And I see from your reaction that my guess was correct. Your Arab friend is probably the Berber who was known to be involved in the affair at Ephesus and the plot against Caracalla. The Praetorians are still very upset about that. The problem, you see, is they are very unhappy at Elagabalus' behaviour. They want a soldier-Emperor, not a young wastrel who prostitutes himself to any man he fancies. I don't think it would take much to galvanise them into action against someone they believed was responsible for what happened."

"You bastard!" was all I could hiss in response.

Caecus was looking at me with an expression of dismay.

"Is this true?" he asked. "Did you help murder Caracalla?"

"No," I assured him. "You were there. You know I tried to stop it."

"But your wife?" he pressed. "And Collinus?"

"Circe had good reason to want him dead," I replied. "But I only learned of her role later."

"So she was the one behind the plot? Not Julia Maesa?"

Caecus was obviously struggling to grasp the details. I had wanted to keep this knowledge from him, but it was too late now.

"They were in it together," I told him. "Maesa wanted Macrinus out of the way so her grandson could be proclaimed heir, then she wanted Caracalla removed. Circe was happy to go along with that, although things turned out differently because Martialis panicked when he thought you and I were about to reveal he had been hired to do the killing."

The Juggler was grinning, obviously delighted to have his guesswork confirmed, but Caecus was shaking his head in confusion.

"So you did let Macrinus die once you learned the truth?" he asked in a low whisper.

"I couldn't betray Circe to him," I confessed weakly.

Caecus closed his eyes, letting out a long sigh.

I told him, "I'm sorry, Caecus. Perhaps I should have told you, but we felt it was best that we kept the secret to ourselves."

He opened his eyes to look at me. If he'd been angry, I would have understood, but his expression was one of deep regret and disappointment.

"You said she had good reasons. What were they?"

I hesitated, glancing at the Juggler who was watching us intently. Did I dare tell him the full story?

I decided it could not put us in any greater trouble than we were already in.

"Circe's original name was Fulvia Tertia. She was the daughter of Fulvius Plautianus. Her step-sister was Fulvia Plautilla."

Both Caecus and the Juggler regarded me with wide eyes. They recognised the names, although many people might have forgotten them by now.

"A man named Plautianus was Praetorian Prefect under Septimius Severus," Caecus frowned. "Is that the man you are talking about?"

"Yes. Fulvia Plautilla was Caracalla's wife until he killed her father and sent her into exile. Circe, or Fulvia Tertia as she was then, was only a small girl, but she went into exile with her older sister."

Rufus put in, "And the sister was executed as soon as Caracalla came to power."

I nodded, "Which is why Circe hated Caracalla so much. He'd murdered her father and her older sister because they both knew he was having an affair with his step-mother."

The Juggler's lips were curled in a faint smile, but Caecus merely gave a weary nod.

"I understand vengeance," he sighed. "But you should have told me."

"It is a secret we would prefer to keep," I said, feeling shame at my lack of trust in him. "Now that you know, I hope you will not reveal it. But I will understand if you wish to leave our service."

The Juggler let out a coarse chuckle.

"This has been an interesting little chat," he smirked. "Everyone has secrets, it seems. But it is time for me to leave you. You should think about what I said, Scipio. Then, when you decide you are going to find out what your brother is up to, you should begin by asking if you can visit his villa down by the Alban Mount."

I was still distracted by Caecus' reaction to learning Circe's story, but Rufus' words demanded my attention.

"What? The Alban Mount? Why would I want to go there?"

"Perhaps you want to send your family there for safety while you continue your investigation."

"Again, why?"

Rufus grinned, "Because it will be interesting to see what excuse he gives for not letting anyone go there."

Dealing with the Juggler was always like this. My mind was racing as I tried to keep up.

I said, "How do you know he won't want us to go?"

He told me, "Because I've seen him send men riding south on an almost daily basis. I haven't been able to follow them, but I did pay an acquaintance to ride out that way. It seems someone is staying at your brother's villa. I'd like to know who it is."

I stared bleakly. He had me, and he knew it. The last thing I wanted to do was become involved in imperial plots, but it seemed I would have no choice.

Rufus placed his wine cup on the tray, picked up his freedman's cap, stood up slowly, stretched, then waved a hand in farewell.

"I'll be in touch soon," he declared as he headed for the door.

"Wait!" I called after him.

He turned, eyeing me expectantly.

I said, "If you've been watching Primus' house, have you seen anyone writing on his walls?" Rufus shook his head.

"No, but I'll keep an eye out for that sort of thing. After all, we are a team, aren't we?"

Then he was gone, and I was left facing more problems than I had begun with.

Chapter 14
A Question of Trust

The Juggler had left me in a state of shocked dismay, but my first concern was what Caecus intended to do.

"I am sorry," I told him again. "I should have trusted you more, but the way you attacked me when we first met in the forum in Leptis Magna meant I wasn't sure you would take kindly to learning the full truth."

It was hard to tell what he was thinking. His face was set in a stern expression, but that was quite normal for Caecus.

I went on, "If it's any consolation, we kept it a very close secret. Until a few moments ago, only five people in the entire world knew the whole truth. I think the reason for that should be clear. Now that the Juggler knows, you see what he's doing with the knowledge."

Caecus barely blinked as he regarded me stonily.

"Julia Maesa must know," he stated flatly.

"No. She wanted Macrinus dead, and she knew someone wanted Caracalla dead. She never met Circe, nor learned her true identity. Collinus did all the negotiating. He also introduced Maesa to Martialis, who had held a long grudge against Caracalla. In fact, Martialis had been recruited by the Alexandrians to murder the Emperor until you and I foiled that plot. But Circe knew his identity, so she passed the information to Maesa who gave Martialis money and empty promises of promotion."

Caecus gave a slow nod as he asked, "So your wife was involved in the Alexandrian plot as well?"

"I'm afraid so."

"So you were on opposite sides, yet you still married her?"

"Love is a funny thing," I shrugged. "Besides, once she explained what Caracalla had done to her father and sister, I understood why she wanted revenge. She was in constant danger of discovery, and you know what that would have meant."

"I can understand vengeance," Caecus agreed reluctantly.

Then, eyeing me coldly, he asked, "Do I know the full story now?"

"Most of it. The bit you don't know is that Collinus was the one who played the part of the prophet. He began the rumour that Macrinus would depose Caracalla. He also played the part of a guide for the Praetorians. He was the one who persuaded Martialis that we had uncovered the plot. That's what made Martialis murder Caracalla."

Caecus scowled, "I never did trust that Arab."

"If it's any consolation, he didn't trust you either. He was ready to kill you if you ever learned the truth."

"And now that I do know?"

I shrugged, "I suppose that depends on what you intend to do next."

If I had been in his place, I'd have wanted time to think the situation over, but Aelius Caecus had been a soldier all his adult life, and an officer for most of his career. He was accustomed to assessing situations and making quick decisions.

He let out a long, slow breath, then said, "I can't deny that I feel disappointed that you deceived me, but to be perfectly honest, I would probably have done the same as you if I'd been in your position. If you'd told me the tale six months ago, I probably would have turned against you. But I've had time to think about things since then. Whatever you did or didn't do, Macrinus made his own decisions. Several of us advised him to get rid of Maesa at the outset, but he ignored us. And he was the one who cut the soldiers' pay. That, and begging Parthia for a peace treaty, damned him in the eyes of the army. Now that I've had time to reflect, I realise he wouldn't have survived no matter what you did."

"What about Caracalla?" I asked. "You served him as well."

"And his father before him. They were good generals, and I was a soldier. I don't suppose that part of me will ever forgive Aurelia for what she did, but I can understand why she did it. For her, it was a war, and she won it."

"So what are you going to do?" I asked, trying to quell a rising hope.

He countered, "What do you want me to do?"

"I would hope you will stay with me as a friend."

His face was as unreadable as a marble statue as he said, "If I were a cynical man, I might think you had offered me a place

146

in your home in order to prevent me spreading word of your whereabouts."

I sighed, "I can't deny that was part of it. But a greater part was guilt. I felt bad about disappearing, even though I know I could not have altered Macrinus' fate. I honestly wanted to help you. For that matter, so did Circe."

Caecus gave a slow nod.

"I only ever knew a soldier's life," he said. "I've always followed orders, and you know better than most what those orders could sometimes lead to. It never bothered me at the time, but these past months have shown me a different perspective. I should have died in that last fight alongside Macrinus, but I think the gods have given me a chance at a second life. You and Aurelia have helped give me that chance. So I'll stay, and I'll keep your secret even though I wish things had been different."

Hearing that, I let out a sigh of relief. Until that moment, I don't think I'd fully appreciated how much I had come to rely on Caecus as a friend.

"Thank you," I told him earnestly.

I stepped towards him, my hand outstretched, and we clasped forearms to seal our pact.

His eyes locked onto mine as he growled, "And you can tell Collinus from me that he's welcome to try killing me, but if he makes the attempt, I'll break his neck."

"I think I'll let Circe tell him that," I grinned.

Fronto, who had watched our exchange in fascination, poured himself another cup of wine, draining it in one gulp.

Then he looked at Caecus and said, "There are two things you ought to know about being Scipio's friend. The first is that you can trust him when he gives his word."

He grinned at me as he added, "And the second is that your life will never be boring. Dangerous, yes, but never boring."

"That suits me," Caecus nodded gravely.

I smiled at him, trying to let him know how much I appreciated his decision. What worried me was whether he was secretly harbouring resentment for the things we had done and the secrets we had kept from him. I supposed only time would tell. For the moment, I had no option but to take him at his word.

147

We all drank another cup of wine, then Caecus, as professional as ever, declared, "Now, you said earlier we have a lot to do. What your fat boss told us about your brother doesn't change that, does it?"

"No. I still want to find out who is waging this vendetta against him. Finding out what else he's up to is a separate issue, although investigating the first might help provide answers to the second."

So we said farewell to Fronto and trudged further up the wide hill, heading for the Colline Gate and the *Via Salaria*.

The Colline is the most northerly of Rome's ancient gates. It gives access to northern Italia, but the *Via Salaria*, which begins here, turns eastwards and crosses the peninsula until it reaches the Adriatic Sea. It's one of the major trade routes, bringing supplies of salt to the city, which is how it received its name. It was also, according to my mother, where I would find Primus' former property factor, Aconius Dardanus. Perhaps dealing with him would help take my mind off the burden Sempronius Rufus had placed on me.

Stalking along beside me, Caecus was also deep in thought. After a while, he announced, "I thought I might take a look at the Praetorian Camp. It's not far away from here."

"What for?" I asked, feeling a sense of alarm.

A grin briefly flashed across his face as he said, "There is no need to panic. I don't intend to denounce you. Remember, I sided with Macrinus when much of the Guard went over to Julia Maesa. I'm at as much risk as you are."

Then why go?" I frowned. "What if someone recognises you? That beard won't fool anyone who knew you well."

He replied, "No, but there's a chance I might still find a friend. If I do, I'll buy them a drink and have a chat. Then I can maybe judge what the mood in the camp really is. Your friend didn't strike me as the most honest of men. He might be lying to you about how the Praetorians feel."

"Rufus rarely tells outright lies," I told him. "But he rarely speaks the whole truth either. He only ever tells you what he wants you to know, and that's to encourage you to do what he wants. He's one of the most devious men I've ever known."

"So do you want me to pay a visit to the Camp?" Caecus asked. "You could come with me if you like."

I knew why he was making that offer. He was telling me that he understood I might be afraid to let him go on his own in case he decided to denounce us. So, while I really wanted to tell him not to go, I knew I owed him some trust.

I said, "I need to speak to the property factor. You go to the Camp and see what you can find out. But be careful."

"I will be," he promised.

We left it at that. Caecus went off to try his luck at the Praetorian Camp which is situated just outside the old Servian walls to the north-east of the city. I must admit I felt extremely nervous as I watched him go, his head held high and his gait marking him as a military man.

Could I trust him? Would he betray us in order to regain a favoured position in the Praetorian Guard? Or had he genuinely become a reformed character?

I honestly could not tell, and I felt a chill of fear at what he might do to us. I wanted to run back to Primus' house and tell Circe we needed to leave, but my rational brain told me that would be a pointless exercise. If Caecus set the Guard on us, there was very little chance we would be able to leave the city undetected.

No, I told myself, I must place my trust in Caecus' promise. It wasn't an easy decision to reach, and I knew I might soon regret it, but if we ran away while he was genuinely trying to help, he'd never trust us again.

Chapter 15
The Property Factor

It wasn't easy, but I did my best to dismiss thoughts of Caecus' potential treachery, and set about my task of locating the property factor.

I asked around until, after a few unsuccessful enquiries, I was eventually directed to the office of Aconius Dardanus. This was on the third floor of a tenement where he occupied a few rooms, one of which he used as an office.

The first room was an ante-chamber where a middle-aged slave greeted me with a welcoming smile. I gave him my name and told him I'd like to talk to his master because I had only recently arrived in Rome and wanted to discuss property matters. He asked me to take a seat on a wooden bench which sat against one wall, and he went off through a door to an adjoining room, returning a moment later to inform me that Aconius Dardanus would see me shortly.

The slave had a desk which bore papyrus and vellum scrolls, and he had an ink pot with several quills close at hand. Behind his desk was a large rack of pigeon holes, each containing a neatly labelled scroll. As if this wasn't enough evidence of his role, I noticed that his fingers were stained dark with ink, showing he did a lot of the paperwork for Dardanus.

I did not need to wait long before I was ushered through to the main office where Dardanus met me. I must say my initial impressions of him were not very favourable. He was a small man with oily features and an even greasier manner. He welcomed me with a smile as artificial as that of a crocodile, and a handshake which was both moist and flabby.

"Valerius Cantiacus, is it?"

"That's right."

"And you have recently arrived in the city? You're looking for somewhere to stay? I have lots of excellent properties I can show you."

"Actually," I told him as we took seats at his desk, "I already have a place to stay."

"You do? But it is perhaps not best suited to your needs? I am sure I can find you something more suitable."

I held his gaze as I informed him, "I am staying at the home of Sempronius Primus. I believe you know him?"

His smile vanished, replaced by a cold, distrusting expression, and he began to fidget in his chair, a clear sign of anxiety.

"I'm sorry," he said icily, "I don't think I can help you after all."

"Really? May I ask why?"

His arms formed a barrier as he folded them across his chest and informed me, "I no longer have any dealings with Sempronius Primus, and I'd prefer to keep it that way. I'm sorry, but that is all I am prepared to say. Good day to you."

I didn't move.

Ignoring his uncooperative mood, I said, "What I'm here about is your disagreement with Primus. I'd like to know what it was about."

"It's got nothing to do with you," he said, the words faint but still audible.

"I'm afraid it does. You see, someone assaulted Sempronius Primus a couple of months ago, and attacks on his house continue. I've been asked to find out who is behind those attacks. So I need to know what caused your falling out with him."

His jaw dropped, revealing a set of crooked teeth.

"You think I did that? You're mad!"

"You know about the assault?"

"Everyone on the Quirinal knows about it," he assured me. "But I certainly had nothing to do with it. The man's a pompous ass, a bully and a gangster. I want nothing to do with him at all, and as Jupiter is my witness, I wouldn't attract his attention by having him mugged."

"It wasn't so much a mugging as attempted murder," I told him.

"Whatever it was, I had nothing to do with it."

"Can you prove that?"

"How?"

"I don't know. Do you have witnesses for the night it happened?"

151

"Possibly, but I don't keep a note of what I was doing on any particular night. My slave keeps my appointments in a diary, but they are for during the day."

"So convince me why I should believe you," I said, hoping there was sufficient menace in my voice to get something out of him.

"I can't," he shrugged helplessly.

"In that case, tell me what your argument was about."

He hesitated, but I think he understood that the best way to get rid of me was to tell me what I wanted to know.

With a long-suffering sigh, he explained, "Money. It's always about money with Sempronius Primus. I used to collect the rents from his various properties, and he claimed I was overcharging the tenants and skimming off the profit."

"Were you?"

Dardanus shifted uneasily, his eyes flicking away from my stare.

"Everyone does it," he mumbled.

"But Primus wanted all the uplift for himself?" I guessed.

Dardanus nodded, "He sends out his own bullies to collect the rents now, but I'll bet they're skimming a slice for themselves as well."

Visualising Primus' gang of thugs, I had to agree with this assessment.

I asked, "How many properties does Primus own?"

Dardanus hesitated, using his fingers to count while he mentally ran through the various places.

"Eleven tenements on the Quirinal," he eventually decided. "Plus a couple down near the Field of Mars."

I could not prevent myself from showing some amazement at that. Primus, it seemed, was building a veritable property empire.

I said, "He's got one on the Viminal as well."

"I know. I warned him that was a bad idea. There are people who regard that part of the city as their own private territory."

"So he bought that before you fell out with him?"

"It was around the same time," Dardanus recalled.

"And the attack on him took place shortly afterwards?"

"I suppose so."

"Tell me," I smiled. "Did you go on your own to collect the rents?"

He knew what I was driving at, but he realised it would be difficult to persuade me a small chap like him could bully the rougher members of society into surrendering their hard-earned cash.

"I have a couple of guys who help me out on collection days," he confessed.

"Handy with their fists, are they?"

"Look!" he exclaimed, "I know you are trying to pin this on me, but I will swear by any god you care to name that it wasn't me!"

He was growing quite agitated now. He was a man who made a living out of being insincere, so it was difficult to know whether I could believe him.

His voice was rising as he said, "Look! I earn a decent living at this. I may not live in luxury, but very few people do. I get by, and I wouldn't jeopardise that by getting into a fight with Sempronius Primus. I know what happens to people who try that."

"Oh? What does happen to them?"

"They end up with broken bones. Or worse. Believe me, I've seen it."

"So you're not worried he might send his thugs after you?"

"Why should he? He can't believe I was behind it."

He was probably right about that. Primus was convinced it was Vindex who was after him, but Dardanus was such a slimy character he could well have hired some thugs to do his dirty work for him.

I asked him, "Well, if it wasn't you, do you know who it might have been?"

"It could have been anyone," he shrugged, his tone sour. "I mean, half of Rome hates him."

"What about his builder? The man who built his new house?"

"Him and a thousand others," Dardanus rasped.

"So you don't know anyone specifically?"

Dardanus slapped a hand down on his desk as he whined, "Look! Sempronius Primus is a nasty piece of work. There! I've

153

said it. I hate his guts, but I'm perfectly happy to have nothing to do with him ever again. If anyone else is daft enough to take him on, that's their lookout. But don't try to set me up as the person responsible."

I doubted I would get much more from him without resorting to violence, but I wasn't prepared to go that far. Primus and Vindex might use such tactics, but I didn't want to bring myself down to their level.

"All right," I said. "Thanks for your help. If you do think of anything that might help me, you can send a message to Primus' house."

"You can forget that," he said defiantly. "I told you, I'll have nothing to do with him."

Then he gave me a very keen look, his eyes narrowing to slits.

"Why are you helping him anyway? What is it to you?"

"I'm a friend of his mother," I replied. "She asked me to track down whoever was behind the attack."

He stared at me for a moment, then said, "Then take my advice and forget all about it. Go back to wherever you came from and stay away from Sempronius Primus. He's dangerous."

"Yes," I agreed, "I'm starting to see that."

Chapter 16
Sinking Deeper

All the way back to Primus' house, I fretted about what I might find. Normally, I'd use such walks to mull over what I'd learned from the person I had just spoken to, but this time, all I could think of was what might have happened if Caecus had betrayed my trust.

Would there be a squad of Praetorians waiting for me? Had the place already been raided? What had happened to Circe and the children?

I confess my heart was pounding by the time I turned into the street, and I let out a long, slow breath of relief, slowing my pace when I saw that everything looked perfectly normal.

I knocked on the door, and was admitted by a surly guard. Lucius was there, too.

"How are things?" I asked him, doing my best to keep my voice as normal as possible.

Lucius has no guile in him, so his answer reassured me.

"It's been quiet," he informed me.

"Is everyone out?"

"Yes, Master."

Which meant, I realised, that Caecus could yet be on his way here with an army at his back. This thought set my pulse racing again.

A few moments later, Circe and my mother turned up, Collinus and a couple of slaves tagging along behind them. I did not want to alarm them, especially when young Sextus could overhear, so I kept my agitation under control when they greeted me with smiles.

My mother beamed, "We took the children to see the chariots training for the races."

Bouncing excitedly, my son blurted, "They were very fast. Mama says we can go to the races soon."

I looked at Circe who returned a sweet smile.

"The day after tomorrow has been declared a Holy Day," she told me. "There will be races at the Circus Maximus."

I frowned, "We have chariot racing in Leptis Magna."

"Yes, but you've never taken Sextus to see any of them. Besides, this is the Circus Maximus. We might not get a chance to see races here again."

I refrained from telling her we might not get to see them at all if my faith in Caecus had been misplaced. I simply smiled and ruffled Sextus' hair, telling him we would definitely go to see the races.

Circe smiled in triumph, declaring that she was hungry after a long day, so we went through to the dining room. While we waited for the kitchen staff to bring our meal, I explained what Caecus and I had learned that day. As I recounted our meeting with the Juggler and his ultimatum, Circe's tanned face grew visibly pale, while my mother sat very still, her eyes studying me intently.

"Where is Caecus now?" Circe asked anxiously.

"He's trying to find out what the Praetorians really think."

"You let him go to the Camp?" she blinked.

"Yes."

"Why?"

"Because he gave me his word that he would keep our secret."

Collinus' hand strayed towards his dagger, but I told him, "Forget that. If I have misjudged, Caecus will return with more armed soldiers than even you can handle."

The flint-eyed Berber scowled at me, and I could see Circe's chest rising and falling rapidly as she hurriedly tried to assess the risk we were facing.

When she spoke, her voice was husky with concern.

"I hope you have done the right thing, Scipio, but if Caecus betrays us, I suppose there is very little we can do about it."

I gave her the most reassuring smile I could manage.

"You could always leave now," I told her. "Take the kids and stay out of the house until we know what's going to happen."

Collinus agreed, "That would be sensible."

Circe gave an absent nod, but her mind was still working at its habitual high speed.

"What about the Juggler?" she asked. "Do you think he was bluffing?"

"I wouldn't count on it," I told her.

156

"And he, or one of his minions, could be watching the house?"

"Very possibly. He saw us arrive, at any rate."

Collinus was rising to his feet, clearly anxious to whisk Circe away to somewhere safer, but that was when we heard footsteps coming down the corridor. The door swung open to reveal Aelius Caecus.

We all froze. The only thought in my mind was that he was alone, and that sent a wave of relief through my entire body.

Caecus looked at each of us in turn, his expression inscrutable, but he must have known we had been talking about him.

Circe, taking control of the situation, rose elegantly to her feet and stepped towards him.

"Come and sit down, Aelius Caecus. I am told I owe you an apology, and my thanks."

Caecus' stony expression softened slightly, and he allowed himself to be seated where he could see all three of us. I noticed the hard look he shot at Collinus, but Circe's openness seemed to have relaxed him.

Looking earnestly at her, he said, "I understand why you did what you did, Lady. I am not saying I condone your actions, for it placed us on opposite sides, but I do understand your motives."

"Thank you, Caecus. I am glad you know the truth. It always tugged at my conscience that we had kept it from you."

He gave a slight nod.

"The past cannot be changed," he said. "Whether we can alter the future remains to be seen."

I didn't like the sound of that last bit, but Circe ignored it.

"Did you discover anything at the Praetorian Camp?" she asked him.

Caecus gave a shake of his head.

"Not really. I couldn't march into the camp, so I hung around outside in the hope of seeing a face I recognised. Eventually, I saw an old comrade I knew I could trust, and we managed to have a brief chat. Once he'd got over the surprise of learning I am still alive, he told me the mood in the Camp is not good. It is as Fronto and Sempronius Rufus said, the Praetorians distrust the Emperor. Only their loyalty to the memory of Severus and Caracalla prevents the soldiers doing away with him."

I asked, "So it is as bad as the Juggler told us?"

"If anything, it is worse," Caecus informed me. "My friend told me there is much division within the Guard. They have the Emperor, his grandmother, and his mother all making demands on their loyalty. The only thing most of them agree on is that young Alexander would make a better Emperor."

"A more amenable one, they mean," Circe observed drily. "He is only a boy."

I asked, "Are they close to revolt, then?"

"It would not take much for their anger to boil over," Caecus replied. "But, as I said, their loyalty to the Severan house remains strong. They swore oaths to the Emperor, and they seem inclined to keep them."

After a short pause, he added, "Until Alexander is a bit older, at any rate."

"What about the threat Rufus made?" I asked. "How would they react if they discovered our involvement in Caracalla's death?"

Caecus shrugged, "I could not ask that question directly. I honestly don't know. But I fear Rufus may be correct. It would not take very much to rouse the anger of the Praetorians at the moment. If that anger was given a target, they may well decide to take matters into their own hands."

I shot a worried look at Circe, but she seemed remarkably calm.

"Can you trust your friend to keep silent?" she asked.

"I did not tell him anything about you," he replied. "I merely told him I had found employment as a bodyguard to a wealthy man from Africa. As for telling anyone I am still alive, I trust him to keep that to himself. Not that it matters overly much. Soldiers understand that former enemies can become friends. It is in the nature of war."

He let that thought hang for a moment, and we all understood it also referred to our own past differences. The atmosphere, still tense, nevertheless eased considerably.

Smiling, I gave him a grateful nod.

"So where does this leave us?" I wondered aloud.

158

With a phlegmatic shrug, Circe said, "It leaves us in the Juggler's power."

I suggested, "We could always return to Africa."

"That would give the Juggler the excuse he needs," she told me. "He would set the hounds on us. No, we have no option except to do as he asks."

"That is not a pleasant prospect," I muttered.

"No," she agreed. "But it does not mean we simply sit around and fret. We may as well try to resolve the mystery your mother asked us to investigate. "

I could hardly believe how calm she was. My own nerves were jangling around like the bells on an Alexandrian dancer's belt. I swallowed an entire goblet of wine in an effort to fortify myself.

Caecus interjected, "I think satisfying the Juggler's demands are more important."

Circe nodded, but gently pointed out, "That may be true, but if we suddenly stop investigating the attacks on Primus, he will become suspicious. That will make it even more difficult to find out what he is up to. For the sake of appearances, we must carry on as if the Juggler had not demanded our cooperation."

We all saw the sense in this, but Caecus was still focused on Primus.

He asked me, "Very well, but how are you going to discover whether your brother is involved in a plot?"

I looked at my mother, and the sight of her calm determination provided almost as much sustenance as the wine. The news that her eldest son was a gangster and possibly planning to assassinate the Emperor must have struck her hard, but she was putting on a display of Roman stoicism. Fronto had told me she was learning to accept the truth about Primus, so perhaps she had half expected this news. What she had not been expecting was the possibility of us being blackmailed into becoming involved in political intrigue. All the same, she looked remarkably determined, her dark eyes radiating resolve.

I said to her, "Could you go and ask Primus whether you can take Circe and the children down to his villa on the Alban Mount?"

Frowning, she asked, "What excuse can I give?"

159

Circe suggested, "You could say it would be a chance to let the children see something more of Italia while Scipio carries on with his investigation."

I added, "Or you could tell him you are still worried about your safety here. Going away for a few days would make you feel safer."

Collinus murmured, "That's plausible."

He clearly was not happy, but nobody reacted to his muttering.

My mother considered our suggestions, then rose to her feet, a look of steely determination on her face.

"I may as well get it over with," she declared.

She headed off to the door which connected the two sections of the house. While she was away, I brought the others up to date with my meeting with Dardanus, the property factor.

"Do you believe him?" Circe asked.

"I wouldn't trust him if he told me the sky was blue," I replied. "He's a sneaky sort of guy, and I wouldn't put it past him to organise some sort of revenge attack. But if he did, he's a bloody good actor. I'll reserve final judgement but, on balance, I'd have to say I'm inclined to think he's innocent as far as Primus is concerned."

Circe treated me to a smug smile as she announced, "Then I have better news."

"Really? I think I could do with some good news."

She explained, "I watched the house across the street where Helvius Oceanus lives."

"The neighbour whose wife had an affair with Primus?" I asked.

"That's the one, although whether he did actually have an affair is not proven. The lady says not."

"She would," I pointed out.

With an impatient frown, Circe retorted, "Are you going to let me tell you what I discovered?"

"Sorry. Carry on."

"As I said," she resumed, "I watched the house until I saw Helvius Oceanus leave. Then I went across and asked to see his wife."

I smiled at that. I could always rely on Circe not to do the obvious. By avoiding any confrontation with Oceanus, she had focused on a more vulnerable target, and her smile suggested it had proved a successful gambit.

She went on, "The poor girl is still in her teens. Oceanus is in his sixties, and he looks it. It turns out he was a ship's captain, mostly on merchant ships travelling to and from Hispania. That's where he met Lavinia. He was growing tired of life at sea and, at his age, I can't say I'm surprised. So he was looking to settle down, and he wanted a wife to look after him. He saw Lavinia on his last trip to Hispania, and he paid her parents to agree to the marriage."

I could tell from Circe's tone she did not approve of this arrangement, but she refrained from making any direct comment as she continued, "The poor girl had never been anywhere outside her home village, so coming to Rome was a bit of a shock for her."

"And Primus turned her head?"

Circe shrugged, "A little, perhaps. She's a pretty little thing, and I'm sure Primus would have noticed her. She says he visited her once or twice, and I think he must have showed off how rich he is, which no doubt impressed her. But she insisted nothing happened between them."

"And you believe her?"

"I think it is more important that her husband believes her. You see, she's pregnant."

That revelation created a moment's silence until I ventured, "Does Oceanus believe he is the father?"

"She says he does, but I think it might be worth asking him directly."

"So he holds a grudge against Primus?"

"Oh, yes," Circe smiled. "According to young Lavinia, her husband was not at all upset when he heard Primus had been beaten up. She said he declared it was about time somebody had taught the fat slob a lesson."

"That doesn't mean he arranged it, though, does it?"

"No, and Lavinia says he didn't arrange the first bit of graffiti either."

From the way she said that, I knew she was expecting me to draw a conclusion.

I guessed, "Not the first, but the rest of them?"

Circe nodded approvingly.

"According to Lavinia, Oceanus saw the first threat scrawled on the walls and laughed about it. Then, once he had taken some time to think about it, he decided to carry on the work. He has a slave who can read and write. This young man waits until the dead of night, watches to make sure the street is deserted, then nips across the road, paints some threat or insult, and runs back as quickly as he can."

"She's sure about this?" I asked.

"She says her husband refuses to give her any details, but she's heard him speaking to the slave, and she's heard the door being unbolted in the middle of the night. Then she hears the slave coming back, and then Oceanus returns to bed in a good humour."

"That sounds suspicious, to say the least," I observed.

Circe grinned, "She also says she's found a pot of black paint."

For the first time since we'd arrived in Rome, I felt a surge of satisfaction. We'd found our culprit at last.

"You are a marvel!" I told Circe.

"I know," she smirked, unable to conceal her delight at having solved one part of the puzzle so easily.

"The question," I mused, "is how we handle it now."

"Confront him," suggested Caecus.

I rubbed my chin while I considered our options.

"It would be better to have some absolute proof before challenging him," I decided.

"What sort of proof?" Caecus asked.

I told him, "What I'd like to do is catch that slave in the act."

"That should be easy enough," he declared. "Now I know where the culprit lives, I can watch out for him and catch him as soon as he dips his brush in the pot."

"We could keep an eye out tonight," I agreed.

"Let me do it," Caecus insisted. "I am well accustomed to checking on young *tiro* recruits and catching them at things they shouldn't be up to."

162

I conceded the point. As a Centurion, discipline would have been high on Caecus' list of responsibilities. I'd wager his recruits believed he had eyes in the back of his head.

"If you are sure," I nodded.

He said, "I'll find a dark doorway from where I can watch Oceanus' house. As soon as I see him make a move, I'll cut off his retreat."

"And then what?" Circe asked. "The slave is only following his master's orders."

"I'm sure Primus won't see it that way," I muttered.

Caecus, his tone reminiscent of the soldier he had once been, stated, "So we confront Oceanus, and we make it plain we won't stand for any more of it. I think I can convince him to stop."

"All right," I agreed. "I'll leave it up to you. But I'll stay awake tonight so I can join you once you've caught the slave."

"If you like," he shrugged.

I smiled to myself. In the greater scheme of things, the graffiti wasn't a huge problem, but solving who was behind it at least meant we were making a little progress. A very little, but that was better than none at all.

At that moment, my mother returned, her eyes blazing and her mouth set in a grim, flat line.

"Your friend, Sempronius Rufus, was right," she announced. "Primus says he is having some renovation work done at the villa, and it is apparently uninhabitable just now. He says we cannot go."

"It's a reasonable excuse," Circe pointed out.

"It's the first I've heard of it," my mother retorted sharply.

I reached out to place a hand on hers, giving her a squeeze of comfort.

I said, "Thank you. I'm sorry you had to find out this way."

She gave a slight shrug, again confirming she had probably always been suspicious of Primus' behaviour.

Caecus wondered, "But what is really going on down there? What is he hiding at the villa?"

"That's what we need to find out," I sighed. "Although I'm not sure how best to handle it."

Circe said, "You need to stay in Rome, but Collinus could go."

We all looked to the tall Berber, but his attention was on Circe.

He said, "I need to remain here to protect you, my Princess."

"I will be perfectly safe," she assured him. "We have plenty of slaves here, and I do not intend to go out on my own."

Collinus sat very stiffly, but Circe knew he would obey her.

She added, "You are the best person for this task."

That, I knew, was true. Collinus was the ideal man for this sort of mission. He could adopt a number of disguises, and he could move very stealthily when necessary. He also possessed one of the coolest minds I'd ever encountered.

He gave a slow, reluctant nod.

"As you command," he said.

"You will need to buy or rent a horse," I told him. "You should allow the best part of a day's travel to reach the Alban Mount."

He nodded gravely, "A day to get there, a day to look around, and a day to return. Three days. I shall leave first thing in the morning."

"Be very careful," Circe cautioned.

He replied, "You know I am always careful, my Princess."

I sat back, closing my eyes as I sought to control the whirl of thoughts racing around in my mind. There was so much happening, and we seemed to be sinking deeper into the mire. At least we had some plan of action. Collinus would check out Primus' villa, which would keep the Juggler off my back for a while, and Caecus would hopefully trap the graffiti artist.

For my part, I had a number of options to choose from.

"I'm going down to the forum tomorrow," I decided. "I think I'll hang around the Senate House. With luck, I'll spot Primus' former guard, Vespillo."

Chapter 17
Dangerous Encounters

Caecus' night vigil was a waste of time. I had a bed made up for me in the small room just off the lobby where my mother's old slave, Lucius, slept. I lay awake most of the night, dozing occasionally while I waited to hear Caecus knock on the door and present Oceanus' slave, complete with paint pot and brush.

Nothing happened. I was roused from my fitful slumber by Collinus preparing to leave at the first sign of dawn, with Caecus trudging wearily into the house as soon as the door was opened. His curt headshake told me all I needed to know.

I said farewell to Collinus, while Caecus gave the tall Berber a distinctly unfriendly nod. Neither man spoke to the other, so I guessed it was going to take some time for them to overcome their mutual antipathy. If they ever did.

Collinus was unconcerned by Caecus' frosty manner. He had dressed in a tunic and long trousers, and he wore a floppy, wide-brimmed hat on his head. I'd never seen him dressed this way before, and I assumed it was part of whatever persona he was going to adopt. He strode off into the early morning light with purposeful intent. I watched him go, then turned my attention to Caecus.

"No luck then?"

"There was no sign of anyone," he reported with obvious disappointment.

"He doesn't do it every night," I reminded him.

"Then I'll wait again tonight," Caecus stated.

He gave me a sharp look and asked, "Do you think your friend Fronto would really have locked his slave, Rusticus, up all night?"

"Very possibly. If only to prove a point."

"But it hasn't proved anything yet. Until we catch the real culprit, Rusticus must still be a suspect."

"You'll catch him soon enough," I said reassuringly.

I hoped I was right about that. I must admit I was disappointed by Caecus' lack of success. I had genuinely thought we would have solved this part of the investigation, but we were still out of luck.

I told Caecus, "Go and get a couple of hours' sleep. Then we will go down to the Senate House."

He nodded and ambled off, leaving me jealous that he didn't look nearly as tired as I felt. I decided to follow my own advice, so I went up the stairs to our bedroom where I slipped into the bed beside a still slumbering Circe, only to be woken a few minutes later when I heard our children getting up. As usual, their first destination was our room. The two slave girls knew Circe didn't mind being woken this way, but I groaned, rolled over and mumbled a few curses when the door burst open.

Circe then lifted Valeria up and placed her down beside me, telling me my daughter wanted a cuddle.

This soon turned into a game which involved both of the kids bouncing on top of me while Circe laughed in delight.

She eventually relented, announcing that they would be going to a bath house as soon as they had eaten breakfast.

"I think we'll try the Baths of Trajan," she told me. "So we might visit the forum ourselves later."

Which was, I guessed, a coded message that she would be checking up on me and, if past performance was anything to go by, discovering a lot more than I could.

I did manage to snatch a short sleep, but the truth was I had too much on my mind to rest for very long. By the fourth hour of the morning, I was ready to set off and so, too, was Caecus. The man seemed able to operate on very little sleep at all, because he looked as fresh and ready as he always did.

We donned our cloaks and headed out, following the *Vicus Longua* which winds down from the Quirinal and leads to the Flavian amphitheatre. From there, it's only a short walk to the forum.

Yet even a short walk can take time in Rome. The streets were as busy as ever, so it was just as well we were in no rush. As we made our way down towards the centre of the city, we found time to grab a late breakfast at one of the many tavernas which provide meals for Rome's thousands of citizens who have no cooking facilities within their own tiny, cramped apartments.

166

The weather was cool, with a damp breeze coming in from the west, but I did not mind. I spent most of my life in the baking, relentless heat of Africa, so it made a pleasant change to be able to walk without breaking into a sweat.

The forum is the ancient heart of Rome. In fact, the city has more than one forum, some being set aside for specific purposes such as cattle or vegetable markets, but the main forum is where Rome's history was made. It is flanked by magnificent temples, libraries and other civic buildings, and statues of heroes and former Emperors abound. Old Augustus, the first real Emperor of Rome, claimed that he had found Rome a city built of brick and had turned it into a city of marble. He was always one to claim great deeds for himself, but his boast probably wasn't far off the mark as far as the forum is concerned.

The place was busy, street vendors doing steady business, rich men striding along with a score of clients scrambling after them, and ordinary citizens wandering around or standing to listen to an orator who wanted to make a speech about some important issue.

"It never changes," Caecus remarked. "It's probably been like this ever since Rome began."

I nodded. The buildings might change, the statues might be replaced, but the people had always congregated here ever since the city was first founded hundreds of years ago.

And here, at the beating heart of the empire, was the *Curia*, where the Senate met.

Ever since Augustus' time, the Emperor has led the Senate. Technically, he is known as the *Princeps*, or First Citizen, the first among equals. It's a nice pretence because the Senate can talk all it wants, but in reality it has little option except to go along with whatever the Emperor says. That's because the Emperor commands the army. Some Emperors have gone a step further and eliminated dissension by doing away with any Senator who disagreed with them. I wasn't sure what Elagabalus' policy was on that front, but I suspected Julia Maesa, who now also sat in the Senate in defiance of the tradition which banned women from attending, was not the sort of person who would put up with any opposition.

There was usually a crowd hanging around outside the Senate House. Some were mere spectators hoping to glimpse someone famous, perhaps even the Emperor himself. Others would be the attendants and guards who were forced to wait outside while their masters, the Senators, debated the events of the day.

Those were the ones I was looking for.

"Vespillo has a broken nose and has lost a finger," I reminded Caecus. "Let's take a slow stroll and see if we can spot anyone matching that description."

Given the size of the milling crowd of people in the forum, that may have seemed an impossible task, but we were able to narrow it down because the waiting guards were rather obvious. They stood or sat in small groups, chatting idly to one another while casting glares at anyone who dared to approach them too closely. Plenty of them were big, broad-shouldered and muscular, and quite a few of them had noses which had obviously been on the receiving end of a fist, but all of them seemed to have the full complement of fingers.

We wandered up and down a few times, pretending to be fascinated by the marble-fronted Senate House with its tall columns and bronze doors. Those doors stood ajar because Roman tradition demanded that government should be open to public view. The reality, I knew, was that the Praetorians who stood in the wide entranceway were there to ensure that nobody was able to get inside unless they had been invited. It was a typical Roman compromise which both recognised and flouted tradition at the same time.

My only interest in the Senate House was that this was where Primus' former bodyguard should be, but I was growing frustrated by the end of our third circuit of the building and the neighbouring area.

"Maybe the Senator he works for is out of the city," I grumbled.

"Maybe not," Caecus responded, touching a hand to my arm.

"There," he said softly, jerking his chin to indicate a man who was swaggering towards the *Curia* having obviously been away on some errand.

168

He was big, tough-looking, with steel-grey hair, and a nose which had been flattened at some time in the past. When I looked at his left hand, I saw the little finger was missing.

I moved to intercept him, side-stepping a number of people who blundered into my path. Caecus stayed close to me, walking a little way behind me.

I stepped in front of the nine-fingered man, smiling as I said, "Excuse me, I'm looking for a man named Vespillo. Would that be you?"

He came to an abrupt halt, clearly irritated that I had blocked his path.

"What if I am?" he growled suspiciously.

I saw his eyes flick towards Caecus, and he tensed, perhaps expecting trouble.

I told him, "I'd just like to ask you a couple of questions. I believe you used to work for Sempronius Primus?"

"What if I did?" he glowered, his demeanour defensive.

"You left his service last year, and then he was attacked and beaten up."

"So what? I wasn't working for him then."

"No, but I heard you left under something of a cloud."

"Bollocks!" he snorted.

He was still nervous of Caecus, but he was more sure of himself now.

He leered, "I moved on to better things. I'm a Senator's guard now, so leaving Sempronius Primus' service was the best thing I've ever done."

"So you don't harbour a grudge against him?"

"No. He's a fat prick, but I couldn't care less what happens to him."

"I see. But is there anything you can tell me about the night he was attacked?"

Vespillo glared, "No. I wasn't there."

"Where were you then? Do you have any witnesses?"

I was pushing hard, but I'd taken a dislike to Vespillo. Even if I hadn't known about his habit of battering women, his bullying manner irritated me.

"I think you should sod off now," he told me, leaning forwards to stare belligerently into my eyes. "Or I might need to rearrange your face for you."

At that, Caecus interposed himself between us, clamping a meaty hand on Vespillo's shoulder, his fingers gripping like talons.

"Easy, soldier," he rumbled. "The man only wants to ask you some questions. This isn't the time or the place for any trouble."

I suppose some long-dead Emperors might disagree with that. The forum had always been a place where trouble was fomented. One, an old man named Galba, had ended his brief reign not far from where we stood when he was hacked down by a bunch of Praetorian cavalrymen who had been bribed by a jealous rival.

As for the present, I held my breath, expecting Vespillo to react violently to Caecus' grip on his shoulder. But Caecus' voice contained all the authority of a Centurion, and perhaps something inside Vespillo recognised the manner. Or perhaps, like most bullies, he knew when he was outmatched. Either way, he remained tense and angry, and I saw his eyes darting around the forum as if he was looking for someone to come to his rescue.

Then, to my dismay, he relaxed slightly and grinned at me.

"All right," he sneered, suddenly full of confidence again. "If you must know, I was at my new boss's house, along with the rest of his guards. Do you want to come and ask them? There are a few of them over there."

So that was what had altered his mood. His pals were close by. He'd called my bluff, but I wasn't going to let him off that easily.

"Why not?" I smiled in response.

He regarded me as if I were mad, then grinned, "Come on, then."

He stalked towards the front corner of the Senate House where I saw a group of five men watching us. In build, they matched Vespillo, and they had that look about them which spoke of them being either ex-military or retired gladiators. They'd obviously noticed how we'd intercepted their pal, and they were all on their feet, most of them scowling at us.

"Good morning!" I breezed as we drew near them, wanting to pre-empt Vespillo. "Can you help me? I was just asking

Vespillo where he was on the night Sempronius Primus was beaten up last year. He says you can vouch for him."

The men looked from me, to Vespillo, then at Caecus.

One of them growled, "What's your problem?"

"No problem," I assured him, doing my best to appear relaxed and confident. These men were trained to intimidate, and they were doing a fine job of it, although I knew I couldn't let them see that.

Vespillo said, "Just tell him I was with you, then he can bugger off and annoy someone else."

There was a short, uncertain silence as the men exchanged looks.

I asked, "Well? Was Vespillo with you on that night? Or did you all go out as a gang to waylay his former boss?"

I could see muscles flexing and fists bunching, but Caecus stepped in again.

He said, "Just answer the question and we'll leave."

"And who are you?" the leader of the group demanded. He was another big man, powerfully built although well past his prime. Still, I wouldn't have wanted to be on the receiving end of one of his punches, and even Caecus would not be able to overcome half a dozen opponents if they decided to turn on us.

Things were in serious danger of turning nasty. There might be hundreds of witnesses within a few paces, but street brawls were not uncommon, and I very much doubted anyone would come to our aid if this lot decided to resort to violence.

Caecus planted his hands on his hips and cast an imperious gaze at the men as if committing their faces to memory.

He said, "I'm a Centurion in the Praetorian Guard. I'm off duty just now, helping my friend here. But if you want me to come back with a cohort of my pals, that will work just as well. It's up to you."

I had to admire his audacity, but this was getting out of hand. Every nerve in my body was telling me it was time to walk away, but I decided to follow Caecus' lead in the hope it might just persuade them to cooperate.

I said, "Leave it. Let's go. This lot must be behind the attack. We'll report it to the Commander and let him decide what to do next."

I turned away, but Vespillo barked, "Wait!"

Turning back, I asked him, "What? You had your chance. Even if they all back your story now, I'm not sure I'd believe them."

I'd hoped to make him angry, but he was almost laughing as he pointed behind me.

"Then why not ask our boss? Here he comes now. You'd believe a Senator, wouldn't you?"

I didn't turn around. That was an old trick, and one I'd used myself in the past. But Vespillo and his companions all stood stiffly, like soldiers on parade, and I heard footsteps on the cobbles behind me.

"What is going on?" a haughty, refined voice asked from over my shoulder.

I spun around to see two men facing me. Both were past middle-age, and both wore formal togas over tunics bearing the thick purple stripe of men of Senatorial rank. The one who had spoken to me was tall, with greying hair and a hawk-like nose he must have inherited from his patrician ancestors. His eyes glared down at me with an expression of distaste.

I'm normally fairly quick with my responses, but it took me a moment to respond because it was the speaker's companion who caught my attention. He was shorter, plumper, in late middle age, with neatly trimmed brown hair which bore traces of distinguishing grey at the temples. He had a smooth, urbane look about him, and he seemed amused at the prospect of witnessing a confrontation. Worse, he was studying me with a look of curiosity as if trying to place me.

Cursing silently, I dragged my attention back to the tall Senator who had addressed me.

"Good morning," I said. "I'm Valerius Cantiacus. I'm looking into the attack on Sempronius Primus a few months back. I was just asking your man, Vespillo, whether he knew anything about it since he used to work for the guy."

The nostrils twitched in disdain as the Senator sneered, "Don't be absurd! I wouldn't let my men assault one of my own clients!"

Oh, Venus! That could only mean one thing.

"You are Herennius Muncius?" I gulped.

"That's correct. And these are my personal guards, so please allow them to carry out their duties without pestering them. Good day to you."

What could I say? I could hear the scorn and laughter from Muncius' guards, and I wanted the ground to open up and swallow me.

I managed to mumble, "Fine. Thanks for your help."

I hurriedly turned away, striding off with as much dignity as I could muster as I tried to vanish into the crowd.

Caecus caught up with me as I wove my way through the busy forum, heading in no particular direction as long as it was away from Muncius and the other Senator who had accompanied him.

"What's wrong?" Caecus asked as he tugged at my arm in an effort to slow my fast pace.

"Didn't you recognise him?" I shot back.

"Muncius? No, I don't think I've ever seen him before."

"Not him. The other one."

"He looked vaguely familiar, but I've seen a lot of Senators in my time."

"Yes, because a lot of them were forced to traipse around after Caracalla. Any Senator he didn't trust to leave in Rome while he was on campaign had to follow him wherever he went."

"He was one of that lot?" Caecus frowned. "What's his name?"

"Dio. Cassius Dio. I met him in Alexandria. He's a very senior Senator. He's also very clever indeed. I'd be willing to bet that, if there are some plots being hatched, he'll be involved in at least one of them."

"He's hanging around with Herennius Muncius," Caecus observed thoughtfully. "If your pal Rufus is to be believed, Muncius is definitely involved in something."

"Which probably means Dio is in it with him," I sighed. "And that could mean we have yet another problem."

"If he recognised us, you mean?"

I nodded grimly. I'd met Cassius Dio several times during my short stay in Alexandria. We had been cooped up in the palace while Caracalla's Legions had been busy sacking the city.

"It depends on how good his memory is," I said. "But he was certainly giving me some very close looks. If he makes the connection, we might be in real trouble. After all, I am supposed to be dead."

Caecus frowned, "I don't see it can be that much of a problem. A man like that isn't likely to bother with people like you and me."

I shook my head. Caecus was far from stupid, but his training and experience meant he was not nearly cynical enough for the situation we were in.

I told him, "If he is part of a conspiracy along with Muncius and Primus, and if he does recognise me, what conclusion do you think he will reach? A man who used to be an imperial spy is living in Primus' house under an assumed name."

To give him his due, Caecus caught up very quickly.

"He'll think you are spying on them?"

"He's bound to. And that will leave them with only two options. Either they call the whole thing off, or they get rid of us."

Chapter 18
Blank Walls

I was angry. Angry at Primus for getting himself mixed up in a Senatorial plot; angry at Mardonius for accidentally omitting to tell me that Vespillo was now employed by Primus' patron; and angry that Cassius Dio might have recognised me and leaped to the wrong conclusion. Above all, though, I was angry with myself. Once again, I'd blundered head on into a problem and created more trouble for myself.

"I'm a bloody fool!" I hissed to Caecus as I stomped along the wide avenue known as the *Via Lata*. "We should have followed Vespillo and made some discreet enquiries instead of confronting him."

"What's done is done," Caecus replied philosophically as he gently placed a hand on my elbow to prevent me colliding with a little old lady who was carrying a string bag full of vegetables.

Slowing my pace a little, I sighed, "Yes, but I've made too many mistakes. I'm so desperate to solve this mystery that I'm not doing it properly."

"Personally," Caecus rumbled, "I prefer the direct approach. But at least you had the sense to retreat from a difficult situation."

"Much good it will do if Dio recognised me," I muttered, still scolding myself for my stupidity.

"So what do you intend to do?"

"There is nothing I can do," I told him.

"What do you mean?"

"Well, we can't run away. Circe won't leave until Collinus gets back, and I don't want to abandon my mother. And we can't hide. If we leave Primus' house, that will only make them more suspicious."

"Then we carry on as if nothing has happened?" Caecus asked.

"That's all we can do," I confirmed.

"That's a risky strategy," he observed. "But I'll admit I can't suggest any viable alternative."

175

I nodded my thanks, trying to conceal my inner dread. During my time as an imperial spy, I'd often taken risks which, looking back, were foolhardy in the extreme. But that was when I was single and had nobody else to worry about except myself. Now, my decisions had placed Circe and my children in danger, and that tore at me like a knife in the guts.

I said, "I'll tell Circe to take the kids home as soon as Collinus gets back."

"That would be sensible," Caecus agreed, although his tone suggested he didn't think I'd have much success persuading the lady to go along with the idea. He probably wasn't wrong.

"So what now?" he asked me, his own mind apparently settled.

I gathered my thoughts. I hadn't chosen any specific direction when I'd left the forum. All I'd wanted to do was put distance between me and the two scheming Senators, but fortune, or perhaps some subconscious impulse, had made my next move an obvious choice.

"We're on the *Via Lata*," I pointed out. "There's the Column of Marcus Aurelius, and that's the Arch of Claudius. If we carry on, it takes us past the Field of Mars."

"I know," Caecus grunted. "I've been here before."

Ignoring his sarcasm, I went on, "And if we turn left before we reach the river, that will take us to the *Via Ostiensis* and Pottery Mountain."

He regarded me stonily, merely raising one eyebrow in question.

"Which is where," I explained, "Primus' builder had his business. Let's see if we can talk to the new owners. They might know where we can find Mallius Tanicus."

Caecus gave a satisfied nod, clearly pleased that we had a plan, so we set off, walking along the busy road. The *Via Lata* is, as its name suggests, a broad avenue. It's one of the main thoroughfares of Rome. It leads out to the *Via Flaminia*, the main route to the north of Italia, and it passes some of the city's most impressive monuments. Caecus and I walked beneath the great Arch of Claudius which held one of the city's aqueducts, then we continued towards the Tiber, passing through the Field of Mars with its myriad public buildings.

176

Before long, we could see another monument rising over the tops of the buildings.

"Pottery Mountain," I said, indicating the huge pile of old jugs and *amphorae* which was now so high it rose above the level of even the tallest tenements.

Pottery Mountain is almost a tourist attraction in its own right nowadays, although it's really just a rubbish dump which has grown out of control. You see, Rome imports huge quantities of wine and olive oil, and these are transported in large, clay *amphorae*. Once empty, though, they have little use. For one thing, the clay absorbs the flavour of the liquid it contained, so it can't be used for anything else. For another, it's not economically viable to have a ship carry empty containers back to Spain or Africa, so people simply get their slaves to take the *amphorae* to this dump site. There are so many discarded pots and jugs that the mountain is higher than many natural hills, and it covers an enormous area of what was once open fields.

With this landmark to guide us, we turned west, following the *Via Ostiensis*, passing various shipyards and other businesses which were based here to take advantage of the river traffic. That included several building operations because heavy stone and marble could be unloaded directly from the ships bringing the supplies upriver from Ostia.

A few enquiries soon directed us towards one of these establishments which was ringed by a tall wooden fence. Inside the open gates, it looked like any such business, with blocks of stone, stacks of bricks, marble cladding, lead pipes, and red tiles spread around seemingly at random. There was timber as well, with some men busy sawing planks and shaping window shutters, while a large kiln was in use, presumably for baking more bricks and tiles. There were two locked store sheds, and a couple of carts stood near a single-storey building to our left. This solid-looking edifice had a painted sign above the door proclaiming it to be the office of Fabius and Didius.

"They must be the new owners," I said as I led the way to the door.

"Are you ready for this?" Caecus enquired. "You took quite a fright back there."

I returned what I hoped was a confident smile.

177

"I'll be fine," I assured him.

So saying, I pushed the door open and stepped through. Inside, the place was neat, well-made but basic. A tiled floor, a couple of desks with wooden chairs, a scroll cabinet and a few chests were the only furniture in evidence. On the walls hung sketches of buildings, all looking magnificently perfect. I presumed these were intended to display the quality of the work carried out by this firm.

There was only one person in the room, a burly man whose florid features suggested a long association with the contents of some of the *amphorae* which now comprised Pottery Mountain. He was, I guessed, in late middle age, and much of his bulk was now comprised of fat rather than muscle.

He rose to his feet and gave us a toothy smile when we entered his domain.

"Good afternoon," he said, his voice hoarse and throaty. "I'm Fabius Murmillo. What can I do for you?"

Forcing a smile, I told him, "Actually, we are looking for someone. A man named Mallius Tanicus used to own this business. We're trying to find him."

I could almost see the shutters coming down on Murmillo's eyes. His smile vanished, and his face grew hard, his entire stance radiating hostility.

"He's gone," he stated. "We bought this place from him a few months ago. I've got no idea where he went."

"What about your workers? Could I ask them? One of them might know something."

"They won't," he almost sneered. "Tanicus had run the business into the ground. He'd got rid of most of his workers, and we replaced the ones he left behind. It's an entire new team."

I suppose I shouldn't have expected much more, but I was growing desperate by now, and I didn't want to give up that easily.

I asked, "You've obviously got the place running a lot better. What did Tanicus do wrong?"

"He just wasn't very good," Murmillo scoffed.

"But you and your partner have plenty of experience?"

"We learned in the legions," he nodded. "Buildings, roads, bridges and aqueducts. We've done them all."

I managed to restrain a sigh. I seemed to be bumping into former soldiers at every turn.

I asked him, "And you got this business at a knock down price, I suppose?"

"That's none of your business," he said coldly. "Now, if you'll excuse me, I am rather busy."

He stood facing us, implacable and unmoving, his legs apart and his arms crossed in a defiant stance. His reaction to hearing Tanicus' name was certainly very odd, but I couldn't fathom why he was so defensive. After an awkward moment, I had no option but to thank him and leave.

"Another dead end," I muttered darkly once we were outside.

Caecus suggested, "We should head home. We have another long night ahead of us."

He was right, and I was too weary to argue, so we trudged back to the Quirinal and home.

Circe had not returned, so I sent Lucius to fetch me a light snack from the kitchen, then I went to bed and slept for a few hours.

When Circe woke me, it was to tell me the children were going to bed.

"You need to say goodnight to them," she informed me in a tone which suggested I was in her bad books.

Once Sextus and Valeria were settled, we went back to our own room. To put off telling Circe about my encounter with Herennius Muncius and Cassius Dio, I asked her how her day had been.

"It was nice," she told me.

It seemed her time had been spent mostly at the baths and in wandering the city centre to have a good look at the various triumphal arches and, naturally, the magnificent Flavian amphitheatre which was still impressive despite not having been used for some years following a lightning strike, a phenomenon which had caused considerable damage, not to mention raising concerns about the place having somehow incurred the displeasure of the gods.

"We saw the Emperor," she informed me.

I raised an eyebrow to encourage her to say more.

"He's a very good dancer," she said after some thought. "He had a crowd of young women all dressed in silks and ribbons, and he led them in a dance from the palace to his new temple. There were flutes and drums, so it was quite a spectacle."

"Did he say or do anything else?" I asked.

"No. He pranced around for a while, then led his troupe into the temple."

"What about the crowd? What was the mood?"

"Unhappy, I would say. If it had been an ordinary group of street entertainers, or dancers in a theatre, I think everyone would have applauded. But the fact it was the Emperor of Rome leading the dance disappointed everyone. There was a lot of angry muttering, and I think quite a lot of the spectators were dismayed to see him behaving like that. I'd go so far as to say one or two seemed disgusted."

"Dancers and actors have always been despised in Rome," I observed. "It's not a good sign, is it?"

"No, it's not," Circe agreed. "Other than that, though, nothing exciting happened. But I'm getting on really well with your mother."

"That's good," I nodded. "Have you broached the subject of her coming back to Leptis Magna with us?"

"Not yet. I'll give her a little more time."

Then, as perceptive as ever, she asked me, "What about you? I can tell there's something bothering you. What happened?"

She knew me too well. When I told her about meeting the two Senators, she became thoughtful, but she rapidly came to the same conclusion as me.

"It all depends on whether Dio recognised you," she decided. "If he did, that could be a problem."

I gave her a puzzled look. She seemed to be taking the news far too calmly.

I said, "That's an understatement. I was thinking it might be a good idea if you and the children went home."

"To Leptis Magna?" she frowned.

"Yes. Just as a precaution."

"It's still the stormy season," she told me sharply. "And I'm not leaving you here with all that's going on."

"But you and the children could be in danger!" I protested.

180

"I've spent my whole life in danger," she reminded me. "Until Macrinus died, I'd always had the threat of imperial vengeance hanging over me."

I argued, "That doesn't mean we should take unnecessary risks."

"No, but I don't think it's as bad as you are making out."

"What do you mean? If Primus' posh pals are planning to assassinate the Emperor, they won't think twice about killing us to keep us quiet."

She treated me to that smile I knew heralded an explanation of why I was wrong.

"Scipio, you haven't thought it through. If they believe you are still an imperial spy, that means they will think the Emperor, or perhaps Julia Maesa, is suspicious of them. If that were true, killing us would only make them more suspicious and would give them an excuse to arrest any suspected conspirators."

I sat back, running that scenario through my mind. She was probably right, although I wasn't entirely reassured.

Circe went on, "At the moment, you have no evidence of any wrongdoing. They know you've only just arrived. My guess is they'll sit tight for a few days to see what you do. That means you should carry on investigating the attack on Primus."

I shook my head.

"You are assuming they will think as logically as you," I argued. "People who are desperate enough to plan an assassination don't always act reasonably or rationally."

"Muncius and Dio are senior Senators," she replied. "They are well used to political life, so they will evaluate everything carefully before reaching a decision."

"Just because they are rich, it doesn't mean they are intelligent," I muttered.

"You said Cassius Dio is a clever man," she pointed out, using my own comments against me.

I sighed, "All right. But what if their plan is nearly ready to go? What happens to us if they kill the Emperor tomorrow?"

Circe gave an infuriatingly relaxed shrug.

"Either they will forget about us because they've accomplished their aim, or they will send soldiers to kill us all. Either way, there is not much we can do about it."

"We can't just sit here and wait for them to kill us!" I exclaimed.

She put a finger to her mouth to warn me to lower my voice, then said, "We have no way of knowing how close they are to acting. If they are still in the planning stage, then I think we are safe enough for the moment. There are too many of us for them to attack us without attracting far too much unwanted attention."

"Maybe," I muttered grudgingly.

"If I were them," she continued, "I'd try to kidnap the children to force us to tell them what we know, and to make sure we said nothing to anyone."

I blinked. Sometimes she was still able to astonish me.

"Kidnap the kids?"

"It would be the most sensible thing to do. If they do anything at all, which I don't think they will. But, just in case, I'll arrange to always have at least four of our slaves close at hand."

I could only admire her calm confidence and the way she seemed capable of setting emotional ties aside. It wasn't that she didn't worry about the children, it was just that she had learned from her earliest years that there were some things you could do nothing about, so it wasn't worth worrying too much over them. On the other hand, she knew that thinking clearly was the best way to deal with those things you could influence.

I leaned over and kissed her.

"You are amazing," I told her.

"I know I am. And so are you, although you don't seem to realise it."

"You're just saying that to cheer me up," I smiled.

"I'm saying it because I think you ought to go and talk to Primus."

"Why?"

"Because it wouldn't do any harm to let him know your only intention is to solve the mystery of who is waging this campaign against him."

"Make him think I know nothing about any conspiracy, you mean?"

"It wouldn't hurt, would it?"

182

"I suppose not," I sighed, not relishing the thought of speaking to Primus again. "I just wish we had some way of getting out of this mess."

"I can't think of anything that would make us any safer," she told me. "Even if we left, we would still be in danger. And, quite honestly, your mother is torn. She knows Primus is involved in unsavoury things, but he is still her son."

"Are you saying she won't come back with us?"

"I don't know," Circe said. "That's why I'm trying to let her see as much of the children as I can. I'm hoping it will help persuade her when I do ask her."

"It might persuade her the wrong way," I joked feebly.

"I doubt it. I've not seen much of Primus' children, but I have the distinct impression Zoe doesn't approve of their manners."

"Zoe, is it? You *are* getting on well with her."

"Yes, I am. And she's very fond of you."

"Even though I abandoned her when I left home all those years ago?"

"Perhaps because of that. But she is certainly relying on you to learn the truth about what is going on. And I don't mean her only concern is the physical attack on your brother. Now she knows he might be mixed up in a plot, she wants to find out the truth about that as well."

Pragmatic as ever, she added, "So we cannot go home now. Besides, as I said, it's still the season for storms. The voyage back to Africa will be even more dangerous than staying here and solving the mystery."

"That's debatable," I murmured.

Circe gave me another smile, showing me the empathy and understanding that had first made me fall for her.

Placing a hand on my arm, she said, "We both know there's another reason you will stay. You want to discover the truth as much as anyone. You want to know what Primus is involved in."

She had me there.

"Yes, I do. I just don't like the idea of you and the kids being in danger."

183

"It's too late to regret what has brought us here," she told me. "So just you carry on asking questions."

She leaned in to kiss me, then gently pushed me away.

"Now go and talk to your brother. Convince him you know nothing."

I grinned, "That shouldn't be too difficult. He thinks I'm an idiot."

I stood up and headed for the door. As I reached it, I turned back and told her, "Lady, I am so glad you are on my side. I'd hate to have you as an enemy."

Chapter 19
Orpheus

I found Primus in his study. He was busy writing on a scroll, an ink-stained quill clenched between his chubby fingers. When I entered the room, he placed the feather in his ink pot and scowled at me.

"What is it this time?" he demanded testily. "I'm very busy."

I was back in deception mode, so I breezed, "I wanted to bring you up to date with how my investigation is going."

"I really don't care," he snarled. "I never asked for your help, and I certainly don't need it. You should go home and take your African tart back with you."

He was goading me, and it almost worked. Insulting Circe was usually a sure-fire way of rousing my temper. Fortunately, I knew all his tricks, so I managed to restrain my anger.

"I told you Mother wants me to find out who attacked you," I reminded him. "Until I do, I'm afraid you are stuck with me. But, if it is any consolation, I'll be heading home as soon as I've identified the culprit."

"If you ever do," he muttered.

"If I can't, I'll not hang around. As soon as I run out of options, I'll be gone."

"Good. Now bugger off and leave me in peace!" he snapped, pointing a fat finger towards the door.

I didn't move, but he made a great show of pretending I had left, looking back down at his paperwork with feigned concentration.

I said, "I met your patron today."

"What?" he blinked, his hand frozen in the action of reaching for his quill.

Speaking casually, I explained, "Herennius Muncius. That's his name, isn't it? Tall fellow. Receding hairline and a patrician nose you could use as a chisel."

Primus was suddenly interested, his upraised hand dropping to the desk and his eyes narrowing as he tried to gauge what I'd been up to.

I said, "You might have told me your former employee, Vespillo, was now working for him."

I knew what he was going to say. It was his usual response to that sort of accusation.

"You never asked me," he frowned.

"No, but I asked Mardonius. He claimed he didn't know who Vespillo was working for, but I am struggling to believe that."

Primus was obviously curious to know what had taken place between me and Muncius, but I guessed he was trying to appear unconcerned.

I told him, "I found Vespillo in the forum, and then Muncius turned up. It was a bit embarrassing, to be honest. If I'd known Vespillo worked for him, I could have crossed him off my list at the outset. I mean, your patron would have no reason to send a gang of his men to beat you up, would he?"

I said it with a laugh, but Primus didn't seem to be amused.

"You were embarrassed? What about me? What am I going to say to Herennius Muncius the next time I see him?"

"Tell him I'm an idiot," I suggested. "I certainly felt like one. Anyway, Vespillo is no longer a suspect, so I suppose I'd better keep on looking for the real culprit. The sooner I track him down, the sooner I'll be able to go back home."

I stalked out, hopefully having left Primus with the impression that my sole concern was investigating his unknown enemy. Whether that would be enough to persuade Cassius Dio and Herennius Muncius to leave me in peace, only time would tell.

I was still on edge by the time I had returned to my mother's wing of the house and made my way to the small chamber off the entrance lobby where old Lucius was preparing to settle down for the night. The main outer door was locked and bolted, but Lucius confirmed that Caecus had already gone out.

"I hope he catches someone this time," I muttered.

While Lucius lay down and soon began snoring, I sat on the bundle of blankets which formed my temporary bed, and I went over all the things I had discovered so far, analysing every meeting in the search for clues. It was a difficult exercise because my mind kept drifting to Cassius Dio and what might happen if he had recognised me. No matter how often I told myself to forget him, visions of armed thugs coming for us haunted my thoughts.

"Snap out of it, Scipio," I told myself. "Concentrate on the things you can do something about."

So I ran over the various suspects again, trying to rank them in order of likely possibility.

Despite what I'd told Primus, his former guard, Vespillo, wasn't entirely out of consideration.

It was always possible the guy had a personal grudge against Primus and had recruited his pals to help him. I couldn't think what that grudge could be, but Primus did have a knack of upsetting people, and guys like Vespillo are perfectly capable of beating someone up just for a bit of fun. Still, all things considered, Vespillo was now low on my list.

Aconius Dardanus, the property factor, was still in the frame. He was a cowardly weasel, but he had admitted to knowing men who acted as his enforcers, so he could easily have hired a few more. I knew I ought to track down the heavies he employed to help him collect his rents. Asking them a few questions might prove useful.

Marius Vindex, the Viminal's crime lord, was also a possibility although, strangely, I had believed him when he said he had nothing to do with the attack. He was a thug who would no doubt order such a thing without a second thought, but his denials had seemed sincere. After all, if he had been responsible, he had no need to deny it.

The prime suspect now, though, was the missing builder, Mallius Tanicus, if only because a process of partial elimination had left him as the only potential suspect I hadn't spoken to. The problem would be finding him. To be honest, I had no idea how I could do that.

I must have sat there for a few hours, but I was roused from my introspection when I heard a fist thumping on the door. Scrambling to my feet, I went into the entrance lobby and began pulling back the bolts. I tugged the door open and, by the dim light of the hallway's solitary oil lamp, I saw the hulking figure of

Caecus standing there, one arm clamped around the neck of a terrified young man who was staring at me in wide-eyed horror.

"Got him!" Caecus grinned over the lad's shoulder.

"Bring him in," I said, stepping back to let them pass.

All the reception rooms off the atrium were being used to accommodate my slaves, so we bundled the poor fellow through the house and into the family room at the back. I took the oil lamp which I set on a small table, then I sat in one of the padded chairs while Caecus shoved the trembling man into another seat facing me. The big Praetorian took up position just behind his captive's chair.

I studied the man Caecus had caught. He was, I guessed, in his early twenties, clean-shaven and neatly turned out, but wearing only a plain tunic and sandals. He wore no rings, so I was able to guess at his status.

"You are one of Helvius Oceanus' slaves?"

He looked almost literally petrified, his face pale and his eyes wide, but he was swallowing nervously while he anxiously rubbed his hands together. After a moment, he did manage to nod in response to my question.

"What is your name?"

"Orpheus."

The word came out as a low, frightened whisper.

"You are Greek?"

Another nod.

I switched to his native language to confirm this.

"How did you become a slave?"

In a quavering voice, he told me, "My parents sold me when I was a boy. There was a famine, and they were very poor."

His Greek was fluent, but I noticed Caecus frowning, so I returned to speaking Latin to let him understand what was being said.

"You have been painting insulting graffiti on the walls of Sempronius Primus' house?"

Orpheus lowered his eyes, but gave a miserable nod of his head.

"On your master's orders?"

"Yes."

"When did this begin?"

188

He hesitated for a moment, and I thought he might be about to clam up, but he was so afraid of us that there was no resistance left in him.

He said, "It began a couple of months ago. Just after Sempronius Primus was attacked in the street."

"Did your master have anything to do with that attack?"

"No, Sir!" he blurted, his face lifting to meet my gaze. "He was entertaining some friends that night. He only learned of the attack the following morning."

I nodded. That didn't entirely rule Oceanus out, but it did reduce the chances of him having been involved. It's not the sort of thing a man could easily conceal from his most trusted slaves.

I said, "All right. But what gave him the idea of scribbling threats on Primus' house walls?"

"Someone else did it first," the slave replied. "I mean, Rome is full of graffiti, but someone used a piece of charcoal to write that Sempronius Primus was a murderer. My master saw it, and he saw how furious Primus was about it, so he decided it would be amusing to write other things."

"As a way of annoying Primus?"

"That's right, sir."

"Because he thought Primus was having an affair with his wife?"

Orpheus lowered his head again, a faint blush appearing on his cheeks.

"It's not my place to say, Sir," he replied hesitantly.

I didn't push that line of enquiry. I really couldn't have cared less whether Primus had been screwing Oceanus' wife or not. What mattered was that the old man clearly held a grudge against my brother.

"So he only told you to do this in order to annoy Sempronius Primus?"

"That's right, Sir. He thought it was funny."

I glanced up at Caecus who gave a slight shrug, his expression saying he believed the young man. He'd had years of dealing with young recruits, so I valued his judgement.

"All right," I said as I stood up. "Let's go and talk to your master. He's probably wondering what's keeping you."

Caecus dragged the lad back through the house. I woke Lucius to tell him to bar the door after us, then we stepped out into the dark street.

"Where are the paint pot and brush?" I asked.

"He dropped them when I grabbed him," Caecus told me.

"Then let's pick them up. There's no point in leaving evidence lying around."

The street was silent and dark, illuminated only by faint starlight which filtered down between gaps in the clouds, but we soon located the brush and a small pot of paint which had spilled most of its contents on the cobbles.

I made Orpheus pick them up, then we marched him across to the home of Helvius Oceanus. It was a modest house, with only a single storey beneath a flat roof. The door was locked, but eventually I heard someone fumbling with a key after I'd thumped on the wood a few times.

The door opened a tiny fraction, and an eye appeared in the crack, candlelight outlining a figure which, for a nice change, was of only average build, about the same height and weight as me, although he was a lot older. His lined, weather-beaten face was framed by thin strands of grey hair and an equally grey beard, and the flesh of his bare arms was tanned and aged.

"Helvius Oceanus?" I demanded before he could speak. "This is one of your slaves?"

Not that he could have said much when faced with the evidence Caecus held. Orpheus hung his head, the brush and pot still gripped in his hands.

I told Oceanus, "My name is Valerius Cantiacus. I'm staying across the road with the lady Zoe, the mother of Sempronius Primus. She asked me to find out who was threatening the family. I now know it was you."

He began to bluster, saying, "I only wanted to annoy Primus. I never threatened anyone else."

"You never threatened anyone at all," I pointed out. "You got your slave to do the dirty work. But it ends now. Do you know what Primus will do to you if I tell him it was you behind the slogans?"

"I'm not afraid of him!" Oceanus retorted as he pulled himself up to his full height in an attempt to impress me.

Needless to say, I wasn't impressed at all.

I told him, "You ought to be scared of him. He has a small army of very vicious thugs working for him. So I suggest you call a halt to this nonsense. Because there have been other, much more serious threats against Primus, and if I thought you were behind them, I'd have no option but to inform him. Do you understand?"

Oceanus glared at me, but he gave the slightest of nods.

"Good," I said. "Now let your slave back in, and we'll say no more about it as long as there are no further threats."

Caecus gave Orpheus a shove in the back, propelling him into the house with such force that Oceanus was forced to step aside. I took the opportunity to move closer to him and hiss, "For what it's worth, I dislike Primus as well. I know it can't be easy living close to him, but you are a lucky man. You have a nice home and a young wife who is carrying your child. Count your blessings, my friend. There is no point in asking for trouble."

"Sempronius Primus is a crook," he shot back, his face flushed with helpless anger.

"What do you mean? What has he done?"

Oceanus faltered at that, and I guessed his main issue was what Primus had or had not done with Oceanus' wife.

"Everyone knows he's involved in all sorts of things," he muttered darkly. "Somebody needs to do something to stop him."

"Somebody probably will one day," I told him. "But you ought to know when not to fight against a storm. Primus is a vengeful man. Believe me, I know. So do yourself a favour and have nothing to do with him."

Oceanus had been a ship's captain, accustomed to command, so I supposed retirement might have been difficult for him, but he was obviously no fool.

"All right," he muttered darkly. "There will be no more from me. As long as he stays clear of my house and my wife."

I couldn't promise that, so I simply said, "Thank you. Good night. I do hope we don't need to talk again."

Caecus and I crossed the street again. I heard Oceanus' door being locked behind us.

"You're not going to tell Primus?" Caecus asked.

"No. Like I said, he's a vengeful sod. He could make life very miserable for Oceanus and his wife. They don't deserve that."

191

"The wife doesn't," Caecus agreed. "I'm not so sure about the old man. He struck me as a cruel sort."

Perhaps being around Circe was rubbing off on the big man. Coming from a former Praetorian, that was quite a statement, but I forbore from pointing this out.

Instead, I replied, "I didn't say he was a nice person, but his wife has done nothing wrong except maybe make a poor decision."

"I doubt she had any choice," Caecus murmured.

I sighed. He was right. But we could not fix all the world's problems. I had enough troubles trying to resolve my own. Still, I felt a lot better now that we had solved one part of the puzzle, even if it was only a small piece.

"Maybe we are getting somewhere at last," I remarked. "Tomorrow might bring us another break."

"Tomorrow we are going to the Circus Maximus," Caecus reminded me.

"Jupiter! I'd forgotten about that."

"You are going, aren't you?"

I nodded, "I promised."

I could have done without going to the Circus, but I knew there was no way of avoiding it. Like Oceanus, I knew when not to fight against a storm.

Chapter 20
Circus Maximus

Early the next morning, I headed down to Fronto's house to bring him up to date with what we had discovered.

"You can let Rusticus out of his locked room tonight," I told my friend. "But for Jupiter's sake, don't tell anyone who was really behind the graffiti. I don't want Primus to find out. It's not all that serious in the great scheme of things, and I don't want him starting another war with his neighbour."

"I won't tell a soul," Fronto promised.

"Thanks. Now, what can you tell me about a Senator named Cassius Dio?"

"Dio? He's an important man," Fronto replied. "I heard a rumour he was considering standing for Consul last year, but he backed out when it became clear the Emperor was going to appoint a couple of his own cronies."

That wasn't welcome news. The office of Consul had traditionally been the most senior appointment any Roman could achieve. In the dim and distant days of the Republic, two Consuls had been elected each year, and charged with ruling the city and its growing empire. Having two rulers with equal power was supposed to prevent any one man holding absolute authority. Rule by a single man had been anathema to our republican forebears after they had thrown out the kings of Rome. Once Augustus became Emperor, though, that situation changed. The office of Consul was still held in high regard, and Consuls were elected every year, but it was a position without real authority. Recent emperors had taken to nominating Consuls as a mark of recognition and reward to their friends. But still, the fact that Cassius Dio was even considered a possible candidate showed just how highly placed he was in Roman society. The fact that he'd been obliged to stand aside for one of the Emperor's sycophants might also explain why he was now in league with Herennius Muncius.

"Can you tell me any more about him?" I asked.

Fronto tapped a finger to his chin while he searched his memory.

"Not much," he admitted. "As you know, he was one of the Senators Caracalla didn't trust, but Macrinus sent him back to Rome as soon as he became Emperor."

"And since then? What does he think of Elagabalus?"

"I have no idea," Fronto replied with an apologetic sigh. "Dio is very clever, and he's also very cautious. I've never heard of him speaking out against the Emperor or any member of the imperial family."

"So he plays it safe in public," I nodded. "But that doesn't mean he isn't doing things behind the scenes."

"What's going on?" Fronto asked. "Why the interest in Dio?"

I briefly outlined my encounter in the forum the previous day.

Fronto rubbed his chin pensively, then said, "It doesn't necessarily mean he's in league with Muncius. Senators need to talk to one another all the time. It could be a coincidence."

"I'm not sure Cassius Dio is the sort of man who does anything by coincidence," I replied.

"You may be right," Fronto conceded. "Tread carefully, my friend. You are in danger of upsetting some very important people."

"I'll be very careful," I assured him. "Now, I must go. We are off to the races today."

I left Fronto and returned to my mother's home to find the rest of the family waiting. My mother had decided to accompany us even though she had never had much time for chariot racing.

"Aurelia has tokens for four adults," she explained. "But your friend Collinus is away, so I may as well come with you."

It turned out that my brother was also going to the Circus Maximus, but he was being carried in one of the public litters because his injured leg would still not allow him to walk any great distance. We saw him hobble beneath the hanging curtains of the litter which was then hoisted up by the bearers, while half a dozen of Primus' guards marched behind them.

"He's going on his own?" I asked my mother.

"Hortensia doesn't like the races," she explained. "But Primus enjoys gambling on the outcome."

I almost said something uncomplimentary about my brother's apparent reluctance to join our group, but I didn't want to drive any deeper wedges between us. Circe had told me my mother was torn, and fuelling the feud would not help her. Besides, I had no wish to sit near Primus, so we let his litter get some way ahead of us, then we set off, with half a dozen of our own slaves tagging along behind us.

It was a long walk, but the day was pleasantly dry and bright, if a little cool. The city seemed to have become infected by a mood of relaxation, and we soon found ourselves joining a great many people who were heading down to the Circus. In fact, the crowds were so great that it took us a while to negotiate the junction where the *Vicus Longua* crosses the *Clivus Suburanus*. The latter is the main road through the low-lying district of the Subura, one of the city's least reputable districts which houses many of the poorer citizens. On Holy Days, these people were always keen to enjoy the entertainments provided by the Emperor. Of course, those entertainments would include theatre shows and gladiatorial games, but it was the chariot racing at the Circus Maximus which drew the really big crowds, so we found ourselves surrounded by a boisterous but good-humoured mob as we headed for the Circus.

Chariot racing has been one of Rome's favourite sports ever since the city was first founded, and the Circus Maximus is one of the city's most popular attractions. The current Circus is mostly built of stone since previous wooden versions of it tended to burn down. On the outside, a multitude of shops and small businesses ply their trade, relying on the hordes of spectators for their custom. Dozens of gates lead into the venue, and tiers of stone benches provide the seating which can hold well over a hundred thousand people.

The Circus Maximus lies in the valley between the Palatine Hill and the Aventine to the south. It's a huge course, well over half a Roman mile in length. The races are run along a long, straight track which is divided in two by a central spine which is decorated by statues, shrines and a great obelisk from Egypt. At each end of the spine stands a gilded column which marks the turning point where the track becomes a semi-circular bend. Essentially, the racing track is an extremely long, thin rectangle with rounded short ends. The chariots race down one side, navigate the tight turn, then come back down the other side and turn again when they reach the end of the central spine.

The Circus Maximus is impressive in its own right, but its setting is quite magnificent. The Palatine Hill sits to the north, with the shrines, temples and elegant houses of the Aventine looking down on the valley from the opposite side. There is also a triumphal arch dedicated to the Emperor Titus at one end of the track, while the starting gates and imperial box are found at the other end.

I gave our slaves some coins and told them to buy some food for themselves while they waited outside, then we joined the crowd and headed towards the nearest entrance. Once inside, we were fortunate enough to find some seats with a good view of the starting gates. These gates were wide, wooden stalls, each having a spring-loaded barrier behind which the chariots would line up. When the Emperor dropped a cloth from his hand, the gates would be sprung open and the race would begin.

I was pointing all of this out to my son who was entranced by the noisy, vibrant crowd who were rapidly filling the seats. The lower benches were for Senators, with equestrians seated behind them, while we were higher up where the plebs and non-citizens sat. I didn't mind this, since it was part of the price Circe and I paid for wishing to be anonymous. Given her wealth, which legally belonged to me, I could probably have applied to the Emperor to be elevated to Senatorial rank. Instead, I had persuaded the local Censors in Leptis Magna to record me as a smallholder. That meant I didn't even appear in the rosters of the equestrians. It cost a small bribe each time a census was held, but we felt it was worth it to prevent anyone in Rome noticing us.

Now, in view of our lowly official status, we sat in the cheap seats at the Circus. I knew my brother would be closer to the track since he was now officially an equestrian and would be wearing his purple-striped tunic to prove it. But our seats gave us a good view of both the track and the imperial box which was only about fifty paces to our right.

The biggest problem with the layout is that the central barrier which runs almost the entire length of the course, is so full of statues, shrines and ornaments that it blocks much of the view of the opposite side of the track. Still, it was a spectacular setting, and our seats gave us an excellent view of the impressive temples and homes on the Aventine Hill which loomed all along the far side of the Circus.

"Do you see those carved dolphins?" I asked my son as I pointed to seven stone representations atop tall poles on the central barrier. "They count the laps. The chariots race round the course seven times, and each time they complete a lap, one of the dolphins is tipped over."

I'm not sure Sextus was paying much attention to me as I tried to explain the finer points of the day. He seemed more fascinated by the sticky pastry Circe had bought him from one of the wandering vendors who patrol the seats with trays hung around their necks.

Not that I was an expert. I'd seen races before, but I could never really get too excited about the contests. To me, they were almost as dangerous for the competitors, both human and equine, as gladiatorial fights. The lives of chariot drivers tended to be relatively short since one of the aims of a race was to force your competitors to crash.

"There are four teams," I told Sextus. "The chariots are painted in different colours so you know which team they represent, and the drivers wear matching tunics. There are Green, Blue, Red and White."

"I like Red," my son declared.

"Then we shall support the reds," I told him. "But they might not win many races."

I didn't want him to become too upset if his favoured team failed to do well. It is the Blue and Green teams which dominate. Historically, several emperors have given backing to one or other of these teams, and they now have more money and can buy better horses and drivers. The White and Red teams generally act as subsidiaries of the two main factions; the Whites supporting the Blues, and Reds backing the Greens. Still, though, a driver who wants to make a name for himself can sometimes succeed as part of the White or Red teams. And, since each team has three chariots

197

in each race, the chance of collisions and crashes is high. This means that even the favourites can suffer, leaving an opening for one of the lesser teams.

Bets were already being placed, with aficionados arguing over the merits of their favourite drivers and horses, but I refrained from gambling. Any win I did have would have been down to luck rather than any knowledge of likely form.

A fanfare of bugles silenced the crowd, telling us that the Emperor had arrived. I looked to my right, pointing for the benefit of my son.

"There he is," I told him.

"I saw him dance," Sextus informed me. "He was very pretty."

The opinion of a four-year-old is not to be despised. I remembered young Elagabalus from my time in Antioch. He had always been an effeminate lad, preferring dancing to rougher pastimes, and he had often dressed in flowing robes which many would have considered more suitable for a girl. Back then, he had been only a boy, but now he was a young man, yet he still seemed to move with a graceful elegance uncharacteristic of most young men.

I recognised his fair hair which marked him out almost as much as the flowing robes of purple silk he wore. His appearance caused some muttering among the spectators, because Romans like to see their Emperor dressed in Roman garb, not decked out like some eastern potentate. Another murmur of disapproval marked the arrival of the Emperor's companion, a short, stocky man with dark hair who was struggling with the folds of a toga as if he'd never worn one before.

"Herakles," I heard someone behind me growl. "He's done all right for himself. He used to drive a chariot, and now he's driving the Emperor."

"He's doing more than driving him," another man chuckled.

Elagabalus must have heard the hisses of disapproval amidst the sparse applause, but he affected not to notice as he took his place, the former chariot driver sitting beside him.

Other people appeared in the imperial box. There's a connecting walkway which allows direct access to the box from the palace, and other members of the imperial family had obviously taken advantage of this. I recognised Julia Maesa even from where I was sitting, while her dark-haired daughter, the Emperor's mother, filed in behind her. They took seats at the back of the box which was then filled by other dignitaries I did not know, presumably friends and advisers of the Emperor.

Two people who were notable by their absence were the Emperor's cousin, young Alexander, and his mother, Julia Mamaea. That was significant. If the Emperor wanted them to attend, they would have been there. That suggested he did not want them with him. The stories of a rift were obviously true.

The reaction of the crowd to the arrival of the imperial party fascinated me. Normally, an Emperor receives applause and adulation, but Roman crowds have been known to jeer and boo an unpopular ruler. Today, though, the mood was almost one of disdain as if nobody could really summon the energy to shout insults. If Elagabalus had hoped to win popularity by providing free entertainment for the mob, it hadn't worked so far. The Romans had come to expect free games, so the Emperor was doing no more than his duty by paying for this show.

Someone, presumably Julia Maesa, had taken precautions in case things did get out of hand, because the imperial box was surrounded by Praetorians, all dressed in full armour and carrying swords. If anyone was planning an assassination attempt, this would not be where it happened. Anyone who approached the box would not get within twenty paces.

Caecus nudged my arm and leaned close to whisper, "Do you see him?"

"The Emperor? Of course."

"No. The man sitting behind him."

I looked again, scanning the faces. And then I saw the grey-hair and beak of a nose.

"Herennius Muncius," I breathed.

"I doubt he'll try anything here," Caecus murmured into my ear. "It's too public."

I nodded, but I still felt the tingle of apprehension, wondering just how far advanced Muncius' plans were.

I was distracted from my fears by a fanfare of trumpets which announced the start of the entertainment. It began with a parade, scores of musicians, whirling dancers and strutting jugglers leading the way along the full length of the track. Behind them came dozens of brightly painted chariots. The drivers, decked in the colours of their teams, waved to the crowd which now became highly animated, cheers and jeers ringing out depending on the allegiance of the spectators.

Some of the chariots were drawn by two horses, others by four. All of the vehicles looked frail and dangerous. They were built of light wood for extra speed, but this made them liable to fall apart in the event of a collision. I would not have dared drive one of these contraptions, but the men who now received the applause of the crowd had little choice. Most of them were slaves whose only chance of reprieve was to win enough races and earn sufficient prize money to allow them to purchase their freedom.

Ahead of each chariot walked a man holding up a sign which bore the name of the chariot driver and the names of his horses, with details of how many races they had run and how many victories they had achieved.

The noise was incredible, so loud it was impossible to talk to anyone. Bugles sounded, people screamed their support for their favourite drivers, and hands pounded approval. The sound grew to a crescendo when the parade ended and twelve of the chariots took their places for the first race. All eyes now turned to Elagabalus who stood up, holding a white cloth in his right hand. He raised it high, held it for a moment, then let it fall.

At this signal, the gates of the starting stalls sprang open, and the chariots thundered out.

The crowd roared, and the race was on.

This was a contest for two-horse chariots, a taster for the more exalted four-horse races which would follow. It was virtually impossible for us to see the first half of the lap because of the restricted view created by the central spine, but we soon saw the first horses skidding around the turning point at the far end of the long stadium. Hooves flung up sandy earth, wheels skidded, and the drivers urged the horses on with shouts and flicks of the reins. Those reins, I knew, were tied around the drivers' waists, which meant they would be hauled out of the chariot if they crashed, so each man had a small knife to cut himself free. That might save

200

him from being dragged around the arena, but it would not prevent other horses trampling him.

The first crash took place not far from where we sat. Two Blue chariots and a Green had completed the first lap, then a White and Green were battling to reach the turning point. They were neck and neck, and the White's horses veered into the Green's, causing one beast to stumble. At the speed they were going, such a stumble was deadly. The Green chariot swerved, hit the central barrier and fell apart in a spray of debris, the driver being yanked headlong by his panicking horses. The White chariot could not take advantage because the Green horses were now blocking its path to the turn, and the driver was forced to take violent evasive action which unbalanced his vehicle. The chariot rose up on one wheel, then flipped over, shattering as it crashed back to the ground in a shower of broken plywood.

The crowd screamed, some in horror, some in excitement, and the following chariots swerved wildly to avoid the carnage. Another one, a Red, also hit the wall, although the driver did manage to cut himself free of the reins and leap to safety on the central barrier.

One of the stone dolphins was flipped over, its tail pointing skywards, and the race continued, while assistants ran from the central spine to try to clear away the wreckage before the chariots returned on the next lap.

"Those poor men!" Circe exclaimed.

Both drivers were being carried away, their bodies limp. I could not tell whether they were dead, but it seemed likely.

Sextus, sitting on my lap, seemed surprisingly calm. He watched, taking it all in, but rarely becoming excited. I think the occasion was rather overwhelming for him.

A Blue won the race, apparently against expectations, which greatly pleased his team's fans, but didn't go down too well with the bookmakers who had to pay out on an unexpected win.

We did give a cheer later, when a Red driver managed to win the third race, but both children were becoming bored of the spectacle by the time the fifth race ended, so we left our seats and made our way outside.

Circe sighed, "I see now why you haven't taken Sextus to the races before. It's very violent."

"That's what the crowd comes to see," I replied. "It's not as bad as the slaughter in the amphitheatre, but it's still the crashes people love to watch."

We were all in a thoughtful mood as we slowly made our way home. By leaving early, we had avoided the crowds, but I think we all had things on our minds.

For my part, I was thinking about Elagabalus. Since I'd not had a great deal of interest in the races, I'd kept one eye on him, and it seemed to me that he would have preferred to be somewhere else. He had applauded politely when the winning drivers had driven on their laps of triumph, but he'd often seemed to be more interested in talking to Herakles. I suppose it must have been something of a chore for an Emperor who dislikes racing to be compelled to sit through a day of watching chariots hurtle around the Circus, but his attitude was obviously noticed by many in the crowd, and it hadn't gone down too well.

As we walked slowly along the side of the Palatine Hill which was dominated by the sprawling palace complex, I had another pang of regret. There, far from the main entrance, was an unremarkable and unobtrusive doorway. Two Praetorians stood outside, both of them looking bored. Behind that door, I knew, was where Sempronius Rufus, the Juggler, had run his spy network. It was where Fronto had worked, and where I had sent my reports. I wondered who was in charge now and, more importantly, who were their spies concentrating on? Was Primus under suspicion?

I shook my head. There was no way of discovering the palace secrets. Yet thinking of the intrigue which had always consumed the occupants of the Palatine made me think of the Juggler and the mission we had sent Collinus on.

Circe, as ever, seemed able to read my thoughts.

"I wonder if Collinus will be able to find anything?" she mused when we stopped at a small taverna to eat some lunch.

I said, "And I wonder what will happen if he does discover something."

My mother put in, "You two should stop worrying. Take a break from your investigation and enjoy the day."

We followed her advice, taking the children to a public garden at the foot of the Caelian Hill where they could run and play. We spent a happy but tiring time as we joined in the fun,

202

most of which seemed to end up with me lying on the grass with the two children jumping on top of me.

After that, we headed for the magnificent bath house built by the Emperor Trajan. With its ball courts and libraries, it is much more than a simple bath house, and it is almost always busy and noisy. Today, though, there was a smaller crowd than usual, and we arrived in time for the family bathing session when men, women and children were all allowed in at the same time.

We enjoyed a good soak, splashing around with the children, then returned home feeling tired but happy.

"It's been a good day," Circe declared as we at last relaxed in the family room. The rear doors were open, giving us a view of the small garden with its shrubs of jasmine and myrtle. Most of the garden was in shade thanks to the bulk of Primus' home blocking the late afternoon sun, yet the sight evoked many old memories for me.

Entranced, I strolled out into the space where I had played as a boy. It hadn't changed a great deal. The raised beds for growing herbs seemed smaller than I remembered, while the bushes towards the rear were definitely taller. I scrunched across the gravel, heading towards the rear wall, and passed between two of the tall shrubs to take a look at the old gate which led out to an alleyway behind the house.

The gate was there, looking rather old, with rust covering the iron lock, and a wooden batten propped against the gate to delay anyone who tried to break it down from the outside.

I was so preoccupied with memories, the low growl made me jump.

I looked to my right and saw a low, wooden hut with an open entrance which was filled by a very large dog.

"Dentes!" I hissed, immediately appreciating why the beast had been given that name. Its top lip was curled back, revealing rows of huge teeth, and its eyes were glaring redly at me, while the rumble of its growl continued.

I saw the heavy collar around the hound's neck, and I also noticed the links of a chain which I hoped was securely fastened, but neither of those things reassured me. The beast was big and powerful, its black coat smooth and gleaming as if it had come straight from Pluto's realm.

Slowly, my heart pounding, I backed away, sidling back between the bushes. The growls subsided, but my heart rate didn't return to normal until I was safely back inside the house.

"Don't let the children out there," I said to Circe.

In response to her quizzical look, I whispered, "The dog. It is well named."

The doors were soon shut as the short day faded, then we ate a light meal and chatted for a while about inconsequential things.

At last, Circe decided it was time to ask my mother the question we had planned.

"We were thinking you might consider coming back to Africa with us when we go," she said with a broad smile.

My mother looked at each of us in turn, her surprise evident.

"Leave Rome?" she responded. "I have lived here most of my life."

"We know, but we would like you to stay with us. If that is what you want, of course."

"I don't know," my mother said, gently chewing her lower lip.

"Well, why not come with us and stay for a few weeks? If you don't like it, you can always come back."

I put in, "The children would love to see more of you. And so would I."

Fronto had suggested my mother would be glad to get out of Rome if the chance arose, but she still seemed uncertain.

"I'll think about it," she told us. "But I have grandchildren here, too. It is a difficult choice you are asking me to make."

"There's no rush," Circe assured her. "We can't travel for a few weeks yet. The sea would be too dangerous. You would be more than welcome, even if you do decide to stay only for a while."

My mother smiled, but I think that was when I realised it was not really Primus who was the anchor she was clinging to; it was his children. I'd seen little of them, and what I had seen had not engendered any feelings of endearment, but I understood that grandmothers can feel a strong bond. Still, at least she seemed prepared to consider coming to stay with us, and that was something to be grateful for.

As for me, I did not sleep well that night. I tossed and turned, eventually rising before the dawn and quietly pulling on my tunic and cloak. If I couldn't sleep, I thought I might as well do something productive.

To my surprise, I found Caecus already up and about. He was sitting in the atrium, perched beside the *impluvium* pool while he sipped at a cup of watered wine.

"Going out?" he asked me.

"Yes. I want to find the builder, Mallius Tanicus. I thought if I went back down to the *Via Ostiensis*, I could ask around some of the other businesses there. Someone might remember him and know where he's gone."

Caecus shrugged, "I suppose it's worth a try. I'll come with you if you like."

"Thanks."

Old Lucius unbarred the door for us, and we stepped out into the street. The sun was up now, heralding a bright day. The dark outlines of the houses seemed to stand out in brilliant contrast to the azure sky, and I noticed a stork flapping lazily high above the rooftops.

"It's a nice morning for a brisk walk," I declared.

Then I stopped, because my ears warned me that other people had the same idea. From down the street, I could hear the sound of marching feet. Curious, I turned to look down the hill. My heart sank when I saw a group of men marching purposefully towards us. I wanted to turn and run, because they wore the armour and cloaks of the Praetorian Guard.

"Ten of them," I hissed.

Caecus snorted, "I can count."

"Do you know any of them?"

"I'm afraid so."

The troop came to a halt a few paces from us, the men behind the leader spreading out to block our path.

"Well, well," said the man in charge, a tough-looking brute with a heavy brow and brooding eyes. "It's Aelius Caecus, isn't it? I thought you were dead."

205

Caecus said nothing, and the man turned his attention to me.

"And you match the description of Sempronius Scipio. I presume that is your name?"

"Who wants to know?" I asked, affecting a bravado I did not feel.

"I'll take that as a Yes," he said. "You are to come with us."

"Where to?"

His grin did not reassure me at all as he said, "To the palace, of course."

Chapter 21
The Palace

Caecus accompanied me on the long march down to the Palatine. I was reasonably sure the Praetorians had been sent to fetch only me, but the lumpen commander made no objection when Caecus fell in beside me. Perhaps he thought capturing a former Praetorian who had been on the wrong side of the most recent civil war might earn him a reward.

I must admit I took some comfort from Caecus' presence. If he had not accompanied me, I am not sure I would have managed to prevent panic taking hold of me. Even with him there, I was feeling lost and helpless. The only real thought in my mind was that the Praetorians had contented themselves with taking me. Circe, the children and my mother were safe, at least for the moment.

Once I had reassured myself with that small consolation, I tried to focus on my immediate future. Pushing aside mental images of possible torture and mutilation, I tied to work out what might be behind my arrest. Perhaps the Juggler had not been the only person watching Primus' house. Had Herennius Muncius and his fellow conspirators already been discovered? No, that made no sense. Why arrest me and leave Primus unmolested?

These and similar thoughts preoccupied me, but Caecus seemed almost content as he marched in step with the armoured men. He might have been dressed in a cloak and tunic, but he quickly assumed the air of a Centurion.

"I remember you," he said to the squad commander. "Canidius, isn't it? Canidius Frequens?"

The man shot him a frown, then nodded, "That's right."

"You were in the Third Cohort."

"I still am," Frequens told him gruffly. "But I'm a Decurion now, not just a ranker."

"Congratulations. I'm sure you deserved the promotion."

Caecus spoke formally, with no trace of irony or scorn in his voice. It was like listening to a General chatting to one of his men during an inspection.

Frequens said, "You chose the wrong side. Everyone said you'd been killed when the usurper, Macrinus, was caught."

"I nearly was," Caecus admitted. "I took a blow to my head. It left me quite mad for months afterwards."

"You should have stayed away from Rome," Frequens told him.

"Why? What's going to happen? Who are you taking us to see?"

That was the question I had wanted to ask, but it did not elicit a meaningful answer.

"I'm only following orders," Frequens growled evasively. "You'll find out soon enough."

The city was waking up now, and we attracted some curious looks from the people we passed as we marched down the *Vicus Longua*, but everyone made way for us. Nobody is daft enough to block a troop of Praetorians.

The centre of the city was already busy, but all I could think as we circled the Flavian amphitheatre was that it might be the last time I ever saw it. I wondered whether I should try to escape, but there was no point. There were too many guards around us, and where would I go in any case? Someone in power knew my true identity, and they also knew where I was staying.

We reached the palace all too soon, but we did not enter by the main steps. Instead, Frequens led us down the western side of the hill where he made for a less prestigious doorway. The guards admitted us without question, and then we were taken deep into such a labyrinth of corridors, stairways and halls that I soon lost my bearings.

In the days of the Republic, ordinary citizens used to live on the Palatine Hill, but now it is entirely given over to a multitude of inter-connected buildings which form the vast palace complex. Back when I had worked for Sempronius Rufus, I had often been inside one of the lesser areas which housed the old information gathering team, but I had never been admitted to the other parts of the palace. I certainly hadn't envisaged coming here under these circumstances, so I was more focused on who we were being taken to see than on our surroundings. What little I did pay attention to confirmed that everything here screamed of luxury. Wooden panelling, brightly painted wall frescoes, statuettes in gold and bronze, decorated pottery from Greece, and marble floors were all of extremely high quality.

I had expected to see more people, but the route Frequens followed took us through an area which was surprisingly quiet. I noticed a couple of scribes or secretaries, and a slave or two carrying trays of cups or bundles of laundry, but other than those encounters, the only other people we came across were more Praetorians who were acting as guards.

Eventually, we reached a gloomy corridor at the end of which stood a set of closed double doors. These were guarded by two more Praetorians. Frequens signalled to them to let us pass, and the doors were pushed open. The Decurion gestured to Caecus and me to enter. When we stepped through, Frequens followed us, but his men remained outside, and the doors were pulled shut behind us.

The room we entered was, it seemed, an ante-chamber. There was little furniture, only some marble busts of the Emperor which were sitting on tall plinths, and a few couches which had no doubt been provided for the convenience of waiting visitors. There was another set of doors in the far wall, but they were very firmly shut. A series of small windows set high in the wall to our left admitted enough sunlight to let me see that the décor and furniture here were extremely expensive even by the standards of the palace. Whoever waited for us beyond the next doors was obviously a person of importance.

It only took a moment for me to take all this in, but my attention was quickly focused on the man who stood in the centre of the room, obviously waiting for us. He was dressed in a formal toga, the long, heavy cloth draped over his left forearm. Beneath the toga, his tunic bore a wide, purple stripe.

I recognised him instantly, and I could not help coming to an abrupt halt when I saw him.

Because it was Cassius Dio himself.

My mind began racing. I'd convinced myself that Dio must be in league with Herennius Muncius, but Dio was here in the palace. Did that mean the Juggler was completely wrong? Was Herennius Muncius loyal to the Emperor after all? Or was there something more complicated at play here?

209

Dio smiled broadly as he stepped towards me, his right arm outstretched in greeting.

"It's good to see you again, Scipio. And you have brought your large friend."

Decurion Frequens snapped a salute as he reported, "The other man is Aelius Caecus, Sir. He was a Centurion in the Guard. He served the usurper, Macrinus. I thought it best to bring him."

"Quite right," beamed Dio, apparently unconcerned at the news of Caecus' former allegiance.

He clasped my hand, then did the same with Caecus before indicating the nearest couch.

"Let us sit down," he invited.

He took his place at one end, with me beside him and Caecus sitting to my left. Frequens, at a signal from Dio, saluted again, then turned and left the room, closing the door behind him.

"You are no doubt wondering why you are here," Dio began, still giving me his self-satisfied smile.

"You obviously recognised me the other day," I replied warily.

"Yes, although it took me a while. It was when you mentioned you were staying at the home of Sempronius Primus that I began to wonder where I'd seen you before. The name you gave Herennius Muncius meant nothing to me, but I rarely forget a face. When I linked it to the name Sempronius, I eventually remembered where we'd met. You did the Emperor Caracalla a great service in Alexandria."

I decided it would be safer to say nothing, so I kept my mouth shut.

Dio went on, "I wanted to check your file, but the fools who now look after the records in the archives are so incompetent it took them a day and a half to locate it."

I was struggling to maintain my composure now. The file he mentioned would have been the one compiled by the Juggler in the days when he had run the imperial spy organisation.

Dio grinned, "You were an accomplished agent. You speak Latin and Greek, of course, but you are also fluent in Aramaic, and can pass for a native of Syria."

I gave a slight nod, not bothering to tell him I also spoke Punic now, although it was with a Roman accent.

"And you served Julia Domna in Antioch. She seemed very pleased with your work."

"I was little more than a household messenger," I told him, trying to play down that part of my career.

"That's not what she reported back to the Emperor," Dio informed me. "She trusted you."

There was a slight pause before he went on, "I understand you were present when Caracalla was assassinated?"

"Yes. I saw it happen."

Dio nodded, apparently satisfied with my admission, although I could feel a mounting sense of dread. Where was this leading?

"And then you disappeared," Dio remarked. "I spoke to Frequens and some other Praetorians who remember you being in the camp when Macrinus proclaimed himself Emperor, but nobody could recall what happened to you."

Something about the way he said this set off an alarm in my head. Was it possible that Macrinus had not told the Juggler about the mission he had sent me on? If so, I could perhaps gloss over that little episode. Then I remembered what Sempronius Rufus had said when he had turned up so unexpectedly at Fronto's house. He had known about the mission, which meant there must be some reference to it in my file.

I told Dio, "Macrinus wanted me to go to Mauretania to track down the holy man who had prophesied Caracalla's overthrow. He wanted to know who was behind it."

"He suspected it was part of a conspiracy?" Dio asked, apparently no more than curious, although I was fairly sure he was still testing me. In view of the fact that the palace was now controlled by a family who had hated Macrinus and who had been aware of the reasons behind the prophecy, I needed to be very careful here. How much did Dio know of the story?

I said, "Macrinus suspected Julia Maesa had wanted to get rid of him. But if it was a plot, it didn't work out the way it had been planned. Whoever was behind it didn't count on Macrinus persuading Caracalla there was no truth to the story. Nor did they count on Martialis murdering Caracalla."

"So the Usurper suspected Caracalla's aunt?"

"He did, but he had no proof."

211

"But instead of finding that proof, you disappeared?"

It was time for me to bend the truth a bit. More than a bit, if I'm being honest.

I told him, "I didn't see the point in going all the way to Mauretania to look for a prophet who had long vanished. It would have been a waste of time. Besides, the prophecy had come true, so perhaps there was no plot after all."

"You think the gods may have truly given the man a vision?" Dio asked.

"I have no idea," I shrugged. "But I knew Macrinus would have ordered the execution of Julia Maesa and all her family if he'd been convinced they had been conspiring to have him killed. I'd known them from my time in Antioch, so I didn't want to be responsible for their deaths. When he sent me on that pointless mission, I decided to leave the imperial service. I dropped out of sight, settled down and got married."

I couldn't tell whether he believed me or not. I hoped so. I also hoped Caecus would back me up if Dio started asking him questions.

Dio, though, kept his attention on me.

He asked, "Would you mind telling me where you have been for the past four years?"

There was no point in lying to him. Anyone who spoke to Circe would detect her African accent, and all the slaves in Primus' house knew where our home was.

"Leptis Magna," I admitted.

"But now you are back in Rome, and asking questions about your older brother."

That was a statement, not a question.

I sighed, "My mother asked me to come. Primus has had some trouble recently. Someone attacked him in the street and almost killed him. And there have been several threats against him. My mother asked me to find out who is behind it."

"Which is why you were talking to Muncius' man, Vespillo?"

"That's right. He used to work for Primus and left under a bit of a cloud. I didn't know he was working for Herennius Muncius now."

Dio steepled his fingers while he considered his next words, so I took the opportunity to try to turn the tables on him.

I said, "I've answered your questions, but I still don't know why I am here. My reasons for coming to Rome are entirely personal."

Dio, instead of responding, looked past me to where Caecus was leaning forward on the couch, his elbows resting on his knees while he listened intently to our exchange.

"What about you, Aelius Caecus? Frequens said you served the usurper, Macrinus."

"As I served Caracalla before him, and Septimius Severus before that," Caecus answered proudly.

"You were in the Praetorian Guard?"

"Centurion. First Century, Second Maniple, First Cohort."

Even a smug Senator like Cassius Dio had to be impressed with that career outline. Centurions were the best and toughest soldiers around, and to lead a Century in the First Cohort meant Caecus' career had been an impressive one.

"And now you serve Sempronius Scipio?"

I quickly put in, "He's my friend, not a servant."

Dio regarded me curiously, then glanced at Caecus who gave a nod of confirmation.

"Sempronius Scipio rescued me from a life of poverty," he stated calmly.

"Ah, the vagaries of life," Dio smiled.

I said, "You still haven't told us why we are here."

"That is not up to me," Dio replied. "I was merely charged with learning why you are in Rome."

The cunning old fox was giving nothing away. He was obviously acting on the orders of someone at the top of the imperial family, but I had no idea which of them it might be. Julia Maesa, one of her daughters, or even the Emperor himself?

I regarded Dio thoughtfully. Which of them would he pledge his loyalty to, I wondered?

Outwardly, he would proclaim loyalty to the Emperor, but that meant nothing. If he was in league with Herennius Muncius, that suggested he was plotting against the Emperor. But the fact we were sitting in the palace told me there was someone else in the

213

imperial family who was actually behind the plot. That meant it had to be one of the three Julias.

Not the younger sister, Mamaea, I decided. Dio struck me as being a man who would want to be on the winning side, so he would not attach himself to someone whose prospects looked bleak to say the least.

The older sister, Soaemias? No, that didn't ring true either. The Emperor may have been trying to wriggle free of her control, but she was his mother, and all her power derived from that position. There was no way she would want to have him killed.

So I looked Dio in the eye and asked, "What does Julia Maesa want with me?"

"You should refer to her as Augusta," he grinned, nodding approvingly at my guess. "And you can ask her yourself. Wait here a moment."

He rose to his feet, striding towards the further doors. He knocked, then slipped through as one of the heavy doors was pulled open just wide enough to admit him.

Caecus and I waited. We exchanged a look, but by mutual consent, neither of us said a word.

After what seemed an eternity, the doors were pulled fully open by a female slave, a very pretty woman with slender arms and a graceful figure. Her brown hair was braided and tied back to show off her sculpted features, and the long robe she wore was made of finely woven cloth which suggested she was a person of some significance in the imperial household. Emperors and their families often rely heavily on slaves and freedmen and women, presumably because they believe they can trust their loyalty. It doesn't always work out that way, of course, as more than one former Emperor could testify.

This woman, whatever her nominal status, behaved as if she owned the palace.

"Augusta will see you now," she informed us, giving a regal wave of a graceful hand to usher us into the audience chamber.

Nervously, I stood up, took a deep breath, tugged my tunic into shape, and headed into the further chamber. Caecus came with me even though it was not clear whether he was included in the invitation. If I had been him, I'd have stayed outside and played

214

the part of an innocent bystander, but Caecus was clearly made of sterner stuff than me.

The dark wooden panelling on the walls gave this next room an air of gloomy secrecy which the arrays of candles and oil lamps could not dispel. There was a window, but the shutters were firmly closed. Luxurious chairs, couches and cabinets were arranged around a low, centrally placed table which bore a jug and several silver cups. Thick rugs covered the floor, their dark colours adding to the room's imposing atmosphere.

Cassius Dio stood to one side, his hands clasped in a deferential pose, but he gave me a smile of reassurance.

The slave closed the heavy doors behind us, then glided past us to take up position behind the only occupied chair in the room. Beyond that chair, standing motionless against the far wall, were two heavily muscled male slaves, but it was the figure sitting in the chair who drew all my attention.

As I'd guessed, it was Julia Maesa.

She had once been a strikingly handsome woman, and even age had not stolen all her looks, but her grey hair and the faint lines around her eyes betrayed that the Emperor's grandmother was now an old woman.

But, while the years may have taken a toll on her physical appearance since I had last seen her in Antioch, there was no mistaking the cool, calculating intelligence behind her eyes.

There were no niceties involved. After studying me closely for a moment, she launched straight in with her challenge.

"You abandoned the usurper, Macrinus," she said, her voice harsh and cold.

"I left the imperial service after he took power," I nodded.

Maesa's eyes flashed towards Caecus.

"But you did not."

"I was a soldier, Augusta," Caecus replied proudly. "I served three Emperors, and I served each of them faithfully until they died."

It was a good answer, but Maesa was not satisfied, and she continued to question him.

"But you chose to remain loyal to Macrinus after the Army declared my grandson Emperor," she pointed out, her eyes boring into him.

"Macrinus had appointed me to lead his personal guard," Caecus told her. "I was raised to be loyal to my superiors."

Then he gave a shrug as he added, "But the Gods turned against him, and he paid the penalty. For my part, I almost died, and was wandering as a starving beggar when Sempronius Scipio rescued me."

He faced her without fear, and I think the old woman respected him for that. After a long, silent moment, she turned her attention back to me, apparently satisfied that Caecus was little more than a follower rather than a leader.

She was silent for a long moment, her finger tapping the wooden arm of her padded chair while she considered me.

She eventually said, "You are staying at the home of Sempronius Primus?"

"He is my brother," I explained.

"And you are investigating who is waging a personal feud against him?"

"Yes."

"A personal matter then?"

"Very personal," I assured her.

There was another long silence during which her eyes never left me. I made a point of returning her gaze, letting her know I refused to be intimidated even though my insides were churning.

At last, she said, "I do not know what to make of you, Sempronius Scipio. My sister admired you, I know that. She always said you were a man who could be trusted. But can I trust you now?"

"I like to think everyone can trust me to keep my word," I told her.

"But what about your loyalties?" she persisted. "If there was some conflict between your loyalty to Rome and your allegiance to your brother?"

"My brother?" I gasped in astonished relief. I had been worried she was going to mention Circe, but it seemed she didn't know the truth about her identity. That was comforting.

I gave Maesa a genuine smile as I assured her, "I have never got on with my brother. He despises me, and I detest him. I am here because of my mother. The fact that I am helping find out who is threatening Primus is coincidental."

"Really?"

This time, I thought she sounded amused, but I could have been wrong, so I said, "Absolutely. Primus is a very unpleasant character. If it was up to me, I'd leave him to deal with his own troubles."

"But your mother wants you to help him?"

"That's right."

"And you love your mother?"

"Of course."

There was another long silence, and I began to wonder whether that had been a poor answer to give. Maesa's own family had once been close, but recent events suggested there were very definite rifts between her and her daughters.

After some thought, she reached a decision.

"I have a task for you," she told me.

I managed not to display my dismay at hearing that.

"A task, Augusta?" I responded, using her formal title for the first time. A little bit of flattery would not go amiss, I thought.

She said, "Your brother is a client of a Senator named Herennius Muncius."

"So I believe."

Maesa hesitated again, and it struck me she was struggling to choose the right words.

She informed me, "You, of all people, will know that there are often plots against an Emperor."

I nodded, but said nothing, so she went on, "I have reason to believe that Herennius Muncius may be involved in just such a plot."

I made sure my expression showed her my astonishment at that news. In reality, things were beginning to fall into place. Dio wasn't in league with Muncius after all; he'd been keeping a close eye on him on behalf of Maesa.

She added, "And, if your brother is one of Muncius' clients, it may be that he knows something of this."

The Juggler had said more or less the same thing, but I needed to act the innocent, so I said, "I really couldn't say. I have barely spoken to my brother since I arrived. Our few conversations

217

have usually ended in arguments, so we tend to avoid one another."

"Families can be like that," she remarked, revealing something of her private thoughts at last.

I said, "I presume the task you wish me to carry out is to spy on Primus?"

"Very good," she nodded, her thin lips twitching in a cold smile. "My sister always said you had a quick mind."

"I'm not sure I'll be able to discover much," I told her. "As I said, I rarely see my brother. My mother lives in a separate house."

I dared not look at Caecus. He knew Collinus was already investigating Primus' activities, and he also knew the Juggler was snooping around. I hoped the big man was maintaining that blank Centurion's expression he was so adept at.

Maesa snapped, "I do not care about the difficulties. You were once an imperial spy. You have just resumed that role."

If I'd been feeling brave, I'd have asked whether I would be paid for my work, but I didn't feel this was the right time to mention that.

"I will do my best, Augusta," I promised.

"Good. I expect results, Scipio. You will report your findings to Cassius Dio."

She flicked her fingers in dismissal. All three of us bowed our heads, then we retreated through the doors. I breathed a sigh of relief when we stepped back into the ante-chamber and the doors were shut behind us. I supposed this must be how a gladiator feels when he leaves the amphitheatre alive.

But, just like a gladiator, I knew I would almost certainly need to go back into the arena for another bout.

Chapter 22
Strange Encounters

The ante-chamber was empty, but that did not necessarily mean we were alone. I would not have been surprised to learn there were secret spyholes which would allow Maesa or her slave girl to listen in to whatever was said here. Cassius Dio was already speaking, all smiles and flattery, but I did manage to catch Caecus' attention and place a finger over my lips to warn him to silence.

Dio was explaining where I could find his house on the Esquiline.

"Report to me there as soon as you discover what your brother knows of Muncius' schemes," he instructed. "Now, is there anything else you need to know?"

"Actually, there is," I nodded.

I moved back to the couch, sitting down and inviting him to join me. That was a bit presumptuous in view of his Senatorial rank, but my legs were feeling rather weak, and I needed to sit down for a few moments. After only a short hesitation, Dio sat beside me.

I said, "I'd like to know a lot more about Herennius Muncius. As I said, I don't know the man other than from that brief meeting in the forum the other day. What can you tell me about him?"

Dio took a deep breath, then replied, "He is extremely wealthy, even by the standards of Rome. He comes from an old patrician family, and he owns some very extensive estates all through Italia. They are mostly farms and vineyards, but I believe he has interests in some other activities such as metal-working, mining and ship-building."

"But his main house is on the Pincian?" I asked.

"That's right. He has a very large property up there."

"What about family?"

Dio told me, "His wife died a couple of years ago, and he has not yet remarried. He has a daughter who is married to a man from Tarentum. I believe he is a local magistrate down there. They have a daughter, I think. Muncius also has a son, Herennius

Agrippinus. He is a junior member of the Senate, and he is one of the new *aediles*."

"So he will have a chance to organise some Games for the public? Or perhaps to make some other contribution to the city?"

"That is correct," Dio nodded. "The *aediles* are responsible for such things."

"Which will do the Herennius family no harm," I observed. "Especially as the father's money will be able to fund some extravagant shows."

Dio merely smiled, so I went on, "What makes you think Muncius is involved in any sort of plot? If you had proof, I'm sure you would have taken action by now."

Dio's smile faded as he admitted, "We were told by an informer that Muncius was planning some sort of coup."

"Really? So why do you need me if you already have an informant?"

"We *had* an informant," Dio stressed. "Sadly, he was found dead. It seems he was murdered and robbed one evening after leaving Muncius' home."

"I take it you don't believe it was a coincidence?"

Dio shrugged, "Who knows? The streets can be dangerous at night. It was certainly unfortunate. Our informer had told us he had been invited to meet with Muncius and a small number of like-minded people to discuss the future of the empire."

"Which doesn't necessarily mean they were planning a coup," I pointed out.

"No, but our spy believed there was something serious brewing. And, since his death, we have done our best to have Herennius Muncius followed. He is being very cautious, but he does seem to be keeping in with some strange bedfellows."

"Like my brother?"

Dio gave another shrug.

"Sempronius Primus is a known client of Herennius Muncius. It is not unreasonable that a patron should visit an injured client. The problem many of us have with that concept is the frequency of the visits. Herennius Muncius is not renowned for his empathy with others."

"Are you telling me he is unpopular?"

Dio smiled again, but there was a hint of mischief as he said, "Let us say that Herennius Muncius has many acquaintances but few friends. And those friends he does have are bound to him by his wealth."

"He buys friendship, you mean?"

"He is not alone in that," Dio replied. "That is how patronage works, but Muncius is perhaps a prime example of the worst features of the system."

"I presume you have been trying to become one of his close associates? That's why you were with him the other day?"

Dio sighed, "Yes, but he has not yet seen fit to take me into any close confidence. Whether he suspects me, or whether he is merely being his usual aloof self, I cannot say."

After taking a moment to gather my thoughts, I said, "Let us assume for one moment that there is a plot to assassinate the Emperor. There are two things which make it difficult."

"Only two?" Dio smiled.

"Two big ones. First, it would also mean murdering the rest of the imperial family. From what I have learned during my brief stay in Rome, the troops remain loyal to the house of Severus."

"That is true enough," Dio agreed.

"Which necessarily means there must be a lot of people involved, and a lot of money changing hands. Have you seen any evidence of that?"

For the first time, I sensed a little discomfort in Dio. He hesitated for a moment before admitting, "So far, it seems to be a small group of individuals, but that is why we believe the conspiracy is not yet very far advanced. As for money, it is hard to say. Perhaps promises have been made, or perhaps gold has been distributed, but we have no direct evidence of that."

"It all sounds very vague," I remarked.

"Which is why we want you to obtain some solid proof," he reminded me. "Herennius Muncius has paid several visits to your brother's house recently. We suspect Sempronius Primus may know what is going on."

"Then why don't you arrest him and interrogate him?" I challenged.

I regretted the words as soon as I'd spoken them. In Rome, interrogation tends to be by way of torture. Much as I detested Primus, I wouldn't have wished that on anyone.

Dio, though, brushed off the question.

"Things are in a delicate balance just now," he explained. "To arrest a man who has a powerful patron could result in some difficult questions being posed."

"You mean Muncius could appeal to the Emperor?"

"Bluntly, yes. There is already a rift within the imperial family, as I'm sure you know. And Muncius, while he generally does not curry favour with anyone, has been at some pains to remain on good terms with the Emperor."

"Which is another reason you haven't taken more direct action against him?" I guessed.

"Indeed."

"I wouldn't have thought Muncius was the sort to curry favour with a young man of the Emperor's nature."

I was skirting around some sensitive issues here, but I had little choice. I needed as much information as possible if I was to avoid blundering into another messy situation.

Dio said, "You are right again. Herennius Muncius is of the old school. But he has been careful not to offend the Emperor, and has always been very formal and proper. Not to mention that he has also been lavish with financial support for the Emperor's many public displays."

"I saw him in the imperial box at the Circus yesterday."

Dio nodded, "Yes, Muncius bore much of the cost of the races."

That explained the old guy's presence at the Circus Maximus. By sponsoring the event, Muncius was making sure he stayed in the Emperor's good books. Not that this was a guarantee of imperial favour.

I pointed out, "Some Emperors have been in the habit of doing away with rich men and seizing their wealth for the Treasury."

"In the past, that is true," Dio agreed. "But our current Emperor has not adopted such habits."

He didn't say "Yet", but I heard it nonetheless.

"All right. But I said I had two points. The second is the question of who would become Emperor if this alleged plot succeeded. Is Muncius working for his own benefit, or for someone else?"

"A good question," Dio nodded. "The truth is, we do not know. Muncius disapproves of pretty much anything which does not benefit Muncius. So far, he has not allowed himself to be seen having clandestine meetings with any Senator who might have ambitions to the Purple."

"So he could be aiming for the job himself?"

"Very possibly. Which may be why he has attracted few supporters. You see, Muncius' view of his own ability is rather higher than everyone else's view. Not that he is stupid, you understand, but his performances in official positions, such as when he was Governor of Lusitania, were competent rather than spectacular. Barely competent, some would say."

I understood what Dio was saying, but the hypocrisy of politicians never ceased to amaze me. They would smile and fawn over each other one minute, then stab one another in the back the next.

"One last question," I sighed. "Can you give me the names of any of the others you suspect are involved? It might be helpful to know."

"I would prefer not to say," Dio responded. "I could give you several names, but whether they are merely associates or fellow conspirators is impossible to say at the moment. Herennius Muncius often meets with other Senators, but those meetings may be perfectly innocent."

That didn't really help me at all, but I could tell Dio was not prepared to divulge any more. Not that I was given an opportunity to ask any further questions because, at that moment, the outer doors burst open and two people barged in on a wave of anger.

One was a middle-aged woman with dark hair and a fair complexion which I knew belied her eastern origins. She had a prominent nose which dominated her thin face, but at that moment it was her angry eyes that were her most noticeable feature. I recognised her immediately as Julia Mamaea, Maesa's younger daughter. She was wearing a long-sleeved robe of dark blue which fell almost to the gilded sandals on her feet, but even this modest outfit could not conceal her outrage.

"Dio!" she barked, paying no attention whatsoever to Caecus or me. "Someone has tried to kill my son!"

I glanced at the good-looking young boy who accompanied her. He was around thirteen years old and, although he was considerably taller than when I had last seen him several years earlier, he had changed very little, so I had no difficulty recognising him.

This was Alexander, the Emperor's cousin who, if the Juggler was to be believed, was a virtual prisoner in the palace. A prisoner who, according to his mother's outburst, had just survived an attempt on his life.

We had all risen to our feet when the two of them burst in, and Dio did his best to appease Mamaea.

"My Lady!" he exclaimed. "That is awful! Tell me what happened."

"You know what has happened!" she retorted furiously. "That nephew of mine, that monster, has tried to have Alexander killed. Again."

"But how?" Dio asked in a soothing tone, doing his best to calm her.

Mamaea's face was pale with anger as she spat, "By weakening the balustrade around his balcony. It gave way when he leaned on it. If it had not been for his own quick reactions, he would have fallen to his death!"

I looked at the boy, who was doing his best to put on a brave face. He was clearly upset, although whether this was as a result of his near-fatal encounter or because, like most teenagers, he was embarrassed by his mother's fury, I could not say.

Dio asked him, "Did you suffer any injury?"

Alexander shook his head.

"I got a fright," he admitted sheepishly, lowering his eyes.

"I will have some carpenters replace the railing as soon as possible," Dio promised.

"Is that all?" Mamaea snapped, her eyes blazing a challenge.

"What else would you have me do?" Dio asked her reasonably. "Is there any proof the balustrade was deliberately weakened? It is an old part of the palace, and the wood may have been rotten."

Mamaea glared at him, her chest heaving and her arms waving angrily.

"Rotten? You know what is rotten, Dio. The Emperor sees my son as a threat, and will stop at nothing to do away with him."

I glanced at Alexander. He was keeping one embarrassed eye on his mother, while casting surreptitious looks at me and Caecus. He obviously did not recognise me, but I gave him a smile which he returned shyly.

Dio said, "My Lady, the Emperor gave solemn vows in the presence of the Gods that he would make no attempt on your son's life."

"Pah! Do you believe that? The boy is deranged. He sees Alexander as a threat, so he is trying to get rid of him."

Dio, still oozing calm sincerity, said, "But he gave his word to the Praetorians. He would not dare try again. His own life would be forfeit if he did."

"Then who else could it be?" Mamaea snorted in disgust.

It was a good question, and one Dio could not answer.

Mamaea flung her hands up in frustration as she blurted, "If only my nephew would marry and sire an heir of his own, that would solve the problem. But he is too far gone in debauchery for that."

Dio flapped his hands at this.

"My Lady! Please! It is not wise to say such things."

Mamaea at last seemed to realise the danger she was courting, so she lowered her voice a notch.

"I wish to speak to my mother," she stated firmly. "Come, Alexander."

She made for the inner doors, sweeping past us, her fury still driving her on. Alexander, head lowered, dutifully followed her. They burst through the doors which were hurriedly slammed shut behind them, blocking us out.

Dio sighed, "Oh dear. This is not good."

"This is not the first time?" I asked.

"There have been some other unfortunate incidents," Dio admitted. "But do not go repeating that, Scipio. There are more

225

than enough wicked rumours circulating without news of this getting out. Besides, it may be a genuine accident."

"I can keep my mouth shut," I assured him.

It was plain to see that even Cassius Dio was a little flustered by this incident. He bustled us out of the room to where Decurion Frequens was waiting for us.

Dio told him, "Sempronius Scipio and Aelius Caecus can be shown out now."

Frequens had clearly learned not to display any curiosity. He merely thumped a fist to his chest in salute, then led us away. This time, he did not bring the rest of his squad along, so it seemed we were now being trusted.

I couldn't honestly say whether the Decurion was leading us back by the same route. The palace is more convoluted than the Minotaur's labyrinth, but this time we ran into a lot more people.

I heard the commotion before I saw it, the tramp of many feet and an agitated voice raised in consternation. Frequens let out a hiss of annoyance, then hurriedly gestured to us to move to the side of the large, marble-floored hallway we had entered. Quickly, we followed him and took our places beside a tall plinth which bore a sculpted bust of Septimius Severus.

The doors at the far end of the hall were flung open. The people we had heard approaching now came into view, moving quickly.

The Emperor himself was at the head of the column. He wore robes of silk which outlined his slender body and rippled as he moved. His was the voice I had heard, and he was still talking loudly to a short, dark-haired, attractive woman who was walking briskly to keep pace with him. Behind these two came a middle-aged man who wore an elegant tunic, while a cluster of Praetorians, eunuchs and slaves made up the rest of the long column.

"I don't understand!" the Emperor was complaining bitterly. "All I was doing was distributing gifts to the people!"

There was an aggrieved, almost petulant tone to his words. As he drew nearer, I noticed his angry expression was enhanced by the layers of make-up he wore. His face was artificially pale beneath his short, fair hair, but his eyes were outlined with dark kohl, and his lips and cheeks were tinged red.

As they drew near us, I confirmed my initial guess that the woman was his mother, Julia Soaemias. She was now well into her forties but, unlike her younger sister, she had aged well. She had a busty figure which exuded attraction, and I knew her reputation as a predatory sexual woman. Even before her husband had died she had been renowned for her affairs, and I guessed little had changed in that regard. Soaemias, dark-haired, with flashing eyes and a lusty temperament, had taken and discarded more lovers than even she could probably recall. After all, who could refuse the mother of the Emperor?

Now, though, she was doing her best to placate her teenage son.

"It was not your gifts the people scorned, my darling. It was the method you used."

Elagabalus seemed genuinely perplexed. For a moment, he came to an abrupt halt, swinging his gaze directly at his mother.

"What do you mean? Do the people not want gold and precious objects?"

"Of course they do, but you were throwing your gifts from an upper window."

"It was the easiest way to pass them out of the palace," Elagabalus replied, stamping one foot in frustration.

"Perhaps so, Caesar," the well-dressed man put in, smoothly taking up Soaemias' efforts. "Sadly, some of the things you threw down were rather heavy. Some people were injured when hit by the statues and golden jugs you dropped to them. Then others were trampled in the crush as some tried to move out of the way, while others came running in efforts to seize the treasures."

"That is hardly my fault!" Elagabalus protested. "The Urban Cohorts are supposed to keep order in the city. I shall have words with the City Prefect about that."

He swung away again, resuming his angry march. He passed within a couple of paces of where we stood, but he paid no attention to the three of us as we silently bowed our heads in deference. Fortunately for me, Soaemias was too distracted to pay us any more attention than a passing glance before she hurried after her son.

The elegantly dressed attendant did pay more notice of us, but he merely gave us a long-suffering look, then walked briskly in pursuit of the Emperor and his mother. Behind him, the guards and slaves stomped past with impassive expressions on their faces.

We could still hear Elagabalus as he and his entourage moved further into the palace.

"Herakles! Where is Herakles? I need him!"

Herakles, I recalled, was the former chariot driver who was now referred to as the Emperor's husband. I must admit that hearing the young man call the name so plaintively struck me quite hard. I had come into contact with a couple of Emperors in the past, and while I knew they could be megalomaniacs, at least the ones I had known had been clever, capable men in their own way. As far as Elagabalus was concerned, it seemed all the reports I had heard were true.

When the last of the slaves had passed beyond the doors and the chamber was clear, Frequens stepped away from the wall and set off for the exit once again. He did not say a word about what we had witnessed.

"Who was the man who spoke to the Emperor?" I asked him.

"That was Publius Valerius Comazon," Frequens replied gruffly. "He is the Praetorian Prefect."

Which explained why he had been able to address the wayward Emperor with such familiarity. As Praetorian Prefect, Comazon was technically the second most powerful man in the empire. Quite how that played with Julia Maesa and her two daughters, I could not tell.

At last, Caecus and I emerged from the palace and stepped out into the open air of the forum. Frequens said a curt farewell, then vanished back inside, leaving the two of us free to go.

"That," I sighed, "was not at all what I was expecting."

Caecus grunted, "I thought the Augusta was going to have us both executed."

"She still might," I told him. "You heard what she said. She expects results. If I don't turn up some dirt on Primus, she won't be happy."

Caecus was silent for a moment, then said softly, "Things were easier when I was a soldier. I just followed orders. It didn't matter who wore the Purple."

228

I sighed, "Our young Emperor isn't exactly inspiring, is he?"

Caecus' silence spoke volumes.

After a long pause, he ventured, "So what do you intend to do?"

"I don't see that I've got much choice," I replied.

After another pause redolent with suspense, he said softly, "You could always join your brother's plot and remove Maesa and her brood."

I looked at him in horror, half hoping he was joking, but he was deadly serious.

And the worst thing was, I knew he had a point. Even that one, short encounter with the various members of the imperial family had confirmed they were not fit to rule.

The big question was whether the alternative was any better.

Chapter 23
Making Plans

Circe was remarkably calm when we told her what had happened, but my mother was appalled. As it turned out, neither of them had realised anything was wrong because they had no idea we'd been intercepted by Frequens and his band of Praetorians. Perhaps, I reflected, it had been just as well Frequens had found us in the street. If Primus had learned a squad of guards was knocking at his door, he'd have had a fit.

Not that my mother's reaction was exactly calm.

"What has Primus done?" she gasped in horror. "This is worse than I feared!"

"We don't know that he's done anything," I assured her. "That's what we need to find out."

"And what will you do when you do discover the truth?" Circe asked softly.

I could only shrug my shoulders.

"I don't know. We will have a decision to make."

"What decision?" my mother frowned.

Circe told her, "Which side we want to be on."

"Oh."

My mother's eyes were large and round as the implications sank in. To give her credit, she did not begin lecturing me on familial duty. She understood as well as any of us that Primus was swimming in dangerous seas.

"What can we do?" she asked, desperate for reassurance.

"Nothing just now. I want to wait until Collinus returns. We need to know what is going on down at Primus' villa."

I suppose I could have carried out my original intention of going down to the *Via Ostiensis* and searching for clues about the missing builder, but I decided I deserved some rest after that morning's experience, so we stayed in the house, waiting for Collinus to return.

It was a long wait. We passed the time by playing with the children, all of us on edge as the day slowly dragged by. Slaves brought wine and platters of bread, olives and honey, but I must admit I had little appetite for food.

Shortly after mid-day, old Lucius announced that Fronto had come to see us. My friend was smiling as he came into the room, but his expression grew sombre when he saw us.

"Is something wrong?" he asked. "You don't look very happy."

While he drank a cup of wine, I recounted what had happened that morning.

"No wonder you look miserable," he said. "So the rumours about what's going on inside the palace are true?"

"It certainly seems so," I agreed.

"What a mess!" Fronto sighed. "Whatever happens, blood is going to be spilled."

I shook my head in frustration.

"I've seen too much of that," I sighed. "I don't want to see any more."

Fronto shrugged, "It's how it's always been, my friend. Few Emperors die peacefully."

He was right, but that didn't make me feel any better, particularly as we now seemed to be in the middle of whatever was going on. Other people being killed was bad enough, but we were now at risk too.

We made small talk for the next couple of hours. The short day was drawing to a close when we at last heard Collinus return. He arrived looking a little tired from travel, his tunic and trousers crumpled, but otherwise he was his usual self.

As soon as he entered the room, Circe leaped up and ran to embrace him.

"You're back!" she exclaimed happily. "Come and tell us what you found."

Collinus first drained a cup of wine, then gratefully accepted a slice of bread and honey which my mother insisted he eat.

"You've had a long journey," she stated. "So have some nourishment before you tell us your story."

We waited with varying degrees of patience while Collinus dutifully chewed on his bread. He took another swig of wine, then told us, "There is no renovation work being carried out

231

at the villa. It was difficult to get too close without being seen, but there was no sign of any work being done."

His raptor gaze swept around us as he went on, "But there are a great many armed men there. They wore civilian clothing, but they had the look of soldiers about them, and they were very organised. They had sentries posted in the woods around the villa, with patrols making circuits of the grounds at random intervals."

Collinus told us this without any emphasis or emotion, merely reporting facts. What he did not say, but what I knew must have happened, was that he had managed to avoid those guards.

He went on, "I spoke to some of the locals. Nobody knows anything except that Sempronius Primus has let a friend use his villa for a few weeks. Nobody knows the name of this friend, but the owner of the local inn did tell me he'd overheard a couple of the soldiers talking about someone they called, 'The Tribune'."

"I suppose that narrows it down a bit," I said distractedly. "Although not much."

Caecus put in, "There is a Legion based down near the Alban Mount. Could it be men from their camp?"

Collinus shook his head.

"The locals say not. They rarely see men from the Legion as the camp is a few miles further south."

I said, "We shouldn't rule it out, though."

"There is more," Collinus told me. "I did manage to approach the house after dark yesterday. There were lamps lit in the rooms at the rear of the villa. I saw a man sitting there. He was obviously someone of importance, because several other men were standing in front of him, listening to his orders."

"I don't suppose you recognised him?" I asked hopefully.

"No. But I would know him if I saw him again. It would be hard to miss him. You see, he did stand up a little later, and it was plain to see he was a giant."

"A giant?"

"He towered over the other men," Collinus nodded. "His whole body is much larger than anyone I've ever seen. He would not have been able to pass through a doorway without stooping. When I say he was a giant, I mean it."

Collinus, I knew, was not given to exaggeration. If he said the man was a colossus, then I believed him. Especially because I thought I knew the person he was describing.

I looked across at Fronto and Caecus, both of whom wore expressions of recognition on their faces.

"A gigantic Tribune?" I asked them. "Are you thinking the same as me?"

Fronto frowned, chewing his lip, but Caecus nodded, "There is only one person who matches that description. Maximinis Thrax."

There was a short silence while the three of us considered the implications of this news, but Circe asked, "Who is Maximinis Thrax?"

"You haven't heard of him?" I asked in surprise. "I thought everyone knew about him."

"I don't," she scowled, clearly irritated that Fronto, Caecus and I knew something she did not.

"He's very possibly the empire's foremost soldier," I told her. "I've never seen him, but I'm told he is huge. Well over seven feet tall, so they say."

Collinus nodded, "At least that. I'd put it at closer to eight."

I went on, "According to the stories I heard, he joined the army not long after Septimius Severus became Emperor. Apparently, this young giant turned up at the army's winter camp where they were having some contests of strength for a bit of entertainment. The boy claimed he could beat any man the Emperor cared to set against him, and he did. He performed all sorts of feats of strength, and he wrestled dozens of the Legions' best men, beating them all. So the Emperor made him a soldier, and he's spent the years since then rising up through the ranks. The last I heard, he was commanding a Legion up on the Danube frontier."

Caecus put in, "That was a few years ago. He retired after Caracalla's death."

"Retired?" I asked, surprised by this news.

"He was loyal to the house of Severus," Caecus explained, "and he disliked the way Macrinus bribed the barbarians to ensure peace. So he left the army and retired to his estates in Pannonia. I recall Macrinus being very annoyed when he heard about it. It was a serious blow to his credibility as Emperor that such a senior soldier should publicly turn his back on him."

Fronto interjected, "But he returned to the Army."

"He did?"

"Yes, shortly after Elagabalus came to Rome. At the time, many people were sceptical of the claim he was Caracalla's son."

"Probably because he isn't," I murmured.

Fronto nodded but went on, "So Thrax was summoned to meet him. Afterwards, he made a public pronouncement saying he was satisfied the boy was Caracalla's offspring."

I said, "I wonder how much he was paid to say that?"

Fronto shrugged, "Perhaps he retained some loyalty to the Severan family. Whatever his motivation, he was appointed Tribune and given effective command of a couple of Legions."

I understood what that meant. Technically, the Emperor appoints men of Senatorial rank to be Legates in charge of each Legion. But these men hold only short-term appointments, and most of them are not soldiers by trade. The senior Tribune of the Legion is the man who really runs the unit. And Maximinis Thrax was as experienced a soldier as the Empire possessed.

It was Circe who voiced the question we were all thinking.

"But if he's in command of some Legions on the frontier, what is he doing down in Primus' villa?"

For some reason, everyone looked at me to provide the explanation.

"It doesn't make much sense," I frowned. "If Primus and Herennius Muncius are plotting to overthrow the Emperor, why have a supporter of the Emperor's family hidden away at the Alban Mount?"

"Unless he no longer supports the Severans," Circe remarked. "Maybe he regrets his earlier decision."

"That wouldn't surprise me," Fronto agreed. "Thrax is a soldier through and through."

"Which still doesn't explain why he is hiding out in Primus' villa," I sighed.

"One possibility springs to mind," Circe put in.

"What's that?"

"If we assume this man Thrax has been persuaded that Elagabalus is going to ruin the empire, he may have been brought into whatever Herennius Muncius is planning."

I nodded, "That must be it. Muncius may be able to bribe the Praetorians to support him, but the rest of the Army will need to be persuaded. There are thirty Legions dotted all around the frontiers of the empire. There are also Legates and provincial Governors, all of whom have ambitions. Caracalla did a good job of doing away with anyone who showed too much of a desire for power, or too much ability, but that wouldn't stop one or two of them bribing their own troops to proclaim them Emperor instead of Muncius. That's why he needs the backing of a famous and influential soldier."

Caecus agreed, "If Maximinis Thrax gives his support, few would dare argue. And if he persuades the *Legio II Parthica* to support Muncius, the rest of the Army will probably fall into line."

Fronto interjected, "But how is Herennius Muncius going to arrange the coup? I thought the Praetorians still favoured young Alexander."

"Most of them do," Caecus agreed. "But not all. It may be that Muncius has enough money to bribe some of them to carry out the assassinations."

"And once the deed is done," I added, "Muncius will no doubt pay the entire Army a hefty donation."

"That is expected," Caecus confirmed. "Every new Emperor pays the soldiers a reward for swearing loyalty."

Circe sighed, "If anyone is rich enough to bribe the entire Army, it is Herennius Muncius."

Fronto let out a soft whistle.

"What are we going to do?" he asked. "Are you going to tell Julia Maesa?"

"Not yet," I replied. "Much as I dislike my brother, I don't want to see him being dragged away for execution."

I glanced at my mother, noticing her pale face and set expression as she kept her jaw firmly clenched. I think she must have understood that it would be difficult to save Primus if he really was involved.

Unless we took his side, which went against my every instinct. I'd heard lots of stories about Elagabalus, but I had years of personal experience of my brother's untrustworthy nature.

With a sigh, I decided, "I suppose I'm going to have to go and talk to Primus."

The *major domo*, Mardonius, must have been busy. For once, he did not loom out of the shadows when I went through the door to Primus' part of the house. But I did meet him as I was crossing the internal courtyard. He was showing a guest back to the house's main door, leading the way with an oil lamp held high.

By the light of that lamp, I recognised the visitor. The tall, grey-haired man who walked with an upright posture, head held high to allow him to peer down his patrician nose at lesser mortals, was none other than Herennius Muncius.

Behind the Senator came four burly guards. Vespillo was not among them, nor was the aggressive ape who had challenged Caecus in the forum, but I vaguely recognised the others.

My heart sank at the sight, but there was no way of avoiding them. I was in the middle of the courtyard, and they were coming straight towards me. My best course of action, I decided, was to bluff it out.

Ignoring the hostile glare from Mardonius, I gave Muncius my broadest smile as he approached.

"Good evening, Senator! How nice to see you again. It's so good of you to come and visit Sempronius Primus."

Muncius stopped, his eyes regarding me with cold contempt.

"You gave a false name when we met," he accused, not bothering with any polite greetings.

"Oh, it's not a false name," I assured him. "It's the name I use back home."

"You are Sempronius Secundus," he rasped. "And you were an imperial spy."

So Primus had told him that? I could feel my insides begin to squirm, wondering whether Muncius was ruthless enough to have me killed right here.

Concealing my fear as best I could, I assured him, "That was years ago. I left the imperial service when Opellius Macrinus

236

became Emperor. I've had nothing to do with that sort of thing ever since then. Besides, you must know the Emperor replaced everyone who worked in old Rufus' department."

I did my best to keep my voice casual and conversational. Muncius continued to stare at me, but I added breezily, "Well, it's nice to see you, and I'm sorry for the misunderstanding the other day. But now, since I assume my brother must be free, I need to bring him up to date on how my investigation is going."

"Your investigation?" Muncius frowned, suspicion showing in every line on his forehead.

"Into the attack on him," I explained. "I'm sure I mentioned that is why I am here."

Muncius gave me a cool nod. Or not so much cool as glacial.

I smiled, "Well, I'd better give him the latest. Good to see you again, Senator."

I moved past him, walking at a steady, confident pace. After a moment, I heard their footsteps on the gravel as Mardonius resumed leading them back to the front door where I presumed Muncius had a litter waiting to transport him back to his luxurious home on the Pincian.

Once back inside the house, I took a moment to gather my wits. Had Muncius come on a routine visit? He'd clearly mentioned me to Primus, and my brother had told him all about me. But did that mean they suspected me of spying on them? I sincerely hoped not, but I waited a few moments to give Muncius time to get out of the house before I continued.

Because I was about to let Primus know he was in trouble.

I needed to take several deep breaths before I entered Primus' reception room. It was the chamber where I'd first met him, the one with all the scenes of military and divine power painted on the walls. He was sitting on his couch, his crutches close at hand, while a slave scurried around, clearing away the empty cups and dishes.

"Close the shutters!" Primus barked at the man. "It's getting cold in here."

The slave dutifully put down the dishes he had gathered and scurried to the side of the room. Reaching up, he closed the shutters on the windows which contained lattice frames rather than glass. He pushed home the bolt, then repeated the exercise on the high window on the rear wall. This done, he picked up the dishes and scurried from the room.

Once we were alone, Primus treated me to his most ferocious scowl.

"What do you want now?" he growled.

I took the seat opposite my brother.

"I came to warn you," I told him.

"Warn me? About what?"

"About your association with Herennius Muncius."

"That's none of your business!" Primus snapped, his eyes blazing.

"Actually, it is. You see, I was arrested this morning and taken to the palace where I had a very uncomfortable interview with a certain Julia Maesa Augusta."

That shocked him. I could almost see the blood draining from his face as he stared at me.

I leaned forwards, hoping to convince him of my sincerity as I went on, "Look, Brother, I'm only here because Mother asked me to help. She's worried about you. But I'll bet she didn't know just what you had got yourself involved in. I don't know either, and I don't want to know. But, for Mother's sake, I thought I'd warn you that Julia Maesa has people keeping a close eye on your Senator pal. If I were you, I'd get out of this mess as soon as possible."

Primus had recovered just enough to hiss, "It's not as easy as that, Secundus. What did Julia Maesa want from you?"

"She wants me to spy on you. She thinks you are up to something, and she wants me to find out what it is and who else is involved."

I held up a cautionary hand before he could interrupt me.

"Don't worry. I'm not going to tell her anything. I've been close to Emperors and their families before now, and I want nothing to do with them. All I want now is to get back to Africa as soon as I can."

His eyes were hard glints of suspicion as he studied me. I really wanted to ask him why Maximinis Thrax was staying at his villa, but I reckoned that would place me in even greater danger. It was, for the moment, best to let Primus think I knew nothing.

238

"You do what you like," I told him. "But leave me out of it. I didn't want to come here, and I don't want to stay, especially if you are playing dangerous political games."

Now I saw his lips curl in a smile I recognised. It meant I was in trouble.

"You need to stay," he told me. "In fact, I insist upon it."

"What do you mean?"

"I mean you and your family must stay in the house. Do not venture outside. My guards will have orders not to let you out."

"What? You can't do that!"

"Of course I can," he sneered. "This is my home."

"Then tell me why. Is Julia Maesa correct?"

"Correct about what?" he retorted, plainly enjoying himself.

"She thinks your patron is planning to assassinate the Emperor."

Now Primus grinned, his expression like that of a gambler whose throw of the dice had just come up Venus.

"That is preposterous!" he barked. "Nothing could be further from Herennius Muncius' mind. I can assure you he has no intentions of doing that."

"Then why keep me prisoner here?"

"Because Herennius Muncius distrusts you. Come to that, so do I. We do not want you wandering the streets, poking your nose into my business."

If anything, that only confirmed to me that, in spite of Primus' vehement denial, he and his patron were up to their necks in something.

"And how long are we to be held captive?" I demanded.

"You are guests, not captives," he smirked. "And it won't be for very long, I can promise you that."

I didn't like the sound of that at all.

"How long?" I persisted.

"As long as necessary," he hissed in response. "Now leave me alone. I have important matters to attend to."

We stared at one another for a long time, but I knew he had me beaten. Eventually, I stood up, gazing down at his bloated figure.

"You're a fool," I told him. "Goodbye, Brother."

He did not reply.

Chapter 24
Choosing Sides

Five pairs of expectant eyes studied me when I returned to the family room.

"Well?" Circe asked.

With a heavy sigh, I slumped down onto the couch beside her.

"It's not good," I told her.

As concisely as I could, I recounted my encounter with Herennius Muncius and my meeting with Primus.

"He wants to keep us out of the way until it's over," Circe reflected, her voice calm as if she admired Primus' tactics.

My mother protested, "He can't do that!"

"He's doing it," I assured her.

"Didn't you ask him about Thrax?" Fronto enquired.

"I didn't see the point. If he knew we'd discovered Thrax is staying at his villa, he might go running to tell Herennius Muncius. And, having met that man up close twice now, I think I know what his next command would be."

I slid one finger across my throat as I said this, and nobody disagreed.

My mother, still obviously shocked, ventured, "Perhaps we will all be safe if we stay here, then."

"Perhaps," I nodded, not knowing what else to say.

Circe, always at her best in circumstances like this, said to Fronto, "You will not be kept here, I'm sure. Perhaps you could take a message to Cassius Dio?"

Fronto's face was serious as he gave a cautious nod.

"I suppose so. But what do I tell him?"

Before Circe could suggest anything, we were startled by a faint knocking sound on the rear doors which led out to the garden.

We all twisted our necks to stare at the wooden doors.

"It'll be the dog," I suggested.

But the sound came again, and it was definitely a human hand rapping softly on the wood.

Caecus and Collinus both stood up and moved to the back of the room. They may have disliked one another, but they worked with a mutual understanding as they took up positions. Collinus drew his dagger, standing with his back to one of the doors while Caecus reached for the locking bar and quietly lifted it out of its brackets. Then he whipped the door open, stepping back to avoid any potential attack.

Instead, we saw the dim outline of a man who cautiously poked his head into the room.

He had a young face, perhaps not yet twenty years old, and he let out a stifled yelp when Caecus grabbed his tunic and hauled him inside, quickly kicking the door back into place. Collinus' blade was at the lad's throat in an instant.

"No!" my mother shouted as she twisted round in her seat to see what was happening. "Leave him! That's Petrus."

The poor lad was terrified. Collinus withdrew his dagger but kept it ready, while Caecus refused to release his grip on the visitor.

My mother insisted, "It's all right. Petrus is one of the house slaves. Let him go."

Warily, the two men stepped back a pace, leaving Petrus gulping for air as he fought to gather his wits.

Circe quickly took charge, waving the young lad forwards.

"Hello, Petrus," she said with a smile. "I think I've seen you in the garden before."

"Yes, Lady," he mumbled, wringing his hands together nervously. "I look after Dentes."

My mother put in, "Petrus raised the dog from a puppy. He's very good with animals."

The lad gave her a grateful smile, but his eyes sought me out. Taking a deep breath, he tried to stand more upright.

"I came to warn you, Sir," he announced, his voice gaining a little strength as he became more confident that he was not about to have his throat slit.

"About what?"

"I was in the garden, Sir, Getting ready to unchain Dentes for the night. I heard the master discussing you with his patron."

Now he had everyone's attention.

"You heard them talking about me?" I asked, frowning. "How?"

"The window shutters had not been closed, Sir. I know I shouldn't have done it, but I climbed up on top of Dentes' kennel and listened through the open window."

I nodded. The windows in Primus' private meeting room had wooden frames to keep birds and cats out, but the latticework of the frames allowed air and light to be admitted. I recalled the slave being ordered to close the shutters when I'd first entered the room.

Petrus said, "I didn't understand it all, Sir, but I did hear them grumbling about some setback they'd suffered."

"What sort of setback?" I asked.

"I don't know, Sir. I'm sorry. But my Master's patron did say it made him very worried about what you are doing here. He told the Master to keep you in the house and not to let you go outside."

"I know," I nodded. "I spoke to your Master shortly afterwards."

Petrus nodded, but continued, "There's more, Sir."

He hesitated, glancing around at the others, particularly Caecus and Collinus.

I told him, "It's all right. You can speak openly here. We are all friends."

"Yes, Sir. I heard you were asking about Vespillo. Mardonius was laughing about how he'd tricked you by not telling you the big bully works for Herennius Muncius."

That, I thought to myself, was one I owed Mardonius for.

"He should never have got away with what he did to Cassia," Petrus stated, his words red with anger.

"Who? Vespillo?"

"Yes, Sir. He beat her so badly she couldn't work for two days. And she had bruises all over her body for weeks afterwards."

I glanced at my mother who gave a sad nod of her head before lowering her eyes guiltily. Not that there was anything she could have done about it, but I knew she felt badly about the way Vespillo had treated Primus' female slaves. I presumed Cassia was the last of those victims who had been harmed before Primus transferred him to Herennius Muncius.

Petrus went on, "They are an evil lot, Sir. Vespillo, Herennius Muncius and your brother."

I looked at him with renewed respect. For a slave to say such a thing about free men in general and his owner in particular was to invite a flogging at the very least. Being branded or sent to the mines was a more likely fate. By saying what he had, Petrus was putting his life in our hands.

I told him, "I think we are all coming to realise that, Petrus. But you said there was more."

Yes, Sir," he nodded. "I heard Herennius Muncius tell the Master that, if you did leave the house, he would ensure that you met with a fatal accident."

We all looked at one another.

Trying to appear calm, I said, "I heard someone else who knew Herennius Muncius met with just such an accident."

Petrus said, "He laughed about it, Sir. He said it would look like a robbery and that you'd end up with a knife in your guts."

My mother interrupted, "What did Sempronius Primus say about that?"

Petrus lowered his head as he replied softly, "He did not argue, Lady. All he said was he'd do his best to keep Sempronius Scipio in the house, but if he got out, he would need to take his chances."

My mother sat rigidly, outrage emanating from every pore.

Petrus still wasn't finished. Looking up again, he said to me, "But even if you stay, you will not be safe, Sir. I heard Herennius Muncius say that, once it was all over, he would make sure you never returned home again."

I suppose I should have been shocked, but the words came as no real surprise. Herennius Muncius had struck me as a ruthless bastard right from the start. He might be wary of killing us before his coup had taken place in case it attracted attention, but once he'd seized power, he'd make sure we were included among the enemies he would dispose of.

I glanced at my friends and family, but there was no need to explain the situation. Everyone knew there was a blood-letting after most new Emperors took the throne, with the death toll often running to thousands, so the five of us would scarcely be noticed among the carnage.

Petrus looked miserable as he said, "I'm sorry, Sir."

"It's not your fault, Petrus," Circe assured him. "We are grateful you had the courage to come and tell us."

"I just want it to stop," he said helplessly. "They treat people like animals, and it's not right."

I'd never heard a slave speak so openly, but I could sympathise with his opinion. There was, though, another worry on my mind.

"Did they say anything about when it would be over?" I asked him.

"Before the Ides of March, Sir. That's what Herennius Muncius said. He was annoyed at the delay, but he wanted it to be over before the Ides."

"Beware the Ides of March," I muttered darkly.

Circe gasped, "That's only a week away! I thought Dio said he was sure the plot was only in its early stages."

I shrugged, "He was wrong, I suppose."

I looked at my mother, whose eyes were damp with tears.

"I'm sorry," I told her. "I didn't want this, but I think Herennius Muncius has just forced us to take sides. Even if we offered to join him, I doubt he'd trust us."

All she could do was nod her head.

I gave Petrus a searching look.

"Was there anything else said that might help us?"

He shook his head.

"I'm not sure, Sir. I did hear the Master say he wanted someone named Marius Vindex added to the list of people who should be executed once they had succeeded. Does that help?"

"Not really," I sighed. "It's no surprise, but it has no bearing on our situation."

Petrus gave me an apologetic look as he went on, "They did say some other stuff about the last plan not working as they'd hoped, but they seemed confident they would succeed soon."

He shrugged helplessly, "I don't know what that meant, Sir."

"Neither do I," I admitted glumly.

"Can I ask one thing, Sir?"

I nodded, "Of course."

Petrus hesitated, his eyes glancing to Circe and my mother as if hoping they would support him with whatever he wanted to know.

Then he fixed his gaze on me and said, "If you find a way to get out, Sir, would you take me and Cassia with you? And Dentes, of course."

I wasn't sure how to respond. Stealing my brother's slaves hadn't been part of my plans at all, but I supposed things could not really get much worse for us than they already were.

I told him, "If I can find a way to escape, yes."

Fronto sighed, "That's a big *if!* What can we do? Do you want me to go to Dio?"

"Not yet," I told him.

"Why not? Surely you know enough now?"

Speaking softly, I said, "Everything we have rests on the word of a slave. I'll not put Petrus at risk after what he's done for us."

I noticed Petrus give a great gulp, but everyone else nodded in understanding. No Roman court would take the word of a slave unless that slave was first subjected to torture. Petrus did not deserve that.

"Then what are you going to do?" Fronto pressed.

I said, "I need to find some positive proof of what they are planning. We still have no idea what Primus is up to."

"Thrax," Fronto reminded me cryptically.

"If we tell Maesa about him, that could start a war. She'd need to send troops to deal with him. I can't see the rest of the Army accepting that. For all we know, he's already got the lads of *II Parthica* on his side."

"I'd be surprised if he didn't," said Caecus. "The Second Legion is Rome's only reserve force. It always stays near Rome. To arrange a coup without getting their support would be dangerous."

Circe said, "It depends on how secretive the conspirators have been. Perhaps they have not yet contacted the Legion. After all, the Praetorians don't seem to know anything about a plot."

Thinking aloud, she added, "And there is always a chance Thrax might be able to explain away his presence."

246

Fronto asked, "Then what do you propose?"

I gave him my most confident smile as I said, "I have an idea. I think there might just be a way we can get out of this without anyone getting killed."

Caecus gave a snort, letting me know what he thought of that hope, but Circe eyed me curiously, while hope flared in my mother's eyes. It was that hope which compelled me to continue.

"What are you thinking?" Circe wanted to know.

"I'm thinking I need to find a way to get out of the house without being seen."

At that, Petrus blurted, "I could help you get out. If you sneaked down into the garden before dawn, I can help you get over the wall. We could all get away."

"No," I told him. "Just me. If we all tried to leave, someone would hear us. We have all our slaves with us, as well as our children. And even if we did get out without being caught, where would we go?"

He looked crestfallen, but I told him, "But if you can get me and Caecus out, I think we might be able to find a way we can solve the problem peaceably."

Petrus did not look convinced, but he gave a submissive nod. He was, after all, a slave, and I was a free citizen.

Circe was looking at me with narrowed eyes as she demanded, "And where do you think you are going to go?"

"I'm going to see Maximinis Thrax," I told her.

Chapter 25
Just Like Old Times

That night, Circe and I made love with a passionate frenzy because we both knew it might be the last time we could share any intimacy. Even afterwards, as we lay side by side in the darkness, I could feel the tension in her body. Circe was normally unflappable in a crisis, but what I planned to do was clearly worrying her.

I reached out to put an arm around her, moving close so our naked bodies were touching, my chest against her bare back.

"It will all work out," I whispered.

"There are too many unknowns," she replied softly. "You are taking a big risk."

"No bigger than staying here."

"That's true," she sighed. "But you could always send word to Cassius Dio. He would ensure some action is taken."

"Action which is likely to end with Praetorians storming this house and killing everyone they find," I countered.

She shuffled round until she was lying with her face close to mine.

"Something else is bothering you," she whispered. "I can tell. What is it?"

"It's just that a couple of things don't make sense," I admitted with a sigh.

"Like what?"

"Like why the Emperor is still trying to kill his cousin after promising the Praetorians he would leave the boy alone. According to what Fronto told me, some of the Guard were prepared to execute him for attempting to have Alexander murdered. Surely he must realise they will blame him if the boy dies? He won't outlive the lad if one of his attempts does succeed."

Circe suggested, "Maybe he isn't thinking rationally. He does seem rather unstable. His jealousy might be overriding his common sense."

I had to admit she had a point. What little I'd seen of Elagabalus certainly didn't inspire confidence that he was entirely rational.

I said, "The other thing is what Primus said to me about Herennius Muncius having no intention of assassinating the Emperor."

"He would say that, though, wouldn't he? You don't expect him to admit it, do you?"

"No, but it's the fact that he said it so definitely."

"You've told me often enough you don't trust your brother," Circe pointed out. "He was lying to you, that's all."

"I suppose so. He's not renowned for telling the truth, that's for sure. It's just the way he said it sounded very convincing."

"That's probably because he's had a lot of practice at telling lies."

I had no answer to that, but my silence told her I was still worried.

"All right," she said. "Let's assume he was telling the truth for once. If he was, what does it mean? What are they up to?"

I sighed, "That's what puzzles me. Julia Maesa and Cassius Dio seem convinced they are planning a coup, and the Juggler has hinted at the same thing. But if they are planning something else, I can't work out what it is."

With a soft chuckle, Circe suggested, "Maybe we should kidnap Primus and have Caecus beat the truth out of him."

"That's a nice thought," I grinned, "although not very practicable in our current circumstances. I just wish I had more answers and not so many questions."

"You are overthinking things, my love," she said.

"It's hard not to," I replied.

"Then let me try to take your mind off things for a little while."

I wasn't sure I had recovered from our earlier lovemaking, but my body responded as soon as she rolled on top of me, pressing herself against me. Once again, we joined our bodies in another bout of gentle but very passionate sharing of physical love until exhaustion left us lying close together on the rumpled bed.

Feeling both physically and emotionally drained, I lay on my back, staring up into the darkness. Circe had one long leg draped across my thighs, her hand resting on my chest.

"Make sure you come back in one piece, Scipio," she whispered.

"I promise," I replied.

"It's a long time since you've done anything like this, so try to remember all the tradecraft you learned when you were a spy. It should come back to you."

"I haven't forgotten it," I assured her.

After a moment's silence, she said, "I want you to know that if anything happens to you, I will kill Primus myself. Then I'll go after Herennius Muncius."

She was not serious. At least, I hoped she was not.

I pulled her even closer, savouring the warmth of her body against mine.

"Nothing will happen to me," I promised.

After that, I drifted into a dreamless sleep, but I was woken before dawn when Caecus knocked gently on our door.

Rousing myself, I pulled on my loincloth, tunic and cloak, slipped my feet into a pair of woollen socks and picked up a pair of boots. Sandals would be no use where I was going, but Lucius had warned us that Primus had two of his thugs guarding the main door to prevent us leaving, so I would need to move silently until I was out of the house.

Circe had tugged on her dress and yanked a comb through her hair by the time I was ready.

I could barely see her in the pre-dawn darkness, but I heard her bare feet padding across the floor as she moved to the door.

Caecus was waiting, holding his own boots in his hand, and Collinus, inevitably, had decided to tag along to make sure Circe remained safe.

Silently, we felt our way down the stairs, cut across the rear of the atrium, then entered the family room.

"I hope Petrus has that bloody dog under control," I hissed.

Collinus unbarred the doors while Caecus and I tugged on our boots. Then, after a final embrace and a lingering kiss with Circe, I stepped out onto the gravel of the garden.

Turning to look back, I told Circe, "Kiss the children for me."

"I will."

250

I hesitated, expecting to hear Dentes growling, but there was only silence. Moving on the tips of our toes, Caecus and I crossed the garden to the row of bushes.

"Petrus?" I called softly.

"Here, Master."

"Where is Dentes?"

"With me. He'll stay quiet, but can you let him get a good scent of you? That way, he won't bark when you return."

I almost said something about his level of confidence that we would manage to get back, but the sound and feel of the big dog left me speechless.

It came up close, and I froze to immobility as its wet nose snuffled around my hands. I dared not look down at it, fearing any movement might trigger a snarl and a snapping of jaws around my hand. Dentes, though, soon lost interest in me and, encouraged by Petrus, gave Caecus the once-over as well. Then, in response to a whispered command from the young slave, the dog lay down on the gravel, making barely a sound.

"Wait a moment," Petrus told us.

I could just make out his shadow in the gloom as he moved to the rear wall, and I heard the scrape of wood on stone.

"I have a ladder," he told me.

"Can't we use the gate?"

"The lock is rusted, Master. And your brother has the key."

So we climbed the ladder, moving as slowly and quietly as we could. Once at the top, I peered over the wall. It was a drop of some ten feet, I knew, so I swung myself over the wall, gripping the top with both hands, and dangled down at full stretch. Closing my eyes and whispering a prayer to Fortuna, I let go and dropped down into the alley. I landed with a thud which I thought would wake the entire street, but I managed to stay on my feet and didn't twist anything. Caecus dropped down beside me a moment later.

"I have no idea how we'll get back in," he muttered.

But we were out, and now we needed to move.

The sky was lightening in the east now, faint tinges of rosy pink creating shadows and outlines where there had been only blackness a few moments earlier. By the time I had led the way along narrow alleys I dimly recalled from my boyhood, we were able to see enough to walk normally. We had travelled in a wide circle around Primus' house, hopefully avoiding any prying eyes which might have been watching for us. Now, as the first of the city's early risers began to leave their homes and walk the streets, I began to relax.

"Don't hurry," I warned Caecus. "We don't want to draw any attention to ourselves."

We had a fair distance to go. We walked across the city to the Porta Capena. Through this gate, we would be able to follow the *Via Appia* which heads south from Rome. By the time we reached this ancient portal, there were a lot of people out and about, and we had to jostle our way through a milling crowd until we reached a stable just beyond the gate. Here, we bought a couple of horses. As I'd expected, the ostler attempted to charge us a ridiculous amount for a couple of nags, but one thing my recent years with Circe had taught me was how to judge horseflesh. We bred horses on our estate, and I'd learned a lot from the experts we employed, so I was able to point out the mounts I wanted, and to haggle for a reasonable price.

"We'll be returning the horses in a day or two," I told the disgruntled horse trader. "You'll make a profit on the deal."

He still managed to grumble, but I left him to it. It was time for us to go.

I'd learned how to ride many years before, although I would never describe myself as an expert. Some of the locals around Leptis Magna are superb horsemen, and I knew I'd never match their skill, but I had learned enough to be confident on horseback, even with a spirited mount like the tall, brown beast I'd selected for this trip. Caecus had spent most of his life as a foot soldier, but he had sometimes been required to ride on horseback, so he sat astride the docile mare I'd chosen for him with only a little reluctance.

"Ready?" I asked him.

"I'll manage," he grunted.

"Then let's go," I grinned.

I felt good. Naturally, I was worried about Circe and my family, but I hoped they would be safe enough. It was me that Herennius Muncius was concerned about, and I had managed to evade his clutches for the moment. A great sense of freedom swept over me as I urged the horse into a canter.

The pace I set was fast by the standards of most travellers. Romans usually reckon on a day's travel to reach the Alban Mount, but that is for people who travel in litters with a long retinue of slaves walking behind them. Carts and wagons move slowly as well, but Caecus and I were able to urge our horses into a canter whenever the road ahead was clear of other travellers. We were often held up, but we still made better time than most of the road's occupants. The pace must have made Caecus suffer, but he never complained.

The ride to the Alban Mount is a pleasant journey. We were fortunate that, with the *kalends* of March now past, the weather was improving. The sky was largely clear of clouds, the sun bright and warm, and there was a definite feeling that spring had arrived.

Beyond Rome's gates, we passed a miniature city of tombs, some of them magnificently decorated. Romans are never buried inside the city walls, so there are hundreds upon hundreds of tombs lining the road on the first part of the journey. Once beyond them, though, we were out into open countryside.

About twenty Roman miles south of the city, the Alban Mount towers above the surrounding land. Its slopes are still heavily wooded, even though a lot of trees have been cleared to make way for the numerous villas built by wealthy Romans who use these second homes to get away from the heat and bustle of the city. Even Emperors have built retreats for themselves in this stunningly beautiful part of Italia.

But it's not only the superb scenery which attracts Romans to this place. Part of the fascination of the area has to do with the history surrounding it. Legend has it that this was where the town of Alba Longa was founded by the son of Aeneas, the Trojan who escaped the sack of his home city. Generations later, the twins Romulus and Remus were born there, but the baby boys were set adrift on the river to dispose of them when their wicked uncle seized the kingship. The polite version of the story says they were rescued from death by a she-wolf who suckled them and kept them alive. The more common legend among the ordinary citizens is that it was a prostitute who found and rescued them, because the

Latin word for "wolf" is also slang for a prostitute. Of course, this version doesn't sit well with the more prudish historians, so the legend of the she-wolf is the official story now.

Whatever the truth, the boys founded Rome, then Romulus killed Remus in a fight to establish supremacy, and the legend of Rome began. Needless to say, the later Romans fell out with their relatives in Alba Longa, resulting in a war which was ended when the old settlement was razed to the ground and its inhabitants either killed or enslaved. This was one of the earliest examples of Rome's great tradition of ending its wars in this manner.

Nowadays, there is no sign of Alba Longa at all, not even any ruins. The ridges and valleys of the mountainside are occupied by villas and a few farms, and nobody knows where the ancient town might once have stood.

There are temples and shrines out here as well, so we found the road quite busy with pilgrims in addition to the dozens of wagons which were loaded with the produce demanded by Rome's insatiable appetite. This slowed us a fair bit, but it was still only a little way past mid-day when we reached an inn which sat beside the road close to the Alban Mount. This place was a proper *mansio*, a large establishment with stables for horses, quarters for slaves, and more elegant rooms for wealthy travellers who could also avail themselves of the inn's common room where food and drink were served.

After leaving our horses with a young stablehand who promised to feed and water them, Caecus and I made our way into the common room. It was busy because this place was a well known resting point, but we found a table where a serving girl brought us bowls of broth and hunks of dark bread.

Neither of us spoke much. I was preoccupied with what I faced, and we could not risk talking about our mission in case we were overheard. So I spent much of the time between mouthfuls looking around the room at our fellow diners. There were a couple of merchants who were discussing the difficulties of the trade in leather goods, a scattering of pilgrims, and a man in an equestrian tunic who had a young woman with him. She might have been his daughter, I suppose, although my initial response was to place her as his mistress. She certainly seemed overly affectionate to be his daughter.

There was one other man sitting on the far side of the wide room who drew my attention. He was alone, and I caught him glancing across at us once or twice. He was in his twenties, I guessed, with dark hair and smooth features. He was wearing a nondescript tunic, and had a cloak draped over the back of his chair.

"Have you seen that fellow before?" I asked Caecus in a low whisper.

He looked around, staring directly at the man who now had his gaze intently focused on his cup of wine.

"I don't think so," he replied after a moment.

"I have," I informed him. "He was hanging around outside the stables when we left Rome."

"Are you sure?" Caecus frowned. "There were a lot of people there."

"I'm positive," I told him.

He shrugged, "So what? The *Via Appia* is the main road south from Rome. Lots of people use it."

"But he must have waited until we'd left before he went in and got a horse of his own."

"You think he's following us?"

"It's very possible," I nodded.

Just as Circe had said, I was slipping back into the habits I'd developed when I'd been sent to spy on the Parthians. Living a solitary life, always fearing discovery, you tend to pay a lot of attention to places and people around you.

Caecus asked me, "If he is a spy, who is he working for, do you think?"

"I'm not sure. It could be Muncius, or maybe Julia Maesa. But at least he is on his own. We should be able to shake him off."

As soon as we finished our meal, I rose to my feet and led Caecus outside, heading for the stables at a brisk walk.

There were several other horses in the stalls, so I asked the stable boy, "Which of those belongs to a young man who has ridden down from Rome on his own?"

I slipped him a silver denarius as I spoke, so he was happy to point to the nearest animal, a black gelding with a white blaze on its forehead.

"That one, Sir."

255

"Do me a favour," I told him. "I think he'll be coming to collect it in a few minutes. Try to delay him a bit if you can. Perhaps have some trouble adjusting the saddle girth."

"Just delay him a bit, Sir?" the boy frowned.

"That's right. A few minutes is all I ask."

He glanced down at the shining coin in his hand, then smiled and nodded, "All right, Sir. I can do that."

"Good lad. Thanks."

Caecus and I mounted quickly and trotted back to the roadway. As we passed the front of the inn, I noticed the dark-haired young man loitering near the front door, making a show of adjusting the brooch which fastened his cloak. Caecus saw him too, and we exchanged a knowing glance.

Turning south onto the cobbled road, I saw the way ahead was relatively clear.

"We should hurry," I told Caecus.

As one, we jabbed our heels into our horses' flanks and set off at a gallop.

There was a slight rise ahead of us as the road crossed one of the many low spurs from the Alban Mount. As soon as we crested it, I began searching for a suitable place where the earth at the side of the road would not leave any trace of hoofprints. I soon found a patch of stony ground which looked ideal. Signalling to Caecus, I reined in, then led him into the trees lining the road. We dismounted, leading the horses deep into the woodland before tethering them, then moving back to a spot from where we could still see the road but where nobody would notice us unless they were looking very closely.

Before long, we heard the sound of clattering hooves as a solitary rider came quickly from the north. As I'd expected, it was the dark-haired man from the inn. He was in a hurry, and his face bore a grim, determined expression.

"I think that settles it," I sighed.

Caecus asked, "Do you want me to kill him?"

"No. Let him go. He'll soon figure out that he's lost our trail. Hopefully he will turn back and wait for us to return."

"He might summon help," Caecus pointed out.

"We can worry about that if it happens," I shrugged.

Caecus frowned, "What happens if he knows we are heading for Primus' villa?"

"I hope he doesn't try to go there," I replied. "I expect Thrax's men won't take kindly to unexpected visitors."

"We are unexpected visitors," Caecus pointed out.

"Ah, but Thrax will want to talk to me."

My companion regarded me speculatively.

He said, "You are enjoying yourself, aren't you?"

I couldn't help grinning as I told him, "It's just like old times."

"I remember the old times," he snorted. "As I recall, you were captured by conspirators in Alexandria and only just escaped with your life."

"Then let's hope for the same outcome this time," I smiled. "But you don't need to come any further. You can go back and wait for me at the inn."

Caecus returned a scathing look.

"I'll come with you," he told me sternly. "I couldn't go back to the Lady Aurelia and tell her I'd abandoned you."

"I can understand that," I told him. "But, whatever your reason, I'm grateful you are here."

His Centurion's stare met my words.

"Don't get me wrong, Scipio," he said. "I think your idea is ridiculous. But I'll come with you all the same."

"Because of Aurelia?"

"Partly that. And partly because there's always a chance your preposterous idea might work. I told you once before I think the gods decided to give me a second chance. Perhaps it will be a chance to avenge Macrinus."

"I want no bloodshed!" I warned. "That's not what this is about."

He grinned, "I know. But, like I said, that is only part of the reason. Mostly, I'll go along with you because I want to meet Thrax. He's a proper soldier."

I wasn't at all sure what to make of all this, but I was hardly in a position to argue with him. We had come this far, so we may as well take the next few steps even if they might prove to be our last.

257

I said, "All right. Let's go, then. I think we should cut across country and approach the villa from the east. We need to avoid the road to make sure that lad doesn't pick up our trail again."

We returned to where we had left our horses, then led them by the reins as we wound our way through the woods. It was tough going, the ground uneven and studded with tree roots and rocks which slowed our progress. The trees also made navigation difficult, but I did my best to stick to a more or less southerly route.

I knew Primus' villa lay quite low on the slopes of the mountain, relatively near to the road, even though it was shielded by trees and could not be seen by anyone riding past on the *Via Appia*. What I did not know, even having heard Collinus' description, was precisely where it lay. Luck, though, was with us, or perhaps not, depending on your point of view, because after a couple of hours spent picking our way through the trees, we stumbled into some armed sentries.

Two of them stepped out in front of me, each holding a *gladius* in his hand. This vicious short sword, so beloved of the Legions, confirmed that these men were more than mere brigands, and the grim expressions on their faces told me they would have no qualms about using their blades.

We had found Thrax's sentries. Now all I had to do was talk my way past them.

Chapter 26
Thrax

I stopped, raising both hands to show I held no weapons, only the reins of my horse.

"I'm here to see the Tribune," I said, addressing the taller of the two men.

A flicker of surprise briefly touched his stern features. He had probably thought we were tourists come to trek the woodlands of the Alban Mount, but my words had quickly dispelled that notion.

"Who are you?" he demanded gruffly.

"My name is Sempronius Scipio," I told him, deciding I may as well use my real name on this mission. If it all went horribly wrong, I didn't want Valerius Cantiacus taking the blame. After all, he was a law-abiding citizen from Africa, not a former imperial spy.

"Nobody sees the Tribune," the man growled.

"Of course they do!" I smiled. "He has been receiving messages from Rome every few days. And he'll definitely want to see me."

The Juggler's information must have been correct, because neither of the sentries disputed my claim about regular messengers.

I paused, making great show of looking around to check for eavesdroppers. Out here, of course, there were only the birds and foxes to hear us.

Turning back to the two sentries, I said, "You see, I have news from Julia Maesa."

That worried them. I saw them exchange glances, each of them clearly hoping the other would make a decision.

After a moment, the shorter man took control.

"Wait here," he commanded. "I'll go and tell the Centurion."

If there had been any doubt about their identity, that remark proved it. These men were either soldiers or former soldiers.

259

The second guard hurried off downhill, picking his way between the trees, leaving his taller companion to watch us.

"Sit down," he commanded.

We complied. Sitting, we presented less of a threat to him. He'd obviously reckoned Caecus, even unarmed, might pose a problem if he decided to cause trouble. That, though, was the last thing we wanted, so we sat, allowing the horses to nibble on the fresh stalks of grass which were beginning to grow now that winter was almost over and spring was in the air.

We waited for about quarter of an hour until the second guard returned. He did not come alone, but brought three more men with him, one of them a rangy, middle-aged fellow who wore a rust-coloured tunic beneath a faded red cloak.

Caecus and I stood up at his approach. The man had a *gladius* at his waist, hung on his left hip, which I knew denoted him as an officer. Ordinary legionaries have the sword hung on their right so they can draw the weapon without needing to adjust the position of their shield. Officers, who tend not to stand in the front line, generally wear their swords on the left.

"You must be the Centurion," I smiled, rising to my feet and holding out my right hand. "I'm Sempronius Scipio. This is Aelius Caecus."

The man stood facing me, his icy expression glaring at my proffered hand. When he refused to return the greeting, I let my hand fall.

He said, "I am Pactumius Melito. And I'd like to know why you are here."

"Didn't your man tell you? I have come to speak to the Tribune. I have some news from Julia Maesa."

Melito's brown eyes studied me closely. He was obviously trying to make up his mind what to do with us. That was a good sign. Men with sharp swords tend to have only one response when faced with an unknown situation.

He said, "I need to know a bit more about you first."

Smiling, I told him, "I used to be an imperial spy. I worked for Sempronius Rufus and served the Emperor Caracalla."

I wasn't sure whether he recognised the Juggler's name, but he certainly knew who Caracalla was. Everyone in the army had adored our now deceased Emperor. Still, his face remained impassive as he switched his gaze to Caecus.

"And you?"

Caecus snapped to attention, slapping a clenched fist to his chest as he barked, "Aelius Caecus. Centurion. First cohort, Praetorian Guard. Retired."

I added, "Aelius Caecus only came with me to make sure I got here safely."

Melito frowned, "And you have been sent here by Julia Maesa?"

"No, not exactly," I replied. "But I'd prefer to explain all that to the Tribune himself. It's important that he knows what is really happening in Rome."

Melito was unmoved.

"How did you find out we were here?" he demanded.

"My brother owns this villa," I informed him.

"So Sempronius Primus sent you?" Melito scowled as he tried to work out what was going on.

"No. He doesn't know I'm here."

"But you said he was your brother," Melito said, sounding exasperated by my answers.

"Which is why I know better than to trust him," I smiled. "He's as shifty as they come."

Melito was plainly perplexed, but he clearly appreciated that a message from or about Julia Maesa could not be ignored. The only real issue was whether he would instruct his men to beat it out of us right here, or let us talk to his Tribune.

He made his decision.

"We will need to search you," he told me.

"Fine. Go ahead. I've got a dagger, but it's really just an eating knife."

I took my knife from my belt, handing it to him handle first. He took it.

Caecus handed over his dagger, a much larger and sharper tool which Melito looked at admiringly. Then he signalled to his men, and two of them stepped up to pat us down.

It was a pretty thorough search. They even opened the small purse I had fastened to my belt. It didn't contain very much, only a handful of silvers and coppers. But, just like Vindex's men,

261

they didn't bother checking my belt which contained my reserve of gold coins.

They did search the bags slung behind our saddles, rummaging through our spare clothing but finding nothing more threatening than clean loincloths.

"All right," Melito nodded. "Come with me."

Caecus and I retrieved our horses and followed the Centurion down the wooded slope until we emerged into an open meadow where flocks of sheep and goats were ranging free. Beyond them was the villa, a sprawling, single-storey building with traditional white walls and red tiled roof. It was not the most imposing place I'd ever seen, but it looked comfortable and large enough to house a couple of dozen people with little difficulty.

Melito told us to tether our horses to a rail which ran around a veranda at the rear of the house. Then, climbing up onto this wooden platform, he led us into the villa.

There were more men here, all of them with the air of the Legions about them. They straightened in their chairs when they saw Melito, but the Centurion swept past them without a word. I noticed the men eyeing us with curiosity, but they showed no signs of any hostility.

Melito led us further into the house. Primus' villa was a pleasant enough place, although it had been decorated in a rather gaudy style, with bright red panels on the walls, and a plethora of bronze statuettes similar to those which infested his house in Rome.

It wasn't the decoration which concerned me, though. It was the man I was about to see.

Melito led us to a small ante-chamber where he told us to wait. He knocked on one of the doors leading off this central room and went inside. I could hear nothing of what was said, but he obviously held a long and detailed conversation with whoever was inside the room. I did my best to appear calm and relaxed under the watchful eyes of the two guards who had followed us here. They had sheathed their swords, which was reassuring, but they remained alert for any signs that we might be a danger to their General.

Caecus, as ever, seemed relaxed but prepared for anything. Perhaps he was feeling at home for the first time since I'd met him in Leptis Magna. These men might not be wearing any armour, but it was evident that they were soldiers, and Caecus had more in common with them than he did with me.

At last, the door opened, and Melito waved us in. He remained in the room, closing the door behind us when we stepped through, but I forgot all about him when I saw the man who had risen to face us. He'd been sitting by a window, reading a scroll which was now furled on a small table beside his couch. He was dressed in a short-sleeved tunic of plain wool, and he wore no distinguishing marks of rank, but, as Collinus had said, you could never mistake this man for anyone else.

He towered above me, his head almost touching the ceiling. His entire body was built in proportion to his size, his tree-like legs supporting a massive body, his long arms as thick as the trunks of saplings. His head was also large, with dark hair and beard. His brow was heavy, protruding over his eyes, and his jaw also projected a little way beyond his mouth to create a prominent chin which his bushy beard did little to conceal. Even so, he was far from ugly or deformed. In fact, some might regard him as reasonably good-looking.

Yet it was not only his physical enormity which created an aura around him. He projected power and strength of will in a way few men I'd ever met. Rumour said he had been born to a barbarian family of peasants, yet he had risen through the ranks of the army as much because of his ability as his strength.

His eyes were clear and sharp, studying us intently. He made no move or gesture, simply standing there, hands on his hips, facing us with a challenge written all over his face.

I decided to bow my head instead of offering him my hand. He'd probably have been able to crush my fingers without any real effort, and he might even have had the strength to lift me up with only one hand.

Collinus had guessed Thrax was around eight feet tall, and I reckoned he must be at least that. A giant in more ways than one, if all the tales about him were true.

"Good afternoon, General," I said. "I am Sextus Sempronius Scipio."

"So I hear," he replied, his voice deep but surprisingly normal.

He sat back down on the couch, but he gave no signal that we should join him, so we remained standing.

"Melito says you have a message from Julia Maesa," he said, one huge eyebrow lifting in question. "You work for her?"

"She thinks I do," I replied. "It's a complicated story. She knows I served her nephew, Caracalla, but I left the imperial service after his death."

"His murder," Thrax corrected sharply.

"Indeed. I was there. I saw it happen."

"You were loyal to Caracalla?" he demanded, his eyes pinning me like skewers.

Loyalty, I guessed, was important to him. In truth, I had come to detest Caracalla, but I had been loyal to Rome, so I was able to answer truthfully, "I served him for several years. He rewarded me for that service when I foiled a plot against him in Alexandria."

"That was you?"

I had his interest now.

"Me and my friend here. Aelius Caecus was then a Centurion in the Praetorian Guard."

Caecus stiffened to attention when Thrax turned his brooding gaze on him.

"You left the army?" the giant asked him.

"I did, Sir. I was wounded in the head, and unable to perform my duties."

Caecus and I had already decided it would be best to gloss over our time spent serving Macrinus. Thrax had, after all, resigned from his own service when Macrinus had taken power.

The giant Tribune gave a ponderous nod before turning his attention back to me.

"So how does Julia Maesa fit into this?" he probed.

Briefly, I explained how I had been in Rome investigating the attack on my brother and how I had been arrested. I missed out a fair bit, making no mention of the Juggler, and only making a passing reference to Circe and my family.

"So Maesa set you to spy on your own brother?" Thrax scowled.

"She knows I do not get on with him. It is no secret."

"But she does not yet know I am here?"

264

"If she does, she has not heard it from me."

"If she knew, her troops would already be here," he grunted.

"But she does know about Herennius Muncius," I told him. "And she suspects my brother is helping him in some way."

He remained silent, inviting me to continue.

I said, "I came here to warn you not to trust my brother, and to tell you that, whatever plan you are working on has already been discovered. You are in danger."

"Only if you tell her I am here," he pointed out with calm, cold logic.

"Unless she has Muncius and his fellow conspirators arrested," I replied. "Under torture, I'm sure one of them would reveal your involvement."

"If she was going to arrest them, she'd have done it already," Thrax countered. "She isn't ready to do that yet. That's why she wants you to spy on your brother."

I must admit I was surprised by Thrax's quick intelligence, although I suppose I should have known better than to judge him by his brutish appearance. He would never have attained his current rank if he had not been very capable indeed.

I forced a smile as I told him, "Perhaps you are right. I don't know enough about Muncius' plans to be sure. But I do know that, if I don't go back, Maesa will know something is going on here. You see, we had to shake off one of her spies earlier today. That's why we were approaching through the woods instead of coming along the main road. Sooner or later, though, that spy will report that we came this way. Maesa is many things, but she is not stupid. She will soon discover this villa belongs to Primus. When she does, she'll send those troops you mentioned to find out what is going on here."

"And if I let you go, you will not tell her?"

I opened my arms in a gesture of helplessness as I said, "I'm sure I can report that the villa is empty."

"Why would you do that?"

"Several reasons. To save my brother's neck for the sake of my mother. To save you because of your service to Rome. To prevent another imperial assassination."

He sat very still, his dark eyes boring into me, his bulk threatening me.

"Who has spoken of assassination?" he asked in a low, menacing whisper.

"I don't need to be told," I replied. "The signs are there. The Emperor is unpopular, Maesa's spies are watching for a conspiracy, and the empire's greatest General is hiding in a villa only a day's march from the city. Something is being planned, and such secrecy usually means only one thing."

"Have you seen the Emperor?" Thrax demanded suddenly.

"I knew him when he was a boy. Not well, but I was in Antioch when he lived there, so I knew him by sight. Since then, I've only seen him a couple of times, and I have not spoken to him."

"Then you have no idea what he is like!" Thrax snapped. "The boy is an abomination! He acts like a woman, giving himself up to men for their pleasure. He disgraces the Empire by prostituting himself in taverns like any common slut, and he shames us all by his wantonness."

Thrax's face was growing red as he spat out the words, and I was left in no doubt that his anger was very real indeed.

Cautiously, I said, "I cannot argue against that, but I do question the wisdom of trying to assassinate him. It will result in a bloodbath, for you will also need to get rid of Maesa, her two daughters and her other grandson, not to mention all their most loyal followers."

"And you are one of those followers?" he growled.

"No. I'm just an ordinary citizen who has got caught up in this mess. But I've seen the chaos that follows an imperial assassination. It's not pretty, and it harms the empire unless there is a strong candidate who can take over."

"You think there is nobody who can rule properly?" he asked.

It was an odd way to phrase the question, but I shrugged, "I presume Herennius Muncius and his pals are squabbling over which of them should be the next emperor. There are around three hundred Senators, but I don't know any of them well enough to say whether they could be a good ruler. Personally, I doubt it. The

Senate has been stripped of any men of real ability for some years now."

I mentally slapped myself for that. It had been Caracalla, Thrax's idol, who had disposed of any Senators who might be powerful enough to challenge him.

"It seems to me," I hurriedly went on, "that your role is to persuade the army to back whoever is selected. But you have already missed your chance. Maesa knows about Herennius, and she's got her spies watching to see who else he talks to. I anticipate another purge very soon. From what little I know of the Senators, even a couple of them being arrested will scare the rest of them witless, and your plan will dissolve."

Thrax considered that for a moment, then asked, "So you are content to let Elagabalus continue to rule even if it ruins the empire?"

"I didn't say that," I countered. "But I am warning you that your current plan is compromised."

"And why should I trust what you say?" he demanded.

"Because I'm here. If I really was working for Maesa, I'd have told her about you instead of risking my life by coming here."

"Julia Maesa is a clever woman," he observed. "She may have sent you here to say just such a thing."

"Why would she send me to warn you that she knows about you and Herennius Muncius?"

"Because she needs me. She knows the army will follow my lead."

"Which brings us back to the same point," I argued. "Either Maesa knows all about you and still wants your support, or she doesn't know, and what I am telling you is true. Either way, your current plan can't work because Herennius Muncius is a marked man."

He pursed his lips, his frown deepening even further while he considered how to react. I did my best to appear calm, but my palms were sweating and my mouth was dry.

To my astonishment, Caecus suddenly put in, "Sir! Sempronius Scipio is telling the truth. He is caught between Julia Maesa and Herennius Muncius. Both of them would wish him dead if they knew he was here talking to you."

267

Thrax merely stared back at him, but then he asked me, "So why are you here? To dissuade me from going through with Muncius' plan?"

"Yes," I nodded, privately tucking away the confirmation that it was indeed Herennius Muncius who was behind the conspiracy. "I don't like seeing people slaughtered, and I want to avoid another civil war."

"That's very noble of you," Thrax growled, his voice dark with menace. "But why should I continue to support Julia Maesa and her grandson? Let me tell you about Elagabalus. Do you remember a man named Gannys?"

"I've heard of him. He was one of Julia Soaemias' lovers, wasn't he?"

Thrax nodded, "That's right. When Elagabalus raised his revolt against Macrinus, Gannys was appointed to command the boy's army. He had no experience of such things, but he managed to win the battles against Macrinus. And do you know what his reward for this service was?"

I shook my head.

Thrax told me, "He was murdered. Some say it was at Elagabalus' own hands that he died, but I doubt it. That pathetic child has no stomach for such deeds, but he wanted Gannys dead for some reason. I think they fell out when Gannys protested about the boy's aberrant behaviour. Julia Soaemias acceded to her son's demands and had her lover strangled."

I said, "Emperors are not renowned for their gratitude. Others have done similar things."

"True enough," Thrax conceded with a grunt. "But most of them were strong rulers. This boy lets his mother and grandmother govern while he prances around with women and eunuchs. We are fortunate that the empire's enemies are in disarray, because if we are attacked, we can expect no leadership from Rome."

"Because they execute their own generals?"

I should not have said that. It suggested Thrax's opposition to Elagabalus was driven by personal motives, but the giant soldier actually smiled.

"That is so," he said. Then, with a sigh of regret, he added, "I should not have allowed them to purchase my loyalty the way I did. But, like you, I wanted no more wars. The empire needs an

Emperor, and I was persuaded that a son of Caracalla would be the right person for the role."

He shook his head as he admitted, "I was wrong, and now I must help right that wrong or the empire will collapse."

I took a deep breath. This was the moment I had been putting off, but I could not delay it any longer.

I said, "Could I ask what Herennius Muncius has offered you in return for your help? I presume he wants you to declare your support for him once the current imperial family has been removed?"

"That is none of your business," he told me gruffly.

"I'd guess he has offered money," I continued, ignoring his admonition. "Men like Muncius always do."

"What if he has? That is how things work."

I said, "Perhaps there is a way you could earn a greater reward. A way we could arrange a change of ruler without needing to kill anyone."

"I doubt that very much," Thrax rumbled, although I could tell that my hint of reward had interested him. Everything I had heard about him suggested he was an ambitious man, so a promise of unprecedented advancement might be enough to sway him.

As for the practicability of my idea, I knew he was probably right, but I honestly didn't think Elagabalus deserved to die. He was thoughtless and vain, but that was a result of his upbringing and his nature. Perhaps he did feel like a woman trapped within a man's body, and there was no doubt this resulted in his behaviour appalling many Romans, but I did not see that killing him, along with his entire family only to replace them with a pompous prig like Herennius Muncius would provide much improvement.

So I told Maximinis Thrax how I thought we could engineer a change which would leave everyone alive, even Herennius Muncius, and I dangled the prospect of further advancement for himself. He listened carefully while I spoke, but he was less than enthusiastic about my proposal.

"It will never work," he declared. "It has merit, but Elagabalus cannot be permitted to live. A faction would gather around him and would cause trouble."

"Not if his guards were men loyal to you," I argued.

"So you will tell Julia Maesa I am here?"

"I can tell her I have spoken to men who represent you. She need not know you are here in person."

"And if she disagrees?"

"I don't think she will. But if she does, Herennius Muncius is a dead man in any case, and if any of his followers are tortured and reveal your involvement, you know what will happen to you. Remember Gannys."

I thought I might have gone too far, but Thrax seemed almost amused. He was, of course, a man who commanded much loyalty with the soldiers, and there was a Legion based only a few miles away from where we sat discussing the fate of the Empire. It crossed my mind that he might have plans of his own, and that he could march on Rome before Julia Maesa could order his death.

Had I blundered? Had I given the conspirators a push towards striking first?

Thrax sat very still, his eyes studying me, and the silence dragged out around us.

At length, he said, "All right, Scipio. I think you are a dreamer, but I tell you what I will agree to."

I suppose I should not have been surprised at how quickly he had reached a decision without discussing it with anyone else. He was a soldier, a commander who was accustomed to making decisions, and he made one now.

"Go and tell Julia Maesa I will support this idea. See what she says. But if she has simply been using you to discover who is involved, you can tell her she won't find me here. I'm moving on, and I'm not telling you where I am going."

"I understand," I nodded.

"And you can also tell her that I'll back Herennius Muncius if she doesn't go along with it. And if Muncius is already dead, I'll find some other Senator who is prepared to wear the Purple. But Elagabalus must be replaced. Do you hear me? He *must* be replaced."

The determination in his voice left me in no doubt whatsoever. What he was threatening was the very thing I wanted to avoid – another civil war. And there was no doubt in my mind that he meant it.

"I will tell her," I agreed.

What else could I do?

Thrax gave another of his slow, heavy nods.

"Then you will stay here tonight as my guest. It is too late now to return to Rome."

He phrased it as an order, not a suggestion. I'd have preferred to return to the inn, but Thrax was not the sort of man you argued with once he had made up his mind. Still, it seemed I had survived another bout in the arena of politics, and that was a better outcome than I had feared.

The only problem was that I would need to go back to Rome and fight another bout, this time with the formidable Julia Maesa.

Chapter 27
A Suburan Welcome

We left the villa rather later than I had hoped. The previous evening had been spent dining with Maximinis Thrax and his officers, and like most soldiers, they indulged in some serious drinking. I tried not to imbibe overly much, but I had little else to do since my status as a civilian rather excluded me from the conversation.

Caecus, on the other hand, was perfectly at home. He and the others swapped stories of their adventures, trying to outdo each other with the horror stories of encounters with the various tribes of barbarians who lurk beyond the frontiers of the Empire. Caecus was careful not to mention his time spent serving Macrinus, but he told a few tales which I hadn't heard before and which shed some light on his earlier career. It seemed he had joined the army as a young man, helping Septimius Severus gain control of the empire before transferring to the Praetorian Guard. He'd served all across the empire, including a short stint in distant Britannia where Severus' dreams of total conquest had been foiled by atrocious weather, endless swamps, forested mountains and intransigent inhabitants.

"It's a dreadful place," he informed us. "And there's nothing of value there. The Emperor soon decided it wasn't worth the hassle of conquering it."

Indeed, there was general agreement that it had been the awful climate of Britannia which had contributed to Severus' death. After that, Caecus had followed his son and successor, Caracalla, on his campaigns in Germania, Armenia and Parthia.

"He was a good general," Caecus declared, earning a murmur of agreement from the rest of the table.

With little to contribute, I drank rather more wine than I'd intended, so I overslept, and I felt rather the worse for wear when I did surface. Even Caecus admitted to having a sore head, so it was late morning before we eventually mounted our horses and set off for Rome. Even as we departed, Thrax's men were also preparing to leave. He may have agreed to let me try to persuade Julia Maesa to go along with my plan, but he didn't trust me enough to sit and wait for the result in a place where Maesa's troops could surround him.

"How will I be able to contact you?" I asked him.

"You won't," he replied. "But I have friends in Rome. If Maesa agrees to your proposal, I will hear of it soon enough."

That was an interesting admission, and I wondered who those friends might be, but I knew there was little point in asking him.

Instead, I enquired, "And if she doesn't agree?"

"Then you and I both have serious problems to contend with."

That was all he was prepared to say, but the implicit threat of armed revolt lingered just beneath the surface of his words, serving to remind me that the future of the Empire was hanging by a very thin thread.

Caecus and I left him to prepare his own departure.

"He is a great man," Caecus said as we rode down towards the *Via Appia*.

I merely nodded. Thrax was certainly an imposing figure, and he had an aura about him that spoke of toughness and capability. It was also obvious to me that his men were utterly loyal to him. It made me wonder whether Maesa would be able to order his arrest or execution if she decided to reject my suggestion. It seemed to me that a man like Thrax might be able to convince men to join him rather than fight him. Perhaps, I reflected, that might help me persuade Maesa to go along with my idea. I knew I would need all the help going, and that prompted another concern.

I asked Caecus, "Are you considering joining up again? I'm sure Thrax would be happy to have a man of your experience."

The big Praetorian's face was as blank as ever as he considered the question.

"It's a tempting thought," he admitted after a while. "Perhaps I will if things don't work out the way you hope. But I don't think he'd be too welcoming if he ever discovers how close I was to Macrinus. Sooner or later, he'd find out. Besides, I owe you and Aurelia a great debt, so I'll stick with you for the moment."

"You owe us nothing," I told him.

"That," he declared, "is for me to decide."

273

I knew I'd never be able to understand what motivated Caecus, but I thanked him and said, "For my part, I regard you as a friend. I'd like to think you feel the same way. I'm glad you are with me, but I will understand if you do decide to rejoin the Army."

He merely shrugged, "Let's deal with Julia Maesa before we make any other decisions."

"That suits me," I agreed.

A few moments later, we reached the paved road and headed north. There was far more traffic than we had encountered the previous day, so our progress was a lot slower. We were often unable to pass wagons or litters which had long trains of slaves because other carts were coming in the opposite direction.

We passed the inn but did not stop. It was already approaching mid-day, and I really wanted to return to Rome before nightfall. Fortunately, we were able to make better time after a while because the road cleared a little, allowing us to increase our pace.

"There's a man on a black horse following us," Caecus informed me.

"Is he alone?"

"Yes. It must be the spy. He was probably at the inn, watching the road for us."

"I expect so. It doesn't matter. If he's alone, he won't try anything."

Our follower maintained pace with us, always staying no more than a hundred paces back. That was closer than a spy would normally ride, but I guessed he wanted to make certain he did not lose sight of us again. If I'd been in his shoes, I'd have been very concerned that my quarry had vanished the previous day. Sempronius Rufus would not have been happy with me if I'd lost a target I was supposed to be tailing, and I guessed Julia Maesa would be an even harsher taskmaster than the Juggler.

We rode on, moving as fast as the busy traffic allowed, reaching the outskirts of the city late in the afternoon. Returning to the stables, we sold the horses back to the ostler who, as I'd expected, cheated us out of a good price. I didn't bother haggling too much because I had far more important things to worry about.

When we stepped out of the stables, I saw the young man with the black horse. He was standing beside his mount only twenty paces from the door of the stables. He made no attempt to conceal himself, so I gave him a wave and a smile before heading back into the city.

"Don't you want to find out who he is working for?" Caecus asked me.

"It doesn't matter," I shrugged. "We'll see Maesa soon anyway. After that, events will take their course."

"What if he is one of Herennius Muncius' men?"

"Then we'd best watch our backs."

Caecus gave one of his habitual snorts, but he did not argue even though I could tell he would have preferred to take direct action. There were, though, too many people around for us to risk a confrontation.

It was a long walk from the Caelian all the way up to the Quirinal, and I expected it would be dark before we reached home. The streets were beginning to clear, so we set a fast pace, but we had only reached the foot of the Caelian and turned off the *Vicus Capitis Africa*e when Caecus nudged my arm.

"We should take a detour," he said.

"Why?"

"There's something I want to check," he replied enigmatically.

"It will be dark soon," I warned.

"I know. That's why we need to follow a different route."

He obviously wasn't going to divulge anything further, so I followed his lead, even when he turned right and headed up the *Clivus Suburanus.*

"This will take us into the Subura," I pointed out.

He nodded, "Yes."

"Are you sure this is a good idea?"

He said, "Trust me, Scipio."

I wondered what he intended to do. As I've mentioned before, the Subura has a reputation as the poorest and roughest part of the city. It lies in the dip between the Esquiline and Viminal Hills and is a festering spot for malaria as well as all the usual vices of a city's less reputable districts. A lot of that reputation is undeserved, because many people who live in the Subura are perfectly law-abiding, but it must be said it has more than its share of less savoury characters, and a crime level which is well above the average.

The sun was low in the sky now, and it would be full dark soon. Twilight doesn't last long in Rome, so most people had already headed home to partake of their evening meal, leaving room for the street girls and their pimps to ply their trade.

Caecus added to my mounting concern when he turned off the main road. His route now took us in a seemingly random series of turns as we followed lesser streets, many of which were almost deserted. He was heading more westerly now, presumably aiming to pass the southern end of the Viminal and then climb back up towards Primus' home on the Quirinal.

"What are you looking for?" I asked him after another sudden change of direction as he cut south again.

"This will do," he replied.

"What will?"

He placed the flat of his hand against my back and gently urged me on.

"Keep walking," he hissed in my ear. "Don't turn around. Just keep walking."

Then he was gone, darting into a narrow alley to the right, vanishing into the shadows.

I kept walking, silently cursing him. I guessed that the man with the black horse was still following us. It seemed obvious that Caecus had decided to ignore my advice and was trying to lure the young man into a trap where he could presumably rough him up until we found out who he was working for.

This street was dimly lit, only a couple of homes having burning lights hanging in wall brackets outside their doors. The sky above was a deep shade of purple now, fading rapidly to black, with a couple of the brighter stars already beginning to appear.

There was nobody else in sight. The street ended only thirty paces further on where it met another, broader avenue, but even that short distance now seemed threatening. My footsteps were loud on the cobbles as I forced myself to stick to a normal pace, and then I heard the sound of someone behind me, closing fast.

I could not help myself. I spun round, my arms raised in a defensive stance, ready to ward off an attack.

The attack, though, never arrived. I saw Caecus leap out of the alleyway, wrap his left arm around the neck of my pursuer, and grab the man's right wrist with his own right hand. There was a dull glint of iron in the stranger's hand.

Caecus' sudden appearance caught the man with the knife off guard. He was able to grab the knife while simultaneously pulling the fellow off balance and dragging him back into the alleyway. I heard the scrabble of feet on the roadway, a strangled cry of alarm, then a horrible groan which was quickly stifled.

Horrified, I ran back to the entrance to the alleyway and peered around the corner. It was dark, but I could see Caecus stooping over a prostrate figure which had a knife buried to the hilt in its chest.

I stepped into the alley, wrinkling my nose at the fetid stink of the place. Piles of rubbish littered the narrow passage, and I was sure I heard the scuttling sounds of rats further along the way. My attention, though, was focused on the man at Caecus' feet.

"What have you done?" I gasped.

"He was going to kill you," Caecus said as he twisted the knife free and stood erect, holding the dark blade for me to see.

"Did you need to kill him?" I asked in dismay.

"Yes. Take a look at him."

Hesitantly, I moved further into the alley and peered down at the dead man. It was difficult to make out his features in the gloom, but I quickly realised it was not the young man who had followed us on the road. This man was much bigger and brawnier, and seemed a fair bit older.

"It's one of Muncius' guards," Caecus told me. "I remember him from when we met them in the forum the other day."

"He was following us?"

"Ever since we got back to the city," Caecus nodded.

I frowned, annoyed that I had not noticed the man trailing us. I'd been too preoccupied with thoughts of how I could convince Julia Maesa to agree to my plan, and that could have proved fatal had it not been for Caecus.

277

I asked, "Do you think he was working with the fellow who followed us up from the Alban Mount?"

"I doubt it," Caecus grunted. "Not unless they spoke while we were inside arguing with the horse trader. This guy picked us up after we'd come through the Porta Capena. The other man was still at the stables."

"Did you see anyone else following us?"

"No. Just this one guy."

I tried to make sense of this, but my thoughts refused to settle.

"Maybe Primus and Muncius know we left the house," I frowned. "They might have men watching all the roads."

"You'd need a lot of men for that," Caecus countered. "But it doesn't really matter whether they are looking for us or whether it was a coincidence."

Frowning, I considered what we ought to do next. The implications of Muncius having sent men to kill me were almost too awful to contemplate, but I knew we needed to be careful with our next course of action.

I said, "Take the knife and empty his purse. If the *vigiles* find him before the rats and dogs eat him, they'll assume it was just another Suburan mugging."

Caecus quickly did as I had suggested, then we left the dead man and hurried back to the Quirinal. My heart was thumping wildly as I drove my legs on as fast as I could go without actually running. If Primus had discovered our absence, what would he have done to Circe and my children?

"Slow down," Caecus warned. "Let me go and take a look first."

"I have a better idea," I told him. "Let's go to Fronto's house. He'll know what's going on."

We reached Fronto's home without incident. Old Rusticus opened the door in response to my frantic knocking, blinking owlishly at me.

"Master Scipio! Come in. You were expected earlier."

That puzzled me, but I was too desperate for news of my family to question him. Fronto would have the answers I needed.

Rusticus showed us into the same reception room with the floor mosaic of Venus where we had met the Juggler a few days earlier. Fronto was already there and so, to my delight and amazement were Circe and Collinus.

I stopped in my tracks as Circe ran to me, her face alive with joy and relief. We embraced for a long time, clinging to one another as if we would never let go.

"The children?" I asked her.

"At home with your mother. They are asleep, I hope."

I reluctantly let her go and stepped back a pace.

"What are you doing here?" I asked her. "Is everything all right? Primus hasn't done anything?"

"Primus? No. Why?"

"Because one of Muncius' men just tried to kill me."

She blinked, then gave a grim nod.

"You'd better tell us the whole story," she decided. "But you needn't worry. Everyone is perfectly safe."

"But how did you get out? Did you climb the wall?"

She smiled broadly as she informed me, "No. Your mother found a spare key for the back gate, and Petrus spent all day yesterday oiling the lock and scraping off the rust. We sneaked out as soon as it was dark. Now, come and tell us what happened."

I made no protest as she led me to a seat. We settled into the chairs, with Circe sitting close beside me, reaching out to hold my hand as I recounted our meeting with Thrax. Then I told them about the spy who had been trailing us and about Muncius' guard who had been planning to kill me.

"I thought something must have happened to you as well," I told Circe, unable to conceal my feeling of relief that she was safe.

She said, "Nothing happened to us at all. We haven't even seen Primus, let alone Muncius. We mostly stayed upstairs, and I made sure the kids made a lot of noise so the guards would think we had accepted being kept as prisoners."

"But why are you here?" I asked her again.

It was Fronto who replied, "I had a visit from the Juggler yesterday."

"Rufus? What did he want?"

"He came to tell me he'd found your builder. Or, rather, the builder's son."

"The builder? Mallius Tanicus?"

279

It took me a moment to push away my thoughts of Thrax and of Muncius' knifemen. Mallius Tanicus, the man who had built Primus' house, was the last of the suspects on our list, but I could not summon any interest in that matter at all.

My lack of concern did not deter Fronto.

He informed me, "It seems Tanicus is dead. But the Juggler found his son, a man named Proximus."

I waved a hand to cut him off.

"I don't have time for this," I told him. "I need to go and see Julia Maesa."

"You can't go to the palace tonight," Fronto told me. "The Emperor is throwing another of his parties. Guests are restricted to Senators and their wives only, so you'll never get in. Even if you did, Maesa will be far too busy to see anyone."

Circe added, "And you really ought to hear what Proximus has to say."

"I'm sure it can wait," I said dismissively.

"No, I think you really need to hear it."

"Why don't you just tell me?"

"Because we only spoke to his wife. Fronto and I went to the house last night. He was still out, but she more or less admitted that he was the one who arranged the attack on Primus."

"Then the mystery is solved. Well done. We can tell my mother, then we can concentrate on saving our own lives."

Circe gave me a stern look, clearly frustrated that I wasn't taking her seriously enough.

"Listen!" she snapped. "There may well be more Proximus can tell us."

"About what?"

"About what Primus is up to."

"All right," I sighed, "tell me."

With a satisfied nod, she explained, "Proximus' wife doesn't know any details, but she does know her husband has been trying to discredit the men who took over his father's business. It seems they are in Primus' pay."

"That doesn't come as a surprise," I muttered.

"No, but Proximus let slip that they won a contract to do some repair and refurbishing work at the palace."

"What are you suggesting?" I asked.

"I'm suggesting we talk to Proximus and find out exactly what he knows. It may be nothing, but if Herennius Muncius is planning to assassinate the Emperor, he'll need men in the palace."

"He'd just bribe some Praetorians!" I blurted.

"That may be difficult if the Guard like Alexander. If Muncius is to become Emperor, the young boy must die as well."

"I doubt a couple of builders will be able to murder anyone and get away with it."

Caecus put in, "They are builders who used to be legionaries."

I still wasn't convinced, but then I had a sudden insight, and my blood ran cold.

"Sweet Venus!" I breathed.

Circe smiled as she said, "You've made the connection?"

"I'm afraid I might have done," I sighed.

Frowning, Caecus asked, "What connection? What are you talking about?"

I said, "We're talking about what Muncius and Primus are trying to do."

He growled, "You'll need to explain it to me. I have no idea what you are on about."

I glanced at Circe. She'd had more time to think about this than I had.

She said, "It is only a theory. But we know the Praetorians are fond of Alexander. Muncius cannot become Emperor if the boy lives, and he'll struggle to find many Praetorians who would dare murder the lad. Even Elagabalus could only find a handful of followers who would dare make the attempt."

Caecus nodded slowly.

"That makes sense."

Circe went on, "But if an accident were to happen, and Alexander died, that would be different."

Caecus caught up with us. Scowling deeply, he guessed, "An accident with a balcony railing, for example?"

"Exactly!" Circe beamed.

I put in, "And the Praetorians would blame Elagabalus. They'd turn on him in an instant. He'd be killed, and there would be no obvious successor."

"And up steps Herennius Muncius," said Circe.

281

Fronto interjected, "This is only speculation, my friends. I know it fits, but you have no proof."

"Then we need to speak to Mallius Proximus," I said.

Circe teased, "So now you do want to talk to him?"

I gave her a smile of admission as I replied, "Yes, but before I rush off to find the builder's son, there's something else we should consider. What happens when Muncius discovers one of his guards is dead? He might decide to make a move against us."

Fronto said, "I doubt Herennius Muncius will find out anything tonight. He's a Senator, and attendance at the palace was compulsory."

Caecus said, "He won't find out for a while anyway. There's nothing to link the dead man to him."

"Fine. Then I'll go and talk to Mallius Proximus."

Circe informed me, "There is more you should know first."

When I raised my eyebrows questioningly, she explained, "You ought to know Proximus is convinced Primus killed his father."

"What? Killed him? How?"

"Proximus' wife said the old man hanged himself, but Proximus blames Primus. She also said she would make sure he stayed at home this evening so you could go and talk to him. But we expected you to return sooner, so when you didn't turn up, I came down here to ask Fronto to go with me."

"Well, I'm here now, so tell me where I can find him. Where does he live?"

There was a short, awkward silence before Fronto said softly, "That's another complication."

"What sort of complication?"

Fronto and Circe exchanged a nervous glance, and I noticed Collinus grinning with amusement.

"What is it?" I asked again.

With a sigh, my friend admitted, "He stays on the Viminal. Down an alley beside a taverna called Xeno's. It's in a square with a fountain. The Juggler said you'd know where it was."

I closed my eyes. The Viminal. Xeno's taverna.

In other words, right in the heart of Marius Vindex's territory.

Chapter 28
The Builder

Circe and Fronto insisted on coming with us.

"We went yesterday and there was no trouble," Circe pointed out when I objected. "But we can always try to sneak some of our slaves out of Primus' home if you are worried."

"No," I sighed. "We're taking enough of a risk as it is. Besides, a large squad of us would only draw more attention. Five of us is more than enough. All right, let's go. The sooner we get this over with, the better."

Fronto took a blazing torch to light our way.

"I may as well do something useful," he said with a self-deprecating smile. "And if there is trouble, I can use it to fend off any attacks."

Collinus, meanwhile, had produced a long walking stick.

"I'm an old man," he explained when he saw me eyeing it curiously. "I need this to help me walk."

The sparkle in his eyes betrayed the lie, but I let it pass. I'd rather he clobbered someone with a length of hardwood than stabbed them with his long-bladed dagger.

"I don't want any trouble at all," I told them all. "We go in, we talk to Proximus, and we get out as quickly and quietly as possible."

There was no point in telling Circe to stay behind. She was desperate to discover the full story, and she had an unfailing confidence in Collinus' ability to keep her safe. I'm not sure whether she had the same confidence in me, but having Caecus to help certainly allayed my own fears.

There were few people out and about. That's not to say the streets were empty, because we could hear the distant rumble of cart wheels as the heavy wagons brought produce into the city or carried refuse away, and the *vigiles* always had patrols out, but it was full dark now, a time when most respectable people stayed indoors unless they were visiting friends, in which case they went out with a retinue of slaves to protect them. The street gangs were always a threat, but we reached the Viminal without incident.

283

Following the main road, we climbed up to the square with the fountain. With fewer people drawing water, the flow was already beginning to spill over the lip of the pool, sending a wide stream of water spreading across the cobbled square.

I studied Xeno's taverna cautiously. The light of candles and oil lamps showed that it was busy, most of the tables occupied, even some of the ones which sat outside its door. Fortunately, there was no sign of the grim-eyed Hestius or any of his fellow thugs. Moving more quickly now, I hurriedly led my friends into the alleyway which ran alongside the taverna.

"Second on the right," Fronto said as he strode towards the door, holding the torch aloft.

It was a typical Roman tenement building in both appearance and smell. Boiled vegetables, urine, dog litter and rubbish all combined to create that pungent aroma.

I told Caecus and Collinus to wait in the entrance lobby. Fronto left the torch with them, then he and Circe led me up to the third floor.

We could hear conversation and laughter from some of the apartments, but the one we went to was silent. I knocked on the flimsy door, and soon heard sounds of movement from within.

The door creaked open and a pretty young woman looked out, her eyes nervous.

Circe said, "Hello, Ignatia. Is your husband in?"

The woman's expression changed into a weary smile as she nodded, "Yes, but he's feeling very low. He couldn't find any work today."

As she showed us in, she added, "The baby's asleep."

Circe assured her, "We'll try not to make any noise. This is my husband, Scipio, by the way."

I nodded a greeting.

Ignatia was small, a little plump, but with a pretty face and a mane of dark hair. She looked tired, but I knew from personal experience that having a baby could have that effect.

The hallway was short, narrow and devoid of any decoration. Two hooded cloaks hung on nails which had been hammered into the plaster wall, but there was nothing else to be seen except two curtained doorways leading to the apartment's only rooms. The first curtain was closed, so I assumed that was the bedroom. The second had been drawn open, revealing the apartment's main living room. This was plain but clean by the standards of many tenements. The furniture comprised a table, a couple of stools, a storage chest and one dilapidated armchair with the horsehair stuffing hanging out of several torn parts of the leather covering.

A man had risen from that chair, his expression clouded by nervous curiosity as he stood to face us. He was, I guessed, in his late twenties. He looked lean, well-muscled and fit, but his hair was untidy and his chin bore several days' growth of stubble. He looked tired and dispirited, but his eyes were studying us warily.

"Ignatia said you were coming," he announced in a dull, resigned monotone.

Gesturing to the table behind him, he added, "I'm afraid we have no wine to offer you."

The table bore the remnants of the couple's evening meal, two bowls, a small jug and two clay cups.

"That's not important," I told him. "We only want to talk to you."

He gave a resigned shrug, leading me to suspect his wife had told him all about her earlier discussion with Circe.

I asked him, "You are Mallius Proximus?"

"That's right," he said grudgingly. "Who are you? If you spun my wife a yarn in order to try to collect any debts, you're out of luck."

It was a poor joke, but I smiled all the same, trying to reassure him. Then I made the introductions before telling him, "We'd like to talk to you about Sempronius Primus."

"You are related to him?" he asked meaningfully.

"I'm his brother. But don't read too much into that. We've never got on with one another."

"Then you won't be offended if I tell you Sempronius Primus is a gangster and a murderous thug?"

"Not at all. But I'd like to know what caused you to have him beaten up. It was you, wasn't it?"

To his credit, Proximus did not try to deny the accusation. He did shoot a glance at his wife, clearly indicating that he knew who had informed us of his involvement, but he seemed almost relieved as he told us, "Yes, it was me and some of the lads who

285

had worked for my father. We all hated Primus for what he did, so we decided to teach him a lesson."

"You nearly killed him," I pointed out.

"At the time, that's what I wanted," he nodded. "I know it wouldn't have solved anything, but we all felt that's what he deserved."

"Tell me why," I prompted.

Proximus stood very still. Then I noticed a tear trickling down his cheek. He hurriedly wiped it away, but his voice was almost choked with emotion as he rasped, "He killed my father."

"How?"

Now there was a hint of angry defiance in his eyes as he looked at me.

"He said we were making a mess of his new house, using shoddy materials and doing a poor job. That was a lie."

"I know. He had his own slaves cause a lot of damage, then he blamed your father."

That caught his attention. He stood a little more upright as he said, "You know about that?"

"I found out a few days ago."

Waving his arms in frustration, he nodded, "And then the bastard refused to pay us for our work. He offered a quarter of the agreed price. When my father argued, we had a visit from some of his heavies. Eventually, we stopped working for him, but it was already too late by that time. He'd insisted on top quality tiles and marble, so we'd outlaid a lot of money, and our creditors were demanding payment."

"I heard your father's business had to be sold."

Proximus snorted what might have been a choked laugh.

"Yeah, we sold it. At a knock down price to a couple of Primus' pals, although I'm pretty sure it was Primus' money they used."

"Fabius Murmillo and someone named Didius?" I recalled.

"That's them," Proximus confirmed. "A right couple of bastards. But my father was too depressed to argue about the deal. Primus had beaten him down to a shadow, and he gave in. He sold the whole business for a hundred gold pieces. It was worth five times that at least."

"That's still a lot of money," I remarked.

"Yeah, but it wasn't enough to pay all the debts we'd run up supplying Primus with the top quality marble and stone he'd demanded. There was nothing left by the time we paid our creditors."

"What happened after that? I suppose it was Fabius and Didius who finished the work on the house?"

"There wasn't much to finish once they'd fixed all the damage Primus had done himself."

I glanced at Circe.

She said softly, "So Primus gets a top quality home, along with ownership of a building firm at a bargain price?"

Proximus gave another resigned nod.

"That's right. And my old man couldn't handle the shame. His creditors were threatening to drag him to court, and he would have ended up being sold into debt slavery. To avoid that, he hanged himself. He'd put his whole life into building up his business, and Primus took it all away from him."

"Couldn't you have taken him to the courts?" I asked.

"Are you kidding? That costs money. We had none."

He gave a bleary look around the room, then added, "We still have none."

"So you and your pals beat him up. What about the other stuff? Was it you who wrote a death threat on his wall?"

"I was drunk," Proximus shrugged. "I only did it once. I know it's stupid, but I just needed to get back at him."

"I can understand that," I told him. "I spent most of my boyhood trying to do the same."

We shared a rueful smile, and I could see him relax a little now that he knew I was on his side.

"So now you know," he said. "What do you intend to do?"

"That depends on what else you can tell me."

"About what?"

"About what your pals Fabius and Didius have been doing at the palace."

This time, the look he gave his wife was one of extreme disappointment.

"I don't want to talk about that," he said defiantly.

"But you know something?" I probed.

"Not really. It's just rumour. Not even that, in fact."

287

"Then it doesn't matter if you tell me," I pressed. "What have you heard? It's important. And if you want to help me punish Sempronius Primus, you should tell me as much as you can."

Proximus blew out a long breath as he ran his hands through his tangled hair.

"Look," he sighed, "I don't know much at all. I just happened to notice a couple of their workmen in a wine shop one evening, so I took a seat close by and listened in."

He hesitated, licking his lips, then continued, "They'd had a couple of jugs, I reckon, so their tongues were a bit loose. They were talking about some extra work they'd done for Didius Pomponius at the palace, and they were gloating about how much he'd paid them to do it."

"What extra work," I asked, doing my best not to let my mounting excitement show.

"I'm not sure. It didn't make much sense, but I heard them mention Primus' name, so I naturally wanted to find out what they'd been up to."

"And what did they say?"

"Like I said, it didn't make much sense. They were talking about a balcony and how Fabius and Didius would be rich men if Primus' plan worked."

And there it was. Our suspicions had been correct. I smiled, feeling my muscles relax as the tension I hadn't noticed evaporated.

"Thank you," I told Proximus. You've been more helpful than you can know."

We had what we had come for, but it would have looked odd to suddenly rush out, so I asked him, "What work do you do now?"

He shrugged, "I get labouring jobs sometimes. It's a case of turning up at a public yard and hoping the foreman will take you on for the day."

That, I knew, was a precarious way to earn a living. Most public works were built by slaves, but sometimes a citizen could be employed if he had specialist skills.

I said, "I'd have thought a trained builder like you would have found no trouble getting work."

288

"It's not that easy," he sighed. "The overseers at public works demand a bribe before they take anyone on. I could set up on my own if I had some capital behind me. I'm good enough, but I can't start from nothing. And the other construction bosses don't like having the son of a known debtor on their staff."

Ignatia moved to stand beside him, linking her arm with his.

She told me, "Gaius does odd jobs for our neighbours, but they can't afford to pay much. They help out with food, but we barely have enough to pay the rent even when he does find work."

I turned to look at Circe. Her expression told me we were in agreement that we must help if we could.

I opened my purse, emptying the contents into my palm. There was not much, only a couple of denarii and a few copper asses. Frowning, I put them back in my purse, then loosened my belt and dug my fingers into the nearest secret pockets. I withdrew three golden aurii.

I decided to hand them to Ignatia. Proximus, I guessed, might feel too proud to accept.

"Take these to a moneylender," I told her. "They'll be able to change them into silver for you."

Her eyes grew damp with tears as she sniffed her thanks, but Proximus frowned at me.

"What's this for?" he demanded suspiciously. "What do you want in return?"

"You've already given me what I wanted," I told him.

He gave me a studied look, and I wondered whether he'd worked things out for himself. He struck me as an intelligent young man, and I would not have been surprised if he had put the clues together. If he had, he had sufficient sense to keep his thoughts to himself.

He said, "You don't need to give us that much. I don't want to be in your debt."

"There is no debt," I assured him. "Consider it a gift. Or a very small recompense for how the Sempronius family treated your father."

The scowl he shot me confirmed that it would take a lot more than three gold pieces to compensate for his loss, but I went

289

on, "I'd like to think there might be a way we can help each other in future."

"What way?" Proximus asked warily.

Ignatia tugged at his arm to tell him to hold his tongue, but I could see that he was very suspicious of my motives.

"I'll think of something. I've got some other things to deal with, but I promise I'll be back in touch with you soon."

Privately, I hoped that was a promise I would be able to keep. Herennius Muncius, Julia Maesa, the Emperor or Maximinis Thrax might have other ideas about my immediate future.

Proximus remained sceptical of my motives, but Ignatia gushed more thanks and promises of eternal gratitude.

"Let me sort out a few things," I told them. "Then I'll speak to you again."

Proximus' only response was another cautious nod.

"Great," I said. "Then we'll say goodnight."

We left them in their tiny apartment and made our way down the stairs of the tenement.

"I wish we could do more to help them," Circe said. "Primus has ruined their lives."

"Perhaps we can," I replied.

"How?"

"By getting the business back from Primus' bullies."

"You'll need to come up with a good plan for that," she told me.

"Actually, I was hoping you'd think of something."

"Perhaps I can, but don't you think we ought to concentrate on the important part of what Proximus told us?"

She was right. What we had discovered could have serious consequences, and we would need to carefully plan how we broke the news to Julia Maesa. By this time, we had reached the entrance lobby where Collinus and Caecus waited for us. The torch had burned itself out, but there was just enough pale moonlight streaming in through the open doorway for me to see that both of them were regarding me expectantly.

I told everyone, "It seems we were right, but let's discuss it back at Fronto's house. I don't want to be overheard."

We stepped out into the dark lane, me leading the way with Collinus and Caecus close behind me, while Circe and Fronto brought up the rear. Stepping carefully to avoid tripping over unseen obstacles in the dark, we reached the end of the lane and entered the square which was lit by a pale moon and a few burning braziers hung on the outer walls of a handful of buildings.

By that dim light, I saw four figures spread in a line ahead of us.

I stopped, recognising them and knowing we could not avoid them.

It was Hestius, Vindex's man. He had the giant youngster, Polus, to his left, while Albius, the angry young man who had wanted to do me serious harm, and Venantius, the fourth man, stood to his right.

"Well, who do we have here?" Hestius asked, his tone light but with definite overtones of menace. "You were told to stay away from here. The boss said he wouldn't like it if you came back."

"We are just leaving," I replied.

"Not yet," he told me. "We owe you for what you did to Venantius and poor Balbo."

His eyes scanned us, lighting up with interest when he noticed Circe.

"A woman? That ought to be fun. I tell you what. Hand her over to us and we'll think about letting the rest of you go."

"I don't think so," I told him. "Why don't you just stand aside and let us pass? We don't want any trouble."

"Tough luck. You were lucky last time, but we can't have you walking around our patch. Not after what you did."

Beside me, Caecus moved forwards to take up position on my right, facing the giant youngster with the brooding brow. Polus wasn't nearly as big as Maximinis Thrax, but he was still one of the hugest men I'd ever come across.

To my left, Collinus stepped up alongside me, his long cane tapping the cobbles.

Hestius regarded my companions with a look of contempt.

"Two old men and a little thing like you? You think we're afraid of you?"

"You should be," I advised him. "Remember what my friends did last time. Why don't you step aside and we'll be on our way. There's no need for anyone to get hurt."

291

Slowly, Hestius reached inside his cloak and pulled out a dagger. It was a short-bladed thing, double-edged and sharpened to a needle point.

"Someone *is* going to get hurt," he promised me. "We're ready for you this time."

Albius, the mop-haired youngster who had taken a dislike to me the first time we'd met, blurted, "Let me gut him, Hestius."

That was enough for Caecus. Being a soldier, he understood the need to take the initiative. Rather than waiting for Hestius to make the first move, he rushed forwards, aiming for Hestius but swerving at the last moment and crashing into the giant Polus, knocking him from his feet. It was an awesome collision. Caecus, as I've mentioned several times, is a big man, but the young bruiser was even larger, bull-necked, with a massive torso. However, he was as slow of movement as he was of thought, and he had no chance to react to Caecus' charge. He went down with a gasp as all the breath was driven from his lungs by Caecus' lowered head and bunched fists.

I had no time to see what happened next. Collinus was already advancing, his walking stick sweeping up as he moved towards Albius and Venantius. I took advantage of Hestius' momentary distraction to close the gap between us. He was looking down at his fallen giant with open-mouthed astonishment, so I was able to grab his right wrist in both hands and twist it in a violent grip which forced him to let go of his weapon. The dagger clattered to the ground as I swept Hestius' legs from beneath him with a swing of my left leg. At the same time, I jerked his arm upwards to throw him even further off balance. I let go as he fell, then I kicked him in the head before he could scramble back to his feet. Just for good measure, I stamped on his right hand with my hobnailed boots, grinding his fingers with my full weight. Hestius screamed in pain, but I ignored him. I felt and heard bones cracking as I hurriedly looked around to see how my companions were faring.

Polus was stretched out on the ground, unmoving, and Caecus leaped past me, heading to my left. Here, Collinus had felled Venantius and was now facing Albius. Caecus came up behind the young thug, but Collinus did not really need any assistance. It was all poor Albius could do to ward off the swinging blows from Collinus' stick. He yelped in pain when Collinus delivered a hard smack to his arm, then tried to turn and run when he realised he was on his own. His escape was cut off by Caecus who grabbed him, wrapping both arms around the young man's chest.

Albius struggled, but Caecus was squeezing him in a bear hug, forcing all the breath from him.

Then Collinus stepped close to the boy, drawing his own dagger, a much more fearsome blade than the one Hestius had dropped.

"Shall I gut him?" Collinus asked me in a conversational tone.

"Best not," I replied. "Let him go. We have more important things to deal with."

Caecus gave another squeeze, forcing a gasping groan from Albius, then he let go, dropping the young man to the ground. Albius gasped for breath, his hands and feet scrabbling for balance as his body flopped to the cobbles. He gave up, rolling onto his back and staring wildly up into the sky, his chest heaving as he fought to pull air back into his lungs. I kicked him in the groin as I passed him.

"Always kick a man when he's down," I told Caecus, recalling my pal Hannibal's mentoring advice.

Caecus grinned in approval.

"You should have been a soldier," he told me.

"No, that's too much like hard work."

I turned back to check that Fronto and Circe were unharmed. They were looking at us in awe, which made a pleasant change for me.

"We have attracted an audience," Collinus warned.

He was right. Several people had stepped out of the taverna to check on what was going on.

"Let's go before someone runs off to tell Vindex," I said.

Caecus snorted, "If that lot are the best he's got, I don't think we need to worry too much."

"I don't want a street war," I told him. "We already have a real war to avert."

Circe hurried over and entwined her arm in mine.

"You were wonderful!" she exclaimed. "All of you!"

293

I can't deny it felt good to know I'd managed to impress her, but I always regretted it when I had to resort to violence to solve a problem, especially as this escapade might well result in Vindex seeking retribution. I had more than enough things to worry about without him sending more thugs after me.

Circe, though, kissed me on the cheek and told me again how wonderful I was.

"I think Caecus and Collinus could have handled them on their own," I told her. "And I hurt my toe when I kicked Hestius. I'll probably have a nasty bruise soon."

"I shall kiss it better," she promised.

"That would be nice. While you are at it, maybe you could think of a way we can solve all our problems without needing to do any more fighting."

She squeezed my arm and pressed close to my side as she said, "I'll see what I can do."

I recognised that tone of voice. Looking at her, I saw the mischievous delight in her eyes.

"You've thought of something," I said.

"Yes."

She explained her plan as soon as we reached Fronto's house. It was a good idea, and I had to laugh at the audacity of it. Caecus, who would have an important role, agreed, and we had it all worked out by midnight. Then we crept back to the rear of Primus' house and whistled for Petrus who unlocked the gate for us and let us in.

It had been a long, tiring day, with far too much excitement for my liking, but I managed to fall into a deep sleep even though my mind was full of plans and hopes. But my slumber was interrupted when the Praetorians arrived at the door.

Chapter 29
Arrest

The shutters were closed, so I had no idea what time it was. It felt very early, but the noise from Primus' house jolted me into wakefulness. There was banging and shouting, and a woman's scream which was cut off with terrifying suddenness.

We'd got to bed so late I hadn't bothered removing my tunic, so I jumped up, scrabbling my feet in a search for my sandals. My sore toe received another jar as I kicked the bed post, but I soon managed to dash for the door.

"Stay here!" I told Circe.

Needless to say, she ignored me. She was clearly intent on following me.

Outside in the hallway, pale daylight was filtering in through a high window. This let me see Collinus and Caecus, both of whom had been woken by the noise and had emerged from their rooms.

"Stay with Circe and the kids!" I told Collinus.

Then I ran for the stairs with Caecus hot on my heels.

The noise had abated by the time I reached the ground floor. Several of our slaves were peering nervously out into the atrium while old Lucius was standing near the front door, his expression a picture of fear and concern.

"It's the Master's house!" he blurted as he pointed to the connecting door. "Soldiers came."

I noticed that the two heavies Primus had left on guard had made themselves scarce. I couldn't say I blamed them.

Signalling to the slaves to remain where they were, I ran for the adjoining door, flinging it open and moving quickly but cautiously into Primus' home.

As I reached the atrium, the first thing I saw was a group of Praetorians in full armour and with drawn swords. They had grim faces and were very definitely not in the mood for any argument. Some of them swung to face me, their blades held upright in warning.

"Who is in charge here?" I barked at them, adopting the role of an outraged homeowner.

"We are," one of them grinned, making his companions chuckle malevolently.

I could not argue with that statement. A couple of Primus' bodyguards were sitting morosely beside the shallow pool of the *impluvium* under the watchful eyes of a pair of Guardsmen, but they showed no signs of being interested in resisting. It would have been futile to try to oppose so many armed soldiers.

Just then, I heard footsteps behind me, and heard my mother demanding to know what was happening. She sounded frightened, but she had not let that prevent her running towards the trouble.

"Stay back!" I warned her, holding out my arm to stop her passing me.

Then I saw Canidius Frequens, the Decurion who had taken me and Caecus to our first meeting with Julia Maesa, march into view. He shot me a glance, then gave a grim smile.

"You'd best stay out of this," he told me.

"What's going on?" I asked him. "Are you in charge?"

"Centurion Laetilius Auctas is in command," Frequens replied.

At that, a man wearing a gleaming breastplate and a helmet with a cross-wise plume as its crest stepped into the atrium, coming through from the interior of the house. Behind him, two enormous Praetorians were holding Primus in a very tight grip as they dragged him between them. Trying to hop, with his left leg hanging uselessly in its splints, primus was yelling and struggling to no avail. He was making such a fuss that one of the soldiers thumped a fist into the side of his head to quieten him. Primus staggered, then slumped, but the two Praetorians hefted him upright and continued dragging him towards the main doors of the house. More soldiers followed close behind them, eyes eager for confrontation.

While this was going on, the Centurion shot me a venomous glance.

"Who are you?" He demanded.

Before I could reply, Frequens put in, "This is Sempronius Scipio, Sir. We were told to leave him be."

296

The Centurion frowned, then turned away from me.

"What's going on?" I asked again.

The officer ignored me, signalling to his men to leave.

"We have the man we came for," he told them as he signalled to them to haul Primus away.

Frequens, though, turned to me and whispered, "He's being taken to the Praetorian camp for interrogation."

"About what?" I asked. "I haven't even reported to Julia Maesa Augusta."

Frequens shrugged, "I just follow orders."

My mother screamed, "Primus!", but Caecus had her in his grip and would not let her pass.

Frequens turned away, hurrying after the rest of the troop, leaving us dumbfounded in a suddenly silent house. It had all happened so quickly, we were left feeling more than a little stunned.

I turned to my mother who was looking at me in horror.

"You must do something!" she told me. "Find out why he has been arrested."

"I think we know why," I told her gently.

"But what will happen to the rest of us?" she persisted. "And what will they do with Primus?"

"He's mixed up in treason," I told her. "I'm not sure anyone can save him now."

She looked distraught, and the sight of her pain wrung my heart, so I added, "I'll go to the palace. I need to talk to Julia Maesa anyway."

I looked at Caecus who had remained in the shadowy recess of the corridor.

"Did you recognise that Centurion?"

He nodded, "Laetilius Auctas. He's a good man. He won't be unnecessarily cruel."

"Yes," I murmured, "they don't seem to have harmed anyone else."

"Hortensia!" my mother gasped, wriggling free of Caecus' hands and hurrying past me.

I followed her, heading through the atrium, across the courtyard and into the main section of the house where we found Hortensia sitting on the floor, her back against a wall, her face in

297

her hands. She was wearing only a night shift, and she was sobbing loudly, while three of her attendant slaves stood by helplessly.

My mother squatted down, putting her arm around Hortensia's shoulders and trying to comfort her.

"Take her to her bed," she ordered the slaves. "Give her a hot herbal drink. And someone make sure the children are all right."

Standing up, she again turned to me.

"You must do something," she told me again.

"I'll try," I promised.

"Do it for my sake, if not for his," she said.

I felt very proud of her at that moment. She knew Primus had become involved with some serious problems, and she also knew he was an unpleasant character when it came to his business dealings, but he was her son, and she did not want to see him executed. It may have been partly because she would never be able to live down the shame of having a rebel son, but I think it was more than that. Seeing her steadfast loyalty, I must admit I felt guilty. My own feelings were that Primus deserved everything that was coming to him.

"I'll go to the palace," I repeated.

I insisted on having one of the slaves give me a shave before we left. I'd have liked to visit a bath house, but I knew I could not spare the time. Putting on my best tunic and cloak, and accompanied by Caecus, I headed outside. None of Primus' guards made any attempt to stop us.

We had a long walk ahead of us. I knew there was no point in going straight to the palace. A veritable army of guards, scribes, secretaries and slaves would need to be passed before I could get close to Julia Maesa. Unless she had left word that I was to be admitted unchallenged, I might never be allowed any further than the front steps of the palace. So we were walking eastwards, heading towards the Esquiline Hill where I knew I would find Cassius Dio.

Neither of us said much. I was too preoccupied with what I would need to say to Maesa, while Caecus was keeping an eye out for anyone following us. It did not take long for him to spot the short, rotund figure who was struggling to keep pace with us.

"I think your friend, the Juggler, wants to talk to you," he told me.

I stopped, turning to watch as Sempronius Rufus jogged his way towards us, his large belly bouncing obscenely and his face flushed with exertion.

"What happened this morning?" he demanded without any greeting. "I heard the Praetorians came to your house."

This wasn't exactly the ideal location to have a conversation about imperial politics. People were moving past us on either side, frowning as they squeezed their way around the obstacle we presented by standing in the middle of the road. But, despite the risk of being overheard, I did not want to waste any more time by finding somewhere we could talk in private.

I kept my voice low as I replied, "They came for my brother."

"Why?"

"I'm not sure."

"What did you discover at his villa?" the Juggler asked me.

"Nothing," I lied.

Rufus shot me a suspicious look.

"Don't keep things from me, Scipio. I sent someone down there and he couldn't get near the place. There were armed men everywhere, he said."

"Maybe there were," I replied, working hard to maintain a blank expression. "But they aren't there now."

That, at least, was true.

"Someone must know what was going on there," Rufus scowled. "Why else would your brother have been arrested?"

"That's what I'm trying to find out," I told him.

He gave me a long, speculative look.

He asked, "Did you find your builder?"

"Yes. He was the one behind the attack on Primus. Not that it matters now."

"But I still helped you. So why don't you tell me what you found out?"

"There is nothing to tell," I assured him.

I don't think he believed me, but I wasn't going to back down, and I think he recognised that.

"I'll be in touch again soon," he promised. "And if I learn you're trying to double-cross me, you'll regret it."

With that ominous warning, he turned on his heel and strode away.

Caecus muttered, "I don't like that man."

"I don't like him much either," I agreed. "He's got no morals or scruples. He wouldn't deliberately set out to harm us, but if he thought he could gain an advantage for himself by helping one of our enemies, he wouldn't hesitate."

"Is that why you didn't tell him the full story?"

"That's right. I don't know what he would do with the information. Things are complicated enough without him getting involved."

Turning round, I set off down the street once more.

"Come on," I told Caecus. We need to find Cassius Dio."

We followed the *Clivus Suburanus* through the Subura and up towards the Esquiline where we soon located Dio's home on the *Vicus Africus*. As you would expect, it was a very large house, and it stood in spacious grounds which were elegantly decorated by many statues set amidst pleasant gardens. Dio must have warned his slaves that I might want to see him, because we were admitted with very little challenge.

We did not have long to wait before Dio met us in one of his opulent reception rooms, a large space decorated in marble and gilt, furnished with very comfortable couches and chairs. The Senator himself, though, looked more than a little tired, with dark patches under his eyes, and his cheeks and chin unshaven.

"It's very early," he said as he greeted us. "I presume it is something important?"

"Yes," I assured him. I did not tell him about Primus' arrest, but I did explain about Maximinis Thrax and the bargain I had struck with him.

"You presume a great deal," Dio frowned when he had heard my account. "But Maesa Augusta will certainly be interested. The proposal solves some very difficult problems."

"That's what I thought," I nodded, grateful that my plan wasn't being dismissed out of hand.

Dio cautioned, "But there are other considerations which may complicate matters."

"There are?"

"I'm afraid so. You see, relations between the Emperor and his young cousin have deteriorated even further since that unfortunate episode with the collapsing balcony rail."

"About that," I said, knowing I would not get a better opportunity to relay what I had learned. "I'm pretty sure it wasn't the Emperor's doing."

Dio cocked his head to one side as he asked, "How do you know?"

"I can't prove it," I told him, "but I am fairly certain it has been Herennius Muncius behind the assassination attempts on Alexander's life."

Dio blinked uncertainly, his mind perhaps dulled by the effects of the previous evening's party.

"Muncius?" he frowned.

"Yes. You see, I've been puzzling over why the Emperor would keep trying to kill his cousin after the promises he'd given to the Praetorians. He must know what they would do to him if he ever succeeded."

Dio gave a solemn nod as he grasped what Circe and I had worked out the previous evening.

"If Alexander were to die, the Praetorians would avenge him by killing the Emperor," he sighed.

"Exactly," I agreed. "That would leave the way open for Herennius Muncius to seize power. The Praetorians would have done his work for him without him needing to bribe them, and Thrax would immediately declare his support, bringing the whole of the army with him."

Dio nodded, "While Julia Maesa and her daughters would lose all authority. Without the two boys, they have nothing."

I said, "I expect Muncius would have them killed anyway, but even if they lived they would not be able to prevent him taking control."

"It's a more subtle plan than I gave Muncius credit for," Dio conceded. "But you say you have no proof?"

"I'm afraid not. Thrax confirmed his own role, but the rest of it is based only on information supplied as hearsay. But the theory does make sense. After all, I doubt the Emperor would botch a second attempt on his cousin's life. He has the resources and opportunities which Muncius does not."

Dio frowned, but he seemed to accept my theory was plausible.

With a sigh, he said, "Whether Muncius was behind the murder attempts or not, he's certainly responsible for recruiting Maximinis Thrax, so we know there is a coup planned. Thanks to you, we may yet have time to stop it."

"I hope so," I said. "But what has happened between the Emperor and his cousin? You said things had deteriorated. I thought it was bad enough already. How much worse has it become?"

With a shake of his head, he explained, "I'm afraid word spread about the accident Alexander nearly suffered. The Praetorians were very unhappy when they learned of it. The Emperor was taken aback by their open hostility, and he is now even more convinced that the Guard prefer Alexander to him. There is a rather dangerous mood surrounding the palace at the moment."

I said, "Then we need to speak to Julia Maesa as soon as possible."

Dio nodded, "I agree. We should be able to see her easily enough. I am sure she will not have arranged much business for today. There was rather a large party at the palace yesterday evening. It went on very late, as usual."

"Was the Emperor there?"

"Of course."

"And Alexander?"

"No. He was, according to the official pronouncement, too ill to attend."

"What about Herennius Muncius?"

"He was there, but kept a very low profile."

"I expect he must be feeling very frustrated," I remarked. "He was overheard bemoaning a recent setback to his plans. I expect that was the failure of the latest attempt to kill Alexander."

Wiping a hand across his brow, Dio murmured, "He came so close. We thought he was still attempting to gather support, but he was already acting."

"Let's hope he doesn't get another chance," I responded.

"Indeed," Dio said. "I know the Emperor is capricious, but I doubt Muncius would be an improvement if he were ever to hold ultimate power. I suspect the days of the proscriptions would return."

That was a sobering thought. In the final days of the Republic, those who seized power would post lists of names in the forum. Anyone whose name was proscribed could be legally killed with no fear of prosecution. Indeed, rewards were often paid when the head of the proscribed individual was presented to whoever had posted the list. Of course, when the next mob took over, fresh lists were posted so that revenge could be taken. It was a sordid episode in Rome's history, and not one I'd like to see return. Nowadays, Emperors merely send out hit squads to dispose of anyone they dislike, but even that wasn't as bad as the proscriptions. Whether Muncius would resort to that, I couldn't say, but an old-fashioned Roman like him might think it a good idea. It was a scary thought, especially because I suspected my name would be on any list Muncius might draw up.

Dio went to don a fresh toga, then we set off for the Palatine with half a dozen of his slaves escorting us. Thanks to his presence, we gained entrance to the palace with little difficulty. The place was eerily quiet, presumably because most people were still asleep after the previous evening's excesses.

Julia Maesa kept us waiting for about half an hour before we were shown into the same room where she had met us the last time, with the same slaves in attendance. Once again, she sat in her chair, while the three of us stood facing her.

Her hair had been pinned up on her head, and layers of makeup had been applied to her face, but her tiredness was evident. At her age, a late night of partying had probably taken its toll even if she had remained entirely sober.

"Well?" she asked me tetchily.

"Herennius Muncius is definitely plotting to seize power," I told her. "I believe he is the one behind the attempts on Alexander's life."

I recounted my story again, although Maesa barely reacted. She remained seated, her expression stern as stone.

"Do you have witnesses?" she demanded once I had explained my theory.

303

I had no wish to place Petrus or Mallius Proximus in the hands of imperial interrogators, so I shook my head.

"No, Augusta. It is hearsay, although it fits the facts. But there is more to tell you, and I can bear personal witness to this."

She pouted slightly, but nodded for me to continue.

I informed her, "I do not know how much support Muncius commands in the Senate, but I know for certain that he has the backing of Maximinis Thrax."

That startled her. She went very still, her face growing even more pale, but she was a tough old bird, and she quickly recovered.

"Thrax will back him?" she asked.

"Yes, but I spoke to Thrax and I have an idea which could foil Muncius. With your agreement, of course, Augusta."

I could see she was rattled, but she did not waste time on histrionics. Maesa was too experienced not to understand the very real threat posed by Maximinis Thrax. Legally, the Senate might be the body which confirmed the appointment of a new Emperor, but the reality was that it was the Army who made the decision. She could probably see her own doom approaching, so she let me explain my plan.

"Tell me," she instructed.

Taking a deep breath, I began, "I think it is no secret that the Emperor is unpopular. His nature is such that he is, in the view of many, unsuited to the role."

Maesa stared at me, but at least she did not disagree. How could she? She was perfectly aware of what people thought of her grandson.

I went on, "We both have a vested interest in preventing Herennius Muncius succeeding, but I think we both realise the futility of opposing Maximinis Thrax. He is adamant that your grandson must be removed as Emperor. He was most insistent that I tell you this."

I thought I saw a faint twitch on the old woman's cheek, but she was too intelligent to make any comment about oaths of loyalty given by a soldier. Thrax had supported Elagabalus at the outset, but he was not the sort who would feel bound by an oath if the Emperor failed to live up to his expectations. In Thrax's eyes, an oath worked both ways.

She asked me, "So what is it you are proposing?"

I told her, "There is another heir of the house of Severus, albeit only due to his mother's family."

"Alexander," Maesa nodded.

"Indeed. It is no secret the Praetorians like him. Thrax was not thrilled at the idea of having a boy Emperor, but he did agree to support his claim in the knowledge that the lad would have some capable advisers."

Maesa did not need me to draw a diagram. She and her daughter, Julia Mamaea, would be those advisers.

She asked, "And what does Maximinis Thrax demand in return for his support?"

There was no point in prevarication, so I simply told her, "He wishes to be appointed as Governor of a Province, preferably in Pannonia or Illyria."

I had expected her to bristle at that, but she merely pointed out, "Provincial Governors are appointed from among men of Senatorial or equestrian rank. Thrax was born a barbarian. What he is asking is unprecedented."

"I know."

I held her gaze, saying nothing more until she gave a brief nod.

"Perhaps it is a price worth paying," she reflected softly.

That gave me hope. I had suspected Maesa would not allow Elagabalus' behaviour to endanger her own position. Without him, she was vulnerable unless she could find a replacement who would be under her control. And that replacement needed the approval of the Army.

There was, though, one other vital point I needed to make.

"The important thing," I said, "is that the current Emperor need not die. He is, after all, a son of Caracalla and your own grandson. As far as I know, he remains popular in the eastern Empire, so I suggest that he should be sent back to his home in Emesa where he can stay in exile and retain his position as chief priest of the Sun God."

Once again I had surprised her. She looked at me with open astonishment.

"Exile?" she frowned, as if the term meant nothing to her.

305

"Why not? The Emperor Tiberius lived in self-imposed exile for years."

Maesa shook her head.

"That was not the same at all. Tiberius remained Emperor. What you are suggesting would create a precedent. Perhaps a dangerous one."

I shrugged, "But what harm could he do? Place him under guard, and put a loyal man in charge of those guards. Everyone knows your grandson is too volatile to be a good ruler, so I doubt whether anyone would want to reinstate him."

"I did not think you were an idealist, Scipio," Maesa remarked as if I'd disappointed her in some way.

"I've seen too many people killed," I told her. "I am sick of it."

"So you seek to replace one of my grandsons with the other, yet keep them both alive?"

"I'd like to keep everyone alive if possible," I nodded. "Herennius Muncius, for example, could be banished. Without Thrax's support, his plans to become Emperor will collapse. Send him away to the Black Sea where nobody will ever hear from him again."

Maesa's thin lips twitched in a faint smile, but she countered, "And what of the Emperor's mother, my daughter, Soaemias? What do I do with her?"

Fortunately, I'd already thought of an answer to this question.

I said, "An idealist would tell you to send her into exile with her son, but a more pragmatic person might suggest you keep her under house arrest somewhere else. Somewhere closer to hand, perhaps."

"As a hostage for her son's good behaviour, you mean?"

"Why not?"

Maesa's manicured fingers tapped thoughtfully on the arm of her chair. Her eyes glinted in the light of the oil lamps as she weighed up what I had said.

After a moment, she asked me, "Is that all you have to tell me?"

"No, Augusta. There is one other matter."

"What is that?"

306

So far, everything I had told her was the truth as far as I knew. Now, though, Circe's plan required me to misrepresent things. In other words, to start lying to the most powerful woman in the empire.

I said, "My brother, Sempronius Primus, was … is … one of Herennius Muncius' clients. I'm afraid Muncius persuaded him to help make contact with Maximinis Thrax. Primus, though, had no idea what it was about. He was merely a dupe used by Muncius to lay some groundwork for his own plans."

I could hear the scepticism in her voice as she drawled, "Really?"

"Yes, Augusta. Primus is a greedy fool, eager to curry favour. He saw Herennius Muncius as a man of wealth who could help his own career, so he foolishly agreed to do things he now knows he should not have done."

"I see," Maesa almost smiled. "So what is it you are asking?"

"I would be grateful if you could write out a formal pardon, Augusta. Primus would be in your debt, as would I."

"A formal pardon? For treason?"

"Not treason, Augusta. For being tricked into aiding someone who was guilty of treason."

"That is a fine distinction the law courts could debate for months," Maesa said. "But I suppose you deserve some reward for your work, Scipio."

She turned to the tall, elegant slave woman who was obviously her principal attendant.

"Fetch a scribe. Tell him to bring ink and parchment."

The woman left through a side door, returning so quickly it was obvious that Maesa kept scribes in close attendance. The man, a tall, thin, pasty-faced individual with his fingers stained by ink, took his place at a small desk, spread a parchment, then opened a bottle of ink and took up his quill.

While Dio, Caecus and I stood there, Maesa dictated an order to the Praetorians to arrest Herennius Muncius and send him to Tomis, a small city on the coast of the Black Sea where he was to remain in permanent exile. It was the same place the first Augustus had exiled the poet, Ovid, and it sounded like a very dreary place indeed if you could trust Ovid's descriptions.

Maesa's next dictation was to write out a formal notice pardoning Primus for his involvement in Muncius' conspiracy. It was short and to the point.

When the scribe had finished, the slave woman took both parchments, laying them on a wooden tray which she presented to Maesa along with a quill and ink. Maesa scribbled her signature, then added her seal, pressing a large ring into blobs of hot wax which the slave poured onto the documents, using a candle to melt the wax.

Maesa told her attendant, "Send for Publius Valerius Comazon. I wish to give him his orders in person."

Comazon, I recalled, was the Praetorian Prefect. If these orders came from Julia Maesa, I knew there was no chance of them being disobeyed.

Once again, the slave woman went through the side door, returning a moment later to confirm Comazon had been summoned.

We waited a few moments for the ink to dry and the wax to cool, then the slave woman rolled up the parchment bearing the pardon and handed it to me.

"Thank you, Augusta," I said, bowing my head.

"And what of you, Scipio? Do you want nothing else for yourself?"

"No, Augusta. All I want is to return home with my friends and family as soon as possible."

Maesa's smile was now as genuine as I could ever recall seeing on her.

She said, "You are an odd man, Sempronius Scipio. Most people would ask for gold or appointment to a position of influence."

"I have gold," I told her. "And I have no desire for a position of influence."

She pointed out, "Yet you have influence matters already."

I merely shrugged. It would not have been sensible to tell her the only reason I had become involved in this messy affair was because she had forced me to.

She said, "You may go now. I have things to attend to. But do not speak of this to anyone else for the moment."

"I understand, Augusta."

"And you can be assured that I will keep Alexander safe until matters have been resolved."

I nodded my understanding. The young boy was now the most important person in her schemes, and he needed to stay alive.

She waved her dismissal. Clutching Primus' pardon, I followed Cassius Dio and, with Caecus hovering protectively at my side, made my way out of the palace.

Chapter 30
Bargains

Cassius Dio was in an ebullient mood as he showed us out of the palace. He slapped me on the back, shook my hand, and warned me again not to do anything which might upset Julia Maesa's plans.

"You've given her a solution to her problems," he said. "But there is still a lot to be done."

"I have done my part," I replied. "I'm more than happy to walk away and leave it to you now."

"It has been a pleasure meeting you, Sempronius Scipio," he said.

As we shook hands yet again, I asked him, "Could you help me with something? I need to find a reliable lawyer."

"A lawyer?"

"Preferably an honest one."

He laughed, "I doubt there are any in Rome, but you could try Oclatius Cornix. He has an office only a few streets away."

He gave me directions to the home of Oclatius Cornix, a man he claimed could be trusted as far as any lawyer. The place turned out to be a modest little house on the lower slopes of the Caelian Hill, so that was my first port of call.

On the way, Caecus broke his silence to observe, "For a man who has little time for the gods, Scipio, you do seem to be blessed by them. Your wife's plan is extremely clever but, even so, I can't believe you got away with that."

"I haven't got away with it yet," I told him. "But at least all we need to do now is concentrate on our own affairs. We can leave Herennius Muncius and Maximinis Thrax to Julia Maesa."

The first thing I needed to do was consult a lawyer. Oclatius Cornix was a beanpole of a man with a scrawny beard which failed to conceal his pointed chin, and he had long, tapering fingers. He clucked and fussed quite a bit, but was very attentive when I told him Cassius Dio had recommended him.

"He's a very important man," the lawyer informed me solemnly.

I knew that already, but I merely smiled and told him what I wanted from him. As an inducement, I paid him his fee plus half as much again.

"That's for your discretion," I told him.

He seemed offended that I might consider him in need of a bribe to keep his mouth shut, but anyone who makes a living pleading cases in the law courts knows how precarious a career that can be, so he tucked the money into his purse, then told me, "What you need is very straightforward. It will not take long to prepare the documents. I can have my scribes copy them out within the hour."

"That's great," I smiled. "It gives us time to get a bite to eat."

We went in search of a cook shop. We'd been up since dawn, and I hadn't had time to snatch breakfast, so we found a place serving bread and olive oil. I ordered two plates, and tucked in ravenously when the food arrived.

While we ate, Caecus observed, "I hope you have time to make this work. We do not know how soon Julia Maesa will act."

I replied, "I reckon she'll need a day or two to make contact with Thrax."

I hesitated, a worrying thought coming to mind.

"What is it?" Caecus enquired.

"She never asked how she was supposed to get in touch with Thrax."

"He said he has his own agents in Rome," Caecus reminded me.

"Yes, but Julia Maesa can't know who they are."

I chewed another mouthful of bread, fretting over this niggling point.

"It doesn't matter," I sighed. "I don't know where Thrax has gone, so Maesa will need to figure it out for herself. Perhaps Thrax will get the message when Herennius Muncius is arrested."

"Speaking of which," Caecus said, "has it occurred to you that Muncius may have already heard about your brother's arrest?"

I shrugged, "There's nothing he can do about it. Alexander will be protected, and Thrax won't back him. All he can do is run away."

"Or slit his wrists," Caecus pointed out.

"That's up to him. I've done my best to keep everyone alive, but I can't stop him if he's going to throw his life away."

"And in the meantime you are going to make your brother sweat?"

I nodded, "It will serve the stupid bugger right."

Caecus, his face a mask of indifference, said, "I would like to be present when you explain that to your mother."

"Don't worry. We'll get Primus out soon enough. As soon as we've fixed some of the injustices he's caused."

We headed back to the lawyer's house as soon as we'd finished our breakfast.

Cornix was as good as his word. I perused the three documents he had drafted and could find no fault with them. Not that I am an expert in legal matters, but he certainly seemed to have covered all the points I'd asked for.

"My scribes have prepared each document in duplicate as you requested," he explained rather needlessly.

"Thank you. Could I trouble you for a case to carry them in?"

He gave me a thin smile as he said, "Of course."

"Excellent. But I also need a small supply of ink and a quill or stylus."

That earned me an odd look, but he produced a small stylus and a vial of ink which he sealed with a tiny cork.

I tucked the scroll case inside my cloak and placed the ink and stylus in my belt pouch.

"It's been a pleasure doing business with you," I told the lawyer.

After that, we crossed the city again, heading to the north-eastern quarter. It was a long walk, and it was past mid-day by the time we reached the Praetorian Camp. This fortress is situated just outside the old city walls, not far from the end of the Quirinal Hill. It has huge walls of its own, forming a strong base where the Guard could hold out against any attack for a long time. Not that anyone had attacked Rome for a few centuries except other Romans, and some citizens joked that the walls were designed to keep the Praetorians safe from the Roman mob rather than anyone else.

Caecus, of course, knew the camp well. He had been a senior member of the Guard, and had spent some years in Rome in the days of Septimius Severus. He strolled up to the main gates as if he owned the place, and asked to see Centurion Laetilius Auctas.

It was Decurion Canidius Frequens who came to meet us and show us inside.

"I take it you want to see your brother?" he asked me.

"Yes. How is he?"

"The lads roughed him up a bit. He was shouting and hitting, so we had to quieten him down."

"He's an idiot," I nodded.

Frequens said, "Since then, he's been very quiet. He's just sitting in his cell, feeling sorry for himself."

Inside the camp were a great many buildings, some of them two or three storeys high. These contained the barracks rooms, the officers' quarters, stores, workshops and everything the Guard needed. There were even a couple of small temples where the troops could make offerings to the gods. There were, though, no stables here because the cavalry element of the Guard had its own base on the Caelian Hill on the eastern side of the city. Other than that, it was like an army marching camp except made of stone, brick and wood instead of having leather tents.

Frequens took us to one of the nearer buildings, a long, two storey affair lined with small windows. There was a door in the nearer end, where I saw the Centurion Laetilius Auctas waiting for us, his hands planted on his hips. He had removed his plumed helmet and was smiling broadly.

"Aelius Caecus!" he grinned. "You are a devious bastard. What is this game we are playing?"

"It's not my game, Auctas," Caecus replied cheerfully as he jabbed a thumb towards me. "It's all his doing."

"You wanted your own brother arrested?" the Centurion asked me. "Why?"

"Believe it or not, it was to save his life. Thank you for helping out."

"It was a pleasure!" Auctas chuckled. "You should have seen the look on his face when I told him he was under arrest."

I said to him, "I'd like you to keep him here for a couple more days. Would that be all right?"

313

He shrugged, "That's no problem. Aelius Caecus vouches for you, so we're happy to help."

"Thanks. I do want to see my brother, though. I need him to sign something."

"Fine with me," he shrugged. "You're the one paying us."

We were certainly paying him well. Circe had come up with this idea as a way to both teach Primus a lesson, to give me a hold over him and, as I'd told Centurion Auctas, to save his life. Julia Maesa had signed the pardon, but I hadn't been sure she would agree to it. But it had been Caecus who had contacted his former colleague, Auctas, and arranged for him to arrest Primus. I reckoned that, if my brother was locked up in the Praetorian Camp, he might just be safe if Maesa decided to send out murder squads to dispose of Herennius Muncius and all his associates. Of course, those murder squads were usually comprised of Praetorians, but Auctas had been asked to keep Primus' identity quiet, and we hoped that hiding my brother in the midst of their camp was as safe as anywhere.

As it was, Maesa had agreed to my proposals without question. That had been a great relief, but it now meant I could use the situation to redress some of the wrongs Primus had committed.

Caecus went to Auctas' office to share a cup of wine, while Frequens led me down into the basement of the building. Here, in the cool of the subterranean lower level, were store rooms and a handful of cells. Rome doesn't generally go in for imprisonment as a punishment for crime. Justice tends to rely more on things like fines, banishment, sending people to work in the mines, mutilation or death. Anyone locked in a cell is usually only there as a temporary measure until their fate can be decided. There are public cells, and there are these ones used by the Praetorians.

The basement was a damp, dark place, guttering torches on the walls creating small pools of flickering light between long stretches of shadow. Frequens had brought a small oil lamp, but it did little to improve the ambience of the place. A cat slunk past me as I followed the Decurion along the stone-lined corridor, the animal's green eyes flashing when it glared at me for invading its home. Cats are essential wherever there are food stores because they keep the rodents in check, but I confess I'm no great lover of the beasts. They tend to treat humans with a sort of disdain I dislike.

Frequens stopped at a thick, heavy door which had a tiny, barred window. He took a key from his belt, placed it in the lock and pushed the door open for me.

"Just shout when you want out," he told me.

He handed me the oil lamp, and I held it high as I stepped into the gloomy cell.

Primus was sitting on a low, stone bunk. He had no blankets or pillow, and he was still dressed in the same undertunic he had been wearing when the Praetorians had dragged him from his bed that morning. His left leg was still encased in its splints and bandages, stretched awkwardly out in front of him, and he looked utterly miserable.

He looked up at me, shading his eyes from the light of the lamp. He must have been sitting here in complete darkness, I realised. His face was haggard, and his eyes were sunken even more than usual. There was a dark bruise on his right cheek, and his lower lip was swollen, his chin streaked with blood where it had seeped from the injury.

"Hello, Primus," I said cheerfully. "I'm glad you are still alive."

I placed the oil lamp on the end of the stone sleeping shelf, then stepped back to take another look at him. He was filthy, his tunic ripped at the shoulder and smeared with grime. The stench in the cell was almost overpowering. I don't suppose the Praetorians bothered much with sanitation for their prisoners.

"What are you doing here?" Primus croaked, his tone full of despair.

"I came to tell you I am trying to get you out of here. I've been to the palace."

"The palace?" he repeated dully.

"Yes. I'm trying to persuade them that you knew nothing about Herennius Muncius' treachery. He's being exiled, by the way."

"Exiled?"

Primus seemed to be having trouble grasping what I was saying.

315

I told him, "But I need your help, brother. It appears people have been investigating you as well."

"Investigating?"

His habit of repeating everything was grating, but at least he wasn't arguing with me. I had the upper hand now, which was what I wanted.

"Yes. I'm told you cheated your builder, Mallius Tanicus, and forced him to sell you his business for a lot less than it was worth. Is that right?"

Primus blinked several times. He looked utterly defeated.

"Did you?" I pressed. "Did you force Tanicus out of business and put a couple of your own guys in to run it once you'd bought it?"

I saw him swallow nervously, and I could tell he was considering lying to me, so I added, "Look, Primus. You are in deep trouble here. Those guys you set up to replace Tanicus were involved in an attempt to kill the Emperor's cousin. We know all about it."

I hadn't thought it possible for him to look any more miserable, but he now seemed utterly deflated.

I persisted, "I need to know the truth. The only way you are getting out of here is to show you are prepared to make some recompense. If you do, there's a chance I can keep your involvement out of things."

I was talking nonsense, of course. If he'd been thinking properly, he'd have realised that the builders would already have been arrested, in which case they'd have named him as being a conspirator. So far, I hadn't mentioned the builders to anyone in authority. If Cassius Dio or Julia Maesa did somehow make the connection, things would soon become even more complicated. For the moment, though, all I wanted was to use Murmillo and his partner as a lever against Primus. Fortunately, he wasn't thinking straight at all, and he nodded his head in miserable agreement.

"Yes."

"Yes you cheated Tanicus?"

Another nod.

"And Fabius and Didius were sent to try to sabotage Alexander's balcony?"

He nodded again.

316

"All right," I sighed. "Thank you. Now, there is something you can do that will help get you out of here."

"What? Tell me!"

His voice was pleading and desperate. Like most bullies, Primus only respected people who were stronger than him, and he knew the Praetorians were controlled by the most powerful people in the empire. This knowledge had crushed his spirit.

Carefully, I drew out the scrolls Cornix had prepared. From my belt pouch, I withdrew the stylus and vial of ink.

"Sign these," I told him.

He took the scrolls, peering at them closely in order to read the finely crafted text.

I explained, "It's a deed of sale. I need you to sell me the builder's business before the imperial Treasury seizes control of it. I'll pay one hundred gold aurei, which I believe is the amount you paid for the business only a few months ago. And I'll put my own people in charge. In case you were wondering, Mallius Proximus will manage it for me. His father killed himself, you see, and you are to blame for that."

I was piling the pressure on him, keeping him wondering precisely why he had been arrested. Adding culpability for a death would, I hoped, keep him confused.

He was still reading as I continued, "I know it's a bargain price, but it should be enough when you consider it will help save your life."

"Will it get me out of here?" he asked plaintively.

"I think so. It shows some remorse, and recompenses Proximus. It also removes any link with the men who tried to murder the young Caesar."

"But you will own the business?" he frowned, perhaps beginning to rally himself. His dislike of me was so ingrained it probably sparked some resentment.

"Only because I have the money," I assured him. "And because I'm working hard to get you out of the mess you've landed in. You're bloody lucky your head hasn't been sliced off. At the very least, I'd expect you to be sent to the salt mines for helping a traitor like Muncius. But if you don't want to sign, I'll go back to the palace and tell them you'd rather take your chances with imperial justice."

That was enough to quash any defiance.

"I'll sign," he muttered grimly.

I handed him the ink and stylus.

"And make sure it's your regular signature," I reminded him. "That will be checked."

He scribbled his name on both copies, then passed them back to me.

"Thank you. Now there are two more documents I need you to sign."

He scowled darkly as I passed over the copies.

"These are Deeds of Manumission!" he blurted.

"That's right. You have two slaves named Cassia and Petrus. I want you to set them free."

"Why?" he demanded, growing ever more suspicious.

"Because you need my help, and this is part of the price."

"They are just slaves! What are they to you?"

"They are human beings. And you let your thug Vespillo beat Cassia so badly she could barely walk. She deserves better than that. Petrus wants to marry her, so I want you to free both of them."

"You are too soft," he muttered, although there was little conviction in his words. He was too far gone in self pity to do more than mouth his usual complaints against me. With a sigh, he signed the two documents and their copies.

"Do I get out now?" he asked.

"Not yet," I replied as I tucked the signed Deeds into the cylindrical scroll case. "It's not easy convincing people of your innocence. I have a lot of work to do on that front."

"How long?"

"I'm not sure. A couple of days maybe."

"Days?" he gasped. "Down here in the dark for days?"

"It's better than the salt mines," I reminded him. "Or the other option."

As I said this, I drew a finger across my throat. Then I called for Frequens to come and let me out.

I know I was being cruel, but Primus had bullied me all my life, and I was petty enough to enjoy taking some revenge.

Frequens arrived at last. He unlocked the door, took the lamp from me, then we left, leaving Primus alone in the darkness.

Chapter 31
A Thief In The Day

Caecus was sitting in Laetilius Auctas' office, the two of them sharing a jug of wine. Auctas offered me a cup which I accepted gratefully.

"I need a couple of witnesses to these deeds," I told them as I took the scrolls out of the case and spread them on Auctas' desk.

Both men grinned as they looked at me. A witness should be present when a deed is signed, but I didn't think anyone would argue with either of them if they said they had seen Primus add his signature.

Like most Centurions, Auctas had ink and quills close at hand, and I was soon able to tuck the completed deeds away in their case.

I said, "Thanks. Now, could you move Primus out of the cell and lock him somewhere a bit less harsh?"

Auctas frowned, "Caecus tells me Julia Maesa has pardoned him. But you still want us to hold him here?"

"Only for a couple of days at most. I need a bit of time to sort things out."

He nodded, "We have rooms on the upper floor. Do you want him to get an easy time?"

"Not particularly. But showing him he can receive a small reward for cooperating wouldn't hurt. And, to be honest, I'm worried he might do something daft if he's left down there alone."

"Fine," Auctas shrugged. "I'll have him taken to one of the upper rooms. They have small windows, so I doubt a fat slob like him could climb out. It's a long drop to the ground in any case."

"Thanks. But don't let him get too comfortable. Small rations of plain food would be good for him, too. He could do with losing some weight."

"You're a hard man, Scipio," Auctas observed.

"Most people think I'm too soft," I smiled, "so I'll take that as a compliment."

"Aelius Caecus tells me you were a spy, yet he still seems to like you."

"There's no accounting for taste," I grinned.

Auctas smiled back. Whatever Caecus had said to him seemed to have convinced the man to help us without any quibbles. Mind you, the hefty bribe we'd paid him probably helped too.

After draining my cup, I told Caecus, "It's time we were heading home. They'll be wondering what's kept us."

I was in a hurry to tell Circe what we had accomplished, so I set a brisk pace as soon as we had passed through the gates. It wasn't far from the Praetorian Camp to Primus' house on the Quirinal, so we reached the door in less than half an hour. To my surprise, it was old Lucius who responded to my knock on the door.

"No guard today?" I asked him as we stepped into the cool of the lobby.

Lucius' face bore an expression of anxiety as he told me, "No, Sir. Most of the Master's bodyguards have left."

"Left?"

"That's right, Sir. They were very worried after the Master was arrested this morning, then they heard what happened to Herennius Muncius, and they all ran away. Well, most of them. There are a couple still here, I think."

Glancing at Caecus, I remarked, "Julia Maesa has acted quickly. I expect Herennius Muncius will be on his way to the Black Sea before sunset."

Lucius frowned in confusion as he said, "The Black Sea, Sir? What has that got to do with it?"

"It's where Muncius is being sent into exile, "I informed him patiently.

Lucius had never been the brightest, but he seemed to be very perplexed by this information. Then he said, "But, Sir, Herennius Muncius is dead."

"Dead? How?"

"Some soldiers went to his house, Sir. They gave him the choice of opening his veins or having his head cut off. He chose to slit his wrists."

Now it was my turn to look confused.

"Are you sure? Where did you hear this?"

Lucius simpered, "Some of his servants brought the news, Sir. They were leaving town, but they stopped long enough to tell us about it."

I was struggling to take this in, but after a moment I protested, "But I saw Maesa sign the document banishing him!"

Caecus pointed out, "But we didn't see her handing it over to Valerius Comazon. I wouldn't put it past her to have burned it as soon as we were out of the room, then written another one ordering Muncius' death."

I exclaimed, "Sweet Jupiter! That sly old witch!"

I felt betrayed. While I'd been drinking wine in the Praetorian Camp, Maesa had sent out murder squads to dispose of the conspirators. My whole plan had been founded on the fact that nobody had needed to die. Julia Maesa obviously had other ideas, but the thought of Muncius' fate left a sour taste in my mouth. If she could deceive me so easily on that front, what else might she do?

I asked Caecus, "Didn't Auctas warn you about this?"

He shook his head.

"I expect the guards were despatched from the palace. Auctas certainly hadn't heard anything. I'll swear to that."

I let out an exasperated sigh. Our plan was already coming apart, and that meant we could still be in very real danger.

I asked Lucius, "Where is Aurelia?"

"Through in the main house, Sir. With your mother and Mistress Hortensia."

I nodded my thanks. At least they were all together, so we would only need to tell our tale once.

The main house was eerily quiet. There was no sign of Mardonius, the *major domo*, and there were only two of Primus' bodyguards slouching in the atrium, sitting beside one another on the edge of the *impluvium*. One of them was Gallicus, the squat ex-gladiator who had guided us to the Viminal on our first day here. The other was a taller, leaner man with craggy features and dark eyebrows set beneath a close-cropped head of mousy hair. They both rose to their feet when they saw us walking towards them. Their expressions were those of men who were sorely in need of reassurance.

"What's going on, Sir?" Gallicus asked me, his manner far more polite than I'd experienced from any of Primus' thugs up until now.

"I'm not sure," I told him. "I've just heard Herennius Muncius is dead."

"Him and a few other Senators," Gallicus informed me.

"Others?"

"Some of Herennius Muncius' associates," he explained. "At least, that's what that mad bugger Vespillo told us. He came running here with the news, then he buggered off, and so did most of the other lads when they heard what had happened."

"Did any soldiers come here?" I asked.

"No, Sir. Not since that mob this morning."

That was something, at least. Perhaps Julia Maesa intended to keep her word about pardoning Primus.

I asked Gallicus, "How many of you stayed?"

He jerked a thumb towards his companion as he replied, "Only me and Casca here. The rest of them reckoned the Praetorians would do away with Sempronius Primus, so they took the chance to run for it before they got caught up in things."

"So why didn't you join them?"

Gallicus shrugged, "I'm not sure, to be honest. It just didn't seem right."

His companion, Casca, mumbled, "I've been here longer than most of the lads, and the Lady was always good to me. I didn't want to run out on her."

It was nice to know some of Primus' heavies had a conscience, but they were the least of my worries.

I told them, "Well, Sempronius Primus is still alive, and I expect he'll be back here in a day or two. So keep your heads. And thanks for staying."

The two men breathed more easily when they heard that, and both of them thanked me profusely.

"We'll keep the house safe until he returns," Gallicus promised.

I doubted whether they would stand firm if the Praetorians did come back, but at least it meant Hortensia and her children had some protection for the time being.

322

Leaving the two guards, Caecus and I walked on, passing through the deserted inner courtyard and making our way to the rear of the house. To my surprise, we found Circe, Hortensia and my mother in Primus' study. They were sitting forlornly around the wide desk, but Circe leaped to her feet when we entered the room.

"You're back!" she exclaimed in obvious relief. "What happened?"

I kissed her, then quickly relayed a short account of our meeting with Julia Maesa.

"She seemed to go along with the plan," I recounted. "But I hear Herennius Muncius and some other Senators have already been executed."

Circe frowned, "Yes, we've heard the news."

My mother interrupted, "But what about Primus? Where is he? You said Julia Maesa signed a pardon."

I hesitated, then like a guilty child being caught red-handed, I admitted, "I'm sorry, but we have a confession to make."

Feeling very awkward, I explained how we had arranged Primus' arrest ourselves.

I told Hortensia, "I'm sorry you had to go through that, but it was important the whole thing seemed real. We thought it was the best way to keep Primus safe. And it seems to have worked. He is still alive."

"Then why isn't he here?" my mother frowned.

"Because we have a couple of things to sort out."

I withdrew the various scrolls from my pouch and passed them to Hortensia. She took them with an almost distracted air, but she scanned the first few lines of each.

"He has sold a builder's business to you?"

"Yes. It's the one Mallius Tanicus used to own. I've bought it, and I'm going to put Tanicus' son in charge of it."

With a sorrowful look at my mother, I added, "Mallius Tanicus killed himself after Primus forced him out of business."

Her face grew sad as she whispered, "The poor man! He was such a lovely person."

Hortensia, meanwhile, had read the other documents.

"He is setting two of the slaves free?" she asked in surprise. "He's never done that before."

323

"I asked him to do it," I told her. "But you can have the pleasure of telling them yourself. And while you're doing that, Circe will bring you the purchase price for the builder's yard."

Hortensia gave a weak smile at that.

"Thank you," she said. "After what has happened here, that will prove useful."

I looked from her to the other women, noticing their faces were still evincing concern.

"What has happened?" I asked.

Hortensia waved a hand towards the rear of the room.

"Mardonius knew where the spare key to Primus' money chest was kept. As soon as he heard about Herennius Muncius' death, he grabbed as much as he could and ran off."

I gaped at her, then moved past to look down at an open chest which sat on the floor behind the desk. There were some small bags of coins, each one neatly tied and labelled, but they barely covered the bottom of the chest, and a quick inspection revealed that they contained low value *asses* and *sesterces*.

"He took the silver and gold," Hortensia explained, her voice hard and angry.

"Did nobody try to stop him?" I asked.

"The other guards had already run away," Circe explained. "As soon as they heard the news, they decided not to hang around."

"When did this happen?" I asked.

"Not long ago," Circe informed me. "Perhaps half an hour before you arrived. Perhaps a bit less."

She went on, "I sent Collinus after him as soon as we found out, but Mardonius had already disappeared."

"Where is Collinus anyway?" I asked.

"Still searching, I think," she shrugged.

I swore.

"I never did like Mardonius."

My mother asked, "Can you not find him for us? He stole a lot of money."

"It's a matter for the *vigiles*," I replied.

The looks on their faces told me what I already knew.

"The *vigiles* won't bother trying to find him," Circe snorted.

324

I said, "Don't be too harsh on them. There are over a million people living in Rome, and finding one man who doesn't want to be found is next to impossible."

"Even for the great Scipio?" she asked, arching a delicate eyebrow.

"I'm tired," I told her. "I've already done one impossible thing today. Asking me to do another is a bit too much."

At that moment, Collinus returned, his swarthy features clouded with irritation.

Without preamble, he reported to Circe, "I discovered he took a litter. Unfortunately, nobody overheard which destination he gave to the bearers. All I was able to learn was that they set off towards the south."

Caecus' brow furrowed as he said, "South? I thought he'd make for the nearest gate and buy a horse. Why would he head into the city?"

Hortensia asked, "And why would he take a litter?"

"Because carrying a large sack of coins isn't easy," I told her. "Money is heavy."

"Then perhaps he has not gone far," she suggested hopefully.

"Perhaps not. But that doesn't help us unless we know where he is heading."

There was a short silence while we contemplated this problem. Then I had an idea.

Turning to Caecus, I asked, "Could you go and fetch those two guards?"

He gave me a puzzled look, but nodded and ambled off.

"What are you thinking?" Circe asked me.

"I'm thinking somebody must know where Mardonius has gone. And the only people who knew him well are those two."

"I suppose it's worth asking," Circe nodded.

Caecus soon returned, bringing a nervous-looking Gallicus and Casca with him.

"Have you heard what Mardonius did?" I asked them.

They both gave cautious nods, perhaps fearing I was about to blame them for not stopping him.

Instead, I asked, "Do you know whether he has any friends or family in Rome? We are trying to figure out where he might have gone."

Gallicus shook his head straight away.

"I've not been here long enough," he said. "Besides, I never took to Mardonius. He was a bit of a blowhard if you ask me."

I glanced at Casca, who didn't seem to be the brightest.

"What about you? You told me you've been here longer than most of Primus' guards."

The tall, craggy man gave a slow nod.

"Mardonius was always full of talk," he recalled. "Like Gallicus says, most of it was just so much horse dung."

"So did he ever talk about his family?"

Casca pursed his lips while he considered this.

"He's from somewhere up north, I think. He never mentioned having any family here."

"What about friends? Was he close to anyone?"

Casca grunted, "Mardonius was only friends with people he thought could do him favours."

"That figures," I muttered darkly.

Then Casca continued, "But there were a couple of guys who used to work here. The boss set them up in business a few months back. Mardonius was a bit jealous, I think, but he kept in touch with them. I know that for a fact because I saw them speaking together one day."

"Who are these guys?" I asked, trying not to get too excited.

His response was as surprising as it should have been obvious.

"Fabius Murmillo and Didius Pomponius."

"The builders?" I gasped.

"Yeah, that's right. The boss set them up nicely there."

Circe hissed, "Mardonius would have kept in touch with them. Somebody needed to carry messages back and forwards."

I made up my mind instantly.

"We need to go there anyway," I said. "Mardonius may, or may not, have gone to warn them, but it's the only lead we've got."

"He's got a good head start on us," Caecus warned.

"Yes, but he's in a litter. They don't move very fast. Come on, let's go."

Chapter 32
Restoration

Gallicus and Casca agreed to come with us. I also summoned half a dozen of our slaves in case of trouble, then I set off, moving in a sort of half-jog, half-walk as I led the way down the hill.

The streets were strangely quiet, word of the murder squads clearly having spread. The Roman mob is notoriously fickle, but there are times when it keeps its collective head indoors. This meant that we made good time, reaching the *Via Ostiensis* in under an hour, although I was sweating profusely by the time we reached the gates of the yard, and we took a few minutes to regain our breath before heading inside.

While we were recovering, I looked at the expectant faces of my companions.

"We want no trouble," I warned, "but be ready for it, all the same."

They each gave a solemn nod.

"All right," I decided. "Let's see who's here."

We marched into the yard, attracting some nervous looks from the workers who were scattered around the place, some sawing wood, others chipping at stone. All of them stopped work when they saw us, and some discreetly slipped away into the further recesses of the cluttered yard, ducking out of sight behind the sheds.

I told the slaves to close the gates and make sure nobody left, then I asked Gallicus and Casca to wait outside the office. They knew nothing about the conspiracy, and I wanted it to stay that way.

With Caecus and Collinus, I strode to the office, flung the door open and barged inside.

There were three men there, and I must admit I felt some relief that we had found them.

Fabius Murmillo was busy gathering various items and packing them into a small bag, while another, much older man with silver hair was muttering under his breath as he rifled through sets of wax tablets.

The third man was Mardonius, standing impatiently to one side, a bulging, heavy leather sack at his feet. I must admit the look of horror on his face was a joy to behold. Like his companions, he stood as still as a statue when we burst into the room.

"Hello again!" I breezed. "I'm so glad we found all of you here. I was afraid you'd already have left."

I treated them to my broadest smile as I went on, "You are leaving, aren't you? I mean, that would be the sensible thing for you to do unless you fancy spending some time in the imperial torture chamber."

Murmillo, reminding me of an unhappy bear, took a step towards us, his fists bunching.

"What are you talking about?" he growled. "Why don't you piss off out of here?"

I wagged a finger at him.

"Don't be stupid," I warned. "If you look out of the window, you'll see we have brought along some friends. But I'm hoping you'll see sense."

Murmillo hesitated, but his older companion, who I presumed was Didius Pomponius, took a step to the side and peered out of the window.

"Casca!" he hissed. "I suppose he led you here?"

"I would have come anyway," I told him. "But when we heard Mardonius was a pal of yours, we decided to pay you a visit a bit sooner than I'd planned."

"So what do you want?" he asked.

Pomponius, I realised, was probably the brains of this operation. He had not wasted time on protestations of innocence. On the other hand, he hadn't admitted to any wrongdoing either. He was, I guessed, waiting to see how much we knew.

I told him, "My brother, your boss, is being held for interrogation. So far, he hasn't mentioned your names, and I've managed to persuade the Praetorians to go easy on him, but if he decides to talk, you know he'll tell them all about you and a certain balcony you weakened."

Murmillo seemed to deflate slightly, but Pomponius merely gave a thoughtful nod.

"So you're not here to turn us in?" he asked warily.

"No. I am trying to make sure as few people die as possible. But I need you to leave Rome and to go somewhere far away. I don't care where, but make sure you never come back."

"That's it?" he asked, his surprise evident.

"That's it. Apart from that bag of coins Mardonius has with him. He stole that. I can go and fetch the *vigiles* if you want, but I'll settle for you handing it back."

Mardonius' face was flushed with anger, but he was too much of a coward to object when Pomponius said, "All right. We can do that."

I smiled, "Thank you. Oh, and there's one more thing. Sempronius Primus has sold this business to me, so I'll be obliged if you leave all the paperwork and tablets here."

Murmillo let out another low snarl of outrage, but Pomponius gave a shrug.

"It's no use to us anyway," he said. "Come on, lads. We may as well go."

"Just make sure you leave all the keys," I smiled.

He took a bunch of keys from his belt, dropping them on the desk with a heavy clang.

"Thanks," I nodded.

I signalled to my companions to clear a path, allowing the three bruisers to reach the door.

Pomponius walked with his head high, giving me a defiant look as he passed. Mardonius followed, his head lowered, and I resisted the urge to smack him in the face.

Murmillo, however, spat, "We'll get you for this, Scipio."

I let him have that one. There was no point in giving him a smart retort.

I followed them outside, waving to the slaves to let them leave. All three of them glared at Gallicus and Casca, but I could not hear the words they exchanged.

Caecus had hefted the sack, checking the contents.

"Gold and silver," he confirmed. "And it's heavy."

"Give Gallicus and Casca a bag of silver each," I instructed.

Caecus looked surprised, but he did as I asked.

"That's for your help," I told them. "And for keeping your mouths shut."

330

I wasn't at all sure the warning would prevent them bragging, but I hoped Murmillo and Pomponius would be far away by the time any whispers did reach official ears.

My final task was to summon the workers. They were utterly mystified and understandably nervous as I stood in front of them.

"There's been a change of ownership," I informed them. "I've bought this business, and I'll be putting my own people in charge. You can close up for today, but be sure to return tomorrow. Your jobs are safe."

That seemed to mollify them, but I waited until all of them had packed up their gear and left before we locked up.

"All right," I declared. "Let's head home."

We trudged back up to the Quirinal, taking our time, and we arrived in time for what I hoped would be an early evening meal. The house, though, was in chaos. Boxes, bags and crates were piled in the atrium, with Hortensia issuing commands to her slaves as they brought more and more items to pack away.

She was amazed when we handed her the sack of coins, and I saw a glint of tears in her eyes.

"Thank you, Scipio," she said. "I shall take half of it and leave the rest for Primus."

"You're leaving?" I guessed.

"Yes. Primus never told me anything about what he was doing. He put me and our children in danger, and I cannot forgive him for that."

"Where will you go?"

"Back to my parents' home in Veii," she told me.

Surveying the growing piles of baggage around her, she gave a weak smile.

"I think I'm going to need to hire a lot of wagons to carry all my things."

Then, with a hint of steely resolve I had not thought she possessed, she added, "But I will stay here until I have spoken to Primus. I wish to tell him to his face why I am leaving."

I'd always thought Hortensia was a rather insipid character, and I rather liked this unexpected display of inner toughness.

Looking past me, she saw Gallicus and Casca watching us.

331

She said to them, "I will need to hire some guards for the journey as well. If you wish, you can accompany me."

The two men exchanged a look, shrugged, then nodded.

"Thank you, Lady," said Gallicus. "We will come with you."

I left Hortensia to oversee her packing, and went through to my mother's part of the house. Here, the atrium was also being filled with luggage.

Circe smiled when I told her that we had recovered Hortensia's money.

"But you let Mardonius go?"

"Better than handing him over to the authorities. He'd spill his guts about the whole plot, and I'd have some explaining to do to Julia Maesa. I assured her Primus was only a small cog in the conspiracy."

"Well, it doesn't matter," she sighed. "We will be able to go home soon."

She gave me one of her looks as she added, "I think we should go to Ostia as soon as we've completed our business here."

I shrugged, "Maesa can find us wherever we go, but I suppose getting out of the city would be sensible. How long before one of your ships reaches Ostia?"

She gave a slight wave of her hand.

"Two weeks? Three or four, perhaps."

I didn't fancy four weeks idling around in Ostia, but Rome was becoming too dangerous.

Then Circe told me, "You'd better go and talk to your mother."

She was right, so I set off through the house, finding my mother sitting talking to Petrus and Cassia. The two former slaves leaped to their feet when I entered the room, both of them looking slightly embarrassed. I realised I'd seen Cassia serving us at table. She was a small, delicate girl, perhaps only fifteen years old, with dark hair and a face which bore more worry lines than it ought to have done.

Petrus gave me a tentative smile as he said, "We owe you our thanks, Master."

"Don't call me Master," I chided gently. "You are a free man now. My name is Sempronius Scipio. And you are now Sempronius Petrus."

I held out my hand. After an awkward hesitation, he clasped it.

"What do you intend to do now?" I asked.

He shot an anxious glance at my mother before saying, "The Lady Zoe asked us to accompany her as part of her household. She said she would help us set up a business of some sort."

I looked at my mother who gave a solemn nod.

"Accompany?" I asked, tilting my head in question.

"I have decided to travel to Leptis Magna with you," she stated. "Assuming your offer still stands?"

"Of course it does!" I exclaimed, moving over to give her a hug. "You will be welcome. All of you."

"Lucius and Justina must come too," my mother told me.

"Naturally."

"And Dentes," put in Petrus.

"As long as you keep him under control," I smiled.

Then my mother rested a hand on my arm as she said, "But I want to talk to Primus before we go. Will you bring him home tomorrow?"

"It will probably be the day after that. We have some things we need to do tomorrow, and we'll need a whole day to reach Ostia."

She gave a sad, determined smile, and I knew how much of a wrench leaving Rome would be for her.

"I'm sorry it has turned out this way," I told her.

She sighed, "It is Primus' fault. He was always your father's son. I tried to steer him away from the cruel side of his nature, but I failed."

"Primus is who he is," I told her. "You did your best. But he is the head of the family, and he made his own decisions. It's a pity they were such poor ones, but you are not to blame for that."

"I wish I had done more," she said, her voice thick with emotion. "But I have had enough of it, as has Hortensia."

There was nothing I could say in response to that. I did not envy the homecoming my brother would experience when I fetched him back from the Praetorian Camp. He'd find a half empty house, with both his wife and his mother wanting to lecture him before they abandoned him. I suppose he deserved it, and it was hard to feel any sympathy for him.

Leaving my mother to begin planning her own packing, I tracked down Hermion, our son's tutor and sent him off with directions to Mallius Proximus' home.

"Tell him to be here at the second hour tomorrow morning," I told the young Greek.

Hermion was evidently puzzled at being given this task, but he did not complain. I had asked him to go because nobody on the Viminal knew him, and he should be able to deliver the message without interference from Vindex's gang.

I scrounged some food from the kitchens while I waited for Hermion to return. When he confirmed that he had delivered the message and that Proximus would meet us as arranged, Circe and I had one more task to complete.

We headed down to Fronto's home, with four slaves tagging along even though it was a short journey. It was growing dark by this time, and the atmosphere in the city was more than a little tense, so I didn't want to make even a short walk without having some protection.

Fronto was, as always, delighted to see us, and insisted on hearing all the news.

Once I'd brought him up to date, Circe told him, "Now, there is something I would like you to do for me, Sestius Fronto."

He looked at her curiously, obviously picking up on her formal tone and the use of his family name.

"You know I will help in any way I can," he assured her.

I smiled to myself. Fronto had always fancied Circe, right back to the very first time they had met several years earlier. That was why I'd asked her to lead this part of the discussion. I reckoned he would find it hard to refuse her.

She informed him, "Primus agreed to sell the builder's business to us. As you know, we plan to ask Mallius Proximus to run the operation on our behalf."

Fronto nodded. He'd been involved in our planning discussions, so he knew this already.

334

Speaking in a formal tone, Circe went on, "But we also want to have someone in overall charge. Proximus is an excellent builder by all accounts, but his business acumen may not be up to the standard we require."

"You want someone to look after the business side of things?" Fronto asked.

"That's right. Specifically, I want you to do this."

Fronto looked from Circe to me.

I shrugged, "Circe runs all our business ventures. My name might be on the title, but I haven't got a clue when it comes to that sort of thing."

Fronto said, "But I have no experience of running a business like that."

Circe dismissed this objection with a wave of her hand.

"You have years of experience of helping to run a spy network. You understand people, and you can take a strategic view of things. Also, I may wish you to purchase some properties and manage them on our behalf."

"You are going to invest in the Roman property market?" Fronto asked, still a little bemused.

"We are. You see, many of the tenements are run down, and the tenants are required to pay extortionate rents. I have a vision of buying old properties, having Proximus renovate them, or even pull them down and rebuild, doing it to a high standard. And we want to charge reasonable rents so that we create a demand for our buildings."

"There is always a demand in Rome," Fronto pointed out. "You can charge whatever you like. Someone will pay it no matter what condition the property is in."

"I don't want to exploit people," Circe stated. "What I need is an honest man in charge. That man is you."

I gave Fronto an encouraging nod.

"It's her idea," I told him.

That, I hoped, would convince him to agree. If I'd put the idea to him, he'd have considered it charity, but Circe was all business-like.

"I suppose I have nothing else to occupy me at the moment," Fronto grinned. "Yes, I'd be happy to do that."

335

"Excellent!" Circe beamed. "You will earn a share of the profits, of course, but we'll agree a regular salary once we've looked at the business's Accounts."

"And when will that be?" he asked, eager now to begin.

"Come up to the house tomorrow at the second hour," Circe told him.

"I'll be there," he promised.

Fronto then sent one of his slaves to summon Faustia and to bring wine. He told his wife what we had agreed, then we had a celebratory drink to seal the bargain.

Faustia, who had perhaps guessed more about what was going on than we had given her credit for, made a point of thanking me.

"Tiberius Fronto now has something to look forward to, and a way of making a living. You have restored his self-esteem."

I shrugged that off as best I could.

"He is my friend," I told her. "And he always will be."

I would have liked to stay longer, but I had a lot to do in the morning and I didn't want a hangover, so we said our farewells and headed home.

When Circe and I finally slipped into bed, I felt drained. It had been a long, tense day, and I was worn out.

"It's nearly over," Circe told me. "And everything is working out."

"Not quite as we'd hoped," I sighed. "Julia Maesa didn't need to have Muncius killed. And I didn't expect Hortensia to walk out on Primus."

"You can hardly blame her," Circe said as she snuggled in close. "As for Julia Maesa, there is nothing we can do about that now. She has made her own decisions."

"I know. But I'm glad we are leaving. I've had enough of Rome and its intrigues."

"It will all be over soon," she assured me.

As things turned out, she was right, although the ending was not at all what I had envisaged.

Chapter 33
Taking Charge

Everyone was up early the following morning, with most people busy sorting and packing for our various departures.

After a hasty breakfast, I went through to check on Hortensia, and found her more determined than ever to leave.

"I could probably bring Primus home today," I told her.

She met my gaze as she stated firmly, "No. I still have a lot to do. I want to be ready to set off as soon as I've spoken to him. Leave him there another day."

Judging by the ever-expanding pile of chests, bags and items of furniture in her atrium, I wasn't sure how much longer it would take her slaves to pack everything. I had the impression she was putting off the moment of her confrontation, but I did not argue with her. After all, it was her life that would be changing.

My mother's home was scarcely less of a riot, with her baggage now being added to ours which Circe was leaving to Hermion to organise.

"There you are," she said to me as I walked back through the connecting door. "Come on. Fronto and Proximus are here."

With Collinus and Caecus in attendance, we left the bustle of the house and went outside to meet our two new employees.

Proximus was freshly shaved and wearing a bright tunic. He seemed nervous but excited, while Fronto was scarcely less on edge. I made the introductions, then, with Collinus and Caecus in attendance as usual, we set off for the *Via Ostiensis* once again.

The city was still remarkably quiet. The few people who had ventured out of doors walked quickly, keeping their eyes downcast, and the usual hubbub was strangely muted.

Down at the builders' yard, I was pleasantly surprised to find that many of the workers had turned up. I'd half expected most of them to abandon the business, but they seemed delighted to learn their jobs were secure. I handed the keys to Proximus, introduced him, Fronto and Circe to the work gang, then stood back and let the others get on with things.

Proximus immediately began making an inventory of the stock, clucking his tongue over the poor quality of some of the material.

"They've been cutting corners," he informed me. "They've been using poor quality wood and stone. I'll bet their bricks aren't up to much either."

I said, "I suppose you'll need to keep a close eye on the workers until you get them working to the standards you want."

"I can do that," he grinned. "I might be able to persuade some of my father's crew to come back and work for me too."

"I'll leave that up to you," I told him. "But it's Aurelia you need to keep happy. I warn you, she can be a tough person to please."

"She won't be disappointed with my work," he promised.

There was one other thing niggling at me, so I made a point of staying with Proximus while he examined every part of the business and spoke to each member of the work crew. I think Proximus believed I was checking up on him until I mentioned my real purpose.

"Do you remember those two workers you overheard talking about a certain bit of work they had done at the palace?"

He gave a solemn nod.

"They're not here," he told me. "I'd have recognised them."

"That's probably for the best," I said.

A few gentle enquiries revealed that two men had failed to turn up for work this morning. That made life a little bit easier.

"If they do decide to come back," I told Proximus, tell them there's no work for them. It's best to make a clean break with the former owners."

"I understand," he assured me.

After that, I left him to sort things out, and I sauntered over to the office. Collinus was sitting cross-legged on the ground outside the door, his eyes always alert. He gave me a silent nod as I passed him.

Inside, I found Circe and Fronto poring over the paperwork. This was well outside my area of expertise, so I was happy to leave them to it, especially as the desk was piled high

338

with scrolls, tablets and scraps of parchment which they were sorting into various stacks.

"It's a mess!" Circe complained loudly when I asked how they were doing. "The Accounts are shoddy, and the records in no proper order at all."

Fronto agreed, "They may have known how to build things, but they had no idea about running a business properly. I'm thankful they have only been in charge for a few months."

"I'm sure you will get it sorted," I grinned.

Circe shot me a scathing look, but then asked, "How is Proximus doing?"

"He seems to know his stuff," I assured her.

"Good, because I intend to keep him busy. Fronto and I were just discussing the possibility of buying up some of Primus' tenements."

I chuckled, "He'll never sell to us."

"He might if we offer more money than anyone else," she answered in her matter-of-fact business voice.

"Why would he sell at all?" I frowned.

"Because he will need to pay back Hortensia's dowry, and even with the money you recovered and the stuff she's taking with her, he'll need to turn some of his assets into cash."

I hadn't thought of that, but I still argued with her.

"He'll try to cheat us," I warned.

"Of course he will," she agreed. "But Fronto knows Primus well enough to watch out for that."

Fronto didn't seem quite as certain as Circe, but he gave a determined nod.

"I'll make sure we get a good deal," he said.

Then Circe gave me a studied look as she asked, "And what are you going to do for the rest of the day? Fronto and I have a lot to sort out here, then we need to go into the city and find a banker so we can arrange for Fronto to draw funds when he needs them."

"I'm at a bit of a loose end just now," I replied.

"Then you should go back to the house and see if you can help your mother. We are leaving tomorrow, and everything needs to be packed away."

"All right. But I'm going for a bath first. I haven't had a decent wash in days."

She rolled her eyes in mock scorn at my indolence, then laughed as she waved a hand in dismissal.

"Go on, then. Get out of here. You'll only slow us down."

With that endorsement ringing in my ears, I left them to their work and went to find Caecus.

"A bath sounds good," he nodded when I told him my plans for passing the time.

In truth, all I wanted was to be on our way, but I knew it would take a full day's travel for us to reach Ostia with all our baggage, and there was no chance of making that journey today. With everyone else busy, a trip to the baths seemed as pleasant a way of filling my leisure hours as any.

"Where do you want to go?" Caecus enquired.

"I thought we should take a look at the baths of Caracalla," I told him.

I swear he almost smiled. After all, everything we had been through in the past days was a legacy of Caracalla's reign. Our former Emperor still cast a long shadow over Roman life and politics. Having met him personally, I knew he was a vain, paranoid, bloodthirsty maniac, but the soldiers had loved him, and even the ordinary people had respected him for his military prowess and his lavish donations. He'd even passed a decree stating that every free person in the empire was considered a Roman citizen. That bestowed some very important rights when it came to the law, although I'm fairly certain the main reason he had issued that decree was to increase the number of people liable to pay tax. Caracalla, after all, had needed a lot of money to finance his wars and the wages he paid his soldiers.

Still, one of the donations he had left was a magnificent new bath house. It had actually been started by his father, Septimius Severus, but the building had been completed and dedicated during Caracalla's reign, and it bore his name. It was a huge building, set in wide gardens surrounded by massive walls containing several water cisterns which were supplied by a new aqueduct.

The baths lie just south of the Palatine Hill, so it wasn't on a direct route home, but I wanted to take a look at this famous new building before we left Rome. Also, as I'd told Circe, I was in desperate need of a bath. Most Romans bathe at least once a day, but I'd had little chance to enjoy this luxury recently.

Bath house is probably a misleading term when it comes to the Baths of Caracalla. There are the usual pools, all of them on a grand scale, but there are also the gardens, the exercise yards and a couple of libraries where people can read or simply chat with friends.

Today, though, after I had spent a few moments admiring the magnificent scale of the building, we passed between the massive columns of the front portico and headed straight for the pools where we enjoyed a restful couple of hours.

The baths can cater for more than a thousand people at any one time, and there was a steady stream of citizens coming and going, although the recent cull of Senators was obviously still affecting attendance, for the place was relatively quiet.

I had expected that the fate of Herennius Muncius and his allies would be the topic of most of the gossip, and I had been looking forward to eavesdropping on some conversations to see how Julia Maesa's precipitate action was viewed by the general populace. However, I was in for a shock, because there was a fresh bit of news which dominated the chatter.

Caecus and I were lolling in the hot pool when a couple of middle-aged men near us began talking about it, and I couldn't resist moving towards them to learn more.

"Excuse me," I said to them. "What was that you were just saying? About events in the palace, I mean."

The two men were only too happy to relate the gossip. The affairs of the imperial family are always on the minds of most people in Rome, and these two were no exception.

One, a flabby, balding fellow with a flushed face, informed me, "It's the announcement by Julia Mamaea. Haven't you heard?"

I shook my head, wondering what Julia Mamaea could possibly have done. According to the Juggler, she was the least influential of the Julia family. She might be the mother of Alexander, but she was allegedly a virtual prisoner in the palace.

"What has she said?" I asked my new friends.

The second man, another plump fellow, grinned, "She's really set the lions loose on the captives, I can tell you."

This allusion to the gory practices in the amphitheatre worried me, especially because of the handful of words I had half heard the two men exchange a few moments earlier.

The fatter man told me, "She has only told the world that her son, Alexander, is also a son of Caracalla."

I felt my heart sink. I'd been hoping I had misheard them earlier, but now they had confirmed my fears.

"It's hardly a surprise," the second man opined. "I mean, he was sleeping with his step-mother and his other cousin, so why not with Julia Mamaea as well?"

"Are you sure about this?" I managed to ask, concealing my dismay.

"Oh, yes. It's all over the city," my flabby pal assured me. "It was an official proclamation."

I was too stunned to react. I simply sat there for a while before dragging myself out of the pool and going in search of a slave to have my body oiled and scraped clean.

Caecus came with me but he, too, was in a pensive mood. It was only once we had been cleaned, shaved and dressed ourselves again that we headed out into the luxuriant gardens where we could speak in relative privacy as we tried to make sense of this latest revelation.

"It must be Julia Maesa's work," Caecus decided. "She's trying to get the Praetorians on her side before she removes Elagabalus from power."

"But there is no need to do it!" I protested. "The Guard already like Alexander. He's the obvious successor. All this will do is provoke the Emperor into doing something rash."

"What can he do?" Caecus asked. "Maesa promised to protect Alexander."

I shook my head in resignation.

"I don't know," I admitted ruefully. "I just don't think there was any need to announce this. Maesa has bungled things again."

"Perhaps it was Mamaea herself who decided to announce it," Caecus offered.

342

"You think she's making her own play for power?" I frowned.

"Why not?" Caecus shrugged.

"I just don't think it makes sense," I argued. "After all, she will benefit anyway if Maesa deposes Elagabalus and installs Alexander as Emperor."

"True enough," Caecus acknowledged. "But we don't know what has been going on in the private parts of the palace."

I nodded glumly. Perhaps Julia Mamaea had been driven to taking drastic action by something the Emperor had said or done. Recalling the tall, angry woman we had encountered when we'd first met Julia Maesa, I supposed it was possible the strain had become too much for her. Was she counting on the Praetorians' love of Caracalla to protect her son from whatever mad impulse had seized the Emperor recently?

"Whoever is behind it," I muttered, "all it will do is make things even more dangerous."

Caecus said, "It's not our problem any longer. We are leaving tomorrow. Let them fight it out between themselves."

"That's what worries me," I muttered. "When an imperial family starts fighting, it's other people who die."

Despite my grumbling, I knew there was nothing we could do other than prepare to leave. Fortunately, my mother did not need any assistance from me. When we returned to the house, we found her issuing commands like Julius Caesar overseeing a battle, her instructions cracking like an overseer's whip.

"Just keep out of my way," she told me.

I was happy to obey that order, so I spent a few hours playing with the children whom I had sadly neglected over the past few days. I managed to tire them out by chasing them around the garden, although I felt in need of another bath by the time they were packed off for their supper and sent to bed.

It was growing late when Circe and Fronto eventually arrived. I could tell from the expressions they wore that they were in a gloomy mood.

"What's wrong?" I asked when they came into the family room. "Didn't you find a banker who would help us?"

Circe flopped down on a couch, waving an elegant hand in frustration.

343

"Oh, that's all sorted," she informed me. "No, it's the news the banker gave us while we were talking to him."

"About Alexander being another son of Caracalla, you mean?"

I felt quite smug that I had anticipated her, but her next words struck me like one of Jupiter's infamous thunderbolts.

"It's not that," she said. "It's the rumour that Alexander is dead."

I gaped at her.

"Dead? How?"

She gave a shrug.

"Nobody knows. But the street gossip is that the Emperor flew into a rage when he heard that ridiculous claim about Alexander being Caracalla's son."

"I feared as much," I nodded.

Circe went on, "According to reports coming out of the palace, he confined Alexander to his rooms, then he dismissed all the Praetorians and set his own slaves to guard the doors to Alexander's quarters."

If I'd felt low when I'd heard about Mamaea's claim that she had slept with her cousin, this latest revelation left a hollow pit in my stomach.

I said softly, "And Alexander is dead?"

"That's what people are saying."

Fronto, looking as appalled as I felt, put in, "It's only a rumour. You know how these stories can grow."

I nodded, but I did not find much comfort in this thought. There were so many people living and working in the palace that keeping something like this a secret was almost impossible.

Circe told me, "I think it could be genuine. The Urban Cohorts are out on the streets in case there's a riot, and the Praetorians have shut themselves inside their camp. They'll be discussing what to do next."

"What can they do?" I sighed. "If they take revenge on Elagabalus, who will rule the empire?"

"Whoever they decide," she replied.

That was a sobering thought.

344

"You should leave first thing tomorrow," I told Circe. "Take the kids and all the luggage with you. Caecus and I will fetch Primus home, then we'll catch up with you."

For once, she was in complete agreement with me.

I wasn't at all sure how any of us would sleep that night, but Hortensia came to our rescue by announcing that she would hold a farewell feast. Fronto and Faustia were invited, and we all lay on couches while Hortensia's slaves served up dish after dish from Primus' larder. I guessed Hortensia had decided to empty the stores of food.

Even so, I found myself toying with a plate of oysters because the day's events had ruined my appetite. I ate, but I did not really enjoy the meal despite the lavish choices laid out before me. I could not help but think that my time in Rome had been almost a complete failure. I had discovered who had attacked Primus, and we'd restored Mallius Proximus, but those were my only real successes. Thwarting Muncius' conspiracy had only led to more deaths, and now Julia Maesa's miscalculations had sparked a crisis on the Palatine.

"We will be leaving at first light," I told Hortensia and my mother.

Both women nodded, but both insisted they would stay in the house until I brought Primus back.

"I wish to speak to him face to face before I go," Hortensia stated. Her voice almost cracked, but she held herself together as a Roman matron should.

My mother was no less determined, insisting that she would wait for Primus to return before leaving.

"You can escort me to Ostia," she told me in a tone which brooked no argument.

Even the small satisfaction of anticipating Primus' ruin could not compensate for the feeling of failure which engulfed me.

"Julia Maesa should have listened to us," I said repeatedly.

But it was too late now, and the only thing we could do was get out of Rome before things turned really nasty.

Chapter 34
Resolution

We were up before the dawn, and Circe oversaw the final preparations. As soon as the first hints of daylight appeared in the sky, our slaves hefted the heavy trunks and bags, and I kissed Circe and the children before watching them go.

My mother had hired some porters who would carry her own luggage, while Hortensia's slaves were already carrying her considerable belongings out beyond the Porta Collina where a column of wagons was waiting.

I was glad to escape the chaos, but our next problem was locating a litter. Primus, I knew, would not be able to walk unaided, and Hortensia needed all the slaves to carry her baggage, so Caecus and I decided to hire a street chair. Unfortunately, most of the public litter bearers were keeping out of sight, and when we did find one, the lead bearer refused to go to the Praetorian Camp even when I explained that we only needed him to carry an injured man home.

"There's trouble brewing, Sir," he told me gravely. "But I tell you what we can do. If you pay the fee now, we'll go and wait at the Porta Sanqualis. If you can get your man there, we'll bring him back the rest of the way."

That was the most I could persuade the bearers to do. The Porta Sanqualis was reasonably close to the Praetorian Camp, so I grudgingly paid them, then Caecus and I hurried off to release my brother from his captivity.

The streets were quiet again. The Roman mob is never backward about coming forward, but today it was as if the city were holding its collective breath while it waited to see what would happen. Personally, I could not foresee any happy outcome at all. If Alexander really was dead, then either Elagabalus would remain in power, or there would be a bloody coup; perhaps even total anarchy.

The feeling of imminent danger increased even further when we reached the Praetorian Camp. The gates were open, but the atmosphere was very different to the one I'd encountered on my previous visit. The entire parade ground was full of angry soldiers, all of them in full armour and wearing their swords. They were talking animatedly, and many of them studied us with hostile eyes when we were escorted to the building where Centurion Auctas had his office and where Primus was being held.

"The litter bearer was right," Caecus remarked under his breath. "There's definitely trouble brewing."

Laetilius Auctas confirmed our fears when we met him in his tiny office.

He told me, "I'm glad you've come. You need to get your brother out of here as soon as you can."

"Is it true Alexander is dead?" I asked him.

He gave a shrug.

That's what we all want to know."

"What's going on here?" I asked, dreading the answer. "It looks as if things could get ugly."

"That's an understatement," he nodded grimly. "At the moment, the lads are waiting for the Emperor to respond to their ultimatum."

"Ultimatum?" I gaped. "What have they demanded?"

"They want to see Alexander," he replied.

When he saw my confusion, Auctas explained, "You heard that Alexander was shut away in his rooms?"

"Yes, and people say he's dead."

"That was what the Emperor said," Auctas growled. "Then, when he thought the lads were going to riot, he changed his story and said he'd invented that in order to see how the Guard would react."

"I bet he knows the answer now," Caecus murmured darkly.

I groaned inwardly. It was no real surprise that Elagabalus had reacted strongly to the transparent attempts to undermine him. But was he so unstable that he would actually have murdered his cousin? Or had he really made up the story to test the loyalty of the Praetorians? Neither of those was the action of a rational ruler, but I supposed Elagabalus could never be described as rational.

Gruffly, Auctas went on, "The lads have sent a demand that the Emperor come here in person, bringing Alexander to prove he is alive and well. Then they want the Emperor to make new oaths in the Temple of Mars."

Feeling a rising sense of dread, I asked, "So what do you think will happen?"

Auctas shrugged, "Your guess is as good as mine. Either he'll come or he won't. But he sure as Hades won't come unless he can produce Alexander alive and well. And if he doesn't come ..."

He left the thought hanging.

"I don't suppose there is anything you can do?" I ventured.

He shook his head.

"None of the Centurions will dare try to stop the lads when they are in this sort of mood."

I understood. Rome may be an autocracy, but the army often operated more like an old-style Greek democracy, where every man had a vote. Those votes were usually backed by swords, so only the bravest of Centurions would try to put a stop to any revolt. Discipline in the army was harsh, and Centurions normally held powers of life and death over the men under their command, but that only worked if the majority of the troops were still amenable to obeying orders. Sometimes, and it seemed this was one of those times, the whole system broke down. That usually indicated a loss of trust in the Emperor. If the troops supported the man at the top, discipline could be maintained, but once that trust vanished, even the toughest Centurion had no chance of imposing imperial will even if he had a mind to do so.

Auctas told me, "That's why you should get your brother out of here now. There may be serious trouble very soon."

Taking my stunned silence for assent, he stood up.

"Let's go," he commanded.

He selected a key from a row of pegs, then led the way to the door.

"I'll come with you. He's on the top floor."

We trudged our way up the stairs to the upper level. Here we found a long corridor with windows on our left looking out onto the parade ground, and a series of doors on the right.

"Your brother is in the third room," Auctas informed me. "These are mostly store rooms, although guests are sometimes lodged here."

"Guests?"

"It happens from time to time," he explained. "Visiting delegations from the Legions, or people the Emperor wants to keep safe."

"This place doesn't feel all that safe just now," I muttered.

We reached the third door which was padlocked. Auctas inserted the key, turned it, and pulled the heavy padlock free, then pushed the door open. Nodding to me, he stood aside to let me enter.

The room beyond was not much larger than the dank cell in the basement where I had last seen Primus, but it was a lot brighter and cleaner. There was a single cot bed, a small table and a waste bucket. Light came in through a square window set high in the far wall, and this revealed Primus lying huddled on the narrow bed. He had no blanket, and his tunic was now rumpled and stained by sweat. The stink of him made my nostrils twitch, and he looked a sorry excuse for a human being. His unshaven face was gaunt, and his red-rimmed eyes betrayed his misery.

He looked up when I stepped into the room, and I saw hope spark in his expression. Awkwardly, he pushed himself up, favouring his splinted leg as he wriggled and heaved, trying to push his bulk upright with arms which seemed to have lost all their strength.

"Secundus!" he croaked. "Have you come to get me out of here?"

"Yes. Julia Maesa signed a formal pardon for you. I'm taking you home."

I didn't have the heart to tell him what was waiting for him because his eyes suddenly filled with tears. Whether they were of gratitude, joy or self-pity, I could not say.

It took a couple of attempts to get him on his feet. Caecus did most of the heavy lifting, placing Primus' left arm around his shoulders and shuffling him towards the door. There wasn't enough room for me to support Primus on the other side, so I followed them, offering moral support by keeping out of the way while Auctas looked on dispassionately.

We had barely dragged Primus into the corridor when we heard a loud roar from outside, the sound of hundreds of voices raised in acclamation. It boomed around the parade ground like rolling thunder, the sound bringing us to an immediate halt.

Auctas' face clouded with concern, but Caecus glanced back over his shoulder to look at me.

"See what's going on," he told me.

I stepped back a few paces to the nearest window, cautiously pushing one of the shutters open a fraction.

I need not have bothered being wary. I doubt anyone in the yard below the window would have noticed if I'd flung it fully open and danced naked on the sill.

The Praetorians had clustered in a large group, a couple of thousand of them clamouring at the tops of their voices, their arms raised in acclamation. The sound reverberated around the camp, amplified by the enclosing buildings and making it difficult to hear anything else. Beyond the crowd, off to my left, I could see the main gates where a group of other people had just entered.

"It's the Emperor!" I hissed.

Auctas, who had moved a few paces along the corridor to the next window, said, "We'd better wait."

Caecus shuffled Primus back to join me. Primus, though, had no interest in what was taking place outside. He leaned his back against the wall, closed his eyes, then slowly sank to the floor with his legs stretched out in front of him. Caecus and I paid no attention to him. We were too fascinated by what we could see.

"Soaemias is there," I said, noticing the dark-haired woman who was, for once, dressed demurely in a long *stola*, the traditional garb of a respectable free woman.

"And Alexander!" Caecus whispered.

He was right. Elagabalus and his mother had brought around twenty attendants with them, but I now saw the slender figure of Alexander stepping out from the crowd. He was alive after all, and the sight of him enraptured the Praetorians. They shouted and applauded, some of them close to tears at the knowledge that he still lived.

Close behind the boy was his mother, Julia Mamaea. Like her older sister, she wore a simple dress of plain wool, and had her hair bound up to signify her status as a married, if widowed, woman.

Alexander, too, was dressed in plain clothing, an everyday tunic covered by a cloak, a gold brooch being the only ostentation.

In contrast, Elagabalus wore a long robe of purple silk, with fluttering ribbons of green and blue waving from his sleeves. He was trying to address the soldiers, but the sight of Alexander, whom they had feared dead, was too much for the Praetorians.

"Alexander!" they boomed.

Then they began a chant, stamping their feet on the gravel in between their shouts, creating a sound like thunder as they flourished their swords above their heads.

"Alexander!"

Stamp. Stamp.

"Alexander!"

Stamp. Stamp.

The Emperor began waving his hands. I saw his mouth moving as he tried to shout to be heard, but the sound of the chanting drowned him out. He looked ridiculous; his lean, dancer's body decked in silks while he faced hundreds of angry men dressed in armour and with swords drawn.

"He's mad!" I whispered to myself. "He needs to get out of there."

But Elagabalus did not seem to be aware of the danger. He twisted, his face contorted with rage, and snarled something at his young cousin, perhaps a plea for him to quieten the crowd, but Alexander, too, seemed overawed by the reaction of the Praetorians. Shaking his head, he edged close to his mother who placed a reassuring hand on his shoulder, steadying him. Neither of them made any move to quieten the chanting soldiers, causing the Emperor to wave his arms wildly as he screamed at them.

Then, realising he would get no help from Alexander, the Emperor turned to another man who had been attempting to remain in the background. I recognised Valerius Comazon, the Praetorian Prefect. Technically, he was in command of the Guard, but I saw him shake his head when the Emperor yelled at him while gesticulating towards the chanting mob. Comazon clearly had no intention of attempting to enforce his authority.

The mood was growing ugly, and everyone seemed to appreciate the danger except the Emperor himself. He continued to shout at his companions, insisting they do something, but he was a lone figure in a sea of peril.

351

I turned to glance at Caecus, and as I moved my gaze, something caught my eye.

It was a movement from one of the buildings on the opposite side of the parade ground. A door opened, and a man stepped out, taking up a position near the back of the crowd. It was a man I knew.

He had to duck low to pass through the doorway. When he stood erect, he towered over the men nearest to him. His long, bushy beard was as luxuriant as I recalled, and his glowering eyes were roving over the scene as if this was what he had wanted to see.

He folded his arms across his massive chest, then gave a nod to the soldiers who stood closest to him.

"Thrax!" I hissed, nudging Caecus to draw his attention. "What is he doing here?"

I understood almost as soon as I'd spoken. The chant began to change. It came first from those men who stood close to the giant Thrax, but others quickly took up the refrain.

"Alexander! Imperator! Alexander! Imperator!"

It was the traditional ovation Roman troops had given to a successful commander after a great victory. Back in the days before the Emperors, a general who was acclaimed Imperator could normally expect to be awarded a triumph, allowing him to ride through the streets of Rome in a chariot, leading a procession in which the booty and captives he had taken would be displayed for the citizens to see. This was how the might and power of Rome had been shown to its people.

But Emperors are jealous, and no general had been awarded a triumph since the days of Augustus two centuries ago. Ever since then, anyone who was acclaimed Imperator was effectively being hailed as a new Emperor because the roles of supreme military leader and ruler of the Empire had been combined in the person of the Emperor.

I felt a shiver of dread run down my spine and simultaneously clench at my belly. This could only mean one thing.

Soaemias realised it before her son did. He was still shouting at Comazon, waving his hands to set his silk robe and

352

ribbons fluttering, but his mother grabbed him and began trying to pull him away.

Except they had nowhere to go. The gates had been shut, and a line of Praetorians stood barring the way. Soaemias, clearly terrified, shouted at her slaves to protect them, then she grabbed Elagabalus' arm and began running towards the nearest door.

The door to the building we were in.

Their movement sparked a response. Like hounds being unleashed to pursue a fleeing prey, the Praetorians let out a ferocious yell as they surged forwards, swords at the ready. They were no longer soldiers; they were a bloodthirsty mob, and their quarry was in sight.

The slaves and eunuchs did their best to delay them, but what followed was a bloody slaughter as some of the armed Praetorians rampaged their way through the unarmed attendants, while another group surrounded Alexander and his mother to protect them. I caught sight of Comazon seeking sanctuary with this group and he, at least, seemed safe enough.

The same could not be said for the Emperor and his mother.

"Oh, Jupiter!" I gulped.

I peered past Caecus to see that Auctas had taken up position in the centre of the corridor. He was facing away from us, looking towards the stairs at the far end of the passage, his arms folded across his chest as he formed a one-man human barrier.

I heard pounding footsteps on the wooden stairs. A moment later, Soaemias appeared, her cheeks flushed and her hair flying wildly around her face as she frantically pulled her son after her.

"Why?" I heard the young man wail. "I am the Emperor! Why are they doing this?"

Soaemias did not answer. She looked up, saw us and stopped dead, the sight of a Praetorian Centurion making her face grow deathly pale. She whirled round, but the sounds of angry pursuit made it plain that there was no escape that way. Panicking, she dashed to the nearest door, flinging it open.

"In here!" she shouted at her son, her voice almost a shriek of desperation.

She dragged him inside, then slammed the door shut.

I have no idea what she was trying to do. It must have been obvious to the men in the courtyard where she had gone. Perhaps she was hoping her sister might persuade the soldiers to stop, but that was a vain thought. Within moments, a gang of armed men stormed up the stairway.

The first soldiers skidded to a halt as soon as they saw us, the others bunching up behind them.

"Where are they?" a man shouted at us as the crowd jostled him from behind.

I felt sick. I had tried so hard to avoid this, but it was happening anyway.

I watched in horrified fascination as Auctas raised one hand to point.

"The first room," he told them flatly.

Guilt swept through me at this betrayal, but I realised Auctas had saved our lives by deflecting the Praetorians' rage away from us.

They kicked the door down and surged inside, even though the room was so small only a handful of them could squeeze through the doorway. The rest remained in the corridor, swords drawn, eyes burning with hate while they shouted encouragement to their companions who had entered the tiny cubicle.

I shuddered when I heard the scream. It was quickly cut off. Then there was a crashing sound, more frightened yells, then shouts of triumph and rage.

"He was hiding in a chest!" someone shouted scornfully.

Then there was a ragged cheer and men began pushing back out of the room. The first man into view held a blood-drenched *gladius* in his right hand and a human head in his left, his fingers clenched in its short, fair hair.

It was the head of Elagabalus.

"Throw his body in the Tiber!" someone yelled, invoking the traditional treatment for criminals and traitors.

The second man who emerged from the room to join the long procession had Soaemias' head dangling from his hand by its long, dark hair.

Cheering enthusiastically, other men went in to drag out the headless corpses. Then they all slowly trooped down the stairs to display their gory trophies to the waiting crowd.

I turned, bent over, and vomited onto the floor.

Epilogue

We waited nearly three weeks before one of Circe's ships turned up in Ostia. It was a pleasant enough stay because we rented some very comfortable rooms, but I spent most of the time fretting over what had happened in Rome and what the new regime might do when it got around to considering my role in events.

"You are worrying over nothing," Circe told me. "You helped Julia Maesa, and she is still in power. She just has a new Emperor under her control."

I tried to tell myself she was right, but I still spent many anxious days until Circe's ship arrived shortly after the *kalends* of April with its cargo of olive oil and wine.

"At least the weather will make our return journey a little easier," Circe told me. "The Captain says they were delayed by storms on the way here, but the season should be much better now."

I hoped she was right. With a trailing wind and calm seas, we could be home in Leptis Magna in eight or nine days.

That evening, I left Circe to oversee the repacking of our luggage and headed down into the inn's public room. We would be boarding the ship early the next morning, so I decided I'd better settle our bill with the innkeeper. I thought I might also take the opportunity for one last jug of wine on dry land.

I had barely taken two steps into the large room when my blood ran cold. Sitting at a table in a corner near the main door was a young man with brown hair who was smiling at me and beckoning me to join him.

It was the man who had followed Caecus and me when we had ridden down to the Alban Mount.

I looked around, checking in case any of the other guests might be part of a squad sent to deal with me, but everyone seemed intent on their own food and drink, and none of them looked like soldiers.

Taking a deep breath, I walked across the room to the corner table.

"Sit down," the man said, his tone light and friendly. "There's someone who wants to talk to you."

356

"Who might that be?"

"You'll see. He'll be here any time now. I sent word to him this morning. I must say you are not easy to find in spite of you having your entire family with you."

Warily, I took a seat. A serving girl came over, and I asked for a small jug of wine.

"You can share mine," the young man offered.

"I'll stick to my own, thanks," I replied, finding it difficult to be civil.

Grinning, he topped up his cup from his own jug, then took a big swig.

As he placed his cup back on the table, he said, "You see? It's not poisoned."

"What's your name?" I asked him.

He shrugged, "You can call me Helios."

I doubted that was his real name. When I'd been an imperial spy, I'd been known as Sigma. Helios was, I guessed, this fellow's code name.

My wine came. I sipped at it, but I didn't really enjoy it.

Helios seemed content to sit in silence, and I had no wish to talk to him, so I watched the door. I'd nearly finished my first cup when it opened to reveal the portly figure of Sempronius Rufus, the Juggler.

He looked around, saw us sitting in the corner, and came to join us, a look of satisfaction on his rotund face. He was wearing a fine tunic of wool, along with what looked like a new cloak. His hair had been trimmed and he was clean-shaven, making him look far more reputable than when I had last seen him.

"Well done, Helios," he said. "And Sigma. It's good to see you again. I worried you might have left by now."

"I wish I had," I muttered in reply.

I did not offer to shake his hand, but the Juggler never bothered about niceties like that. He took a seat opposite me, called for a cup, then helped himself to some of Helios' wine.

I shot a glance at Helios.

"I thought you were working for Julia Maesa."

He smiled, "You were wrong."

"So it seems."

Turning back to the Juggler, I said, "I'm leaving in the morning."

"I know."

"So whatever it is you want from me, the answer is No. I'm going home."

He studied me for a long, silent moment, then spoke in a tone of disappointment.

"You lied to me, Sigma. You met someone at your brother's villa, and you did not tell me about it."

"I wanted it kept secret," I shrugged. "I had an idea that would have saved a lot of bloodshed, but I couldn't afford for word to leak out."

Rufus gave me a wry smile.

"Well, it doesn't matter. Things turned out well enough in the end."

"I'm glad you think so," I retorted. "I doubt Elagabalus or Herennius Muncius would agree."

"You are an idealist, Sigma," he sighed. "That is your greatest weakness."

I did not bother responding to that. Instead, I stared at him impatiently.

"What is it you want?" I demanded. "Why are you here?"

My bad temper had no effect on him at all. He simply sat there, studying me with those calculating eyes, letting my words wash over me.

After a moment, he said, "All I want is for you to keep in touch with me."

"Why?"

"Because I have been reinstated at the palace. I have my old job back, and I need information."

There was a lot contained in that comment, but I played the innocent.

"I live well outside Leptis Magna," I told him. "If you want information on the weather and the harvests, I can probably supply those. But don't expect anything more than that. I retired, remember?"

"And Julia Maesa recruited you again."

"She hasn't paid me. I don't regard that as employment."

To my surprise, the Juggler let out a soft laugh.

"That's very true," he chuckled. "Well, forget that for the moment. Your friend, Fronto, did tell me you wouldn't be interested in working for me."

"You've spoken to Fronto?"

"Naturally. But, for some reason, he doesn't want his old job back either."

Rufus shook his head as if he could not understand this.

"I don't blame him," I said. "The palace is a dangerous place to work."

"It can be," the Juggler admitted. "Things will settle down soon, I am sure."

He took another sip of wine, then leaned towards me, his elbows resting on the table.

Speaking softly, his tone serious, he said, "Never mind all that. The main reason I came here was to give you some news."

"What news?" I asked cautiously.

His voice remained low as he informed me, "It's about your brother."

I did my best to keep my face impassive as I asked, "What about him?"

I wasn't sure I wanted to know the answer. My mother had spent a long time talking to Primus once we'd carried him back home from the Praetorian Camp. She had spoken to him in private after Hortensia had delivered her own speech to him. Afterwards, my mother had refused to divulge what she had said to him, only telling us that she did not wish to speak of him again.

"He is no longer my son," she stated, her jaw set firm, but her eyes damp with emotion.

Now I looked at the Juggler and waited for his news.

"He's dead," he told me bluntly.

I will admit that shocked me. It seemed all my efforts to keep my brother alive had been wasted.

"Dead? How?"

Rufus explained, "A gang of men broke into his house and murdered him."

I gaped at him, scarcely believing what he was saying.

After a moment, I blurted, "But he had a pardon from Julia Maesa herself."

"It wasn't her who ordered it," Rufus told me. "In fact, it wasn't anyone in the palace."

"Then who?"

He gave me a knowing look as he explained, "None of the neighbours saw anything. Well, the old man who lived opposite did, but he's not saying anything except that he's glad your brother is dead."

"Old Oceanus? Yes, that sounds like him."

"But the slaves who survived the attack gave some decent descriptions of the attackers. They said one was a very large young man, and the leader had his right hand heavily bandaged."

I slumped in my chair, closing my eyes. That sounded like Hestius and the ox-like Polus. Marius Vindex had obviously decided to take revenge for the way we had overpowered them on the night we had ventured onto the Viminal.

"But that was nothing to do with Primus!" I protested.

"What wasn't?" Rufus frowned.

I mentally kicked myself for voicing my thoughts.

"It doesn't matter," I replied, waving his enquiry away.

I supposed the feud between Primus and Vindex would have ended in a confrontation whether I had become involved or not. I recalled Vindex telling me that, if he ever decided to go after Primus in his own house, he would do it properly. It looked as if he had. He'd taken advantage of Primus being unprotected, and he'd sent his thugs in to end their dispute permanently.

"What's going to happen about it?" I asked as I fought off waves of guilt that my actions had resulted in another death.

The Juggler shrugged, "Nothing. We can't prove anything. And those on the Palatine aren't sorry that a supporter of Herennius Muncius is dead. It removes a minor problem for them."

I sighed. So Primus was dead. That meant his young son would inherit his estate, which would give Hortensia's father control over things until the boy reached manhood. I knew nothing about Hortensia's family, but I knew deep in my gut that Circe would have Fronto offering to take the various Roman properties off their hands in exchange for cash.

I suppose I should have felt some sort of satisfaction at the outcome, but my brother was dead and, although I had hated him, I was sick of people being killed.

That thought prompted me to ask Rufus some other questions.

"Were you working for Julia Mamaea all the time?"

He grinned, "Very good, Sigma. I see you haven't lost all your faculties, even if you did make some foolish mistakes over the past little while."

"Well, you obviously weren't working for Soaemias, and I knew you couldn't be working for Maesa because she spoke to me in person."

He confessed, "I always knew Elagabalus would come to a bad end. And I quickly realised his cousin was the obvious choice to succeed him unless we wanted another civil war."

"So why did you fake your own death?"

"I would have thought that was obvious. Maesa wanted her own people running her informers, and she would not want anyone loyal to the previous regime being free to provide information to her enemies. It was safer to disappear."

"But Julia Mamaea didn't feel the same?"

"She was in need of allies," Rufus explained. "She and her son were in constant danger. I could not do anything to prevent attempts on their lives, but I did try to help move things along so that their position improved."

Sourly, I muttered, "I would have thought you'd have found Herennius Muncius a safer bet. He almost succeeded."

Rufus shrugged, "Muncius was too secretive. I never could find out what he was up to. Besides, he would never have trusted me."

"So you threw in your lot with Julia Mamaea and Alexander. Was it you who engineered the Praetorian revolt?"

With an air of false modesty, he said, "I merely facilitated the relaying of some messages."

"Between Mamaea and Thrax?"

"Thrax?" he asked, his face bearing an expression of apparent innocence.

"Maximinis Thrax. The man who sparked the Praetorians into action."

Rufus shook his head again, his demeanour suggesting he deplored my ignorance.

"No, Sigma, Thrax was not there."

361

"I saw him!" I argued.

"No, I think you will find that the official reports of what happened that day in the Praetorian Camp will not mention him. He has, though, been recalled from his post at the frontier because he is to be appointed to govern a province."

I sighed. It was all a cover-up, but everyone was getting what they wanted. Maesa had a compliant teenager to control, although the boy's mother, Julia Mamaea, might have something to say about that; Maximinis Thrax was being promoted, and Sempronius Rufus, the Juggler, had worked his way back into his old job. It wouldn't have surprised me if Cassius Dio was appointed Consul as a reward for his part as well.

"So everyone is happy?" I muttered.

"It could have been a lot worse," Rufus told me.

"A lot of people still died," I countered.

He waved a dismissive hand.

"Your idea was ridiculous," he told me. "I said as much to Mamaea when she heard of it from her mother. Sending an Emperor into exile, even one as hated and despised as Elagabalus, would provide a rallying point for any disaffected factions. It would have ruined the empire. No, I'm afraid he had to die."

"And his mother? And their slaves? Did they have to die as well?"

"That was an unfortunate side effect," Rufus stated flatly.

I gave a snort of disgust.

"That's why I'm glad I retired from the imperial service," I told him.

He gave me a thin smile of amusement as he said, "Nobody retires from imperial service, Sigma. You can go home now, but one day, if I have need of you, I will send word."

I drained my cup, slamming it down on the table.

"Don't bother!" I snapped.

Then I stood up, glaring at him.

"Goodbye, Sempronius Rufus. I'm going home tomorrow. I won't be back."

His only response was a mocking smile.

Angrily, I turned my back on him, heading for the door which led upstairs to where my family waited for me. I think every pair of eyes in the room watched me go, my outburst having

362

attracted everyone's attention. I did not care. I had had enough of Rome and its intrigues. I was going home.

And, once there, perhaps it would be time for me to disappear again.

Author's Note and Acknowledgements

Elagabalus, also sometimes known as Heliogabalus, is widely regarded as one of the worst Emperors Rome ever had the misfortune to be ruled by. In modern times, he has become something of an icon for the LGBT community, but that cannot disguise the fact that he was totally unsuited to be granted absolute power. There are several examples of young men being elevated to rule the Roman empire, and few of them turned out well for either the ruler or the ruled. Nero, Caligula and Commodus spring to mind, yet Elagabalus outdid them all.

However, he was probably as much a victim of circumstances as anyone. His scheming grandmother and ambitious mother worked hard to have him acclaimed Emperor, and they attempted to rule through him. This in itself was an outrage for traditionally-minded Romans because women were not supposed to hold positions of authority beyond the occasional role as a high priestess.

As if that were not bad enough, Elagabalus' desire to be worshipped as a god was all too reminiscent of the worst days of Caligula's rule.

As he grew older, his wilful temperament alienated almost everyone. Only his mother, Julia Soaemias, remained loyal to him, but even she attempted to build her own following to counteract Elagabalus' habit of appointing sycophants to high office.

Some of the reports of what he did while in power are scarcely believable, and we must bear in mind that writers of the day may well have invented some of the tales in order to justify his murder. But rumours of lavish feasts at which guests would be given random gifts ranging from immensely valuable items to insultingly cheap gifts of everyday junk are impossible to disprove, as are the reports that he often insisted on his dinner guests spending the night in the palace, and would then have wild beasts like lions released to roam the corridors.

Whether these stories are true must be questioned, but Elagabalus certainly seems to have been thoughtless in much of his behaviour. Again, though, holding absolute power will affect anyone, let alone a teenager who is struggling to come to terms with his sexual identity.

Above all, it was his scandalous sex life which outraged many among the Roman elite. Homosexuality was not considered a bar to being Emperor, but Roman opinion was very much of the view that it was unmanly to be a passive partner in a homosexual affair. Elagabalus not only brazenly paraded himself as a passive partner, he openly declared his desire to be a woman. For Romans, that was too much to bear, and he paid the ultimate price.

As for the story involving Scipio, I will admit to interpreting the recorded events in a way which suited my narrative. In fairness, there are few accounts of this time period, and the few that do exist often contradict each other. There was, however, no Senator named Herennius Muncius, and as far as I know, no conspiracy involving Maximinis Thrax who is a genuine historical figure. He was allegedly over seven feet tall, and he was one of Rome's most famous soldiers. His career under Alexander Severus is difficult to ascertain in detail, but it seems fairly certain that, in an unprecedented move for a man born a barbarian, he was appointed to govern at least one Province during Alexander's reign. Whether that was due to any involvement in the overthrow of Elagabalus is a matter of speculation.

I should also point out that Cassius Dio, another genuine historical figure who wrote a history of these and other events, may not have been in Rome at the time Elagabalus was murdered. It seems probable that he was actually in a sort of self-imposed exile in Bithynia in Asia Minor. He certainly did not seem to be in favour with Elagabalus, but his career did take off spectacularly under Alexander Severus. He is an interesting figure in his own right, and I hope readers will not mind me bending the truth a little to give him an important role in my story.

The other main area where I took some liberties was in the events surrounding the actual murder of Elagabalus. Cassius Dio reports that the entire imperial family was summoned to the Praetorian Camp in order to prove that Alexander was still alive. The Praetorians then held the family as virtual captives within a temple inside the barracks. After a couple of days during which nothing seems to have happened, Julia Soaemias, fearing for her son's life, tried to smuggle him out in a large chest, but he was discovered and the furious Praetorians then slaughtered him and his mother. Somehow, this didn't quite ring true, and I decided to follow an alternative account which, while from a less reputable source than Dio, states that the decision to murder the Emperor was an impulsive one, carried out almost as soon as he arrived at the Praetorian Camp. It is impossible to know which version is correct.

However the coup was achieved, it was fortunate for the empire that Alexander was a very different character to his cousin. Following the advice of his mother, he soon adopted the family name of Severus in order to reinforce his links to the dynasty of which he was reputedly a scion, although few historians believe the claim that he was another son of Caracalla. Still, his mother, Julia Mamaea, helped guide him through some turbulent early months, and he then went on to rule for several largely peaceful years, so there should be no need for Sempronius Scipio to come out of retirement for a while.

Probably.

As always, I owe thanks to a team of friends and family who helped enormously with the production of this book. Moira Anthony, Stuart Anthony, Ian Dron, Stewart Fenton and Liz Wright valiantly waded through the innumerable typos in the early drafts, and also contributed helpful comments on various aspects of the plot. My thanks to them all. Stuart also did an enormous amount of research on the geography of Rome since I have yet to find a way of reading a map when I have no vision. If I've misinterpreted any of Stuart's excellent work, that is down to me. And, being a man of many talents, Stuart also designed the book cover. I'm sure it looks terrific. He tells me it does.

As for the actual history, I relied heavily on Paul Pearson's excellent book, "Maximinis Thrax, From Common Soldier to Emperor of Rome. If anyone wants to learn more of the actual history, I'd recommend that book as a good starting point. I also learned a great deal from "Emperor Alexander Severus; Rome's Age of Insurrection" by John McHugh. In addition to those, I waded through the translated works of Cassius Dio and Herodian which cover this period in frustratingly sparse detail, as well as countless other online articles. If any reader does tackle the actual history, they will realise that there is still plenty of scope for Scipio to become involved again.

GA
July, 2020

Other Books by Gordon Anthony

All titles are available in e-book format from the Amazon Kindle store. Titles marked with an asterisk are also available from Amazon in paperback.

In the Shadow of the Wall*
An Eye For An Eye*

Home Fires*
Hunting Icarus*

The Calgacus Series:
     World's End*
     The Centurions*
     Queen of Victory*
     Druids' Gold*
     Blood Ties*
     The High King*
     The Ghost War*
     Last Of The Free*

The Constantine Investigates Series:
     The Man in the Ironic Mask
     The Lady of Shall Not
     Gawain and the Green Nightshirt
     A Tale of One City
     49 Shades of Tartan

The Hereward Story:
     Last English Hero*
     Doomsday*

The Sempronius Scipio Series:
     Dido's Revenge*

A Walk in the Dark (Charity booklet)

About The Author

Born in Watford, Hertfordshire, in 1957, Gordon's family moved to Broughty Ferry in the early 1960s. Gordon attended Grove Academy, leaving in 1974 to work for Bank of Scotland. After a long but undistinguished career, he retired on medical grounds in 2008 without having received any huge bankers' bonuses.

Registered blind, Gordon had more time on his hands after retiring so, with the aid of special computer software, he returned to his hobby of writing and had his debut novel, "In the Shadow of the Wall" published in 2010. Gordon's books are now being read by a world-wide audience. As well as his historical adventure stories, he has ventured into crime fiction with some spoof murder mysteries in the "Constantine Investigates" series. He is also kept busy with speaking engagements, visiting libraries, schools and community groups to talk about his books.

In addition to his novels, Gordon devotes some of his time to raising funds for the RNIB. As well as visiting schools and social clubs to talk about his sight loss, he has self-published a charity booklet titled, "A Walk in the Dark", a humorous account of his experiences since losing his eyesight. The booklet is available from Amazon Kindle Store. Gordon will donate all author royalties to RNIB.

Now completely blind, Gordon continues to write stories and, in his spare time, attempts to play the guitar and keyboard with varying degrees of success.

Gordon is married to Alaine. They have three children and one grandchild. The family lives in Livingston, West Lothian.

You can contact Gordon via his website or by sending an email to ga.author@sky.com

Printed in Poland
by Amazon Fulfillment
Poland Sp. z o.o., Wrocław

62236750R00210